There w̶a̶s̶ t̶h̶a̶t̶ u̶n̶n̶e̶r̶v̶i̶n̶g̶ f̶e̶e̶l̶i̶n̶g̶ t̶h̶a̶t̶ s̶o̶m̶e̶o̶n̶e̶ else w̶a̶s̶ t̶h̶e̶r̶e̶. I̶ s̶t̶r̶a̶i̶n̶e̶d̶ t̶o̶ h̶e̶a̶r̶ o̶v̶e̶r̶ t̶h̶e̶ w̶i̶n̶d̶ a̶n̶d̶ t̶h̶e̶ cacoph̶o̶n̶y̶ o̶f̶ t̶h̶e̶ s̶t̶o̶r̶m̶. I̶ t̶o̶o̶ c̶o̶u̶l̶d̶ l̶i̶s̶t̶e̶n̶. B̶u̶t̶ t̶h̶e̶ howli̶n̶g̶ s̶t̶o̶r̶m̶ w̶a̶s̶ p̶i̶c̶k̶i̶n̶g̶ u̶p̶ s̶p̶e̶e̶d̶ a̶n̶d̶ f̶o̶r̶c̶e̶. W̶a̶s̶ t̶h̶a̶t̶ a̶ f̶o̶o̶t̶? The m̶o̶o̶n̶ d̶i̶s̶a̶p̶p̶e̶a̶r̶e̶d̶ a̶g̶a̶i̶n̶. I̶t̶ w̶a̶s̶ p̶i̶t̶c̶h̶-̶d̶a̶r̶k̶. M̶y̶ s̶h̶o̶u̶l̶d̶-ers were soaked t̶h̶r̶o̶u̶g̶h̶. M̶y̶ f̶e̶e̶t̶ w̶e̶r̶e̶ w̶e̶t̶, and my legs were spattered w̶i̶t̶h̶ m̶u̶d̶.

If I could just . . . olive grove, I'd be safe . . . grove, there'd be a wid . . . where young olive trees . . . e-foot swaths of dirt between each heagerow of olive trees, with the drip irrigation hoses secured out of the way just a foot or so to each side of the tree trunks, made for a neat and orderly series of wide alleyways through the orchard. Moreover, Dad's young trees were pruned to no more than ten feet high to accommodate his adapted blueberry harvester that would mechanically gather olives in a few weeks. For me, all this translated into a grove of clear, flat paths that were perfect for running. Short trees would make it easier to see at night.

GRUMMPH.

That was definitely a gunshot . . .

ONE FOOT
IN THE GROVE

KELLY LANE

BERKLEY PRIME CRIME, NEW YORK

BERKLEY
PRIME
CRIME

An imprint of Penguin Random House LLC
375 Hudson Street, New York, New York 10014

ONE FOOT IN THE GROVE

A Berkley Prime Crime Book / published by arrangement with the author

ISBN: 978-0-425-27722-5

PUBLISHING HISTORY
Berkley Prime Crime mass-market edition / January 2016

PRINTED IN THE UNITED STATES OF AMERICA

10 9 8 7 6 5 4 3 2 1

Cover illustration by Sarah Oberrender.
Cover design by Anne Wertheim.
Interior text design by Laura K. Corless.

Penguin
Random
House

For Wyatt and David

ACKNOWLEDGMENTS

It's an understatement to say this book wouldn't have been written at all were it not for my literary agent, John Talbot. Thank you, John, for sharing your ideas, foresight, and trust in my abilities. You saw something in me that I didn't know was there. Through your inspiration, patience, and tutelage, I'm thrilled to discover my greatest passion in life as I take these first steps down a new and exciting path into the world of fiction.

To senior editor, Michelle Vega, I can't thank you enough for believing in the proposal that led to this series. Editorial assistant, Bethany Blair; copyeditor, Marianne Grace; production editor, Stacy Edwards; and publicity guru, Danielle Dill—along with the rest of the talented and hardworking team at Berkley Prime Crime—thank you for your expertise and support. Cover designer, Sarah Oberrender; and cover illustrator, Anne Wertheim, great props for your wonderfully whimsical and ever-appealing cover. Dolly gives it a five-woof rating!

For inspiring the series, kudos to the intrepid Georgia farmers who figured out how to resurrect the long-dead olive industry in the American Southeast. Many activities in the series rise up from stories shared by the folks at Georgia Olive Farms. Also, the Georgia Olive Growers Association has been a key source regarding olive tree farming. Additional thanks go to the staff at Oil & Vinegar in Charlottesville, Virginia.

I owe a great deal of gratitude to the Sisters in Crime Guppies group; I've learned so very much from the information shared by the many talented and generous members. Mary

Buckham, your sharp eye and quick wit (and red pen) during your Guppy classes always hones my writing . . . and, still, I've got so much to learn!

Speaking of learning, it's been a *long* time, however, I'm indebted and honored to have studied under my mentor John Irving, who taught me the importance of humor, perseverance, and everyday observation; the lure of a great storyteller's voice; and the joy of following beloved and memorable characters as they come to life on the page.

Johanna Farrand, your kind nurturing over the years has not gone unnoticed. Thank you for believing in my success. Martha Austin, Bibiana Heymann, Jean Pearson, and Michele and Charles Pellham, thanks for the steadfast friendship, enthusiastic support, and putting up with my quirks and blathers. Conner Puryear, your reminder on a crucial day that there's *never* room for negativity opened my eyes. Ryan Taylor, seeing your eyes light up on the day you learned I was writing a book was inspirational!

Most important, Wyatt Morin and David Eddins, to whom this book is dedicated, from the bottom of my heart, I owe everything to you. I'm forever humbled and indebted to your everlasting love, patience, compassion, and encouragement.

CHAPTER 1

Okay, I admit it. I was curious. I'd lagged a bit, stepping past the beauty shop doorway. Maybe I'd wanted to check out Tammy Fae Tanner. See who her clients were. Hear for myself what they were saying about me.

Shear Southern Beauty was the only salon in Abundance County, Georgia. It was the place where every woman in town had her hair and nails done. The place where each woman sitting in shop owner Tammy Fae's swiveling chair received an earful of her up-to-the-minute, down-home Southern dirt. And since my return home from New England a week earlier, I'd heard that all the pernicious drivel had been about me. So, naturally, I thought I'd check it out.

I'd gotten an earful.

Of course, Tammy Fae's animosity wasn't completely out of the blue. She happened to be the mother of Buck Tanner, the man whom I scandalously left standing at the altar, right before I ran out of town eighteen years earlier.

And I'd never returned.

That is, until another wedding-day blowout sent me packing from Boston.

Anyway, most folks weren't out and about on that steamy August afternoon in Southern Georgia. Like my dad always said, summertime in town was hotter than blue blazes. Only tourists, mostly Northerners on vacation, fanning themselves with their "Welcome to Abundance" pamphlets from the Information Booth, ambled under the tropical palmettos, past the Victorian buildings and quaint Main Street shops that showcased hand-painted signs, charming window displays, and perfectly potted plants along the brick sidewalk.

After delivering my dad's fresh olive oil to the Palatable Pecan restaurant, I picked up my dry cleaning and hustled a couple of doors down to Hot Pressed Tees, where, a few days earlier, I'd ordered some custom-printed shirts to promote my family's new olive oil business. Each shirt read GEORGIA VIRGIN across the chest, with OLIVE OIL in smaller letters above an illustration of an olive branch imposed over the state of Georgia.

"These look great, Tommy!" I said to shop owner Tommy Burnside. I threw my purse strap over my shoulder. "Hopefully, we'll sell out in no time." I fitted the lid over the thin cardboard box of tees on the counter before loading up two more boxes of shirts in my arms. I tossed my plastic-bagged dry cleaning on top.

"Y'all have a real nice day, now," said Tommy as he held open the door for me.

"Thanks!"

Stepping into the summer sultriness, I weaved in and out of tourists on the sidewalk as they rubbernecked and took selfies in the picture-perfect village. Then, I spied the open door at Shear Southern Beauty ahead.

I couldn't resist.

Slowing to a stroll and peeping around my armload of bagged clothes and boxed shirts, I stared into the bay window with the giant purple shears painted on the glass. Standing in the middle of her shop, fifty-something Tammy Fae Tanner hadn't changed much since the last time I'd seen her. That'd been at the wedding rehearsal party she'd hosted for her engaged son and me—the night before I'd run out of town eighteen years earlier.

Petite, with brown cocker spaniel eyes, a turned-up nose, and perfectly curled, shoulder-length, whiskey-colored hair, the former Miss Abundance and presiding president of the Abundance Ladies Club wore a purple apron and held a big cup, slathered full of hair color. She stood behind a tall, slender woman who sat covered in a smock with purple flowers patterned over it. With her hair all spiky in foils, the woman looked like a metallic hedgehog. As I neared the propped-open shop door, I could hear their drawly voices tittering away inside.

"Sweet-talkin' thing'll *never* land a fella," said Tammy Fae, slapping a blob of bleach on a spike of the hedgehog's hair. "Not the way she's carried on. Fancy that . . . runnin' away from *another* weddin'—and, in front of the whole world to see!"

The hedgehog giggled. "Even after a dog's age, she ain't changed a bit since high school."

"Well, y'all just can't piss on a man's leg and tell 'em it's raining. No decent fella's gonna touch her with a ten-foot pole now."

Tammy Fae loaded up another glob of bleach and spun the hedgehog in the swiveling chair toward the door. That's when I stopped short, recognizing the hedgehog. It was Realtor Debi Dicer. My old nemesis. Back in high school, the popular blonde, cheerleader, and student council president had looked over my shoulder and copied all my test answers in class. And she'd adored my high school sweetheart, Buck. Often, she'd followed him to Knox Plantation when he'd been visiting me.

"Y'all know, not a one of those three Knox girls can keep a man," sniped Debi, looking down as Tammy Fae slathered more bleach on the back of her head.

"Back in my daddy's day, women like that would've been locked in the attic. The whole lot of 'em are pretentious, shameless tarts," sniffed Tammy Fae. "Just like their mama."

As I stood transfixed in the doorway, a young man taking

snapshots bumped my elbow. My plastic-covered dry cleaning slid to the sidewalk, right in front of the shop.

"Sorry, miss. May I help you with that?"

"No worries, I'll get it!" I whispered, shooing the man away.

Kneeling to pick up my big baggie of cleaned clothes, I tried to balance the tee shirt boxes in my arms, hoping Tammy Fae and Debi hadn't noticed me. Except, I'd unwittingly stepped on the corner of the plastic bag. I got all caught up in myself when I tried to pull the bag from the sidewalk and not drop the boxes.

"And if y'all ask me, she's the worst of the lot," said Tammy Fae with a snigger. "Luring a man right to the altar, then shamelessly runnin' away. That hussy's stuck-up higher than a light pole."

"For sure, that Miss Eva's got some kinda itch that needs scratchin'!" Debi chortled. "She just can't stop herself."

Embarrassed at their words, I felt a rush of blood flush my cheeks. Still stooped over, I hurried backward, out of the doorway. Except, the hot plastic bag was caught on my sneaker, wrapped around and sticking to my bare leg under my cutoffs. My shoulder bag swung wildly, putting me off-balance.

"Goodness knows, her man antics and fame whoring are givin' Abundance a bad name. Folks in the ladies club are real upset about it," Tammy Fae huffed indignantly.

"For sure, that minx has got some balls, settin' her foot back in this town," laughed Debi.

"She's no better than a common criminal, comin' back to the scene of the crime."

"It's just like my honey always says, 'A leopard can't change her spots!'"

Finally, I snatched my dry cleaning from the sidewalk. Just then, the flimsy shirt boxes tumbled out of my arms, thudding and splitting open in the doorway. I looked up. The two women stared at me.

"*Bless her heart*, there she is!" hissed Tammy Fae.

I scrambled to hang on to my purse and dry cleaning

while seizing the torn boxes and spilled tees from the ground. Tammy Fae gave me that disdainful, if-looks-could-kill, Southern-woman stare. Debi plastered a big ol' pompous grin on her face.

"Eva Knox!" Debi flapped her hand to wave. "Bless your little ol' pea-pickin' heart! Tammy Fae and I were *just* talkin' about y'all. Weren't we, Tammy Fae?"

Tammy Fae's expression morphed from deadly stare to supercilious smirk.

"Imagine. Y'all comin' back to town, after *all* these years!" Tammy Fae sneered.

"Afternoon, ladies! So *lovely* to see you both."

I scrambled to stand, squashing the battered boxes, tee shirts, dry cleaning, and purse to my chest. My heart raced, and my ears burned. I'd gotten a bigger dose of Southern scuttlebutt than I'd bargained for, and I'd made a fool of myself doing it. I was embarrassed to hear the things they'd said about me, and my family. And the duo had caught me snooping, to boot!

Mortified, I backed away from the doorway, onto the sidewalk. I couldn't escape fast enough. Hugging my disheveled armload, I racewalked past Beasley's Butcher Shop next door, and the Lacy Goddess Lingerie Boutique after that. I remembered how years ago, Tammy Fae had told her son, Buck, that a farmer's daughter wasn't good enough for him. Of course, somehow, the fact that *she* was a farmer's daughter hadn't mattered. She'd told Buck that I'd break his heart, like my mother had done to Daddy. And all through high school, and later when I'd gone to college and he'd waited, Tammy Fae had done her best to put the kibosh on her son's relationship with me. In the end, she'd gotten her wish. *So, why keep after me now?* I wondered if Buck Tanner was even around anymore.

I hurried across the boulevard to my car parked in front of Duke's Donut Shoppe. With a few minutes still left on the parking meter, I dropped the busted tee shirt boxes on the rear seat and yanked open the door of my green BMW 3 Series convertible—an engagement gift from my

last fiancé. I'd be damned if I'd ever give that louse the car
back. I tossed my purse on the passenger seat and draped
my bag of dry cleaning over it as I slid behind the wheel.
The blistering black leather seat burned the backs of my
legs. Should've put the top up, I thought. I twisted around
to the back, yanked a new tee from one of the torn boxes,
and shoved the shirt under my thighs. Popping on my sunglasses, Maui Jims—another gift from my ignoble ex—I
noticed in the rearview mirror that my face was beet red.
Equal parts heat and humiliation.

"Welcome home, Eva." I rolled my eyes.

I turned the key, shifted into drive, and shot onto the
boulevard, heading out of the village, toward home. As I
cruised past one freshly painted, gingerbread-trimmed Victorian building after another, my strawberry-blonde hair
whipped around my head, free and tangled in the hot summer wind. About a mile outside town, I passed a white farmhouse with painted gnomes on a dirt lawn with scraggly
rosebushes under an ancient live oak tree. An American flag
hung from a pole mounted to the porch, where old Mister
Moody pushed himself up from a rocking chair and waved
as I drove by. I tapped the horn and waved back. Mister
Moody didn't know who I was. It didn't matter. He'd been
on that porch, waving to folks passing by, since I was a little
girl. It was one of the things that I loved about my hometown.

I took a deep breath. I was starting to feel better.

In fact, despite Tammy Fae's scurrilous beauty shop
gossip—and the dubious future of my hair and nails, given
that her place was the only salon in town—it felt darn good
to be home. Back in Boston, the cost of living had been high.
Winters had been long and cold. And friends had been few
and far between. Most New Englanders were often too busy
to chat as they blustered busily along crowded, noisy city
streets. And, inexplicably, a woman with just a hint of a
Southern accent didn't rank as being as "smart" or "indus-
trious" as her Northern counterparts.

By contrast, Southern Georgia's Abundance County was
a calm, bucolic place, with temperate weather and a realis-

tic cost of living. Folks, like Mister Moody, were always ready with a neighborly wave. And, more often than not, locals meandered and stopped on the sidewalk to chitchat, saying, "I reckon," before sharing thoughts and a smile.

In Abundance, neighbors welcomed neighbors at their kitchen doors with just-made, warm peach pies and friendly embraces. On balmy summer evenings, verandas sheltered friends and families lounging in wicker settees, playing cards, sipping sweet iced tea. And always, it was about the food. Homemade, delicious, down-home cuisine. Fried, salted, sugared, buttered. It was all good.

My stomach growled as I contemplated the evening's menu at my family's Knox Plantation. Chef Loretta had planned to serve up pan-fried Georgia trout with cracklin' biscuits and a peach and pecan cake made with Daddy's Knox Liquid Gold Extra Virgin Olive Oil. *Yum.*

I was real proud of Daddy and his new olive oil business. After a series of droughts, a poor economy, and decades of crummy returns for Georgia farmers, a few years earlier, he'd almost lost the family farm. Then, he'd decided to try tapping into the huge, growing domestic olive oil market. Everyone knew that cultivating olives in Georgia was a risk—although Spanish missionaries had grown olive trees in the region five hundred years earlier, no one had tried or successfully grown olives on a large scale since Thomas Jefferson's day. And Jefferson's vision of olive trees flourishing throughout the American Southeast had never come to fruition, mostly because winters were too long and cold, even in the South. Still, thanks to Dad's painstaking research, new technologies, and improved cultivars, the oils made from his first crop had already garnered awards. In fact, his was the first-ever successful commercial olive operation in the Southeast. And it was my job to let the world know about it.

After my mortifying wedding-day blowout in Boston, Daddy had offered me a job as head of PR and guest relations for the family plantation. Also, behind the main plantation house, where I'd grown up—we called it the "big house"—

the tiny, antique cook's cottage was to be mine for as long as I wanted. And my dad had gotten my big sis, Daphne—who was running her own business, a guest inn at the big house—to spruce up the one-room cottage for me.

Several miles beyond the village, a heavy-duty pickup truck towing a livestock trailer passed me going the other direction. Then, another truck, towing harvesting equipment, rumbled by as I whizzed past gracious Georgian- and Federal-style mansions set well back from the road on exquisitely manicured lawns. Long, cobblestoned drives were lined with flowering peach trees, tall magnolias, ambrosia-scented camellias, and mound after mound of blooming rosebushes. The car motor hummed as I took in a heady breath of the sweetly scented air.

I zipped by dusty pickups and faded cars parked in the gravel lot outside Carter's Country Corner Store. Inside, undoubtedly, weatherworn men in grimy overalls were sipping RC Colas and playing checkers. Same way they'd been doing for generations.

Closer to home, I passed a couple of longleaf pine forests. Typical of Southern Georgia wire grass country, the forests teemed with wildlife, including deer, turkey, rabbit, quail, and largemouth bass. And every now and again, I passed swaths of flat, sandy-soiled farmlands that harvested cotton, onions, soybeans, peanuts, pecans, blueberries, peaches, and more. The neat fields were laid out next to antique barns and rambling farmhouses—several were built before the Civil War, like my family's place, Knox Plantation.

This was quintessential Deep South countryside. Land of exquisite charm. Natural splendor. Southern pride.

A wrinkled, old codger in a rusted Chevy pickup loaded with manure honked and waved as he accelerated and passed by. The truck backfired, enveloping me in a noxious cloud of blue smoke.

Okay. So, on the other side of Abundance there was a chemical plant and a prison. Plus, there were some spooky cemeteries and a couple of big, scary swamps in Abundance County. And lots of crappy little cinder block homes on unkempt lots on the far side of town near the railroad tracks. And if you weren't from Abundance, you never *would* be from Abundance, even if you lived there the rest of your life. Honestly, when you get right to it, folks were always meddling in one another's business—Tammy Fae Tanner and Debi Dicer weren't the only ones. For that matter, most Abundance women could smile at your face while happily stabbing you in the back. And although they'd rather be caught dead than admit it, the men in Abundance could be just as bad.

Of course, as cold as New England winters had been, Southern Georgia summers were crazy hot and stiflingly humid, with the wildest electrical storms I'd ever seen. And bugs—well, I'd forgotten how huge they could be—the Hercules beetles were bigger than my thumb. Then, there were snakes—copperheads, diamondbacks, cottonmouths—and they were just the venomous kind. As little girls, my sisters and I learned right quick how to tell a bad snake from a good snake. Good snakes got a free pass; bad snakes got the spade—a job always left for middle sister Pep and me because our oldest sister, diva Daphne, couldn't be caught dead handling a "tool," even if her life depended on it.

I glanced at the speedometer and clucked my tongue. "Not too fast."

I still had Massachusetts plates on the car. And I knew to watch for speed traps. As long as I could remember, deputies considered it "sport" to catch speeding out-of-town motorists. Growing up, everyone knew Sheriff Titus rewarded deputies who'd dispensed the most traffic tickets with gift certificates to Woody's Gun Shop.

Oh—there's that. Guns. And hunting. People came from all over to hunt in Abundance. I hated guns. And I disliked hunting. Still, tourists who came to hunt and fish in Abundance helped stave off development and maintain the longleaf pine and grassland forest, one of the most diverse and endangered ecosystems in the world.

I rounded Benderman's Curve, and a giant white heron soared across the road ahead of me. Moments later, I motored through a tunnel of live oak trees that made a green canopy over the road. Gobs of Spanish moss hung from the ancient, twisted branches overhead. I slowed, breathing in the summery sweet scents of the Southern Georgia countryside. Lush and alive, Abundance County was my home. Heading out of the verdurous tunnel, I punched the accelerator and cruised toward Knox Plantation. Happy to be home, I was eager to get back on my feet again.

CHAPTER 2

Blusters of wind exposed the undersides of leaves on giant live oaks lining the Knox Plantation drive. As I motored toward the big house, surrounded by acres of sprawling lawns and gardens, dark clouds crowded an early-evening sun, bruising the late-summer sky. A storm would roll in soon.

Scents of freshly cut grass mingled with the sweet perfumes of roses and fragrant "August lily" hostas seduced my senses as I pulled up to the white clapboard Knox family plantation house. A mix of neo-Gothic and Victorian styles with peaked red metal roofs and second-story balconies, the pre–Civil War home was fairly modest as far as antebellum plantations go. Like most Southern Georgia settlers who'd been independently minded and poorer than their Northern Georgia cousins, my ancestors had labored on their farmland almost entirely without slave labor. The main house at Knox Plantation had been built for a large, working family.

I parked at the side of the house below the wraparound porch, put up the convertible top, and stepped out onto the gravel drive just as an earsplitting engine roared from the backyard. A vintage "superbike" Kawasaki Zephyr 1100 motorcycle—restored, repainted red with a retro paint scheme, and upgraded to the max with top-of-the-line performance parts—blasted around the corner of the house, spewing gravel everywhere. Billy Sweet, my middle sister Pep's husband, never acknowledged me as he hurtled past, hunched over the handlebars, wearing black-leather everything with silver chains, studs, motorcycle boots, and a big red helmet. Sporting over-the-knee leather boots and some sort of strapless, miniskirted, black-leather affair, my thirty-something sister, Pep, sat behind her husband on the bike, her bare arms wrapped tightly around his waist. "Pep" is short for Pepper-Leigh, but don't tell her that I told you that—the only person who calls her "Pepper-Leigh" is our oldest sister, Daphne, and Pep can't stand it. Anyway, with the earsplitting engine roar and a huge silver helmet domed over her tiny head, it was difficult to hear Pep as she waved and called out, "Seeeee yah-wwwwwl!" The couple peeled down the drive in a spray of smoke and gravel.

A screen door up at the house slammed shut.

"Thank goodness y'all are *finally* back!" cried Daphne from behind the porch railing. Daphne's Southern drawl was thick and deep. Although we'd all grown up together, Daphne spoke with a far more pronounced drawl than Pep, and certainly way more than me, with my watered-down accent from all my years in New England. Still, I loved Daphne's manner of speaking. It was all part of her elegant Southern veneer. My forty-something sister reveled in being the quintessential Southern belle, and she played the role to the max.

Tall and lithe, the epitome of perfection, and usually dressed in soft, feminine designer clothing, on that evening Daphne wore an uncharacteristically long, baglike linen tunic. Even more bizarre, her head was completely covered by a fancy silk scarf. Like a burka, she'd wrapped the big silk square around her head and shoulders, leaving just a slit for her eyes.

Daphne had four girls—Meg, Jo, Beth, and Amy. She'd named them after the characters in *Little Women*, one of her two favorite books. Up on the porch, she gripped the hand of her youngest daughter, six-year-old Amy, who was wrestling to free herself as she clutched a metal lunch box to her chest. Like a perfect doll, Amy, was donning a beribboned pink dress with a poofy tulle skirt, suggesting a model little Southern belle. Unfortunately, the dress looked like a Halloween costume on poor Amy, who was anything but a "belle."

Like her mother, Amy was pretty, slender, and fair skinned. Except, unlike her mother, who cherished all things ethereal and feminine, little Amy had a hankering for all things dark and creepy. During the children's summer visit to Daphne's ex-husband—pro ballplayer Bernard "Boomer" Bouvier, who'd remained in the marital home in Atlanta after the divorce—Amy had gotten ahold of some hair color and had dyed her waist-length, strawberry-blonde hair jet-black. Most likely, an older sibling had conspired in the offense, but no one copped to it. Regardless, against her fair, freckled skin, pale eyes, and blonde eyelashes, Amy's long raven hair gave the child an eerie, otherworldly appearance. In the froufrou mini belle outfit, Amy looked like a wee Vampira dressed for a cotillion. And she didn't like it one bit.

"Eva, I need y'all to help me tonight!" Daphne sounded completely exasperated as Amy wriggled to get free. "Earlene Azalea just dropped off Amy from her Bloomin' Belles cotillion class in town."

Daphne had convinced her best friend, Earlene Azalea Greene, to send her youngest daughter, Ertha Mae, along with Amy, to a finishing school, of sorts, for kindergarteners and first graders because, according to Daphne, "it's never too early to learn good Southern manners."

"Oh, that's nice," I said. "Amy, sweetie, did you have fun at your cotillion class tonight?"

Amy just scowled as her mother lamented, "Oh, Eva! I'm so chagrinned! I don't know how I'll face anyone in town, ever again! Amy was dismissed early after they discovered she'd brought that dreadful pet snake with her to class—in her new Amelia Bedelia lunch box!"

Amy stamped a foot and let out a grunt. Daphne's heavy gold charm bracelet jingled as she kneeled down and hugged Amy still.

"Fiddle-dee-dee, child, stop your fussin' this minute!"

No surprise, after *Little Women*, Daphne's second favorite book was *Gone with the Wind*. Growing up, her role model had been Scarlett O'Hara, and she used to quote Scarlett ad nauseam. Unfortunately, she still did on occasion, and "fiddle-dee-dee" was one of her favorites.

Amy let out a yowl.

Daphne scolded, "Miss Amy! We've got important guests inside. They've come all the way from New York for our Southern hospitality and a little peace and quiet—I don't reckon they're takin' kindly to your yammerin' out here."

"Daph, what's with the head wrap?" I stepped in front of the car to the edge of the porch.

"Don't y'all know? I've had a *drrrr-eadful* accident," said Daphne as she stood.

Amy spun herself free from her mother's grasp and twirled over to a big wicker chair on the porch, where she plopped down, kicking the chair leg and scowling with her arms folded against the lunch box cradled to her chest. Daphne studied her daughter for a moment before clucking her tongue and looking down at me in the parking area below.

"Eva, I'd be much obliged for y'all to help. Everyone's abandoned me, and Chef Loretta can't handle all the cookin' and servin' by herself. We've got important guests from New York, it's the first week of school, and I've got to help the children with their homework and get them fed and ready for bed. Amy's bein' quite contrary, and Little Boomer is coming down with the sniffles."

Daphne's fifth and youngest child was Boomer, named after his athlete father. To distinguish one from the other, the child was known as "Little Boomer" and his father up in Atlanta was "Big Boomer." The *Little Women* thing was bad, but how Daphne could name her child "Boomer," I'll never know, especially given her high-mindedness.

Amy kicked the chair. Daphne prattled on.

"Daddy is away in Texas this week. Pepper-Leigh just took off with that hooligan husband of hers for some sort of rock concert that she swears they bought tickets to a year ago." Daphne pulled the wrapped scarf down from her nose and honked into a lacy handkerchief. "I hesitate to say anything negative about anyone, but I must say, I've never understood what Pepper-Leigh sees in him. Although, I guess we should be grateful he decided to step away from the gamblin' table for at least one night."

I waited as Daphne honked into the hankie again.

"And, much to my utter astonishment, Charlene and Darlene took the night off without telling me in advance, presumably so they could go to the same inauspicious concert! Who's goin' to serve our guests tonight? I should've never hired those twenty-something twins of Earlene Azalea's . . . they're too immature, not at all hardworking or conscientious like their mama. And I can't fire them because I'll insult my best friend. Honestly, if Charlene and Darlene spent half the time cleaning around here as they do texting, we'd have a five-star rating in no time. At least they're each cute as a button, and the guests do seem to appreciate that. Anyhoo, other than you, the only other person left to help me tonight is Leonard."

"Leonard?"

"Yes. You know, the field guide I hired last month. He's out driving around somewhere in Chef Loretta's car, supposedly getting ice. We're nearly out. And apparently, he doesn't have his own car. Who doesn't have a car these days? I can't believe that I hired a guide without a car. Oh well. So, y'all can see, Eva, *dahhwr-ln'*, the place is goin' to hell in a handbasket, we've got hungry guests inside, and y'all are the only one around to help me."

"Gee, Daph, thanks." I rolled my eyes.

"Why didn't y'all answer my calls? I've been tryin' to reach y'all on the cell phone for an hour!"

Daphne's "hour" sounded like "aowah."

"I never carry my phone anymore." I grabbed my dry cleaning from the convertible. "When it rings, it's always reporters. Hassling me about Boston."

Daphne sighed.

"Well then, we need to get y'all a new number if that's what it takes to end this runaway bride nonsense. Y'all can't be goin' around willy-nilly without a phone. It gets busier than a moth in a mitten around this place, and y'all need to be available, twenty-four, seven."

"Daph, you haven't answered my question. Why is your head trussed up?" I reached into the backseat and piled the busted boxes in my arms. In a minute, I'd be cross the back lawn, to my cottage.

"Who knew! I'm *deathly* allergic to lye!" she wailed. "My face, neck, chest—everything—is all red and swollen!"

"Lye? What . . ."

Daphne waved her arms dramatically.

"I was infusin' olive oil and making lavender soap with our lady guests from New York while their husbands were fishing with Leonard."

"Omigosh, Daphne, that's terrible. I'm sorry."

"I can't let folks see me like this. And we've got the big Chamber of Commerce meetin' comin' up in two days. I've been plannin' it for months—with Daddy's new olive oils, and our new hospitality business, it's our Knox Plantation comin'-out party, of sorts. And now, *this*!"

Daphne clutched her bosom, bent over, and made a high-pitched birdlike squeal. Amy looked up from the wicker chair, studying her mother. Showing such overt emotion amounted to an unacceptable lack of decorum, which was a big Southern social taboo. Even Amy knew that. Daphne would never do such a thing in public. Still, I'd seen Daphne do it on occasion, when it suited her, no doubt, while in the privacy of family. Drama Queen Daphne, "DQ" for short—

that's what Pep and I had nicknamed her growing up. Often she'd been prone to bouts of clutching her frail, undernourished bosom as she lamented about one unspeakable calamity or another. Moreover, given that things rarely lived up to Daphne's exacting expectations—her ex had called her "impossibly" perfect—she'd spent a good deal of her life reacting to the tribulations of being Daphne. Although, I'd always suspected that her big boo-hoos were more for effect. Still, I couldn't stand it when Daphne wailed. No one could.

Squinting up at the house against the early-evening sun, I noticed a curtain move in a second-story window behind one of the small balconies. That would be in the room belonging to the Gambinis, one of the two New York couples visiting for the week.

"Alright, I'll help. As long as I don't have to cook. You know I can't cook."

Just then, my little black dog, Dolly, came skittering around the corner of the house and jumped up on my leg to greet me. All whimpers, licks, and happy wags. As Dolly hit my leg, the cardboard shirt boxes in my arms tumbled to the ground.

"Dolly!"

I cradled Dolly and smothered her with kisses. Daddy and my sisters had given me the pup a week earlier to keep me company, and no doubt, to act as a distraction from the heartache of my broken engagement. I named her after Great Grandma Knox.

Amy climbed down the porch stairs, still holding her lunch box, and followed the rose-lined gravel path flanked by Daphne's carefully pruned shrubs and flower gardens until she stood next to me. I put Dolly on the drive, and the pup was more than happy to jump all over Amy and deliver more licks.

Picking up the spilled boxes and shirts, I caught a smile flicker across Daphne's face, before she dabbed her eyes with her hankie and said, "I knew I could count on y'all, Eva."

CHAPTER 3

Black smoke billowed from the skillet on the range. I plugged my ears as the smoke alarm screeched overhead.

"What the hell!" muttered Chef Loretta.

Loretta was a large, oddly quiet woman with dark features, big hands, and no neck. Daphne had hired the native Rhode Islander a few months earlier after she'd shown up in response to an ad for a chef to cook for Knox Plantation guests. Despite her New England background, Daphne said Loretta had prepared the most delicious Southern-style meal she'd ever tasted. My sister hired Loretta on the spot and gave her a small basement apartment to live in, rent free.

Loretta shut off the blender and marched across the kitchen floor to the imported, fire-engine red, double-oven Lacanche range. Grabbing the skillet handle with a mitt before yanking it off the gas burner, she tossed the smoking pan and its charred contents into the farmhouse sink.

"Now you've messed up my timing," Loretta shouted over the screaming smoke alarm. "I need those cracklin's for the biscuit batter!"

"I'm so sorry!" I dragged an oak chair across the wide-pine floorboards before racing around the kitchen, looking for something to fan the smoke away from the overhead alarm.

Except for the huge red range and the Sub-Zero refrigerator, both of which Daphne surreptitiously yanked from her Atlanta home during her divorce, the spacious, smoke-filled kitchen was pretty much as it had been while I grew up, with red laminate countertops, white farmhouse sink, creamy painted cupboards with glass-fronted built-ins for china, and a round claw-foot oak table and six pressed-oak Larkin chairs.

"I told Daphne that I *can't cook*," I shouted. "She said I was just helping serve the guests."

Grabbing a thin wood-composite cutting board, I jumped up on the chair under the alarm and furiously started fanning the smoke near the screeching ceiling device. Loretta turned up the fan in the giant ventilation hood over the red range. As I continued flapping on the chair, Loretta marched around, muttering to herself, tending to her various in-progress dishes. Finally, the screeching stopped. I jumped from the chair and ran to open the back door, hoping the remaining smoke would drift outside.

At the range, Loretta stirred her crowder peas and butter beans, a classic Southern side dish flavored with savory ham hocks and spicy hot peppers, as they simmered on a back burner. Oil in a big cast-iron skillet heated on another burner while a second skillet was half filled with olive oil, ready for the fresh trout that Loretta would dredge in buttermilk, spiced panko, and pecans.

Big Loretta turned and stared at me, like a thug who wanted me gone. Her look gave me the creeps. She grabbed a third cast-iron skillet and thunked it on an open burner. Next, she marched across the floor, yanked open the refrigerator, grabbed a package of salt pork, and tossed it on the cutting board before unwrapping it and slicing off a hunk. With freakish speed and precision, she diced the salt pork and tossed it into the skillet.

"Start again. This time, don't stop stirring until the bits

are browned. Then, right after the cracklin's are done, you'll have to drain them on paper towels and make the biscuits right away," she ordered. "Guests will be down to eat in another thirty minutes, and I've got okra and trout to fry."

"But I can't cook!"

Loretta brushed a baking sheet with olive oil and placed it in the oven to warm.

"You don't have a choice," the Rhode Islander said tersely. "I worked too hard to get here. I'm not letting the likes of you screw this up for me." And she gave me that if-looks-could-kill stare again. It occurred to me that it was remarkably similar to the Southern-woman stare that I'd gotten from Tammy Fae earlier. I'd never noticed the look while I'd lived in New England. But then, there were lots of things that I hadn't noticed during my eighteen years in New England. Apparently, the stare was a universal expression. At least when it came to me.

So, for ten minutes I stood, as instructed, under the tutelage of dour Chef Loretta, stir-frying salt pork bits until they were suitably browned and brittle. At one point, I took the skillet off the heat, ready to dump the cracklin's on a paper towel to drain, but Loretta grabbed my arm and said, "More!" So, I returned the skillet to the burner and stirred the bits until they were extra crispy.

Meanwhile, Loretta hustled about stoically, working next to me as she used a slotted spoon to scoop up and drop sliced okra dredged in a panko and buttermilk mixture—this one with cornmeal, eggs, and hot sauce—in and out of the hot oil on the range top. Somehow, at the same time, dredged and fried the trout filets in pairs, bumping my leg for me to move aside when she needed to open the oven in front of my knees to keep the already fried filets warm while she worked on the next batch.

She thumped my arm, and I dumped my cracklin's on a paper towel and placed the hot pan in the sink to cool.

"Here," ordered Loretta as she directed me to a large bowl filled with flour. The flour was arranged so that there was a deep well in the center. Loretta poured cream into the well, stirring with a spatula until the flour was moistened. "Dump in the bits."

I dumped the drained salt pork cracklin's into the flour mixture and stirred.

Loretta and I continued to work that way, side by side, with Loretta occasionally barking out instructions. I transferred my dough to a slab of lightly floured marble and carefully followed Loretta's commands, patting the dough down with my floured hands, folding and patting down the dough again. She handed me a drinking glass, and I pressed the rim into the dough to make each biscuit round, before placing each round onto an already-greased baking sheet. Loretta brushed on some whisked egg whites over the biscuit tops before grabbing the baking sheet and sliding it into the oven. Wisely, I noticed, she wasn't letting me near the ovens.

Although it was the kitchen where I'd grown up, prepping the meal with Chef Loretta seemed so different from the days I remembered as a child. After Mother left, Daphne, Pep, and I used to cook together—Pep and I had been so young, we stood on stools at the counter. We'd laugh and tease one another, almost always screwing up whatever it was we were preparing. Of course, we'd fooled around— spaghetti ended up on the walls, ketchup on the counters, and we ate more cookie dough than we actually baked. And fried food? Forget it. Daddy'd be cleaning up spattered grease from the walls, counters, and floors for hours after we'd gone to bed. Afterward, we'd all sat around together at the kitchen table for our family meals. I can't imagine what it must've taken to clean our clothes. Finally, after a year or so of blackened and raw dinners—it's a wonder someone didn't end up in the hospital from burns or food poisoning—Dad hired a woman from down the road, whom we affectionately called Auntie Ella, to come and cook dinners for us.

Behind me, I heard a light footstep in the kitchen.

"Gracious, me! All this smoke!" I turned to see my sister, Daphne, still in her head wrap and ugly linen tunic, fanning her face with one delicate, lily-white hand, her heavy gold charm bracelet jingling away. In her other hand, she held something poofy, made of black-and-white fabric. It looked like another one of Amy's froufrou Blooming Belles dresses.

"How are y'all gettin' along?" Without waiting for an answer, Daphne said lightheartedly, "Good! Now, the guests are already downstairs in the living room, and they'll be ready to eat any minute. Eva, I brought this down for y'all to wear."

As she spoke, my sister fitted a short tulle petticoat around my waist and pressed it closed with Velcro. Like a tutu, it barely covered my shorts.

"What the . . ."

"I see you're wearin' a black tee shirt. That'll work just fine," she fussed. Something dropped over my head, and Daphne's arms were around my waist again, pulling the sides of an apron to the back where she tied a big bow.

"Daphne, what is this?" I looked down to see I was wearing a full-waisted black apron with a white top skirt in the front. It was miniskirt length. Both the black sweetheart-shaped neckline and white top skirt were bordered in thick rickrack trim. The overall effect screamed French maid.

Daphne stepped back and took me in.

"Oh, that's just *dahhwr-ln'* on y'all!" She clucked her tongue. "I wish we had time to style your hair . . . Your little ponytail will have to do."

The apron and tutu-like miniskirt circled all around me, completely covering my shorts.

"I'm not wearing this."

"Of course you are," cooed Daphne. "I need y'all to look like a legitimate server, and the twins took their uniforms home. Last time they did that, I heard they wore them to some sort of fraternity debauch at the college." Daphne shuddered. "Besides," she said, looking me up and down, "if it's good enough for me, it's certainly good enough for y'all. I used to wear this little outfit all the time."

"You used to wear this outfit? This?" I looked down at the French maid getup, with its ridiculous miniskirted crinoline. "Wait. No. *Oh no!* It's a French maid costume . . . for the bedroom! Isn't it?"

"Isn't it precious?"

I pictured Big Boomer ripping off the Velcro-wrapped crinoline from my sister's lithe frame before he pounced . . .

"Eeeew. No way. I'm sorry, sis, there is no way I'm wearing this ridiculous thing. Get it off me."

I reached back to untie the bow at my waist. Daphne grabbed my hand, firmly leading me toward the dining room door.

"Boomer used to love me in this little number! He said I looked like every man's dream." She sighed wistfully. "Now, y'all just go on out there and serve the guests. With the black tee underneath, it looks perfectly normal. Y'all look adorable."

"Forget it! Daphne, what are you thinking? This is a guest inn, not a brothel."

She gave me the look.

"Eva, this is an emergency! Y'all can't go out there looking like Daisy Duke." She turned to Chef Loretta. "Doesn't she look like a classy French server, Chef Loretta?"

Loretta grunted.

"See? I told you. Now here, take these out to the guests."

Daphne plopped a delicate china plate brimming with food in each of my hands before pushing open the swinging door and shoving me into the dining room. Before I could turn back, the door swung closed and the guests looked up expectantly from my granny's antique mahogany table.

Seated at the formally attired table, under the dimmed crystal chandelier, the two men from New York, Sal Malagutti and Guido Gambini, wore pastel-colored polyester golf shirts with wide collars that framed their thick necks and heavy gold chains. They looked like a pair of grumpy toads.

There were big gold rings on their stubby fingers. Sal, seated on the left, with a pristine white linen napkin tucked into the collar of his shirt, appeared to be a bigger, older toad than Guido, who was seated on the right.

Across from her husband, under an overprocessed bee-hive hairdo, Bambi Gambini wore ginormous false eyelashes that looked like black butterflies had landed on her blue eyelids. Glossy pink lipstick drew too much attention to her artificially puffed lips. She'd pulled the zipper on her bright pink velour jogging suit low enough to expose her balloon-like boobs bursting from a teeny white scoop-necked tee. Next to her, Judi Malagutti was slightly older looking than Bambi—maybe in her forties—but still young looking for her age. Big boned, she was olive skinned with near-black eyes and a very low forehead. A straight hairline defined the thick, somewhat unruly, long black hair. Judi also wore a velour running suit—hers was yellow. And she wore lots of gold jewelry. Although not beauty-pageant, plastic-pretty like Bambi, Judi was attractive in a smoldering, earthy sort of way. Judi barely looked up at me as she continued speaking to her husband.

"Why not, Sal?" she said. "Women have used olive oil in beauty routines forever, right, Bambi?"

"Um-hum," said the blonde as she nodded. The expression on her face didn't change at all.

I set each china plate—filled with pan-fried Georgia trout drizzled with pecan brown butter, pork-seasoned simmered crowder peas and butter beans, buttermilk coleslaw, and pan-fried okra—in front of each woman. Then, I went to the kitchen door, where Loretta waited with two more plates of food.

"It's a cockamamy idea," growled Sal. "You girls waste my time with harebrained crap."

"I remember mother heating olive oil and putting it in my hair as a conditioner. And great-grandmother used to mix it in her night cream. Didn't you guys do the same, Bambi?"

"Uh-huh." No change in her expression. Bambi placed a pressed linen napkin in her lap and studied the food on her plate.

I served a plate of food to each man.

"Sal, we could feature all sorts of skin care products," continued Judi. "We could call the company 'Olive Glow Bath and Body' or 'Judi's Natural Beauty.' What's wrong with that?"

From the kitchen, Loretta handed off a basket of cracklin' biscuits and pitcher of sweet lime tea.

"I like 'Beauty from Bambi,'" said Bambi in a soft, sultry voice. "Remember, we talked about it on our walk today, Judi."

I set the biscuits on the table and began working my way around the guests, pouring tea. As I reached around Judi for her empty glass, Sal banged the table hard with his fist.

"I'm not havin' any wife of mine gettin' into any business," croaked Sal sharply. "Business is man's work. Besides, like I said, the only way to make money in olive oil is how we've been doin' it for years. Bottling and distribution. *That's* our biz. So, stay out of it and shut up about it."

I finished pouring and gently set the last glass down on the linen tablecloth in front of Sal's plate.

"You know, Sal, I'm getting tired of the way you treat me," scolded Judi. "Bambi and I've got good ideas. The least you could do is listen."

"Yeah," echoed Bambi. "We know lotsa stuff." She stabbed a single crowder pea with her fork and held it up to examine it. "How about 'Bambi's Beaudacious Beauty'? I like that name."

"What does that have to do with olive oil?" asked Judi. "It's supposed to be about olive oil."

"You're both stupid," said Sal, grabbing a biscuit. "Right, Guido?"

"Right, boss." With coleslaw on his chin, Guido shoveled a huge forkful of trout and crowder peas into his noisy mouth.

"I don't see why we can't have our own business. It gets boring around the house all day long. Hey, speaking of olive oil, that reminds me," said Judi. "Miss." She turned in her chair and looked up at me as I crossed behind her. "Bambi and I were on our power walk earlier, and we noticed some of the olive trees didn't look too good. Are they sick?"

"Say!" interrupted Bambi, looking at me. "You're that girl in the YouTube video, aren't you? The runaway bride? From Boston?" Holding a single piece of fried okra on her fork, Bambi's hand froze midair as she stared at me. With her batwing eyelashes and pouty, poofed-up lips, she looked like a surprised blowfish. The fried okra dropped to her plate. "Oh, phooey!"

"Damned if it isn't!" said Guido, staring at me as he pushed a mound of trout and coleslaw into his plump face. Then, with a mouthful, he said, "You're that *crazy bitch* who decked the weatherman! They were showing you on that *Celebrity Sneek Peek* TV show the other day. Guys, we got a real wacko servin' us!"

"Sal, why do you always have to be so nasty and rude?" Judi scolded.

"Maybe 'cause I ain't getting enough." Sal sulked.

Judi squinted up at me. "Say, it *is* you, isn't it!" She looked delighted.

Still chewing, Sal leered, as he looked me up and down. I shrunk back, hiding behind the big silver pitcher of iced tea in my hands. If being the "wacko" from Boston wasn't bad enough, dressed in Daphne's French maid outfit, I was sure that I resembled a cheap call girl.

"You know, you're the reason we found this place, isn't she, Sal?" said Judi.

Sal ignored his wife and just kept leering. Then, he shoved a pile of coleslaw into his mouth, followed by half a biscuit. He never took his eyes off me.

"Sal!"

"Yeah, sure," he said, finally looking down.

"We saw the TV show about you being a runaway bride in Boston. The lady on TV said that you ran away from your hometown in Georgia once, and that your family had just started an olive plantation where guests could visit. Right, Sal?"

"Yeah, sure. Could ya pass the biscuits?"

"So, I looked up your place on the Internet and made last-minute reservations for our thirtieth anniversary. We were so lucky you had a cancellation! I knew this place was your family's and all, but I never actually expected to see *you* here. You're almost famous!"

"We're glad that you could join us on the plantation for your anniversary," I said calmly.

Guido wiped his mouth with his sleeve. Like Sal, he lasciviously looked me up and down. He slathered a biscuit in butter and shoved the entire thing in his mouth, still not taking his eyes off me.

"Please enjoy your dinner," I said with a smile that I hoped didn't look too insincere. "I've left the iced tea on the table so you may help yourselves to more, if you like. Chef Loretta has a wonderful, homemade Georgia peach and pecan olive oil cake she'll be offering for dessert."

I backed into the kitchen door before anyone could say more. Chagrinned about the runaway bride comments, I was even more irked at the sleazy way the men had eyed me. In the kitchen, Chef Loretta picked her teeth with a toothpick as I yanked Daphne's big bow behind my waist and tossed the French maid apron. Then, I ripped off the stupid crinoline.

After traveling twelve hundred miles to take refuge back home, I still hadn't managed to leave the stupid Boston scandal behind me.

CHAPTER 4

Dolly snored loudly from her cushy dog bed on the floor. Sitting on Granny's antique four-poster bed, laptop across my knees, surrounded with books, magazines, news clippings, and printouts about olive oil, I looked out a rain-spattered window. Fat spikes of lightning, angry cracks of thunder, and sideways rain pummeled the tall palmettos and live oaks in the yard. Between gusts of howling wind and rain, I could see the big house hulking in the night across the lawn. The place was completely dark except for a small light coming from my sister Daphne's room on the third floor. The five kids, also on the third floor; the two couples from New York, the Malaguttis and the Gambinis, in their second-floor guest rooms; and Chef Loretta in her basement apartment were all sound asleep, no doubt.

Restless and unable to sleep, I closed my laptop and picked up a magazine. Still, my mind kept wandering. No wonder. I'd suffered from insomnia as long as I could remember. And, often when I did sleep, my kooky dreams would awaken me. Then, I'd be unable to get back to sleep again. Although people said exercising before bed kept you awake at night, in my case the opposite was true. I'd found that running at night cleared my head from all those annoying, anxiety-ridden thoughts that kept me from sleep. And on that stormy Monday night, there were plenty of reasons to run. Still, the storm outside made it impossible. So, I fretted.

An old ceiling fan churned around and around overhead. Still, it didn't seem to move the stiflingly humid air. I blotted my forehead with the sleeve of my oversized GEORGIA VIRGIN tee as my mind wandered back to dinner, when perfect strangers had reveled in the realization that the infamous, "wacko" runaway bride from Boston was serving them.

Of course, they'd been referring to the event two weeks earlier, on my wedding day, when I'd very publically ditched my fiancé, popular Boston weatherman Zack Black, whom I'd foolishly mistaken for the love of my life. Afterward, the TV network damage-control team for my not-to-be husband, Zack, made sure that he was still a paragon and that I'd lost all credibility—both with my clients and the public at large.

In a heartbeat, my weatherman, our shared condo, our future home in the suburbs, and my career as a pubic relations consultant had all gone up in smoke. I was homeless, broke, and single.

Worse still, because my ex-fiancé was an up-and-coming network "star," sensational details of the wedding drama made all the national tabloids. And, of course, once word got out that I'd run away before, my miserable, mascara-stained mug began circulating on the Internet, big-time. Folks were messaging, tweeting, and hashtagging all about the antics of notorious runaway bride Eva Knox. One late-night television host even made a joke about me during his monologue. Worse still, YouTube videos of my unseemly behavior outside the Boston church ensured that my cringe-worthy fifteen minutes of fame would haunt me forever. Like the Malaguttis and the Gambinis, folks all over the country couldn't be happier to feast on my wretched heartbreak.

Sitting on the bed, absently flipping the pages of a

magazine, I wondered if it was some sort of karma. After all, eighteen years after running away from Buck, I'd finally been forced to run back home, tail between my legs, to face folks like Tammy Fae Tanner. Folks who despised me.

And as much as I tried pretending Tammy Fae's and Debi's harsh words hadn't mattered, they'd really gotten to me that afternoon. That, and the fact that people considered me some sort of unhinged celebrity, worthy of derision, only worsened my distress about the Boston affair.

Leave it to me; I'd handily served up another juicy helping of wedding-gone-wrong fodder for the Abundance Ladies Club to dish over. No wonder I was Tammy Fae's perennial topic du jour. A wave of tear-ridden anxiety heaved up from my chest. I grabbed a tissue, blotted my eyes, and blew my nose while a crack of thunder sounded off outside. Actually, I'd first thought it was a gunshot. However, nose deep in tissue, I hadn't been able to tell for sure.

"Get a grip, Eva. Focus on the olives."

I tossed the spent tissue on the bed and ripped out an article titled "Olive Oil's Dark Side" from the *New Yorker* magazine. It was all about rampant fraud ingrained in the olive oil industry, and how it'd been going on since Roman times. Intentionally mislabeling schlocky oils as coveted, more expensive "extra virgin" oils—a moniker reserved for only the naturally finest and purest of oils—was a common trick, said the article. Moreover, new technologies made it possible to chemically treat bad oils, camouflaging their impurities and aiding in the masquerade. I put the pages down. Could an honest small-town farmer like my father really make it in this business? Or would Dad's venture to produce blue-ribbon oils ultimately end up being nothing more than a big, expensive boondoggle that would result in our losing the family plantation after all?

An earsplitting *CRACK*, followed by a *BOOM*, echoed outside. The teeny cottage shook as wind-driven rain spattered through an open window. Dolly woofed from her cushion beside my bed.

"It's only thunder, Dolly."

I reached into my nightstand drawer, pulled out a dog biscuit, and tossed it to Dolly. She nabbed it from the air and chomped it to bits in a flash. My grandparents' black Victorian clock on the mantel chimed musically. It was eleven o'clock at night.

Dolly jumped up and barked again.

Someone knocked on the screen door.

"Eva, sweetie, are y'all up?" called a soft, honeyed voice. "It's Pep."

"Coming!" I tossed another spent tissue and slid from my bed.

Dolly sat, wagging her tail, as I unhooked the screen door latch. Outside under a big moon, crickets and katydids *chicka-chicka-chicked* like noisy maracas. The rain had slowed to a pitter-patter, and the air smelled of sweet, earthly freshness. Leaves of tropical palmettos, along with gnarled limbs of centuries-old live oaks in the yard, swished and rolled in a balmy wind. Underneath the dogwood tree, light from my cottage fell on Pep's vintage Schwinn bike. A wicker basket hung on the handlebars.

"Hey, sweetie, how's tricks?" Pep gave me a big bear hug and a kiss on the cheek. "Sorry to bother y'all. I spied a light on and figured folks were up, so I pedaled over when the rain slowed."

In her thirties, like me, and just two years older, standing no more than five feet two inches, Pep was curvier and shorter than I was. She wore no makeup on her flawless porcelain skin except for smoky eye shadow and mascara around her big, soulful gray eyes. She had a small nose, like mine, and a pouty mouth—she got that from Mother. Her natural strawberry-blonde hair—we *all* got that from Dad—was short, spiky, and bleached platinum. Pep maintained and fixed everything from engines to hard drives on the farm—that is, when she wasn't tending bar at the Roadhouse, a grungy watering hole located in an abandoned train station on the edge of town. She and her motorcycling musician husband, Billy, lived in a little brick ranch on the other side of the farm.

"Love your GEORGIA VIRGIN tee shirt," said Pep, stepping inside.

"Thanks. Hot Pressed Tees printed up a bunch for us."

"It's cute. Don't wear it to the Roadhouse, though. With your looks, there'll be more googly-eyed men on your tail than y'all can shake a stick at." She snorted.

I latched the hook on the screen door.

"You're looking quite glam, yourself," I said.

As usual, Pep was totally gothed out. She wore a black leather skirted corset with a big silver zipper that ran between pointed leather bra cups down the center to the frilly leather miniskirt—it was so short that it was more of a ruffle than a skirt, really. There was a wide black choker with an oversized satiny bow that draped over her chest. Lacy black bootie-leggings hugged her legs up to her thighs, where they were held high with black garters. She looked like a glamorous white mink in a biker tutu.

"Like I said, sweetie, I'm sorry to be a bother. I hope y'all aren't entertaining . . ." Pep smiled and raised her eyebrows as she stood on her tiptoes and peered over my shoulder.

"Entertaining?" I laughed hard. "Are you kidding? I've got a self-imposed moratorium on men these days. Just a bad case of insomnia, that's all."

"Whoa, Eva!" gasped Pep. She made a face and ran her fingers through her spiky hair as she took in the cottage.

My cottage was little more than a shoe box with a bizarre furniture arrangement. Shoe box because it was small. Bizarre because Daphne—who considered herself a decorista of sorts—said the room looked best with Granny's big four-poster bed placed just inside the front door. And of course there was no arguing with Daphne.

As Pep and I stood between the fireplace and an antique steamer trunk at the foot of the bed, I followed her gaze. On top of the bed, there were lots of squishy pillows, a rumpled matelassé quilt, my laptop, as well as magazines, books, and other materials that I'd been reading. Littered on top of all that were a couple of empty Kleenex boxes and—easily—fifty or more spent, wadded, and balled-up tissues. Next to the bed, an antique maple nightstand and small crystal lamp were nearly obliterated by more wads of my tear-stained tissues.

Pep whistled quietly. "Holy cow!"

Along the front wall, between the front door and an open window, the top of my Sheridan dresser was just about the only clean surface in the room. The dresser stood below a matching mirror hanging on the whitewashed wall.

"Okay, so, it's a little gross around here. I've been . . . working through some things."

I swept my arm across the foot of the bed to make a space to sit down. Accidentally, I knocked a small mountain of tissues to the floor. Dolly hastened over to inspect. She picked her prize and trotted with it over to her bed on the floor next to mine.

"I'll say. About this man moratorium of yours, sweetie, I wouldn't stick with it too long. There's no heartbreak that an orgasmic night with a hot stud can't fix. Believe me."

I rolled my eyes.

"Hon, y'all think I'm kiddin', but it's *way* better for your psyche *and* your complexion than sittin' around bawling all night." Pep gave a tiny snort as she took in the room again with her hands on her hips. "Maybe y'all should wear your VIRGIN shirt to the Roadhouse after all."

"Seriously, Pep, no men. And certainly, not one of your Roadhouse cronies."

"Have it your way, hon. When y'all change your mind, just let me know. I'll set you up with a fella who'll make y'all forget *everything*." Pep smiled provocatively.

"I'm afraid I may never be ready for that!" I laughed.

"Y'all know what they say about Southern farmers . . ."

"No. And please, don't tell me. Pep, you're scaring me." I changed the subject, "So, why are you here? Is something wrong?"

"Naw, there's nothin' 'wrong,' really . . ."

"How 'bout a late-night snack, then?"

"Thanks, no snack. Billy is waitin' on me. We went to the Creamed Peaches concert at the college. You know, part of the Monday night concert series."

"I heard. Darlene and Charlene didn't work so they could go. Daph was fit to be tied."

"Well, it was worth it. The stadium was packed. Unfortunately, party pooper Billy insisted we leave early 'cause after the last concert there was so much traffic we ended up trapped on the interstate for five friggin' hours."

"Uh-huh."

"Anyway, I s'pose that y'all know Billy and I've been havin' some 'issues' lately."

"Uh, I guess so . . ."

"I think he's been gamblin' again—stayin' out late, sometimes not comin' home at all. Last week, I discovered money missin' from the household account. And I'm worried that one of my gold rings—the one shaped like a skull with ruby eyes—may be gone, too."

"I'm sorry."

Pep shrugged. "Anyway, tonight we finally got to spend some quality time together, and Billy's actually in the mood for some nookie." She smiled, and the room lit up. "It's been months. I wanted to slip out of this outfit and into something 'more comfortable.' Well, really"—Pep rolled her eyes—"nothing at all."

I cringed. "Thanks for sharing—sure we're not headed into the 'too much information' category?"

Pep ignored me.

"Except . . . I can't."

"You can't? Can't . . . what?"

"I'm stuck."

"Stuck?"

"Yeah. Right, hon. Stuck."

Pep reached up and grabbed the giant silver zipper between the cone-shaped bra cups of her leather corset and yanked on it, hard. Nothing happened.

"See?"

She yanked again, this time even harder.

"Even Billy couldn't get it down." Pep blushed. "And believe me, he tried!"

"I see!"

"So, I was wondering, do y'all have any of Daddy's olive oil? We're out. And if I can just get a little oil on the zipper, maybe I can get it to move again." Pep's eyes wandered over to my collection of olive oils. "I like this outfit and all, but I'm not game to wear it forever," Pep said dryly.

"I have tons."

Under a turn-of-the-century cranberry glass lantern, a tattered Oriental rug stretched out under a round gateleg table and a couple of whitewashed Provincial-style side chairs in the center of the cottage. To the right of the table, a high counter with a reclaimed marble top separated my central "dining room" from a sparsely outfitted galley kitchenette that was next to the fireplace. A couple dozen clear bottles of olive oil lined the countertop between the kitchenette and dining table.

"By the way," I chatted, "I see that Daphne's become quite the gardener. I had some of her tomatoes today. Chef Loretta paired them for me with fresh chèvre on a baguette and drizzled it all with garlic- and basil-infused oil and balsamic vinegar. It was heavenly."

"Chèvre—that's fancy talk for goat cheese, right, hon?" Pep rolled her eyes. "Sounds good. But I'm still a meat and potatoes girl myself. I reckon I'd need to have a big New York strip with that. And a cold beer. Don't get me wrong, hon—I love olive oil and all, but I'm more likely to drizzle it in my hair than over Daph's precious organic fruits and veggies." Pep sniggered like a little piglet.

"I hear you." I chuckled, motioning to the bottled olive oils. "Pick your poison."

Instead of the usual dark green glass to preserve freshness, the sample bottles were clear so they showcased richly colored gold, green, and amber olive oils inside. Each bottleneck had a purple ribbon tied around it securing a handwritten tag that identified the oil, its origin, and flavor notes. Like wine, each reflected its terroir—the geography, soil, and climate in which the olives were grown. Several were harvested from olives at our farm. Some were from California. Others were imports from Spain, Portugal, Greece, France, Argentina, and Chile. A few were infused with flavorings, like lavender, lemon, and rosemary.

"Cracky girl! Y'all weren't kiddin'! There's an olive oil smorgasbord over here!"

"I'm taste testing. To educate myself."

"Better you than me. I'd be on oil overload. Still, I reckon my hair would shine and my skin would glow like crazy." She tipped her head and batted her eyes in fun as she studied the bottles. "Fresh pressed. Not the rancid crud from the market we had growing up."

"I've been reading how Americans have been buying crappy, out-of-date oils sent over from Europe for years, thinking that's the way fresh, good oils are supposed to taste."

Pep picked up a bottle. I pointed to another one at the end of the row.

"Still, there are wonderful, fresh, premium oils available today," I said. "I like that fruity one from Portugal with the light, peppery finish. It surprised me. The pepper doesn't 'bite' at all. And the California one next to it, see? It's lighter green in color—it has a fresh, grassy flavor. I'm thinking it'd be perfect with pasta. Of course, Daddy's own Knox Liquid Gold, rich, buttery, and creamy with the sweetly floral, slightly green flavors of the Arbequina olives, is hard to beat."

Pep rolled her eyes at my effluent descriptions.

"I see you *have* been brushing up on your olive oils!" She laughed. "Darn tootin'. Daddy's is best. Although, I like the lemony one from California. Loretta made some mini muffins with it for a morning wedding here last month. They were killer."

Pep uncorked the lemon-infused oil. She poured some on her fingertips before kittenishly licking it off her fingers.

"Hey, how come I haven't seen you mornin's in the big

house for breakfast? Billy and I eat over there every day. Everyone does. We all have a sit-down in the kitchen."

"You mean, like old times?"

Pep slipped the cork out of a bottle of Dad's olive oil. "Daddy's there early—he comes over from his place usually by the crack of dawn, before chores. Billy and I show up a little after that. Daphne comes down . . . well . . . when she gets there with the little ones."

"Daphne, mother of five, the oldest just twelve. What was she thinking?"

"I dunno, hon," said Pep. "She and her ex were busy as bunnies, that's for sure. And I'm sure he's payin' for it now, up there with his new squeeze in Atlanta. At least he should be. Of course, with Daphne, he could pay her until the cows come home and it'd still never be enough."

"I'll be at breakfast tomorrow. I *love* Chef Loretta's cooking! I'm miffed because I missed dinner tonight. Loretta had some trout warming for me in the oven. Only, when I meant to turn down the oven, I turned on the broiler instead. While I set a place for myself at the table, the trout went up in flames."

"I see your cooking prowess hasn't changed over the years." Pep laughed.

"No kidding. That was my second fire of the night. I can still smell the smoke in my hair."

"About breakfast tomorrow, hon, didn't y'all get Daphne's text?"

"Text?"

"Yes. She texted me earlier; I just assumed she texted y'all, too."

"Everybody texts me. I hate my phone. I never check it. It's always nut-jobs proposing to me, or rag reporters and paparazzi."

"Oh yeah. The runaway bridey thing, right? Sorry, hon. Anyway, Daphne texted to say that Loretta left a note. Daphne found it in the kitchen when she went down a while ago for some ice." Pep poured a bit of olive onto her fingertips.

"Pep, you're killing me here. What did the note say?"

"Loretta and that new guide Daphne hired last month—Leonard? They ran off to get hitched in Vegas."

"You're kidding!"

"Sweetheart, I'm dyin' if I'm lyin'!" Pep snorted and dabbed more oil on her fingers before working them into the zipper again. "Gosh, this zipper really is a stinker."

"I never heard Loretta say anything about leaving."

"That doesn't surprise me. Something about her always struck me as being 'off' somehow." Pep fiddled with the zipper some more.

I had to agree, Loretta was strange. And the fact that she'd been seeing someone romantically shocked me. I couldn't imagine ungainly, grumpy Loretta on a date. Let alone being intimate with anyone. However, who was I to judge someone's love life, especially when my own was in the toilet—once again? As far as I knew, Loretta had been a decent employee; she took directions well, and she was a fierce cook. We needed her, grunts and all.

"Pep, this is serious. Who's going to *cook*? What about breakfast? We've got guests!"

"I dunno, sweetie. It's not my cup of tea. It's Daphne's bailiwick, and she made it clear that I'm not ever to meddle in 'her' guest affairs. I think she's afraid I'll make everything black . . . you know, hang black lace curtains, set out black leather placemats, and burn all the muffins. And I probably would. Actually, I think it might be kind of fun to try it once—just to see the look on her face." Pep broke into little piglet snorts again. "Although, you seem to have that covered."

"Very funny."

I watched Pep furiously massage the oil into the fixed zipper. The woman who couldn't get a simple zipper to work was a mechanical genius. Growing up, while all the girls were playing imaginary fairy games, Pep had been off with the boys, picking at frogs, daring one another to eat crickets, and mooning over John Deere tractors. From the time she was little, Dad taught Pep the intricacies of farming and heavy equipment, and he'd made her his right-hand gal on the farm. Household affairs were definitely not her thing.

"Seriously," I said, "who's going to cook for the guests at breakfast . . . Dinner?" Fortunately, Daphne had made the executive decision not to serve regular lunches at Knox Plantation, unless it was by request for a picnic or special event. That was one meal we didn't have to prepare.

"Tell me about it, sweetie. Oh . . . hey . . . voilà!" Pep yanked the zipper up then down to reveal a lacy confection under her mini leather corset dress. She smiled, showing off beautiful white teeth. "Billy's gonna be *so* excited to see this! She patted her bosom. Listen, I've got to skedaddle before he falls asleep—if he hasn't already." Pep frowned. "I don't want the 'magic' to wear off, if y'all know what I mean."

"Here, then. Take the whole bottle." I stuck a cork in the top and handed Pep the bottle of olive oil. "I'm sure you'll think of something romantic to do with it . . . It's all natural," I teased.

Pep let out a hearty laugh and batted her eyes. "We'll put this naughty lube to good use!"

"*Lube?*" I blushed. "Oh gosh . . . Pep, you're one step ahead of me. I was thinking *massage*!"

"That, too. Okay, I'm off to rock and roll."

Pep's tiny leather skirt flounced as she trotted across the floor. She unlatched the hook, pushed open the screen door, and jumped over the stoop into the wet night. The door banged shut.

"Have fun." Then, I remembered. "Hey, Pep, did you hear a gun go off earlier?"

"I don't reckon so. Just thunder. Or I thought it was thunder. Anyway, it's not huntin' season, far as I know." She thought a moment as she grabbed the bicycle and dropped the oil in the basket. "Although, folks can shoot wild boar anytime, night or day. Some of the big huntin' lodges advertise boar huntin' parties. Maybe they go out at night. Although, it sounds kinda sketchy."

"Must've been thunder."

"Okay, I'm off. And don't forget about my offer!"

"Offer?"

"About finding y'all a hunk to hook up with." She reached into the basket, pulled out the oil, and wagged it in her hand. "You could try a slip and slide!" Pep broke into giggles and snorts before dropping the oil back into the basket and straddling the bike.

I slapped my hand on my forehead. "I'll pass on that for now, thanks."

"And Eva!" Pep called out as she pedaled away. "Don't worry about the guest meals—Daphne will have a plan. She always does!"

Too late. I was freaking out about all that had to be done. I needed to plan a breakfast that was just a few hours away. Obviously, I wasn't going to sleep.

Now that the rain had stopped, maybe a quick run would help me think.

CHAPTER 5

I yanked open a drawer in the dresser and grabbed from a small pile of clothes. There weren't many to choose from—I'd been in such a hurry to get away from the throngs of people camped outside my apartment in Boston—not to mention Zack—that I'd walked away from almost everything I'd owned. I threw on a sports bra and pulled on cutoff shorts before slipping back into my GEORGIA VIRGIN tee and my running shoes.

Still, before I knew it, rain pounded on the roof again and the palmettos swished wildly outside the door. A lightning bolt lit up the sky, and a rumble of thunder followed. The weather had turned in a snap. Mother Nature had given Pep just enough time to pedal home. But for me, it wasn't safe to run.

I sighed.

"No running for us, Dolly."

I wrestled my limp tresses into a knot on top of my head. Over in the kitchenette, I grabbed a loaf of olive bread that Chef Loretta had baked. The last loaf, I thought disappointedly. I knew it'd be delicious. Loretta had made the bread after I'd asked if she could re-create a loaf that I'd tasted in New England, figuring it'd be a slam dunk to go with Dad's olive oil. The inspiration bread came from a little Moroccan restaurant just outside of Boston proper in nearby Brighton, Massachusetts. My fiancé, Zack, had liked the restaurant because it was dark and people didn't recognize him. Zack's proclivity for going unnoticed when he wasn't on TV, or making public appearances to further his career, should've been a red flag.

My chest tightened.

Forget him, Eva.

I pulled the cork from a bottle of French oil and poured thick, iridescent liquid into a Blue Willow teacup. Then, I shuffled back to bed, armed with Loretta's loaf and my teacup of olive oil. I ripped off a hunk of bread, stabbed it into the vibrant green oil, and shoved it between my teeth.

Outside, there was a *CRACK* and a flash followed by a thunderous roar. The cottage shook. Dolly huffed quietly in her bed. I reached into the nightstand drawer, grabbed another doggie biscuit, and tossed it to Dolly. I tore off a second chunk of bread and ripped it into smaller pieces while still munching on the first big bite. The hard outer crust in my mouth hid surprise bits of soft, savory black olives in the bread. As I chewed, the olive bits infused a piquant brininess that contrasted with the rich, buttery flavor of the bread. Prophetic for my life, I thought. Everything looks good on the outside, but when you bite into it, there's an unexpected, salty twist. *Like Zack.*

Zack Black. Fair haired, blue eyed, and oh so charming. The Massachusetts native was heralded as Boston's "very own" prime-time weatherman for WCVB-TV. We'd met and literally fell in love—or so I thought—five years earlier when a runaway goat crashed into us and we'd fallen together into a giant tub of ice and beer at the Most Beautiful Goat Contest. The contest had been my idea. It was a publicity stunt sponsored by a microbrewery client launching a spring bock beer.

Anyway, our crash into the icy tub—along with the goat

named Destiny, who'd landed smack in my lap along with
Zack and a TV light stand—had been broadcast all over
New England as "soft" news. The public had loved it. The
TV station had promoted the hell out of it. Soon after, Zack
and I'd begun making appearances together for public and
charitable events. New Englanders had come to adore their
"very own" couple, Zack and Eva. It was "Destiny," they'd
said. The couple is sure to get married, they'd decided. And
when our engagement finally had been announced, people
celebrated with parties. School kids sent us cards. For everyone, it'd been a romantic fantasy come true.

There was another flash of lightning and a loud grumble
of thunder.

I pushed a piece of oil-soaked bread into my mouth and
closed my eyes, trying to concentrate on the flavors . . .
trying to block Zack, the stupid goat, and a million unpal-
atable memories from my mind. Loretta's loaf was definitely
better than the restaurant inspiration, I thought. The burly
Italian cook had done a masterful job reinventing what I
remembered.

I stared up at the creaking ceiling fan, watching it churn
uselessly in the hot, balmy air. Like my mind, it went round
and round, but nothing came of it.

I needed a meal plan, I thought. I wiped my hands on a
tissue, opened my laptop, and typed "Southern breakfast
recipes." However, probably because of the storm, the Internet connection had quit. My mind rambled. What was
Zack doing back in Boston? What were my old clients thinking? Did they believe the stupid, flack-spun story?

A big *BOOM* echoed outside. Again, it didn't sound right.
Gunshot? I listened. The rain slowed; yet, I heard nothing
more. Pep was probably right, I thought. There must be a
boar hunting party somewhere in the woods. Still, they
sounded awfully close to our plantation. Dolly woofed from
her cushion, looking up with winsome dark eyes and girly
lashes, her long black tail hairs waving back and forth like
a feathery flag.

I opened my nightstand drawer, pulled out yet another

doggie biscuit, broke it in half, and tossed Dolly a piece. Dolly gobbled it up instantly.

"Last one for the night, Dolly."

Rain spattered hard and fast through the open back window. I picked up a *Wall Street Journal* article about olive oil titled "Can American Virginity Be Saved?" From somewhere, perhaps the drawer of my nightstand, my iPhone made some sort of soft burping noise. I had a phone call. Or maybe it was a text message. Or an e-mail. I didn't know which. It didn't matter. I wasn't responding. Whomever it was, I just wanted them to leave me alone.

I wiped my hands together. Already, I'd absently consumed an entire loaf of bread. *Who cares*. My mind flashed to Boston. The horse-drawn carriage had been parked on a quiet side street outside the Beacon Hill church before the wedding. Zack and I had planned to enjoy our first minutes as Mister and Missus Black by taking a carriage ride through Boston Common after the ceremony. After that, a vintage Rolls-Royce would whisk us away to the North Shore yacht club reception. The livery man had looked surprised when I'd approached the horse. All I'd wanted to do was pat the horse's muzzle before following my sisters inside to the church anteroom. Yet, something wasn't right. I heard whispers and giggles coming from inside the rollicking coach. I'll never forget Zack's startled, yet smug expression after I'd thrown open the coach door. I felt a sickening, heavy panic in my gut as I realized not only Zack's infidelity, but also, the enormity of his egregious indiscretion. He didn't, hadn't ever, loved me. Our impending marriage was no more than a colossal publicity stunt to enhance Zack's career. I felt nauseous. My world went black. Next thing I remember was the slick, icy feel of well-worn cobblestones under my bare feet as I rounded the street corner and bolted up Beacon Hill. Once they caught sight of me, a gaggle of reporters and photographers who'd set up outside the front of the church shouted and bounded up the hill after me. Of course, that was my mistake. I should've stopped and led them back

to the discreetly parked carriage around the corner. I
should've let them see for themselves.

Just read, Eva.

Still, I couldn't help myself. I wondered what happened
to my fairy-tale lace wedding gown, with the princess-like
full-length skirt, fitted three-quarter-length trumpet sleeves,
and corseted sweetheart bodice. It'd taken me eight long
months to find it, and five fittings at the chichi designer
boutique, Prunella's of Boston, to get the fit just right.

I'd ripped it off and left it in a heap.

And what happened to the custom-designed wedding
cake from the award-winning North End Italian bakery,
Anthony's Awesome Pastries? I'd made half a dozen trips
to the pastry shop, carefully designing and planning the
eight tiers of luscious raspberry- and chocolate-filled lemony
layers covered with blush fondant in a subtle, quilted diamond pattern decorated with a cascade of delicate Cherokee
roses representing Georgia and mayflowers representing
Massachusetts, all topped with a painstakingly accurate
sugar sculpture of Destiny the goat. Had four hundred guests
gnawed at my scrumptious custom confection without me?

Poor Daddy, had they made him pay for the ritzy yacht
club reception that took place without me? I'd make it up to
him. I'd promote the heck out of his olive oils. I'd make his
business world famous. I'd make him a wealthy man. More
important, I'd make him proud of me again.

My phone burped. I tried to concentrate on the olive oil
article. Still, my mind kept torturing me. Already in my
thirties, would I ever find my soul mate? Get married? Have
kids? *Oh gosh.* I needed to think about something else.

Anything else.

Another flash.

I remembered Zack's familiar touch on the back of my
neck. It used to comfort me. Now, I shuddered. Tears welled.
My chest tightened. My heart pounded fast. I'd been a fool.
And no one would ever know. I was so embarrassed. They
blamed me. Not him.

This time, it was his fault.

I dropped the article on the bed.

It's too damn hot to read.

I shoved away piles of books and papers and brushed a tear with the back of my hand. I pulled another tissue from the box. I wasn't sure which felt worse, the small humiliated part of me that somehow still ached for the man and the wedding that wasn't, or the smarter part of me that was mad that I still wanted any part of either.

Dolly jumped up, ran to the door, and let out a piercing, loud bark.

CHAPTER 6

The mantel clock chimed a dozen times. It was midnight.

"Yooo-hoo! Eva, dear, are y'all in there?"

Dolly woofed again. Then, she sat down next to me at the screen door and wagged her tail.

I recognized my oldest sister's light, singsongy voice. Flowing across the wet lawn like an apparition, Daphne held up folds of her long white satiny bed robes that billowed in the blustery wind. Her other hand carried a silver bucket. My slender sister's face was still covered with a big pastel-colored silk scarf tied over and around her head, like a fairy burka. Only her watery blue eyes peeked out through an opening in the headdress that fell to her shoulders.

"*Dahhwr-ln*', it's meeeeee, Daphneeeee!"

"Daphne. Is everything alright?" Standing at the screen door, I brushed bread crumbs from my GEORGIA VIRGIN tee. Dolly quickly scoffed them up from the floor.

My wraithlike sister stepped lightly inside the cottage. On Daphne's petite feet were heeled mules with sodden white marabou-feather pom-poms that covered her perfectly painted toes. Daphne was one of the few people in

the universe who could carry off such ridiculously imprac-
tical footwear, and make it look perfectly normal. In the
rain, no less.

"I have something for you . . ." Daphne sang, as she
floated past me, through my "bedroom" and "dining room"
areas, and headed to the "living room" on the far side of the
one-room cottage. A waft of pricey floral perfume trailed
behind her. French, no doubt.

Daphne alighted on a rumpled off-white linen love seat
with rolled arms that squatted behind a glass-topped coffee table with a metal frame with clawed feet. Dolly lay
down by Daphne's feathered feet on the shabby Oriental
carpet.

I plopped into a comfy armchair that was newly slip-
covered in perky floral chintz. The chair and matching ot-
toman, both of which had been in my bedroom as a girl,
were nestled under a tall wrought iron lamp alongside a
Chinese garden stool in the corner. On the rear wall behind
the chair, shelves were built around an open window where
lacy curtains billowed and puffed in the wind. The shelves
were jam-packed with my beloved books—mostly fiction—
as well as some of my most favorite things, including a
decoupaged box from my childhood that was filled with
special trinkets, some first-place ribbons I'd won running
cross-country, a few cherished photos, and my "emergency"
cash—although, already, I'd spent nearly all of it and was
down to a one-hundred-dollar bill. Also on the shelves was
my collection of tiny landscape paintings, along with some
glass baubles, old cameras, and my printer.

Daphne reached into her silver ice bucket and pulled out
a slender green bottle adorned with a sprig of lavender and
a purple ribbon. Then, she pulled out a brown bottle of
liquor.

"Eva, *dahhwr-ln*', I wanted to give these to you earlier.
They're little housewarming tokens to welcome y'all back
to Georgia—some peach whiskey and some lavender-
infused olive oil. The oil is wonderful for your skin. Smells
like a garden. And it's ever so relaxing."

I took the bottle of whiskey and the smaller bottle of oil.

"Thanks, Daph. I'll enjoy these, I'm sure."

"Wendel, over at the package store, just started carryin' the whiskey last month. It's made locally, so I thought I'd help support our neighbors. And I made the lavender-infused oil with the ladies from New York a few hours ago before . . . before . . . ooh *my*!"

Daphne let out a wail and made squeaky sobbing sounds of despair before putting her head in her delicate, manicured hands. Her "my" was drawn into a two-syllable word. Very dramatic. Daphne searched a pocket somewhere in the folds of her satin, pulled out a lace handkerchief, reached up to the slit in her headdress, and dabbed her eyes.

"You couldn't have known that you're allergic," I said. Daphne nodded her shrouded head and sobbed. Dolly whimpered and licked the pom-poms on Daphne's feet. The drama was getting on my already-primed nerves. I had enough to worry about, I thought. Honestly, I couldn't imagine why she'd been using lye, anyway. If she and the guests had just used olive oil to make a pure castile soap, lye wasn't necessary at all. And making castile soap would have boosted our olive oil business. I'd give her a hard time about it when we were both feeling better.

"Daphne, it's late. Is there something I can do to help you?" Hopefully, I didn't sound too harsh. I was overtired. And I was anxious to ask her about Chef Loretta running off with the guide, Leonard. Because he'd been out on a hunting and fishing spree when I'd first arrived back home, I'd never met the man. Given Loretta's distinctive demeanor, I was curious to get Daphne's take on the couple.

Daphne pulled part of the wrapped scarf down and blew her nose, loud and hard, into the dainty hankie. Her normally flawless porcelain face was blotchy red and swollen. I actually felt sorry for her.

"I've cold-compressed for hours (hear her, when she says 'aow-wahs') and used up all our ice. I'm not sure we'll even have enough for the guests. Do y'all have some ice that I may borrow?"

Although the notion of "borrowing" ice is ridiculous, I decided not to be smart about it.

"I have ice. Also, I have some freezer packs. I'll get you what I have."

"Thank you, Eva, dear. I'm sorry to be a bother. I know y'all have a lot on your mind."

"It's no problem. I keep cold packs around for when I run and overdo. Or for when I do something stupid, like jog into a pothole."

"Heavens! You're not likely to find potholes in these parts." Daphne pulled the scarf back up over her nose, muffling her voice. "I reckon we've got plenty of gopher holes, though." She dabbed her eyes. "Anyhoo, I'm glad to hear y'all are still runnin' these days. The exercise will do your mind some good. I do worry about y'all frettin' so much. Y'all have always been a bit of a fretter."

Daphne held out the ice bucket. I was pretty sure it was sterling. I took the bucket and went to my mini freezer in the kitchenette. Yup. Sterling. And antique. With a big "B" engraved on the side. Must've been from her Atlanta ex's family. I wondered if Big Boomer knew she had it. Probably not. Kudos for Daphne. I pulled out ice cubes and packs— all I had in the freezer—and plunked them into the fancy bucket.

"Daph, would you like a little bite to eat? Some tea?"

"I'd love a little bite, nothing to drink, thank you. I missed dinner and I'm rather famished."

"That makes two of us. Missing dinner, that is. Sweet or savory?"

"Savory sounds lovely. If it isn't too much trouble. Thank you."

I grabbed a baguette and sliced it on a wooden board. I opened a jar of Chef Loretta's tapenade—it was just about the only thing I had left in the cupboard. I slathered the bread with the briny paste of black olives and fresh olive oil, anchovies, capers, garlic, figs, fresh mint, basil, parsley, and dried herbs from Daphne's garden before placing the treats on a blue and white transferware plate. I crossed over to where Daphne was seated and shoved aside stacks of papers and wads of tissues on the coffee table before resting the plate on the glass tabletop. I set the icy silver bucket on the corner of the coffee table. Dolly came over to investigate and began licking the cool, sweaty sterling bucket.

"How lovely," said Daphne as she stiffened her back and wrinkled her nose, trying to look past the piles of papers and tissues obliterating the coffee table. "I see you're usin' grandma's Blue Willow."

Like the Blue Willow patterned plates, except for my very personal and most cherished items, almost everything in the cottage had belonged to someone in my family, or was some sort of vintage find, recently purchased and re-habbed by Daphne.

With two dainty fingers, Daphne picked up one of the slathered slices of bread from the plate and pulled her head wrap down below her chin, biting off a chunk of bread and tapenade.

"Ummmm," she mumbled. "Good."

"Glad you like it. Loretta made it. Speaking of Loretta, what's this about her leaving tonight?"

I grabbed a piece of the tapenade-topped bread. After noshing on an entire olive loaf earlier, you'd think that I'd had enough. But . . . no.

"Umm." Daphne picked up another piece of bread and tapenade. "Frankly, I'm relieved. Don't get me wrong; she was a wonderful cook. However, I found the woman to be a bit brusque."

"Brusque?"

"If y'all ask me, she went about butchering with a bit too much gusto." Daphne pushed the entire piece of bread and tapenade into her little mouth. "I watched her hack a side of beef once, and I swear, it's the only time I *evah* saw her smile. I worried about the children." She raised her hand in front of her lips as she mumbled through the big mouthful.

"But what about tomorrow? I mean, today! How are we going to serve the guests?"

I shoved a slice of bread piled high with the chunky topping into my mouth. *Instant pleasure*.

"Well actually, we were counting on *you* to see it through. Didn't you get my text earlier?" Daphne licked her lips and raised her scarf back up to just below her eyes. "I mean you *are* in charge of guest relations. I told Daddy that y'all could handle it just fine," she mumbled through her headdress.

My chest tightened and I swallowed hard. I nearly choked on the tapenade treat.

"But, Daphne, I . . . I can't cook," I gasped. The treat went down like a lump. "I nearly burned the big house down today . . . twice!"

"Of course y'all can cook, Eva. Y'all are just a little out of practice. And, I daresay, y'all have been a bit distracted by your heartbreak and this deplorable runaway bride nonsense. Y'all will get over it. In fact, cooking will be good therapy. Every woman can cook. Except, of course, Pepper-Leigh." Daphne sighed. "You know, I've wondered if she's a changeling. All that nasty black. And leather. She's just so out of step! Why does she have to be like that? She distresses me. Remember the time she used bird skulls as place card holders on Thanksgiving?"

Daphne brushed bread crumbs from her lap and put them in a neat pile on the edge of the serving plate. Dolly inched closer to the table.

"Dear me, Eva, you must do something about all these piles of papers! And, my, my, my! The tissues! They're not all *used*, are they?"

I sat silently and rolled my eyes. I knew that up until that moment, Daphne'd tried really hard to be polite and not say anything about the mess. Still, the answer was obvious.

Daphne swallowed hard and her back stiffened. "How will you *evah* entertain . . . in such . . . a . . . place?" Looking around and taking in all the balled-up tissues scattered over nearly every surface in the room, I knew that Daphne was horrified.

"Entertain? Me? Not an issue, I assure you," I said dryly.

"I know y'all have been distraught, dear, but it's time to

pull yourself up by your bootstraps. After all, y'all are a *Knox* woman."

"Right."

Daphne flapped her hand and changed the subject.

"Anyhoo, y'all can take care of the meals until I find someone suitable. We can't go willy-nilly and just hire *any-one*, of course. It may take a few weeks." She honked her nose again. "Maybe months."

A chunk of bread caught in my throat as I tried to smile. Knox woman or not, how was I going to prepare meals for people? Paying guests, no less? And even if I could—and I couldn't—I'd still never live up to DQ Daphne's exacting standards. I doubted anyone could. Chef Loretta was as close as anyone'd come, and apparently, even she'd failed the test because she'd been too "brusque." Whatever that was. Who used words like "brusque," anyway?

I stood up and headed to the kitchenette.

"Maybe we can find y'all a man right quick. That should help y'all feel better."

"Really, no man. I'm taking a break from men."

"Well, I suppose that's fine for now. At least until y'all get this place cleaned up. Maybe next week, then."

I rolled my eyes.

"Alrighty. I'll not keep y'all," continued Daphne. "The snack was delish, thank you." Daphne stood up with her bucket. "Y'all should make some of this tapenade for our guests," she continued cheerily as she made her way over to the door. "It's quite tasty."

"Sure," I said. "Of course."

I was kidding. I choked down some water. When it came to *preparing* food, there was no way. I couldn't understand how Daphne didn't know better. She'd raised me. And she'd seen—and smelled—the smoked-out kitchen in the big house earlier. Twice in a day. She must be desperate, I thought.

"There are grits in the cupboard for breakfast," continued Daphne. "And some of Boone Beasley's marvelous thick-sliced, nitrite-free bacon and low-fat spiced sausages in the fridge. And blueberries. Yes, do make some blueberry pancakes. And biscuits. And sausage gravy, of course. One can't have biscuits without sausage gravy. There's plenty to work with in the pantry. And there's fresh eggs from the Spencers' farm, some of Daddy's peaches, and all sorts of fresh fruit and veggies. Can y'all carve those little rose-shaped butter patties like Loretta did? Guests just adore those! We'll need ice. Maybe y'all can run down to Carter's Country Corner Store and pick up ice. They still open at six, don't they?"

"Daphne, aren't you getting carried away? It's not like we're feeding an army."

"Yes. Still, we want our hospitality to be nothing short of extraordinary. Our reputation is paramount. Guests write *reviews* on the Internet, you know!"

"Trust me. I know all about the Internet." I rolled by eyes. "No worries. You just get some rest. I'll take care of all the details. It's no problem."

Liar, liar, pants on fire!

Daphne's pom-pommed feet tip-tapped to the door as satin gowns swirled about her lithe frame. She pushed open the door and floated outside.

"Don't be worryin' about all this, Eva. Y'all will do just fine. Nighty night!"

A gust of wind ripped the flimsy screen door from Daphne's hand and slammed it shut.

CHAPTER 7

Daphne drifted across the yard under wads of dangling Spanish moss that cast eerie shadows on the wet lawn. My sister floated through her lush, well-tended flower and vegetable gardens, then up the stairs onto the big wraparound porch of the farmhouse. The kitchen door opened and closed silently as she stepped inside.

I saw the back stair light flick on and then off. Except for a glow coming from Daphne's curtained master bedroom window in the third-floor family quarters, I didn't see a light on anywhere. Sleeping guests probably hadn't noticed the fast-moving tropical storm. After stuffing themselves silly with Chef Loretta's mouthwatering, mammoth meal and finishing it all off with a slew of cocktails, they'd all tumbled to bed, completely unaware that their cook had absconded with their fishing guide—off to Vegas. *Sigh.* At least they'd had one good meal. The Last Supper.

Make no mistake, "cooking" for me was, at best, heating up takeout. Or stir-frying tofu and a bag of frozen veggies. To prove it, I had nothing in my cupboards, except for a few of Daphne's fresh herbs that her oldest daughter, twelve-year-old Meg, had picked and made into a bouquet for me. Moreover, the notion of me preparing food in any sort of "professional" capacity—worse still, preparing meals capable of meeting Daphne's demanding, perfectionist standards—was, in a word, insane. My chest tightened again just thinking about it. I'd never get to sleep.

"Come on, Dolly. There's a breeze outside. Maybe we can think better in some fresh air."

I pushed the screen door, and it creaked open easily—too easily. Trees swirled above me as a burst of wind grabbed the flimsy door and slammed it back into the cottage's wooden exterior. Dolly yipped as she shot between my legs then skidded and tumbled across slippery grass. The rickety wooden door caught the wind again, flew back the other way, and smacked shut behind me.

Gardenia-scented air, thick and heavy with moisture, hugged my body close. I pulled my hair from its topknot and gathered it into a ponytail before tightening and retying my shoelaces. A drift of Spanish moss blew from a twisted tree limb to the lawn. Dolly pounced on it and shook the heathery wad.

I tried to think how I could fix a meal and serve guests in just a few hours. *Obviously impossible.* My stomach churned. Maybe I could pick up some donuts and coffee at Duke's Donut Shoppe.

The full moon peeked through fast-moving clouds, then disappeared.

"I sure hope they like donuts, Dolly."

I'd tout the donuts as a local delicacy. An Abundance tradition. Maybe I could order some take-out eggs and bacon at Carter's Country Corner Store.

Daphne would just die.

"I'll call Earlene Azalea and beg her to take Daphne shopping for the day," I said to Dolly. "Daphne'd never have to know about the donuts."

The moon peeked through the clouds. Dolly made a little circle and wagged her tail. Her eyes twinkled in the moonlight, and she panted with excitement. She jumped up on my knee and made another circle.

"Yes, yes. I know. *You* like donuts! Okay, Dolly. We'll go for a quick run."

I figured the deep-woods trail would still have decent footing despite the rain. I'd be back in bed in less than an hour. I crossed the lawn behind the cottage, jogged past the gazebo and pond, and headed toward the hardwoods. I'd make a big loop through the longleaf pine forest before heading back home.

Dolly jumped excitedly in the air and gave a little yip before trotting past me on the trail. Shrouded by foggy darkness, I heard the little dog sniffing and skittering across the sodden, muddy ground as I started out, jogging slowly behind her. After a minute or two, I picked up my pace and started to find my running rhythm—one foot in front of the other—with regular long breaths.

Admittedly, bringing along a flashlight, or my phone with flashlight app, would've been prudent. Still, trying to run by the light of a flashlight as the beam jiggles with each step is just plain annoying. I could never see past the beam, anyway. Besides, I was taking a break from my phone.

It wasn't long before we were on the other side of the pond and running through an ancient forest of longleaf pines. The trees whispered and howled in a confused wind. Towering straight and tall, many of the trees were more than three hundred years old, stretching as high as one hundred feet. On other Abundance properties these majestic pines would be felled for use as telephone poles. However, at our place they remained safe in conservation. I remembered playing hide-and-seek in the forest as a girl. And as a teenager, I'd walked many nights under the tall trees, hand in hand with Buck Tanner.

"Let's pick up the pace, Dolly."

Deeper in the darkened forest it felt almost cool. An eerie mist rose up from dank blackness and twisted around my calves. I sensed something—or someone. Stopping to listen, I heard nothing but rustling trees and the loud *shicka-shicka-shickaing* and tweeting of night creatures.

I pressed on. Clouds blew over the moon, shrouding the woods in inky shadows. We ran though blackness across a slick, spongy carpet of pine needles and itchy wire grass that grew past my thighs. When clouds opened up, shafts of moonlight highlighted little dots of purple, blue, pink, red, yellow, and white wildflowers that looked like Christmas tree lights scattered in the wire grass under the trees. The air here was uncomfortably muggy. My breathing was getting heavier. My nose tickled with the smell of decay and musty dirt mixed with minty pine.

Dolly trotted through the night as fireflies flashed and bats fluttered, dove, and squeaked overhead. I turned right at the first fork, then right again. Slivers of moonlight hit the trail, and a bat flew swiftly and silently toward me. I ducked. It shot up abruptly and over my head. Clouds covered the moon, and it was dark again. Suddenly, Dolly sat down, put her nose to the ground, and whined.

"Don't worry, Dolly. We'll be out of the woods soon. It won't be so scary, I promise."

I had to admit, even for an experienced night runner like me, it was creepier than I'd thought it'd be. Creepier than I'd remembered from my childhood days. I'd gotten used to Boston city streets, with solid pavement and streetlights. By contrast, in the forest when the moon hid behind clouds, it was as dark as any place I'd ever been. Everywhere I ran, it all looked the same to me. I wasn't as familiar with the old trails as I'd imagined. Had I made a wrong turn? The run that normally would have relaxed me seemed to be setting me more and more on edge. The woods gnawed at my nerves.

A little later, I took a left fork, and after just twenty minutes or so, I decided to head back toward the cottage. I turned my head away from the wind to listen. All I heard was a cacophony of crickets and night creatures. There was some kind of screeching bird—at least I thought it was a bird—and wind whistled though high boughs. Spatters of rain hit my face and arms.

Dolly started off down the trail again. I followed.

Minutes later, some sort of animal cried out. I stopped and clutched at my chest. It was a terrible, wretched cry—it sounded like a screaming baby. Fox? Bobcat? Maybe it was a wild boar. *What does a wild boar sound like?* I was losing my nerve.

The moon popped out and made ghostly, wavy shadows on the ground. Dolly stopped and cocked her head. I pulled up and looked around, to get my bearings. I couldn't see a thing except glowing fireflies, wire grass, and tall pine trees, their boughs surging in the blustery wind.

There it was again. That unnerving feeling that someone else was in the woods. I wanted to quell the wind and the cacophony of screeching critters so I could listen. But the howling storm was picking up speed and force. Was I lost? The moon disappeared again. It was pitch-dark. My sneakers were soaked through. My feet were wet, and my legs were spattered with mud.

If I could just find my way to the hundred-acre olive grove, I'd be safe and close to home, I thought. In the grove, there'd be a wide-open space cut out of the forest where young olive trees were planted together in rows. Twelve-foot swaths of dirt between each hedgerow of olive trees, with the drip irrigation hoses secured out of the way just a foot or so to each side of the tree trunks, made for a neat and orderly series of wide alleyways through the orchard. Moreover, Dad's young trees were pruned to no more than ten feet high to accommodate his adapted blueberry harvester that would mechanically gather olives in a few weeks. For me, all this translated into a grove of clear, flat paths that were perfect for running. Short trees would make it easier to see at night.

GRUMMPH.

That was definitely a gunshot, I thought.

"Come on Dolly, this way!"

It was pitch-black. I didn't have a light. I wasn't wearing

hunter orange or anything reflective. Dolly and I sprinted in earnest. We reached an intersection—three trails. Dolly sniffed a tree trunk. Rain was beginning to spatter. I guessed that the olive grove was left. Quickly, I scooped up my wet pup before taking off. Racing with Dolly in my arms made me unbalanced over the uneven terrain.

Still, I pressed on.

Soon after, the moon peeked out from behind clouds and I saw an opening in the pine trees. *Yes!* Daddy's olive tree orchard was just ahead. Rows and rows of young Spanish Arbequina trees—known for high-quality oil and early fruit bearing—along with super-pollinator varieties, Arbosana and Koroneiki planted every twelfth tree, were not much bigger than tall shrubs. Their slender trunks and narrow sage green leaves shimmered in the wind-kissed moonlight.

The hundred-acre plot was long and narrow. All I had to do was run down a row and find the path to the house through the woods at the other end of the grove. After just five or six minutes, I'd pass the old cabin, then go around the pond through the hardwood forest, past the other side of the pond, over the field, and I'd be home. I put the pedal to the metal, so to speak, and sprinted down the trail as fast as I could. Clouds covered the moon, and it was suddenly inky dark again.

I had one foot in the grove. Then, I tripped.

CHAPTER 8

Coming out of the forest, something rubbery caught my
toe and I went flying. I managed to keep ahold of Dolly
until we hit the ground, then with a yelp she shot out of
my arms. I landed like a deadweight on the edge of the
grove. Dolly was somewhere in the dark ahead of me. I had
a hard time getting my breath—the unbroken fall had
knocked the wind out of me.

Finally, I found a little air.

"Dol-ly? Whe . . . where are you?" I gasped. I listened
for my little dog, but I couldn't hear or see her anywhere.
The damn night creatures were too noisy. Wind howled. Big
raindrops slapped the ground. I gasped for another breath.
However, like a deflated tire, my chest wouldn't open. I
huffed short little sniffs of air.

My ankle hurt. I tried not to move my foot. Tears filled
my eyes. My ribs and forearms ached. I worked to breathe.
Covered in dirt and mud, I was shaky and weak—the way
you get when your body knows something is hurt. Before
you go into shock. Or faint.

GRUMMPH.

The sound was soft, but loud. Like a muffled cannon. It was close. My heart raced. There was a crazy hunter on the loose, I thought. I might as well be a deer. Or a wild boar that Pep said anyone can shoot. Anytime.

"Dolly!" I tried to sit up, but a sharp stab in my ribs caught me by surprise. Hot tears of panic and pain streamed down my face. I cried out again, this time louder, "Dol-ly!" Thunder rumbled as I carefully pulled my sprained ankle toward me.

"Dolly! Where are you?" I whimpered. Of all the dogs in the world, mine had to be coal black.

I twisted around to examine my ankle. The moon peeked out for just a second. And that's when I saw the foot. The moon disappeared behind the clouds, and it was dark again. Had I tripped over someone's foot? My head started spinning. I felt nauseous.

Somewhere in the dark, just a few feet ahead of where I'd landed, Dolly started barking. Shrill and sharp, she wouldn't stop.

"Dolly! Come here!" I cried.

Dolly barked as I dragged myself to the foot. Then, I saw the man. Facedown, in the tall grass. His rain-soaked khaki pants matched the wire grass. Only his foot, clad in a worn black sneaker, lay in the path on the edge of my dad's olive grove.

And I'd tripped over it.

I put my head between my knees to keep from fainting. *Breathe in. Exhale. Breathe in.* I knew that I needed to check the motionless man on the ground next to me—maybe I was wrong about him. Maybe he was alive, I thought. Maybe I could save him. I took a deep breath before I dragged myself to his head and bent down to see his face . . .

Suddenly, Dolly barked like crazy—shrill and frantic. I turned my head against the wind and thought I heard a rhythmical, low thumping from somewhere behind me in the woods. Menacing gusts wailed, and stinging rain slapped against my skin as titanic drops pelted the already-drenched cotton khaki pants on the morbid body next to me.

There was a blinding red flash. Earsplitting crackle. Earth-splitting *BOOM*.

I was engulfed by a deafening explosion.

CHAPTER 9

I thought it was another one of my kooky dreams. It was inky dark and I couldn't see. I was cold and shivering as big gusts of air—first icy, then blistering hot—blasted over me. Was I on the ground? I smelled dirt. My heart felt like a trapped bird, wildly fluttering inside my chest, thudding in my ears. I felt sick. Weak. Tired.

There was blistering heat crackling and roaring around me, along with eerie howling and loud snapping sounds. Then, the ground rumbled. I felt a massive creature, breathing . . . no . . . snorting. Fire and snorting . . . a dragon? The ground shuddered. Metal clanged. Someone cursed.

"Ye're alright, lass," whispered a voice. A man? Yes. I felt a hand brush across my cheek. A big, warm hand. Soft. Okay, a big man with soft hands. He had a Gaelic accent. And he'd called me "lass." Was I in Scotland? I'd always wanted to visit Scotland. In fact, I'd dreamt of Scotland often.

"Ahh crikey. You're drookit and bloody Baltic," he mumbled.

There was frenzied motion. My heart raced, yet I felt powerless. Dead. His arms wrapped around me, and my face fell into his warm, muscled chest as he moved us as one. I inhaled his masculine, musky scent—a seductive bouquet of earthy oakmoss, vetiver, and leather with the tang of pine and the smooth, lingering pungency of grayed smoke. It was the unmistakable scent of a wealthy outdoorsman. Although I'd never known a wealthy outdoorsman, I was sure this was what he'd smell like. Maybe he was a Scottish prince and we were in the Scottish Highlands? My ancestors were Scottish.

I sensed the unmistakable tang of horse sweat, and suddenly, we were moving through the darkness. Fast. Holding me tight in his strong arms, my Scottish prince and I jostled and careened up and down through the murky Highlands, racing over rough terrain, through angry rains and howling winds. Creaking, clanking, and whacking of metal and leather echoed in my head as I jostled over the front of the saddle, safely encircled by his brawny arms. I felt his heavy, warm breath in my hair. We must be headed to the castle, I thought.

I didn't want to wake up. Still, I had to see him. I peeked open one eye. Just inches from the tip of my nose, my handsome prince's dark, wavy hair fell over his smooth forehead to frame intense green eyes. They flashed bright with alert intelligence. His lean face was both rugged and handsome, with a strong jaw and day-old beard.

Then, unexpectedly, we rode out of the ruinous forest and into a car wash.

Which reminds me, I thought, I need to wash my BMW. The one sleazoid Zack bought for me as an engagement present. The dark green paint showed all the dirt. With no saved money, no assets, and questionable income, it'd be a while before I could afford another car; I needed to take good care of it. *Oh crappy!* Speaking of no money, *I forgot to pay my auto insurance.* Again. Must remember to do that in the morning when I wake up, I thought. Must not forget . . . But don't wake up! Not now. Not yet.

Water wooshed over me. My mind rambled back to the car wash.

It was the cleanest, whitest car wash I'd ever seen. White tile everywhere. It hurt to look. I snapped my eye shut. Hot, soapy water sprayed over me as my sexy Scotsman's big, warm hands carefully undressed my frigid, shaking body. He ran a cloth over me, rinsing free the mud and muck that was caked on my skin and trapped in my hair. He was strong, but he held me ever so gently. Like I might break. Big, warm hands pressed against my backside as the water rinsed over us. Still, I felt cold. My teeth chattered. I tried to speak, but nothing came out. My heart raced.

"Easy. Ye'll be alright, lass," he whispered in my ear.

He held me tight against his drenched shirt. I pressed myself deep into his warm, wet body. He held fast. My stomach flipped. I heard him call me "precious."

Best dream ever.

CHAPTER 10

Someone burnt the toast. The earthy, acrid smell was everywhere. Must've been Pep, I thought. She never could cook anything . . . even toast. Although, when you think about it, Daphne never could cook, either. Nor could I. That makes three Knox women who aren't worth a lick in the kitchen. It's no wonder none of us can keep a man. Maybe Tammy Fae was right after all.

Pep was still married, at least. Only, hadn't she told me she and Billy were having troubles? *Oh well.* Was it only a matter of time before she, too, would fall off the man-wagon?

I pushed the charred, burnt toast smell out of my mind as I rolled over. Icy cool sheets, pressed smooth, caressed my skin as I buried my nose into the lavender-scented pillow. I tried to reclaim my dream, tried to remember my tall, dark, and handsome Scottish prince as he rinsed my nearly naked body in the steamy car wash. I wanted to feel his strong, unshaven jaw against my neck. His warm, steady hands caressing me, holding me against his big, taut frame. Ancient tribal tunes pulsated in my head. I heard his hunky Gaelic voice whispering to me . . .

"Mornin', Sunshine!" chirped a deeply Southern woman's voice. I heard the *swoosh* of heavy draperies sliding across a rod. "Doc says you'll be back to your old self in no time. I brought you some chamomile tea."

I pried one eye open. Bright sunlight filtered through an ornate lacy curtain decorating a floor-to-ceiling window flanked with voluminous folds of heavy velvet cerulean blue draperies. I lay ensconced on a gilded four-poster bed, heaped with embroidered linens and pillows.

"Where . . . ? Uh . . . is this the castle? Wait . . . Versailles?" I thought I'd been in Scotland. However, perhaps it was France.

Okay, so I wasn't totally awake yet.

"Child, this is anyplace y'all want it to be!"

The woman laughed as she sashayed to my bedside. She was extraordinarily tall with a large frame, like a great warrior maiden, with copper-colored skin and close-cropped hair in the same rich copper color. She had full lips and dark, almond-shaped eyes. Her skin was flawless, and her face was impeccably made up. It was hard to tell how old she was. Not old. Not young. She wore giant gold hoop earrings, a tight-fitting black skirt, and a ruffled, contemporary yellow chiffon blouse with butterflies patterned on it. The butterfly blouse looked pricey. Had to be a designer piece, I thought.

I blinked and took a better look around. Well, if it wasn't the Palace of Versailles, I thought, it certainly could've been. The resplendent room had ceilings that were at least fifteen feet high, with elaborate moldings, chair rails, and carved panels that surrounded blush pink and ivory damask wallpaper. At first, no doors were visible anywhere. It took me a moment to figure out that invisible doors were built seamlessly into the walls.

Oriental rugs sprawled over European oak floors that supported gilded rococo furnishings, including tufted slipper chairs, oversized and heavily framed mirrors, ornate wardrobes and matching dressers. It was a palatial space fit for a queen. You could fit two cottages like mine inside the room.

Suddenly, the resplendent luxury was pierced by raised, angry voices from somewhere outside the room. The woman pinched her lips, put her hands on her hips, and rolled her eyes.

"Miss Sunshine, y'all just sit back and sip some chamomile tea if you can," she said to me. "I'll be back in a few minutes after I call Doc and tell him you're up. First, I need to straighten out those men. I swear, the two of 'em think the sun comes up just to hear 'em crow."

"What's . . . going on?" I stammered. My head ached so bad I felt like it would explode. My mouth felt like a desert, and I barely recognized my hoarse voice. I was thirsty. My heart was racing. My ribs hurt terribly. And I was realizing that every bit of me was sore and achy. I felt a bandage wrapped around my left foot.

"Nothing y'all need to worry about, Sunshine. Just let ol' Precious Darling here take care of everything." She stepped to the table next to the bed and poured a little tea from an ornate silver teapot into a delicate china cup. She patted me on the shoulder. Her large hand was warm. I realized that I was cold. And shaking.

"Wait!" I croaked. I wanted to ask where I was. Find out who she was—Precious Darling? *Who is Precious Darling?* But I never got the chance. The warrior woman strode swiftly to the wall—red-lacquered soles of her spiky yellow Christian Louboutin pumps flashing with each step. She grabbed a lever in the wall, yanked open a hidden door, stepped forward, and was gone. Quietly, the door clicked shut behind her amply endowed butt.

I pinched myself.

It hurt.

"Nope. Not a dream," I mumbled.

Bright sun made my eyes water. I turned toward the antique tea service on the carved table next to me. As I pushed myself up and off overstuffed pillows to reach for the cup, voices outside the room got louder. Arguing. I froze to listen.

"I said, you can't go in there!" scolded Precious Darling. "Doc needs to examine her. Her condition is quite precarious. It's her heart. She's not well. You'll *have* to wait."

"Darlin'," calmly purred a man with a smooth Southern drawl. His low, sotto voce voice was muffled behind the heavy door. It was almost familiar. "Out of respect, I've been coolin' my heels since before sunrise. And I thank you for the coffee and homemade muffins. They were mighty fine. Better than Mama's—but don't you let Mama know I said that, or she'll have my hide."

"Why, thank you," quipped Precious Darling. I could hear the pride in her voice.

"However," the man cautioned, "unless this woman is in a hospital and Doc tells me she's too ill to speak, I'm going in. Now."

I heard quick, heavy footsteps on the other side of the wall.

Precious Darling raised her voice. "No! I see what you're up to—praisin' my muffins! You're not smooth-talkin' me. No, sireee!" She raised her voice. "Mister Collier will see to it that y'all leave his home right quick. In fact, he's on the phone talkin' with his friend the judge right now!"

I imagined her standing outside the door, hands on hips, feet planted firm.

"Please, step aside," he asked quietly.

"Over my dead body!"

"I don't think you mean that," he said flatly. I heard scuffling.

"Like hell I don't!"

"Given the circumstances," he continued coolly, "I can't admire your choice of words."

Still weak, I pushed as hard as I could to sit up against the huge pile of flouncy pillows. That's when the bedcovers fell away. I realized for the first time that I wasn't wearing any clothes. How could I've been so out of it that I'd not noticed my own nakedness?

"What the . . ."

The hidden door flew open. My trembling fingers snatched at the sheet to cover myself.

Just in time.

The man marched in. He stopped short at the foot of the bed.

"Well, I'll be damned," he said.

My mouth dropped open, and the sheet fell from my shaky fingers.

Standing before me in boots and sheriff's uniform was a rock of a man. Thirty-something, tall, tanned, and sexy by anyone's standards, he had an immense chest and shoulders, well-muscled neck, and strong farmer's hands. His dark brown hair was cut short, and he wore aviator sunglasses. A pristine, short-sleeved, collared white button-down shirt fit him to a T—almost as if it'd been painted over his finely muscled form. On one shoulder, he had a large patch and bars denoting his rank. There were small gold pins with the letters "ACSD" embellishing his lapels, and a gold badge with a star in a circle covered his right chest pocket. Loaded with little pouches all around, a heavy-looking black belt holstered a large gun over his hip.

"Eva Knox!"

And when he smiled, he still had those damned cute dimples.

"Buck Tanner!" I gasped.

My high school sweetheart. Eighteen years earlier I'd left him waiting for me at the altar—standing in a rented tuxedo like a soldier in the blistering Georgia summer heat—while two hundred and fifty wedding guests sat fanning themselves on hard wooden pews. The story goes that when I didn't show up, Buck refused to leave the church. He was sure of our love. Sure that his beloved sweetheart would be there. Still, with each passing minute, as folks watched him standing there, waiting, proud and sure, they felt sorrier and sorrier for him while they grew angrier and angrier with me. Finally, after hours passed and all the guests had crept quietly from their seats, someone dragged poor jilted Buck from the church and took him back to his mother's house.

I never showed up. I never spoke to him. I ran straight from Abundance to New England. The fallout from that dreadful day was the very reason I'd never returned home.

Even so, when the sheet covering my naked body fell suddenly from my grasp, Buck Tanner never missed a beat.

"Lookin' damn good, Babydoll," he said with a smile.

CHAPTER 11

"Buck!" I woke with a start. Tears streamed down my face.

"That tomcat's long gone," Precious said, looking up from a paperback novel with a tawdry cover illustration of a half-dressed woman in the arms of a princely man. "You know, Sunshine, you scared Sheriff Sweet Cheeks to death when you fainted."

She stood up from the chair next to my overstuffed bed, tossed the book, and opened a drawer, pulling out a pressed white cotton handkerchief. She handed it to me, and I dabbed at my tears. No common Kleenex boxes in this place. No, sir.

"Fainted?" I mumbled. "I don't understand." Had I fainted?

"Doc says you need bed rest, Sunshine."

I still felt groggy and confused. I just stared at the woman as she spoke.

"The lightning didn't hit y'all direct, but it seems you got yourself quite a jolt of juice when it blasted the big oak in the woods next to your Pop's olive orchard. The oak tree's completely gone. Smells like a dirty barbeque everywhere."

I blinked, trying to take it all in. And after she mentioned it, I detected the whiff of smoke. *The burnt toast.*

"We would've taken y'all to the hospital 'cept there was a terrible pileup on the interstate after the concert at the college last night. The hospital is full up. In fact, they said on the news that there's no beds in *any* of the hospitals nearby. They had to helicopter injured folks to trauma centers all over the state. Y'all are better off here anyways. No germs."

I gulped. My throat felt like I'd swallowed sand.

Precious Darling smiled. Probably had a good dentist. Her teeth seemed unnaturally perfect. Was she a nurse? She just kept right on talking.

"Your big sis, Daphne, she says you're a mite tougher than you look. And that's a good thing, 'cause to tell you the truth, Sunshine, up till now, y'all ain't been lookin' too good."

"Daphne? Is Daph here?" I whispered. My lips felt cracked.

"Well, Miss Daphne *was* here. She's back at your place in the big house, workin' on getting things started for a late breakfast. That's where I'm headed, in a few minutes."

Precious started fussing, straightening the bedcovers around me. "Hey, I never seen anyone from these parts all wrapped up like your sister. Vintage Pucci, no less. Just one little slit for her eyes. I swear, I don't know how she sees to get herself around. I wanted to ask about it, but I didn't want to offend. I figured it must be on account of her religion or something."

"Not her religion," I whispered. "Just . . . Daphne." It would take too much energy for me to explain Daphne's allergic reaction to lye, and her desire to never be seen as any less than perfect. Explaining my oldest sister didn't seem to matter anyway. Precious never came up for air.

"Your other sister was here, too," she continued. "Ain't that Pep a pistol! Promised she'd find me some big dangly skull earrings like what she's wearin'. Now, mind you, when

it comes to accessories, I'm more of a classic designer gal—
not usually into that dark, goth stuff, ya know?"

Precious flapped and waved her hands around and nodded her head emphatically as she spoke. Still, she never
waited for me to say a word. Just kept right on smiling and
talking.

"They got a full house over there with six guests. I said
I'd sit with you here a bit, but I gotta head over now. Promised I'd cook a late breakfast for everyone after the detective
and his deputies left."

"Guests? Six?" I'd thought there were only four. Then, I
remembered how I'd promised Daphne I'd take care of the
New Yorkers. "Oh my God!" I croaked. "Guests! Breakfast!
I shot straight out of bed, flailing around stark-naked, hob-
bling on one foot, looking for my clothes. "What time is it?
I've got to cook! Buy *donuts*!"

"Hold on, Paula Deen." Precious tapped a finger to my
shaking shoulder. I was weaker than I'd imagined and keeled
backward onto the bedcovers. Jumping up quickly had only
made my colossal headache worse. Made my ankle throb.
Made me want to throw up. My head pounded, and my left
ribs hurt. My heart fluttered and flip-flopped. I wanted to
cry. Precious calmly picked up my bare legs and swept them
under the sheets. She pulled up the covers to my chin and
tightly tucked everything under the mattress. She wagged
her finger.

"There's no cookin' for you today, missy. And there's no
gettin' out of bed, either, for donuts or anything else," she
scolded. "Like I said, it's all taken care of. Mister Collier
'loaned' me to your folks. I'm helpin' out, for as long as your
big sis needs me."

I opened my mouth to say something, but I couldn't, for
the life of me, figure out what to say. My mind was racing
to put it all together. I felt worse than crap. I was totally
confused. Who was Mister Collier? Where was I?

"Since your sister's staff—the Greene twins?—went to
the concert and got laid up from the accident on the inter-

state, Miss Pep is helping with the servin' this morning. We got it covered."

"Daphne's letting Pep help? Really?" I couldn't fathom it. She must be *more* than desperate. "Please. I have questions . . ."

"I'm just glad I could help y'all out. Things have been mighty quiet over here." Precious looked up at the ceiling for a moment. There was a beat before she mumbled, "Too quiet."

"Wait. I'm all confused. Where am I? And who is Mister Collier?"

"Why, Sunshine, I thought you knew. I mean, surely, where *else* would you be? I work for Mister Collier, right next door to your place. At Greatwoods."

"Greatwoods? You mean, this is Greatwoods Plantation? Next door?"

"Yep. Greatwoods. Right next door," chirped Precious. "Didn't I say that?"

Built during the Gilded Age of the late nineteenth century by cotton broker Duke Dufour and his wife, railroad tycoon heiress Dina Abbot Dufour, the opulent, mega-thousand-acre Greatwoods Plantation featured a grandiose French-style mansion; hunting lodges; stables; guest cottages; and more. The estate was once a summer playground, hunting retreat, and ostentatiously rich and lavish party place for some of America's most wealthy and famous people. A century later, when I was growing up, the mansion was inhabited by a crotchety spinster descendent, Doris Dufour. The place was rumored to be in general disrepair, and the old woman was rarely seen in town. A manservant took care of her needs. Most of the land was neglected and became a playground for poachers. I'd been told that during my eighteen-year absence, Doris had perished, Greatwoods had changed hands, and the new owner, a mysterious and reclusive man from out of town, had brought the estate back to its former grandiloquence.

"Now, Sunshine, you just set back and rest," said Precious.

"No! Stop! Please. Why was Buck Tanner here? He *was* here, wasn't he?"

"Sheriff Tanner? That man's as hot as a dog on a stick. Yeah, he was waitin' and wantin' to ask you about the dead fellow Mister Collier found layin' with you in the woods."

"Wha . . . what?"

"Mister Collier found you two out there in the fire, and when his cell phone wouldn't work, probably on account of the weather and all, he brought you back here early this mornin'. We weren't sure who you was at first. Then, when Doc got here, he said he thought it was you, on account of your hair and all. Doc said all you Knox girls have that pink hair."

Floyd "Doc" Payne was old and decrepit looking when I knew him as a child. He'd always reminded me of photos I'd seen of Albert Einstein, with knotted hands; big, bushy eyebrows; and untamed, wiry white hair. Plus he had bad breath. Worst ever. I couldn't believe he was still practicing medicine—surely he was well into geezerdom.

"It's not pink. It's strawberry-blonde." I frowned, trying to assimilate everything Precious was saying. It was all too much, too fast, for me to process. Worse still, I didn't remember any of it.

"Whatever. Your hair looks pink to me. Anyway, once we figured out who you were, we called your folks right away. And the sheriff, of course, on account of the dead fella."

"Dead fellow?" I was starting to remember. I'd been running in the woods . . .

"Now don't go botherin' yourself about things—your big sis told me that y'all fret too much." Precious waved her hand in dismissal. "And Doc said you need to stay calm and rest. No fretting. Besides, I'm sure the dead guy deserved what he got. Men usually do. Maybe it was some sort of accident, like the time my cousin Dewanna shot her husband, Tyrell, when she came home early and found him doin' the deed with the babysitter on top of the portable dishwasher. Dewanna wasn't thinkin' straight when she ran into the bedroom, opened the closet, climbed up on the chair, opened the shoe box, and grabbed Tyrell's gun and started wavin' it around—just to scare him, ya know? Well, before y'all know it, the silly gun goes off and Tyrell is plumb dead as a doorknob. Anyway, Dewanna's always been a good girl, and since the babysitter took off and was never seen again, there was no one to say it *wasn't* an accident, so Dewanna made out just fine. And I think you're a good girl like Dewanna. So, no matter what other folks are sayin', I think that whatever happened was accidental, ya know? Anyways, y'all have got time to think about it. Sheriff won't be botherin' us again for a bit. We sent him away, cute, pinchable ass and all."

"Stop! Stop! Stop!" I whined in a squeaky voice that I didn't even recognize as my own. I put my hand to my forehead, closed my eyes to concentrate, and continued, mustering all the strength I could in my voice. "I remember now. What was the guy from Anthony's Awesome Pastries— in Boston—doing here? In Abundance? And he was dead. Right? Dead!"

"Now listen, Sunshine, I don't know nothin' about no pastry guy from Boston."

"It was him—the guy I ordered my wedding cake from. In Boston." A wave of confusion and anxiety washed over me. Nothing made sense. "He was here. The pastry guy! From Boston."

"Hon, I don't have the faintest notion what you're talkin' about."

"I tripped over his foot. In the woods—our woods! Oh my gosh, he was really dead, wasn't he?" I felt tears welling.

"Now listen, Sunshine. You're not makin' sense, 'cept the part about there bein' a dead guy. You must be confused . . . What would some 'pastry guy' from Boston be doin' here in Abundance? Doc said your heart had a shock—literally— and you need to rest and remain calm. So, we're not gonna think about a pastry guy anymore today. Or donuts. And we're not gonna think about whatever it was that happened in the woods, either. Doc's orders. I promised to keep you calm."

"But I have to know! Please, why was the guy from Anthony's Awesome Pastries here?"

"Sunshine. This conversation is over. Ya hear? I'm not
gonna be the one callin' Doc to tell him you keeled over on
account of your fussin' and havin' a big ol' heart attack
about some Boston pastry fella. It ain't gonna happen. Not
on my watch. Nuh-uh."

"But it doesn't make any sense!"

"If it don't make sense now, then maybe it'll make sense
tomorrow after y'all have had some rest and Doc has been
out to check on you again." Precious fluffed my pillow.
"Now, I promised your big sis that I'd head on over to make
breakfast after you were up. So, that's what I'm gonna
do. Y'all just stay here, cool your jets, enjoy your pretty
room, and relax. There are some snacks on the bedside table.
Someone'll check on y'all in a little while."

With that, Precious turned on her yellow Louboutins and
marched toward the hidden door.

"Wait!"

Precious reached for the latch in the wall, pulled open
the door, and stepped into the hallway.

"Are you *seriously* telling me that Buck Tanner is the
sheriff?

The door clicked shut.

CHAPTER 12

I tried to sort out what had happened. I remembered that I'd been running in the woods with Dolly when the storm changed direction and got decidedly dangerous. Then, apparently, I'd tripped on a dead man's foot just on the edge of Daddy's olive grove. Just as I'd recognized the dead man as the guy from behind the counter at Anthony's Awesome Pastries in Boston, according to Precious, lightning hit a big oak tree behind me and I got zapped. Ian Collier, the new owner of Greatwoods next door, found me in the early morning and brought me to Greatwoods where Doc Payne examined me. I had a sprained ankle, probably a cracked rib or two, and was suffering from the aftereffects of a lightning strike, which somehow affected my heart. Still, it couldn't have been too serious, or I'd be in a hospital. Right? But then, Precious said the hospitals were all full, on account of a big accident on the highway. Also, Precious said she was helping Daphne prepare meals for the guests—six, not four—until we hired a chef to replace Loretta, who'd vanished without giving notice to marry our guide, Leonard, who'd also vanished.

That's all I could put together before Precious said she had to run off to help Daphne. I still didn't know what happened to Dolly. And, more important, I didn't know what happened to the pastry guy before I stumbled over him. Or why he was here in the first place. I shuddered thinking about the rubbery foot and his deathly face.

Also, I didn't remember seeing Daphne, Pep, Doc Payne, or Ian Collier. Although, I'd been told that they'd all been at my bedside. On the other hand, I did remember seeing Buck Tanner. And he'd most definitely seen me.

All of me.

My stomach flipped. I felt myself flush at the thought.

"Crap."

I needed to find Dolly. And I needed to figure out what happened to the man in the woods and how he got to Knox Plantation. Not to mention how the hell Buck Tanner had become sheriff.

I threw off the quilt and slid down the bed to the floor. *Ouch!* Still bandaged in elastic, my left ankle hurt when I put weight on it.

"Ignore it, Eva."

I wrapped myself in the satin quilt and hobbled to the foot of the bed where, lo and behold, sitting on a tufted velvet bench, were my clothes. My GEORGIA VIRGIN tee, cutoffs, underwear, and all were clean and folded. Except, my sneakers. They were nowhere to be found.

"I have to get out of here."

I grabbed my clothes. Every muscle in my body ached as I tried to dress quickly. I was clumsy, holding on to the bedpost for support as I stepped gingerly though my panties and shorts, ever-so-carefully placing weight on my wrapped-up foot.

"Just don't flex it," I thought. Since I could put weight on it, I knew that I could get pretty far if I just kept the joint immobile. The elastic wrap would help. My aching ribs were another story.

After I'd finally managed to dress myself, I tossed the quilt back on the bed and rested on the bench. It was hard to breathe. My ribs were killing me. My head ached, and I wanted to puke. What about the dead pastry guy? I shuddered. Why was he here in Georgia? I shuddered again. Then, another reality began to set in.

Wait till the tabloids get ahold of this.

Already, I could see the headline: "Runaway Bride Trips Over Dead Pastry Guy." Tammy Fae Tanner and Debi Dicer would have a field day. Not to mention everyone on the Internet. They'd probably blame me for the poor guy's demise.

And what about Buck? Was he actually sheriff? *Impossible.* Growing up, Buck had been everyone's favorite bad boy. After his dad had left his unwed teenaged mother, Tammy Fae, when she was pregnant, Buck had been raised to work on his granddaddy's farm. From the time he was a little boy, mornings before school he'd milked cows by hand. When he was in high school, after football and swim team practices—he led both teams to state championships—he'd worked in the fields, mowing, plowing, seeding, and hand-picking weeds until after dark. Buck was anything but shy. He'd irreverently spoken his mind whenever he pleased, even when it meant a whipping from his granddaddy. He'd been a cutup in class. His coaches had made him do extra laps—on the field and in the pool—during almost every practice. He hadn't cared. In fact, I think he'd rather enjoyed the extra challenge.

When he was a junior and I was a freshman, Buck's football coach had arranged for me to tutor Buck in English. Buck was smart; he'd just had no time for studies. Months later, much to the dismay of every other girl in Abundance, the most popular guy in school had made me his sweetheart.

Still, Daphne always said Buck would never amount to anything once he got out of high school. She often described him as a "sweet talker" and a "loose cannon." And, on those counts, Daphne was right. Buck had played pranks on everyone at school. Even the principal. He'd raced cars on the interstate. He'd gone with the boys and hunted illegally. Buck and his chums had done silly things with snakes and alligators in the swamp. They'd partied all night. Still, Buck never got in trouble. And the one time he was caught red-handed, Buck was so damn cheeky that he got away with it.

Now, could this man actually be Abundance County sheriff? No, I'm sorry. Thinking of irreverent Buck Tanner as sheriff was a total stretch.

No way.

CHAPTER 13

I turned the handle to the secret door in the wall. The door opened silently to reveal a freakishly tall, bald, Lurch-looking manservant with a long nose, sallow skin, and sunken eyes standing in a grandiose hallway. When he saw me, he skulked toward the door and mumbled something about Miss Precious telling me to stay in bed. With over-sized, boney hands, he ushered me back toward the bed where he poured more steamy, hot tea into the tiny Limoges cup. Then he shambled away. The door clicked shut.

I felt like a prisoner. I needed to find out what happened, I needed to find Dolly. And I wanted to get home. Lurch's raspy breathing echoed from the other side of the door. My heart stopped. I held my breath, listening to Lurch, listening to me.

An eternity passed.

Finally, I heard his footsteps thump slowly down the hall.

Knowing Lurch was roaming about the hallway compli-cated my escape. I slipped out of bed. "Ow!" Then I inched to the big window to check out my options. Happily, the window wasn't a window at all. It was a French door that led to a balcony outside. I turned the key to unlock the door. It clicked. The door swung inward with a creak.

It never occurred to me that there might be some sort of alarm. Or camera.

I heard the sound of rushing water. I limped outside into a smothering blanket of muggy morning haze. The humid air was at least twenty degrees hotter than the air-conditioned bedroom. Like a fish out of water, I gulped for breaths in the oppressive mist. I tiptoed awkwardly to the balcony's edge and peered over the massive marble railing.

This was definitely Greatwoods. The ground was a *long* way down. Below, a garden with evergreens, flowering shrubs, and perennials wrapped around a patio decorated with giant, cherub-festooned fountains gushing with falling water and the most grandiose, turquoise, Gatsby-like pool I'd ever seen. I'd climb down the woody wisteria vine and drop into the garden, sneak across the pool area, climb the iron fence, navigate the lawns, and slip into the woods before heading home.

Ironically, I'd had a good deal of experience with this type of situation. Late nights, back when I'd been a teen, I'd snuck out of my bedroom on the second floor of the big house, crossing the veranda roof before climbing down a dogwood tree to where Buck waited for me in the garden. From there, we'd embark on our late-night trysts, moseying and hanky-pankying about the farm.

One time, we'd been misbehaving in the old cabin by the pond when my dad and his friends stopped by after some late-night fishing. Like the slaves whom my family helped hide a century and a half earlier, Buck and I had thrown open a little trapdoor disguised in the floorboards and dove down into an underground chamber. Buck had held me re-assuringly while Dad and his friends chatted, cleaned fish, drank beer, and smoked cigars above us. I was scared to death we'd get caught. Finally, after the fishing party had broken up, Buck and I'd clambered out of our hiding place and headed quickly and stealthily home, where he hoisted me up into the dogwood tree and I'd climbed to the roof,

then through the window, back into my room and to bed.
No one ever knew.

"I can do this," I chanted under my breath, trying to
psych myself up. "I am stealthy." I peered over the edge of
the massive balcony. It looked to be more than 30 feet
down. The ancient wisteria vine twisted around one of the
pillars. I thought of the dogwood tree outside my room back
home.

"I can do this. I am stealthy."

There were acres and acres—miles, actually—between
where I was on the balcony and my cottage behind the big
house. Even so, I was sure that once I'd hit the ground, I
could be home through the woods in less than an hour. Unless something went wrong.

Suddenly, the hallway door clicked open.

Lurch!

Without thinking, I grabbed the massive marble railing
and threw myself over the balcony.

CHAPTER 14

"Wow, Eva, what happened to you?" Pep raised her eyebrows over big smoky gray eyes. "And what are y'all doin' here? Aren't y'all supposed to be resting at Greatwoods?"

She took a stack of plates from the dishwasher and set them on the red laminate countertop. Standing in black leather biker boots, her flawless pale skin and short platinum hair were a stark contrast to her all-black teeny leather skirt and fitted sleeveless tee. Her nails and lips were painted a deep plum color. A silver skull earring dangled from one ear.

"Eva, sweetie, it is good to see you up and about. We didn't expect to see y'all today." Daphne opened a drawer, pulled out a handful of spoons, and handed them to Pep. "Pepper-Leigh, be a *dahhwr-ln'*, please, and set the dining room table for breakfast while I finish ironing." Daphne's "ironing" sounded like "*ahhr-wrunun.*"

I stepped into the kitchen from the back porch. The clock above the sink read nine fifteen.

"Well, lookee who the wind blew in!" Precious Darling stepped out of the walk-in pantry near the back door. She gave me a big wave and a toothy white smile. "I told y'all that Doc said to stay in bed and rest today."

Precious looked mammoth compared to my two sisters. She pulled open one of the doors in the range. Studying the contents of the oven, she looked like a giant peering into a mouse hole. She shook her head and shut the oven door.

"Eva, is that some sort of tree growing in your hair?" asked Daphne.

I reached up and grabbed a small branch from my hair before picking pine needles off the front of my GEORGIA VIRGIN tee and tossing them all out the back door, in the general direction of Daphne's garden. I hobbled into the kitchen and plunked down onto the caned seat of an antique pressed-oak chair at the table—it was the same oak table and set of Larkin chairs that I'd grown up with as a girl. Only they looked better than I'd remembered, because Daphne had used some of her divorce money to have the wood refinished and the seats recaned.

"What happened to the pastry guy?" I rubbed a sore shoulder. My ankle throbbed and my arms and legs were covered with cuts and scratches. My ribs hurt. "I can't find Dolly. Has anyone seen Dolly?"

Daphne, standing behind an ironing board, pressing and folding creamy linen napkins, answered brightly, "Miss Precious told us that y'all said you knew Leonard from Boston. How did y'all know each other? Did y'all date up North?"

My sister wore a crisp white linen blouse and a pair of white designer jeans with a skinny yellow belt and yellow slingback Kate Spade pumps. The blotches and swelling on her willowy arms and hands had disappeared completely. Still, loosely wrapped around her head was another over-sized silk scarf. It had horses, bits, and leather straps printed on it and fell over her shoulders. Hermès, no doubt. Daphne's gold charm bracelet jingled as she vigorously worked the iron across the linens.

"Leonard? The hunting guide? I don't know Leonard."

"Of course y'all know Leonard, Eva. He works for us here." Daphne looked at me sideways, trying to sound casual. Still, her voice was higher pitched than usual. She was trying to hide it, but I knew she was eager to hear my answer.

"Daph, you mean Leonard *used* to work for us," said Pep, rolling her eyes. She pulled open the refrigerator and scanned the contents.

"I've still never met Leonard," I said. "Remember? He was out on a fishing trip when I got here. I just keep missing him. Anyway, I wasn't talking about Leonard. I was talking about the pastry guy from Boston. The dead man. In the woods."

"Exactly, the dead man in the woods. Leonard."

"What are you talking about?"

"Honestly, I can't believe I'm doin' this," Daphne murmured under the scarf head wrap as she sprayed in inordinate amount of starch on a napkin. "I'm talking about the man in the woods with y'all last night. Leonard."

"You mean, the pastry guy."

"Pastry guy?" asked Pep.

"Eva, what in the world are y'all talkin' about?" demanded Daphne.

"I'm thinkin' head injury," said Pep.

"Well, yes, I suppose we could take her for a CT scan."

"Doc says it's her heart, not her head." Precious tossed an ice-filled plastic baggie into my lap. "There ya go, Sunshine. Put that on your ankle. You shouldn't be on it like that. Glad to see my elastic wrap held up."

"Thanks."

Pulling another chair close to me, I set my foot on the seat and draped the ice baggie over my sprained ankle. The cold compress felt good. Daphne came around the end of the ironing board. She looked at my ankle. Then, the rest of me. I sat hunched over, as my ribs were killing me.

"Don't y'all have clean clothes? A pretty little sundress, perhaps?" asked Daphne. She sounded exasperated. "And look at your feet!" cried Daphne. "Why, they're positively filthy, Eva. What happened to y'all? Where are your shoes?" She sounded as if she were scolding an unruly child. Daphne shook her head and crossed to the laundry room near the back door, across from the pantry.

"I couldn't find my shoes."

"They melted," said Precious. "Did Mister Lurch bring you home?"

I turned to her. "Mister Lurch? *Lurch?* You mean that's actually his name? *Lurch?*" I pinched myself. "You've got to be kidding."

"Of course that's his name. Why would I be kidding?" asked Precious. She actually looked serious.

"Look, you guys, it took me more than an hour to get here this morning—and without my sneakers. I had to jump off a balcony. Climb through strands of electric fence. Disentangle myself from barbed wire. *Barbed wire!* Why is there barbed wire next door? It wasn't there when we were kids."

"Sunshine, a whole lot has changed since you were a kid," laughed Precious.

"If only," snorted Pep.

The dryer door in the laundry room slammed shut, and Daphne reappeared, heading for the ironing board, carrying a wad of linens.

"Eva, if y'all are well enough to be jumpin' from balconies and running through the woods in your bare feet like a savage banshee, you're well enough to help us with the guests. Except, y'all can't serve the guests or be workin' in the kitchen in your filthy bare feet, wearing that nasty 'virgin' shirt and those teeny cutoffs. We have board of heath rules to consider. Honestly, I know you're not one hundred percent, but did you even bathe today?"

"Speaking of which, what happened to that shirt?" asked Precious. "I *know* that I washed and pressed it. It was spotless when I laid it out on the bench."

"You *pressed* a tee shirt?" asked Pep incredulously.

"Of course."

Precious stomped her four-inch spiky yellow heels past

me on her way to the pantry. She looked so tall that I imagined her having to duck under doorframes.

"Ya know, Sunshine, Mister Lurch would've given you a ride home," said Precious. "All you had to do was ask."

"Yes. Mister Collier and his staff have been most gracious and accommodating. I daresay, he may even have saved your life, Eva. Such a *lovely* man." Daphne swooned. "And frankly, dear, it looks to me like they took better care of you than y'all do yourself. Y'all looked positively radiant and rested earlier, all tucked into your beautiful gold-leaf bed surrounded by luxurious, silky linens and gorgeous antiques. Honestly, you haven't looked that good in *years*!"

"Thank you," said Precious.

"I'll second that," Pep said, scuffing across the floor toward the Sub-Zero. "But what a difference now. Maybe a CT scan wouldn't be a bad idea. Eva, you look scary."

"That says a lot, comin' from Pepper-Leigh," said Daphne.

Pep scowled at Daphne. "And you look ridiculous, Daphne—with that scarf wrapped around your head. Why can't you just be yourself, for once, and let people see who you really are?"

"If your face were disfigured like mine, you'd not be lettin' folks see you. Why look at a bloated woman when you could look at Hermès? Besides, you're no fashion goddess yourself, Pepper-Leigh!"

"Like me," said Precious with a smile.

I rolled my eyes.

"Honestly, Pepper-Leigh, who wears black leather in the summertime?" Daphne asked.

"Let's be real, here, Daphne. Your face is a little puffy," said Pep. "Not disfigured. I mean, really, just look at Eva. She's scratched, bloody, and bruised, and her clothes are torn and smeared with disgusting debris. Still, she's obviously fine with *her* wracked-up appearance."

I glared at both my sisters while Precious sniggered as she stomped her four-inch spiky yellow heels on her way to the pantry.

"We don't have time for chitchat," said Daphne, looking exasperated. "We're late with breakfast on account of your, er, accident, Eva."

"Plus Daphne's shorthanded again. The twins are out today," said Pep.

"And the detective and his deputies woke everyone early and interviewed us before they scurried all over the property, snooping for heaven-knows-what. We've heard nothin' but ATVs buzzin' back and forth to the spot where they found you and *that man*. We're *all* tired and cranky. And we have six guests, the foursome from New York and two young women from Tallahassee who came in this mornin' after the accident business on the interstate."

"And," said Precious, "the bus for the antebellum tour is comin' soon."

"Exactly. Eva, the guests will all be down any minute. They're scheduled for the antebellum plantation tour today, and they've got to eat breakfast first. A wonderful breakfast. So, please, pull yourself together. Try to look cheerful. Now that y'all are here, we need your help."

"And, don't forget, Boone Beasley is comin' with a delivery," said Precious.

"I can't wait to see Boone Beasley." Pep smirked. "He was at the Roadhouse all afternoon yesterday. Hopefully, he's slept it off." Pep rolled her eyes.

"Pepper-Leigh, no sarcasm, please. Boone has worked hard at his recovery. It's when folks won't give him a chance that his soberness becomes problematic. Besides, his spicy sausages are heavenly, and he gives us a deal on them."

"Ahhh! The man has wooed you with his spicy sausage!" said Pep. She broke out into little pig snorts. Precious let out a chuckle.

"That's disgusting, Pepper-Leigh." Daphne shot Pep a stern look.

"Daphne, with five kids, you can't be half the prude you pretend to be." Pep kept snorting as she checked out the contents of the cupboard.

"Eva," continued Daphne, ignoring Pep, "please, go to

the back door and put on my green Wellies. In fact, y'all can consider the rubber boots yours; I have another pair. At least your feet and legs will be covered, which—judging from their condition—will be a blessing, and we won't be in violation of any health codes. I daresay, some of my homemade olive oil salve and a nice pedicure are in order, and right quick. Y'all can go tomorrow. I'll even pay for the pedi."

I ignored my sister's offer. I wasn't in the mood to think about going to Tammy Fae's for a pedi. Not in this century, anyway.

"Can someone please tell me what the pastry chef from Boston who made my wedding cake was doing, here in Abundance, lying next to Daddy's olive grove? Was he hunting?"

"Mornin', good folks of Knox Plantation!" called a man from the front of the house. "Missus Bouvier, are you somewhere about?"

"We're in the kitchen, Boone!" Daphne called cheerily. Then she turned, gave us "the stare," and waged her finger. "Now, y'all listen up," she whispered. "We'll hear no more about this dead-man business in front of the guests, or while Boone Beasley is here. Not a word! Boone's the biggest gossip in town. And since we don't know what really happened to poor Leonard, it's business as usual. If anyone asks straight-out, we say it was a terrible accident. If we don't nip it in the bud, this type of scandal will *kill* our business."

"Wait, wait, wait!" I whispered. "Are you guys telling me that Leonard, the hunting guide, is dead? And he's the same guy who used to work behind the counter at Anthony's Awesome Pastries in Boston?"

No one said a word. Then, almost in unison, they all looked at one another, raised their eyebrows, and shrugged.

CHAPTER 15

When I was a little girl, I thought Boone Beasley looked like a pig. And, I admit, I still thought of him that way. With beady eyes, a stout nose, and puffy pink cheeks, he wore khaki pants and a chambray shirt, bursting at the buttons so much that it showed his yellowed tee shirt underneath.

The butcher handed my sister a large string-tied package wrapped in brown paper. He didn't seem fazed a bit by the silk scarf wrapped around her head. Or by Pep, in all her goth gloriousness. Or by Precious, the Herculean woman in an apron, ducking through doorways and clomping around the kitchen in four-inch yellow Louboutins.

"Here's your order, Missus Bouvier—oooh, isn't that a pretty scarf you're wearing! I've added some of my special spiced low-fat sausage that y'all like so much."

"Why, thank you for the delivery, Boone. I so appreciate it!" Daphne accepted the package.

Boone Beasley had been the only butcher in Abundance County for as long as I could remember. I used to go to his shop downtown when I was a little girl. First with my mother, then later with Auntie Ella. We'd go several times each week to purchase the freshest, best cuts of meat.

"Precious, can you deal with this, please?" Daphne handed the wrapped meat to Precious.

"Sure can, ma'am." Precious hustled to the far end of the kitchen to unwrap and inspect the goods.

"Say!" said Boone with a smile. "Y'all must be quite frightened, knowing there's a murderer running around here! Everyone in town is talking about it! Do you have a gun to protect yourselves? Can't be too careful these days."

Before Daphne could answer, the butcher turned to me.

"Why, Miss Eva! Folks said you were back. I haven't seen you since you were a child. You're just as lovely a woman as your father said you were. You remind me of your mother—oh, perhaps I shouldn't have said that?"

"No, it's fine, Mister Beasley. Thank you."

My mother had run off and left Abundance for who-knows-where when I was a small child. I was long over being sensitive about it. I plopped the ice baggie from my ankle on the table and raised myself up from the chair to face the butcher. He kept talking.

"I've been seein' your pretty picture in the *Supermarket Stargazer*. And I saw you on TV! What's the name of that new show? Oh yes, *Celebrity Screwups*! Sorry about all your troubles lately. I just want y'all to know that I've been payin' no mind to what folks in town are sayin' about you."

"Thanks, Mister Beasley," I said. If that wasn't a back-handed compliment, I don't know what was. But it only got worse.

"So," Boone Beasley continued, "who killed the man in your daddy's olive grove? Was it you? I heard that someone found you layin' right there on the ground next to him, right by the lightnin' fire! Tell me watchya know! Folks in town are just all abuzz about it." He took a breath and turned to Daphne. "Tammy Fae Tanner said it was a love triangle." Then he turned back to me. "I heard he was the plantation's field guide. Was the man your secret lover? Your 'rebound' guy after you dumped that Boston weatherman? Or, since he wasn't from around here, did y'all know the dead fellow before comin' back home? We were thinking that you and your lover get caught by the other woman." He turned to Daphne. "Wasn't she your cook?" He turned back to me. "Before she shot him. Or did you let 'em have it yourself? Did you catch the two of *them* together?"

Boone was gushing with excitement. His face was all red, and he looked like he might pop.

Daphne forced a polite laugh. "Oh, Boone, you have such a naughty sense of humor!"

Tina Turner's song "Simply the Best" blared from the countertop. Precious reached over and picked up her cell phone, cased in gold sparklies.

"Hello?" Precious turned away and mumbled to someone on the other end of the line.

"Mister Beasley always entertains me," said Pep with a big smile. She popped a couple of blueberries into her mouth.

"Huh-huh," said Precious into the phone.

I crossed to the sink to wash my hands and face, thinking Boone would get the hint and stop asking his ridiculous questions. No such luck.

"Why, I'm not tryin' to be funny," said Boone. "People in town want to *know* what happened. Of course, since I was coming out here, I said I'd speak to y'all and let folks know what happened. Kind of gettin' it straight from the horse's mouth, so to speak."

"Y'all don't say!" Precious chimed into her phone.

Boone Beasley chortled and put his arm on my elbow. Shutting off the faucet, I turned to face him. He leaned in close and gushed, "Tell me, he *was* your illicit lover, wasn't he? He followed you here from up North, didn't he?"

I smelled alcohol on his breath. Still, was this guy kidding? I felt my cheeks flush. Daphne slid his arm away from mine and stepped in between us.

"Oh, don't be silly, Boone," she said cheerily. "Why, *everyone* knows that Eva is a lesbian!"

"What?" I turned to stare at Daphne.

Precious spun around and stared, making little choking noises. "I gotta go," she stammered quickly into her cell phone, before tossing it on the counter. Pep just kept popping blueberries into her mouth, her gray eyes twinkling.

There was a knock on the dining room door.

"Excuse me," said a woman's bedroomy voice. "I have a question." The door opened a crack, and our guest Bambi peeked in.

"Please, Missus Gambini, do come in," said Daphne. She cleared her throat.

The door swung open, and we were faced with ginormous batwing eyelashes, puffy pink lips, and boobs so about to pop that they looked ready for the Macy's Thanksgiving Day Parade. Bambi's unnaturally blonde hair was loosely piled on top of her head. It looked like a lopsided bird's nest. Boone Beasley's mouth dropped open.

"I'm sorry to intrude," she said in her sultry voice. "I was wondering, is there somewhere in town I could get my hair and nails done?"

"Y'all can get your hair and nails done at Shear Southern Beauty on Main Street," said Daphne with a smile. "The owner is Tammy Fae Tanner. She'll take good care of y'all."

"Oh yes! Miss Tammy Fae is a whiz with hair!" gushed Boone, still bug-eyed. "I should know—my shop is right next door to her salon. And she's *so* much fun to talk to . . . She knows absolutely everything about *everyone* in town!" Boone winked at me.

Boone sounded enamored with Tammy Fae. I couldn't imagine her putting up with the porky butcher. On the other hand, they both loved gossip mongering. And she was probably always eager to have the ear of anyone who would listen. With his shop next door to hers, he was a sitting duck.

"Thanks!" Bambi said to Boone. Then to me, "Maybe she can take me this evening."

"She has very flexible hours," I said. "Please, make sure you tell Tammy Fae that her *good friend*, Eva Knox, sent you to see her."

Pep stared at me with an amused expression as she hand washed a serving platter at the sink.

"Okay. I'll be sure to tell her that you sent me." Bambi pushed her hair up before yelling over her shoulder, "Oh yeah, I almost forgot. Is there a spa or someplace that does Botox?"

"Botox?" Daphne, Pep, Boone, and I all said the word at the same time.

"No Botox in these parts, deary," shouted Precious from the other side of the kitchen as she rewrapped the meat. "Y'all gotta go to Thomasville or Valdosta for that kinda stuff."

"Oh. I see." Bambi pursed—or tried to purse—her puffy lips as she tried to furrow her creaseless brow. I think it was her pout face, but her expression looked the same as it always did, like a sad blowfish who'd spent too much time at the makeup counter. Then she said, "Darn. I was kind of hoping for a little filler. Thanks anyway."

"You're welcome," said Daphne. "Please tell folks breakfast will be ready in a few minutes."

"Okay. We'll be in the living room."

Bambi blew us a kiss—easy for her, because her lips were permanently positioned that way.

"If you ask me, that gal has had more than her share of filler already." Precious chuckled.

"Precious!" Daphne sighed.

"Ladies, it's been lovely," said Boone. "I must run." He blinked several times, almost as if he had a nervous tick. "Miss Pep, as always, you look stunning, I might add."

"Thank you."

"My bill is in the package." He tried to smile, except he looked like a man who was out of practice.

"Got it right here," called out Precious.

The butcher looked expectantly at Daphne. But he'd made her mad, with all his impudent questions. I knew there was no way he'd get paid that day. Daphne would make him wait. And she was such a good customer he'd not dare to ask for immediate remittance.

"We'll have it in the mail first thing tomorrow," said Daphne curtly. "And I do thank you for bringing the order over today. It will give us a big jump-start on preparations for the important Chamber of Commerce meeting we're hosting tomorrow."

"Always happy to have your business, Missus Bouvier. Ladies, have a nice day."

Boone Beasley turned up the corners of his mouth and puffed out his chubby cheeks. He waved to Daphne, Pep, and Precious and avoided my gaze before walking out the door.

I whirled to face Daphne.

"What the hell were you thinking? I'm not a lesbian and you know it!"

CHAPTER 16

"I'm sorry, Eva," said Daphne. "I don't know what got into me. Boone Beasley just ruffled my feathers, talkin' to you like that, speculating and suggesting terrible things! I had to say *something* to stop him. It just came out."

Precious was laughing. "Now, Sunshine, if that fella is fixin' to believe it, then let him have at it. Anyway, it's a mighty improvement over what they been sayin' about you around town. Go with it, Sunshine. Who cares?"

"Eva, listen, Precious does have a point here. Having folks talk about y'all's sexual preferences is a lot better than having folks call y'all a slut and a murderess."

"Murderess? That's ridiculous. And who's calling me a slut? People are calling me a slut? Why? Because I chose not to marry a person? Someone who isn't right for me? Someone who deceived me? Someone who . . ."

"Simpletons around here are just jealous, that's all," said Precious.

"Yes. It looks easy for you to get a man, when it's not so easy for others," said Daphne. "They're just takin' potshots because they wish they could be more like y'all and they don't know how to go about it. They'll tire and move on. Eventually."

"If brains were leather, most of these folks wouldn't have enough to saddle a june bug," said Precious with a chuckle.

"Too bad about Leonard, huh?" Biting into a fresh peach, Pep grabbed a folded pile of ironed napkins, placed them on top of the stack of plates, and topped it all off with a handful of silverware before she kicked her boot into the swinging door and sashayed into the dining room. The door swung with a big squeak.

"Don't get peach juice on the clean linens, Pepper-Leigh!" warned Daphne. "Yes, it's a shame about Leonard."

"What did happen to Leonard?" I asked. Finally, I would get some answers.

"Detective Gibbit seems sure the guy was bumped off," said Pep from the dining room.

"Shhh!" hissed Daphne through the door. "Pepper-Leigh, why must you always be so dark?"

"Bumped off? You mean, someone killed him?"

No one paid attention to me.

"I don't like him much. Do you?" Pep called from the dining room side of the door.

"Don't like who?" asked Precious. "The beady-eyed dweeb detective?"

"Don't forget his skinny ass and jug ears," snorted Pep. "And the bucktooth."

"Yeah, that boy could eat an ear of corn through a picket fence!" laughed Precious.

"Hush, Pepper-Leigh! Precious!"

"And I'm not being 'dark,' Daphne," said Pep from the other side of the door. "The detective clearly thinks there was a murder on the farm. Why else would he have been questioning everybody and snooping around for 'evidence' today?"

"Please, Pepper-Leigh, don't talk about this in the dining

room," begged Daphne in a loud whisper. "The guests will hear y'all! They've been through enough this morning. I'm hoping they can forget this unpleasantness and still enjoy their vacation."

Pep kicked open the door again. Daphne jumped back and shot her an exasperated look.

"Now, mind y'all, until this terrible event is figured out, I want us to keep everything hush-hush. A scandal like this is deadly in the hospitality business!" warned Daphne. "Especially you, Pepper-Leigh. Don't you go talkin' about any of this down at that sleazy bar of yours. Just comport yourself as if nothing out of the ordinary has happened out here. All of you."

"What happened to Leonard?" I asked again.

"You're kidding, right, sis?" Pep said, pouring herself fresh-squeezed orange juice. In a flash, she'd chugged the juice and grabbed another napkin pile. She kicked the dining room door open.

"Pepper-Leigh, *puhhl-eeze* do not kick the door!" scolded Daphne. "Y'all make scuff marks."

"C'mon, guys! What happened to Leonard?"

Daphne's eyes returned to me. She stopped for a moment to study my face.

"Why aren't you telling me what happened to Leonard?" I stood with my hands on my hips, waiting for someone to answer. "And where's Dolly? Has anyone seen my dog?"

"Dead as a doornail," said Precious.

I let out a little shriek, then doubled over in pain from my ribs. "What!"

"Shhh, Eva, not so loud," Daphne scolded.

"Leonard, that is. He's dead. Kaput. Gonzo," said Pep.

"That's the guy you were layin' next to," said Precious.

"Well, I gathered that much," I said, rolling my eyes.

"Only his name wasn't Leonard. Did y'all know that?" said Precious with her eyebrows raised. "Tilly Beekerspat, down at dispatch, said on the phone when we were talkin' earlier that the fella's driver's license is a fake. Until they get a make on his prints, no one knows his name. Y'all got any ideas, Sunshine?" Precious looked over at me.

"Me?" I shook my head "All I know is that he used to work at Anthony's Awesome Pastries. In Boston. I'm sure it was the same guy. And I'm still waiting for someone here to tell me what he was doing here and *how* he died. And what happened to Dolly?"

"I think folks have been waitin' for you to tell *us* what happened, Eva," said Pep.

"Me . . . ?"

Precious interrupted, "I don't know anything 'bout no Dolly, 'cept that's who you've been callin' for when you was out of it earlier. That is, when you weren't blubberin' for the sheriff." Precious let out a husky laugh, plopping dollops of something white and creamy into the blender.

"I've seen Dolly running around," said Pep. "She's fine. Daphne had the kids feed her on the back porch earlier today, right, Daph?"

I whirled around to face Precious, "I was *not* 'blubbering' for Buck." Then to Pep, "Why is Dolly loose? She's still a puppy. Have you checked to see she's alright?"

"Oh yes, ma'am, you was blubbering *and* callin' out his name, over and over." Precious waved her arms and in a falsetto voice cried out again, "Buck! Buck!" She laughed like it was the funniest thing in the world. She turned on the blender and the engine whirred.

I could feel my face and the back of my neck heating up.

"See, I told you so. She still wants him," Pep said to Precious.

I glared at Pep. Then Precious.

Daphne stared hard at Pep. Then, she turned to me and said, "Dolly will come home when she sees y'all are back, Eva." Then to Pep and Precious, she warned, "I told you two not to fret Eva. She'll tell us what happened when she's ready. And I don't want to hear that man's name in my house, Pepper-Leigh."

"Who, Buck Tanner?" asked Pep, raising her eyebrows.

"Dolly is a dog?" Precious shook her head as she shut off the blender. "All this time I thought she was a relation or somebody important. Or somebody else bumped off in the woods."

"Dolly *is* important," I snapped.

"Gee whiz, Daph, why don't you want to hear Buck Tanner's name?" said Pep with a smirk.

Daphne glared at Pep but didn't answer. Then, she shot Precious a warning look.

"Dolly brings great comfort to Eva." Then she turned to me. "We'll find her. Don't fret, Eva. Y'all know how your sensitive mind wanders. Meanwhile, back to the question about Leonard, since, apparently, y'all really don't remember anything about it. Folks seem to be thinkin' it was some sort of lovers' quarrel between him and Loretta."

"Like, they were running off to get hitched, they had a fight, and Loretta offed him before she disappeared," said Pep dryly. "Of course, then there's the other theory . . ."

"Pepper-Leigh! I *told* you before. Not a word!"

"What 'other' theory?" I asked.

"Never you mind. It's all silliness," said Daphne. "Ouch! Oh, how I loathe ironing!"

"Pep, what other theory?"

"The one where folks says *you* killed him, Miss Eva," answered Precious.

"Precious!" Daphne scolded.

"Me? I killed him? That's ridiculous. Why would I kill someone?"

"Yup," said Precious. "You killed him. My girlfriend, Coretta Crumm, she works at the bank, y'all know, well, she called and said Tammy Fae Tanner has folks worked up about it already."

"Tammy Fae? Oh my gosh." I put my hands to my head.

"No surprise there," said Pep dryly.

"The woman is a demon," I said. "Will she *ever* quit? What possible reason could she be telling folks I had for killing someone?"

"Well, you were layin' on the ground next to the poor

fella when Mister Collier found you. Seems pretty easy to figure something happened between you two, then, whatever you two was doin' got interrupted by the lightnin' and all," said Precious. "Tilly Beekerspat says Detective Gibbit is comin' to arrest you this morning."

Daphne gasped.

"Arrest me! Are you kidding?"

"Dyin' if I'm lying," said Precious. She sounded smug. "I mean, what would *you* think?"

"Miss Precious!" cried Daphne.

"The man was already there—on the ground—when I got there! I tripped over his foot and didn't even know what it was until I started looking for Dolly . . ." I shuddered again. "I wasn't sure he was dead. I thought it'd been some sort of hunting accident. Or maybe a heart attack."

I thought I saw Daphne heave a sigh of relief.

"Wow. Now, that's a lifetime achievement if I ever heard one. How many people get to say they tripped over a dead guy?" said Pep.

Daphne shot Pep a disgusted look.

"Did you all actually think I had something to do with the man's death?"

"Well, of course not," sniffed Daphne. "I hoped y'all would have some sort of reasonable explanation. But then, you said that you were acquainted with the man, from Boston."

"Hoped? You mean, you weren't *sure*?"

"Well, findin' you out there like that . . . It did look kinda bad, Eva," said Pep.

"I believe you," said Precious. She didn't sound convincing. "Of course, Miss Tammy Fae says you must've killed the Loretta woman, too. Folks just haven't found her body yet."

"Good grief!"

"Anyway," said Precious, "What I hear you sayin' sounds good to me, hon. Like I told you before, I'm not judging. Sometimes, folks get what they deserve. Like with my cousin Dewanna."

"But I'm telling the truth! How could I kill someone? *Why* would I kill someone, *anyone*?" I could feel my heart race. "You mean it wasn't an accident?"

"Please, Eva, don't raise your voice," said Daphne. "And don't excite yourself. Y'all are gettin' red in the face."

"Coretta Crumm said it wasn't accidental on account of somethin' 'close range' had happened," said Precious. "Coretta knows 'cause her brother, Bigger, works at the morgue."

Daphne shot a look to Precious and then wagged her finger toward Precious and Pep.

"Y'all are just upsetting Eva. And I warned y'all earlier not to do that!" scolded Daphne. "Of course, Eva had nothing to do with any of this. I'm sure there is a perfectly logical explanation for the bullet hole in the middle of the man's chest. Now, let's just have a nice day and focus on our guests. Can we please, ladies?" Daphne slammed the iron down and shut off the switch.

"Bullet hole? You mean he was shot? Up close? On *our* farm? And they think I did it?"

"Just put it out of your mind, dear," cooed Daphne. She sounded the way she had when she'd comforted me after I'd had a nightmare as a little girl. "Put the green rubber boots on."

"We've got to do something! What about this man's family? *I've* got to do something! Is it in the paper yet? We've got to have a PR plan!"

"Hon, you got more to worry 'bout than some silly PR plan," laughed Precious.

"Shh!" scolded Daphne as she gave Precious a disapproving look.

"Local paper doesn't come out until Tuesday," said Pep. "Oh. That's today! Or is it Wednesday that the paper comes out?"

"Usually Tuesday. Unless there's no news. In that case, they just wait until something happens," sighed Daphne.

"Well, somethin's sure happened!" laughed Precious.

"I've seen 'em whip out a paper in hours," said Pep. "Remember the time they finally found Maisy Merganthal's prized pig stuck in the Laundromat dryer? Crazy porker had been missing for three days. They had a special edition out that very afternoon."

"I remember. Folks had to use the Jaws of Life to get the pig out," laughed Precious.

"Now that Eva's back, they won't be lacking for news anytime soon," chortled Pep.

"Yes, well, undoubtedly, this news is every bit as big as a pig in a dryer," sniffed Daphne. "I'm sure they've already written the story to Tammy Fae's specifications."

"Oh crappy." I shoved my foot into Daphne's ugly green rubber boot. "I'm so glad I can entertain everyone in Abundance County."

"Speaking of lost animals," Daphne cried from the laundry, "I nearly forgot to tell you. Amy neglected to put the lid on the fish tank. Her pet corn snake is loose. We need to find it before he slithers into a guest's room."

"Noose is loose?" asked Pep. "Again?"

"Snake?" Precious was bug-eyed.

"Oh jeepers," said Pep, looking at the wall clock. "It's gettin' late. Billy's givin' me a ride to work in a few minutes, and I've got to powder my nose first. If he gets here while I'm upstairs, just tell him to wait and I'll be right down." Pep ran from the kitchen and tore up the back stairs.

"There's a runaway *snake* in this house?" asked Precious. "And y'all are just tellin' me now?" Her face turned white. "Better hope I don't find that critter in my kitchen! I ain't got a bit of tolerance for a slitherin' snake. Pet or otherwise!"

"He's harmless. As long as you don't startle him," said Daphne weakly, stepping back into the kitchen. "Big Boomer gave the snake to Amy this summer for her sixth birthday— against my strong objections, of course. That made the gift even more delicious for him, I'm sure. Anyway, the child won't hear of getting rid of it. Believe me, I've tried. It was all I could do to convince her that she couldn't sleep with it." Daphne shuddered.

CHAPTER 17

Why I let Daphne convince me to hide in the pantry, I'll never know. But when we heard that Detective Gibbit was in the living room waiting to see me, Daphne insisted I take cover. In fact, she was adamant.

"That man'll take y'all away in handcuffs over my dead body!"

Moments later, too beat-up and tired to argue, I sunk quietly to the pantry floor, surrounded by floor-to-ceiling shelves stocked with jars of peaches and tomatoes; pickled cucumbers; canned peas and corn; beets and eggs; boxes of cereal and crackers; bags of brown and granulated sugars; salt and spices; bottles of vinegars, relishes, sauces, and much, much more.

A small oval window directed a beam of morning sunlight onto a shelf filled with dark green, long-necked bottles of our olive oil. I noticed there were a few infused varieties that I hadn't tried before, like lime and chipotle, and one label in Daphne's meticulous calligraphy read, BACON-INFUSED. *Interesting.* Was that even possible? I wasn't sure that I wanted it to be possible.

In the kitchen, I heard Precious moving around, opening drawers and cupboards, clanking bowls and utensils, and running water as she prepared more food. The mumble of people talking, the creaking of floorboards, and the clinking plates and silverware drifted from the dining room as guests began serving themselves a big buffet breakfast. The dining room door squeaked open, and Daphne's voice rang out.

"Detective, it's lovely to see you *again*! Won't you take a seat out there in the living room, while I bring you some coffee or a glass of our sweet lime iced tea."

Daphne's over-the-top conviviality was Southern-woman-speak that really meant she was peeved. Her airy footsteps moved across the kitchen floor. The refrigerator door opened, and I heard something slide onto a shelf.

"Thank you, ma'am." It was a man's voice. Whiny. Not pleasant. There was a heavy footfall, then a chair scooted across the floor. "No need to be formal. I'll just set here in the kitchen. I'll have tea."

"Oh! Bless your heart, I see you've already seated yourself, Detective," said Daphne. I imagined her giving him "the stare."

"We're fresh out of donuts, Detective," said Precious. Y'all want one of my *dee-licious* peach pecan muffins to go? Still warm! I'll wrap one up and you can take it with you."

"Miss Precious . . . Darling? Isn't it?" asked the detective in a pseudo-innocent tone.

"Yes, sir."

"Let's see if I have this right, now. You're the estate manager for that fella at Greatwoods, Mister Ian Collier—is that right?"

"Yes, sir."

"And that's where Miss Eva Knox was, d'reckly after the incident in the woods this morning, is that right?"

"Yes, sir."

"You been nursing her?"

"Yes, sir."

"You a nurse?"

"No, sir."

"Huh? She hurt bad? Seems to me if she's hurt bad, she should be in a hospital with a real nurse and a doctor."

"I've had my share of experience nursin' folks. Besides, there weren't any rooms in the hospital. Doc Payne's been comin' out and doctorin' her. He says her heart's kinda iffy."

I grabbed my chest. *What the hell is wrong with my heart?*

The dining room door squeaked open.

"Is there more sausage?" It was Judi.

"Why, yes, of course, Missus Malagutti. I'm so sorry," apologized Daphne.

"Got some comin' right up," called Precious. I heard something sizzle on the grill.

"Ma'am, if you don't mind, I'd like to ask you a couple of questions," said the detective. I heard paper rustling. "According to my notes, you said earlier that you and Mister Malagutti didn't go upstairs together last night."

"Right," said Judi. "During dinner, I chucked biscuits across the table at Sal and he was pissed."

"Biscuits?"

"Yeah. He'd been busy checking out the little waitress in the French maid outfit. So, later, I chucked a biscuit at him. That made him mad 'cause I'd already buttered my biscuit and when it hit Sal, it stained his favorite shirt. After dinner, he just had a couple of drinks then huffed on upstairs while the rest of us finished up."

"So, you were angry with your husband?"

"We always argue."

"Go on."

"Anyways, the rest of us went upstairs about twenty minutes later."

"And when was it that you came downstairs?"

"I couldn't sleep, on account of the thunder outside. And Sal's snoring always keeps me awake at night anyways. So, I decided to come down and watch TV in the living room."

"What time was that?"

"I think it was about ten. Maybe eleven o'clock."

"Did you see anyone?"

"Like I said earlier, I met Bambi. The two of us came downstairs in the dark so's not to wake anyone up. We helped ourselves to a couple more of those Georgia peach whiskeys."

"And you left your husband alone in the bedroom?" The detective sounded humorless.

"Yup."

"For how long?"

"Oh, a couple of hours, probably. Can I finish eating now?"

"Yes, ma'am. Thank you. Could you send over Missus Gambini, please?"

"Sure." She shouted into the dining room, "Bambi! The detective, here, wants to talk with ya!"

I laid my head back against the wall and exhaled slowly. With all the goods in Daphne's pantry, all I wanted was an ibuprofen, and of course, there was none to be had. I closed my eyes. I heard the detective clear his throat importantly before he said, "Missus Gambini! You're looking lovely today!"

"Thanks!" answered Bambi's hushed, bedroomy voice.

"Now, if I recall correctly, you said earlier that you were downstairs between the hours of eleven at night and one o'clock in the morning. Correct?"

"I couldn't sleep on account of Guido puking in the john—he had too much to drink."

"Was anyone with you?"

"Judi was with me. We met upstairs in the hall. I told you that earlier, didn't I?"

"What television show did you watch?"

"We didn't. We just sat in the dark and talked."

"Did you see anyone else?"

"Nope."

"Was your husband in your bedroom when you left?"

"I think so. Wait. I forgot. He was in the bathroom puking. He'd had a lot to drink."

"Did you go anywhere else?"

"Just the library. To get more drinks."

"And where were you seated in the living room?"

"In the front corner, on the big couch."

"What time was it when you went upstairs?"

"Oh gee. I don't know. Late."

"And was your husband in your room?"

"Yes. Nope, actually . . . I'm not sure. I think he was still in the bathroom."

"In the bathroom? Again?"

"Yes. He slept there."

"Why?"

"He was hammered. When he gets like that, I don't let him back into bed with me, so he usually just sleeps on the bathroom floor."

I couldn't help making a face. *Gross.* I heard more sizzling from the grill, then some clattering of utensils and china. My stomach gurgled. The sausages smelled yummy.

"Thank you, ma'am. That's all."

"Here, I'll come out with you, hon," said Precious to Bambi. "I got more sausages here."

I heard Precious clomp across the floor, and the dining room door squeaked open and shut.

"More tea, Detective?" cooed Daphne. I marveled at how remarkably cool Daphne was. After all, there'd been a murder at our place and she was hiding the prime suspect in her pantry. But then, she was our modern-day Scarlett O'Hara.

"Why, yes, I think I will have more tea," said the detective.

I heard the dining room door swing open, and Precious clomped back into the kitchen.

"Miss Precious Darling, you work here, at the Knoxes', too?" asked the detective.

"No. I'm just helpin' folks over here until they find new kitchen help."

"Uh-huh. I see. Yes. That's right. Miss Loretta Cook has disappeared."

"Just like we told you earlier," said Daphne. "We don't know anything about Chef Loretta or where she is now."

"Right, ma'am. Got it. And none of you folks have seen or heard from Miss Loretta Cook since she supposedly left. Let's see . . . sometime after dinner last night?"

"I ain't even met the woman, so I wouldn't know her if I saw her," said Precious haughtily.

"That's right, Detective, no one has seen Chef Loretta since after dinner. All we know is what we read in her note."

"Funny thing, that note," said the detective.

"Yes?" Daphne said.

"Just odd, that's all, don't you think?"

"I'm not sure what y'all mean, Detective."

"The note says she and Mister Leonard Leonardo were runnin' off to get hitched, right?"

"That's correct, Detective."

"But then why wouldn't she have packed her suitcase?"

"I don't understand."

"Her suitcase. It was in the closet in her apartment, downstairs."

"It was? Well, then, perhaps she had another one."

"Maybe. But the note made it sound as if the couple wasn't comin' back. And she left some personal things down there. Clothes. An alarm clock. Even her phone. Stuff like that."

"I honestly can't say, Detective."

"Your guide left personal things in his cabin as well. I just came back from there. In a way, it doesn't seem as if either one intended to leave."

"Well, *he* sure ain't comin' back." Precious chuckled. "And I hear his name wasn't even Leonard Leonardo. Ain't that right, Detective?"

The detective didn't answer. *Leonard Leonardo?* Was that the name he'd given Daphne? That did sound stupid, I thought. She should've known something was wasn't right with that.

"Perhaps they were just swept up by the moment and couldn't wait to be married?" suggested Daphne.

"They argued, and she blew the guy away. Like my cousin Dewanna and her late husband," offered Precious. "Or maybe she figured out the guy was some sort of fugitive from the law and she bumped him off, savin' y'all the trouble of a trial. Say, maybe he was tryin' to kidnap her!"

Their conversation brought no clarity. I mean, why didn't Loretta tell me she was leaving when we were preparing dinner? And as far as Daphne's suggestion of being "swept up in the moment," well, Loretta didn't strike me as the type to get "swept up" in anything. And thinking of Loretta in any sort of romantic relationship seemed impossible. Running off willy-nilly to get married? It just didn't fit. Could she have killed the pastry guy trying to protect herself? Maybe. But then, why didn't she come back afterward? And what about the pastry guy, coming here and getting hired under an assumed name? What was that all about? Could he have been part of the paparazzi following me for a story? No, I thought, that didn't work. He'd shown up *before* I ran away from Boston. What on earth was a pastry guy from Boston doing working as a field guide in Abundance?

My mind flashed back to the woods. I saw the still black sneaker in the grass. I remembered the rubbery way it hadn't yielded when I'd stumbled over it. Then, I saw his ghoulish face. I blanched and a whirl of dizziness hit me. *Please, don't puke!* I bent down and took a deep breath.

That's when the snake slithered out from behind a wicker basket in the corner.

CHAPTER 18

Before I could think, my body reacted and recoiled. Flying backward, I smacked myself hard against a shelf behind me. As I *kur-thunked* loudly into the shelf, stifling a shriek of pain, almost instantly, out in the kitchen, I heard a jumble of pots and pans tumble to the ground.

"Why, Miss Precious!" said Daphne. "How could y'all be so clumsy as to knock over an entire pot rack? That's my heavy Enclume stand!"

"Sorry, Miss Daphne. I just backed into it by mistake." There was more clattering as Precious righted the wrought iron pot stand and loaded all the pots and lids onto the shelves. "I'm afraid the linens that were stacked on top are all dirty now."

"There are more in the pantry."

"Okay. Thanks."

If Detective Gibbit had heard me in the pantry, he didn't let on. Precious had made enough of a hubbub to cover up my ill-timed commotion.

Daphne and the detective chatted tersely as Precious clomped to the pantry and threw open the door. She stared down at me as I sat completely still, cross-legged in the corner. When she saw the four-foot grayish brown and orange patterned snake in front of me, Precious nearly tripped over herself, flying backward, eyes big as saucers. At the same time—careful not to bother Amy's pet snake, Noose, slithering happily about twelve inches from my knee—I reached up to a shelf, grabbed a handful of clean linen dishtowels, and held them out to Precious.

"Found 'em!" she called out to Daphne. Precious stepped gingerly into the doorway, leaned way in, and stretched out her hand as far as she could, seizing the linens from me with her fingertips. Her terrified expression never changed. She slammed shut the pantry door before clomping quickly back to the kitchen counter.

I leaned back as far as I could and held my breath as Noose raised his head, flicked his little tongue, and began slithering over my right knee. It tickled.

"Now, Detective Gibbit, as I told you before, my sister is not here," said Daphne in the kitchen. "She doesn't live in this house anymore."

"Yes, ma'am. I know all that. I tried her place out back and she wasn't home. So, I thought she might be here with y'all. Especially since you say she's ill."

The first foot and a half of Noose had slid over my right knee.

Someone ran down the back stairs and into the laundry room.

"Did Billy show up yet? Oh. Detective! Sorry, I didn't realize you were here," said Pep.

Fully draped across my lap, Noose paused.

"Miss Pep Sweet. *Always* a pleasure to see you. You look ravishing today!" Detective Gibbit actually sounded like he was gushing. But then why not? Most Abundance men found Pep irresistible. I called it her Pep Appeal.

"Detective Gibbit is here to see Eva," said Daphne. "Although, of course, I explained to him that Eva is not here."

"Oh. Yeah. Right," Pep said slowly.

"The detective seems to think Eva might know something about how poor Leonard died."

Noose raised the front part of his body and flicked his tongue.

"Hummm. I see," said Pep.

"'Cept, his name wasn't Leonard, was it, Detective?" asked Precious again.

There was a loud metallic tear. Precious and the aluminum foil. Noose froze on my lap.

Again, the detective ignored Precious. "It does seem fishy," he said. "Your field guide turns up dead, and Miss Loretta Cook disappears just a week after your little sister comes back home, after all these years away. I'm just tryin' to get to the bottom of what happened, that's all. It'd just be terrible if Miss Loretta Cook has passed on like your guide, now, wouldn't it?"

"Oh my goodness, that *would* be terrible." said Daphne. "Are you tellin' me that you suspect *more* foul play, Detective? Surely, you don't suspect my sister?"

Noose turned his spoon-shaped head and stared up at me. I tried staring him down.

"Ha-ha. Eva? Murder? That's a hoot!" laughed Pep with her little pig snorts. "Especially with a gun. Eva won't go near a gun."

"I didn't say it was a gun," said the detective. "Where did you hear that? Did your sister, Miss Eva Knox, tell you that? By the way, that's whom I came to see. Where is Miss Eva Knox?"

"Crikey, detective, folks all over town have been talking 'bout how it was a gunshot that killed that fella. And at close range, too," boasted Precious. "Fella had a big hole in his chest."

I wrinkled my nose as Precious spoke. *How awful.*

"Are you going to arrest Eva?" asked Daphne.

A loud engine roared outside. Noose and I continued to face off. He tickled my legs.

"This is a homicide investigation. Your sister was found

lyin' next to the victim. I need her accounting of the events that happened. She's just a person of interest, that's all. All we want to do is talk to her. Downtown. Once we get some answers, we can have this matter all wrapped up, nice and neat, and you folks can go about your business. Besides, we can't have her running around the county with a bad ticker, now, can we?"

"Person of interest?" Precious sniffed. "Ain't that what you folks always call the prime suspect before he or she gets formally charged?"

The back door squeaked open, and I heard a heavy footfall.

"Hey, folks!" I recognized the voice. It was Pep's husband, Billy. "Pep, you ready? We gotta go, or I'll be late for a session. Oh . . . uh . . . Detective?"

"Mornin', Mister Sweet."

"Don't y'all worry, Billy. The detective isn't here for you, hon," said Pep. "Be out in a jiffy."

I heard the back door open and shut before Billy shuffled in his motorcycle boots down the back steps outside.

"I've gotta go," said Pep. "Billy's givin' me a ride to work today. Sorry, Daphne. I know you're slammed here, but we've got an all-morning meeting at the Roadhouse and I'm scheduled to work the bar for the midday crowd."

"It's alright, Pepper-Leigh. I know your little bartending job is important to you. Miss Precious has agreed to help out all day today. We'll manage, won't we, Miss Precious?" said Daphne.

"Damn right we will," answered Precious. The coffee grinder started whirring.

Noose was getting on my nerves. Not because he was on my lap—I was okay with a snake on my lap, as long as he wasn't a copperhead, diamondback, or cottonmouth. But he was annoying me because he kept changing his mind. He started to slither toward my hip. I held my breath.

"Don't forget, Daph, I've got to work at the Roadhouse again tomorrow. I can't be here for the Chamber of Commerce thingy in the afternoon."

Noose, either get off my lap or settle down to sleep, I thought. I heard Pep march across the floor in her boots. The back door opened and banged shut.

"Detective, my sister is not a murderer."

"Of course, I understand. This is your little sis we're talkin' about. Still, it could be that Miss Eva Knox don't like comin' home after eighteen years and finding strangers livin' and workin' in the home where she grew up. After all, it's pretty common knowledge that she's got a temper. Maybe she just threw another one of her fits. And this time, it ended up with someone dead."

"Temper? Eva?" Daphne sounded genuinely incredulous.

The motorcycle outside revved up before peeling out of the drive.

"I think you may be seein' your dear little sis through rose-colored glasses. On her very wedding day, she punched that Boston television guy she was supposed to marry. Poor guy, said he never saw it coming! Then, there's the video on the *Celebrity Sneek Peek* television show where she shoved and clawed her way through a bunch of bystanders before she tore up the road in her bare feet. Found out later she'd thrown her shoes at the poor weather guy after she punched him. Yes, I'll say your little sister has got a temper."

"Surely, Detective, y'all can't be serious," said Daphne calmly. "Besides, Eva didn't punch that scoundrel. Believe me, if she had punched him—and she didn't—she'd have done it for good reason."

"Folks in town are anxious," continued Detective Gibbit. "We got a murderer on the loose. And now your cook is missing. Heck, she could be dead. The county has its good reputation to protect. I aim to close the case as soon as possible."

"I'm as anxious as you are, Detective, to get to the bottom of this. I daresay, more so. After all, this is our home and place of business. I have children to protect. And, our livelihood depends on getting this mystery solved. However, you're barkin' up the wrong tree if y'all think my little sister has anything to do with this."

"It must be some kinda coincidence that nothing like this has ever happened in Abundance until right after your baby sister comes back to town. And it happens right in her backyard. Involving two people from outta town. Two Yanks. Just like her. You ever think that she knew the victim from when they were both up North?"

My heart started racing. I closed my eyes and tried to relax. *Breathe, Eva.*

Noose flicked his tongue at me.

Precious interrupted. "Here's your muffin, Detective. All wrapped and ready to go. It's loaded with fruit and olive oil to keep you healthy and regular."

I tried to take a deep, slow breath.

"Precious's muffins are absolutely *wonderful* for constipation! Do you have constipation, Detective Gibbit?" asked Daphne brightly.

I blew out my breath as noiselessly as I could.

"Uh . . . no, ma'am. Can't say as that's a problem."

"Thank you for stopping by, Detective. Don't forget your muffin. When I see her, I'll let my sister know y'all are looking for her. I'm sure that when she's feeling up to it, Eva will be happy to put all your scandalous theories to rest. Perhaps she's down at the station now. Meanwhile, I'm sure you'll be keepin' busy lookin' for Chef Loretta and collecting your evidence in the woods."

"The woods, *that's* the scene of the crime," piped Precious.

"However, Detective, don't hesitate to find a judge before stopping by the house again." Daphne sounded just as chipper and cheerful as she would at a luncheon party with girlfriends.

"Thank you, ma'am. I'll do that."

"This would be a crime scene if y'all could find any evidence, but since y'all haven't found any yet, y'all need to stop houndin' the good folks here, or get a warrant," Precious said. "You boys have been though the place once; now y'all need to scram 'cause we got a business to run!"

"Miss Precious!" Daphne sounded shocked and amused

at Precious's chutzpah. Of course, it was everything Daphne wanted to say, but decorum wouldn't allow it.

"I know all about this stuff. I read mysteries."

A chair scooted. Several pairs of feet moved across the floor. Precious's Louboutins clomped. The dining room door squeaked open into the hubbub of the dining room crowd, then it swung closed again.

Noose slithered from my lap and headed for a sunny spot in the far corner of the pantry. The kitchen was silent.

CHAPTER 19

"Okay, Eva," Daphne said, yanking open the pantry door. "Coast is clear."

"There's no love lost between you and Detective Gibbit," I said, unfolding myself from the pantry floor. I scratched some bug bites on my arms, battle scars from my trek home through the woods earlier.

"Oh, Eli's still sore from third grade. Instead of 'Gibbit,' we called him 'Giblet'—a nickname that's haunted the poor fellow forever. And we used to make turkey sounds. I s'pose it was cruel, and we probably made him meaner than he already was, but y'all would think that thirty-five years later he'd be over it." Daphne shook her head. "Don't scratch, Eva. It'll leave scars."

"You think?"

"Word is, Eli has his knickers in a twist because last year Buck Tanner came back and got the sheriff's job that Eli thought he deserved. To be fair, when Sheriff Titus finally retired, everyone figured Eli would be sheriff. He'd campaigned to get the job for years. But somehow, even after he'd been gone for so long, Buck returned and snagged the job. A bunch of folks are nettled about it. And it looks like ol' Eli is bent on proving he's the better man. He's got people behind him."

I nodded.

"Putting away a murderer is just the feather Eli needs in his cap to boost his image," continued Daphne. "And if he can tie the deed to you, a celebrity of sorts, and a Yankee to boot, well then, all the better."

"Daphne, he can't honestly think that I *killed* somebody. And aren't you worried about the real murderer? What about the kids? And, in case you forgot, I am *not* a Yankee."

"I called the sheriff's office. They've assigned someone to watch the place at night. And although I want this terrible crime solved more than anyone, I don't want our future guests to hear about it and cancel their reservations. And I don't want Big Boomer to hear about it up in Atlanta. He'll use this to take the kids from me. So, it's business as usual. In fact, now that I think about it, I'll call the sheriff's department again after breakfast. They need to understand that I'm mighty serious about our safety and gettin' this solved quickly. As long as we find the right person, of course. And *you're* not that person. Y'all need to stay out of sight while they come to their senses."

"I'm gonna need a big platter for this ham!" Precious called out.

"In the lower cupboard, next to the sink," replied Daphne. "It's gettin' so a person can't find anything around here."

Precious grabbed the platter, plated the ham, and was out the door into the dining room where the guests were clattering merrily over their big buffet breakfast.

"That reminds me. I found Noose. He's in the pantry."

"Heavens to Betsy!"

"It's like a feeding frenzy out there!" huffed Precious as she stomped in from the dining room, carrying two empty platters and a pitcher.

"Well, I'm not touching a snake!" whispered Daphne about Noose. "And Amy's at school."

Precious plopped the platters on the counter.

"I'm not wrestling with him, either," I whispered back. "Not with my sore ribs. It's sunny and warm in the pantry. He should stay put, as long as we keep the door closed."

Daphne looked at Precious. "What about her?"

"Just keep the door closed. Noose will probably stay curled up in the corner."

"Here, fill these muffin tins." Precious shoved a big bowl of blueberry muffin batter toward me and handed me an ice cream scoop before she started filling empty plates with more hoecakes and ham. "You two gonna get rid of that slitherin' beast in there? 'Cause I ain't goin' in that pantry till it's dead and gone."

"He's sleeping." Daphne said brightly as she crossed to the pantry. I saw her surreptitiously check to be sure the pantry door was firmly closed. "We'll have Amy catch him after school."

"Crikey!" Precious took some dirty dishtowels and shoved them along the opening under the door. "I see it's slitherin' ass in this kitchen and I'm outta here, for good!"

"Oh for goodness sakes! That looks awful." Daphne went to the pantry door and pushed her toe into the dishtowels, pressing them tight between the bottom of the door and the floorboards so they were nearly impossible to see. "There. Much better."

Ice cream scoop in hand, I looked at the muffin batter. "I can't . . ."

"Just scoop and fill each tin. Surely, you can do that, Sunshine?"

"I guess, as long as there's no fire involved, we should be safe."

One by one, I scooped out the blueberry muffin batter made with lemon-infused olive oil and plopped each scoopful into the muffin tin.

"Now what?"

Precious stepped across the floor, grabbed the tin, whipped open the range door, and shoved the muffins into the oven. Then, she went over to the dining room door and pushed it open an inch or so to see the guests.

"Still need more," she whispered. "I've never seen so few folks eat so much food."

In the dining room, passing behind Judi, who was seated at the table, a young woman with a nose ring and a camera around her neck carried a plate piled high with pancakes and fruit. She bumped Judi in her chair.

"Hey!" Judi said over her shoulder. Then, Judi saw me in the kitchen and smiled.

Precious squeezed past me in the doorway and placed newly filled platters of ham and eggs on the buffet and clomped back into the kitchen. Judi got up from the table.

A man's voice boomed across the dining room, "Judi, sit your ass down here! I told you not to bother the girl."

"Oh, it's fine, Sal. She doesn't mind." Judi shouted across the room. "Besides, she's a *woman*, not a girl. When will you ever learn? I don't call you a *boy*, now, do I?"

She dismissed Sal with a flip of her hand. "Men." Then she said to me, "We were just talking, Bambi and me." She waved toward Bambi, who was delicately fishing for a fallen bite of muffin from between her breasts. "You know," continued Judi, "I may have mentioned this, but you're the reason we found this place. Did you know that olive oil is our business?"

"How wonderful!" I said. "I'm sure my father would love to talk shop with you all."

"Sal would love that."

"Missus Malagutti, I don't mean to interrupt," said Daphne warmly from behind me. Appalled that a guest might see me covered in dirt, dressed in a tacky tee shirt, green Wellies, and cutoffs, my sister pushed me aside. I rolled my eyes as she stepped in front of me. A camera flash went off from somewhere in the room as folks laughed and chatted amiably at the table. Precious's mammoth meal was a hit.

"The antebellum tour bus will be arriving any minute," continued Daphne. "It's a wonderful look at some of our most exquisite plantation homesteads. Y'all don't want to miss it." Daphne smiled as she continued to push me behind her.

"Sal, we need to get ready to go," Judi shouted. "Bambi, Guido, are you guys finished breakfast? They say the bus will be here any minute."

Judi let go of the dining room door, and it swung toward us, nearly hitting me in the face. It opened again on our side as Judi walked to her companions at the other end of the table.

"Bambi, hurry and come upstairs with me. I gotta pee, big-time."

Daphne pursed her lips as the door took its final swing shut. "New Yorkers," she mumbled. "They have such a *way* about them, don't they?"

"As far as I can tell, our New Yorker guests are big-time olive oil distributors," I said to Daphne. "Given they decided to stay on here, even after what happened to Leonard, err, whomever the guy is, I'm still hopeful that if we can keep them happy, they might do some business with Daddy. Where is Daddy, by the way? I haven't seen him in days."

"Daddy's still in Texas."

"Texas?"

"Yes. Something about the olive trees not being like they should. He took samples and went to confer with the fellow at the processing plant. I don't think he was satisfied with state lab results."

"You mean, something is wrong with the trees? This year's crop?" I remembered Judi Malagutti saying something during dinner the night before about some trees not looking right.

"Honestly, Eva, I don't know. I've had my hands so full with the kids and the guests, and all the craziness that's been going on around here, I was distracted and wasn't listening when he told me about it the other day. Ask Pepper-Leigh. She knows all the about the farmy stuff."

"I can't believe he's not here. Whatever's going on with the crop must be important."

"He'll be back in a few days. By then, all this murder business will've been solved."

"Listen, Daph, I've been thinking. About Detective Gibbit—don't do that again," I said.

"Do what?"

"Hide me. It won't help. Public relations lesson number one: Never hide from the problem. It's always best to get out in front of it. If you hide, it only makes you look guilty."

"Eli Gibbit isn't the brightest bulb. With Tammy Fae drumming up gossip, plus your jilted boyfriend bein' sheriff, and the community clamoring for this all to be over and done with yesterday, and y'all bein' an outsider, they're likely to skip the trial and lynch y'all right here and now."

"I'm not guilty. I've got nothing to hide, and I can't stay squirreled away here forever. Besides, I've got work to do for you and Daddy, and I can't do it hiding in a pantry closet."

"Well, you can't do it if you're in a jail, either, now, can you?"

"Amen to that," said Precious from the table.

"You're being dramatic. I'm not going to jail."

"You're bein' naive. This is Abundance," said Daphne.

"Amen to that," Precious echoed.

"The detective was here to arrest you. And once he does, you're hardly in a position to afford a decent lawyer. Although, of course, I'll hire one for you. And I'll probably have to post some sort of bail. Maybe my lawyer in Atlanta knows a top-notch criminal defense attorney . . ."

"I didn't do anything wrong! We just need to give the detective a little time to sift through the evidence. And I need to swing public opinion my way a bit. Still, I don't want my 'story' to overshadow the family business."

"That horse has already left the barn, Sunshine," said Precious with a chuckle.

I glared at her.

"Look," I said, "I've been thinking a lot about how to stop all the ridiculous runaway bride gossip. Now, with the dead man in the olive grove, I think we need to put my plan into play."

"What plan is that?" asked Daphne.

"We manage what people are saying about me—about us, the family, the business—by making up the fodder ourselves."

"Huh?" asked Precious.

"We generate more and more outrageous gossip ourselves. Something new every week. Every day, if we have to. Eventually, people will be sick of it. And me. They'll move on."

"You mean, like a homeopathic approach to public relations?" Daphne asked.

"Homeopathic?"

"Why, yes. If you suffer from the ill effects of gossip, the homeopathic remedy would be to introduce *more* gossip, in smaller amounts, to cure the larger flow of gossip."

"What the . . ." mused Precious.

"Exactly."

CHAPTER 20

The three of us marched into the empty dining room and stopped short. The room, decorated with my grandparents' finest antiques, was littered with piles of dirty dishes, empty bowls and platters, soiled napkins, and food-encrusted silverware. Daphne's white linen tablecloth was blasted with multicolored globs of food and drink.

"Well, I'll be damned," whispered Precious.

"It's alright," Daphne sighed. "We have all mornin' to clean. The antebellum tour will take most of the day."

Outside, there was a loud *pssssshhhttt* of air brakes. We all went to the foyer and looked out the front door. A big white box truck was parked next to the house. Printed on the sides of the truck were the words DIXIE SHINDIGS under a cartooned pair of dancing magnolias.

"Daphne, what's this?" I asked.

"Oh fiddle-dee-dee! I completely forgot. Since y'all have come back, Eva, there have been *so* many last-minute RSVPs for tomorrow's Chamber of Commerce meeting that we simply don't have enough room for everyone. I've leased a tent."

"A tent? Like, the kind people use for weddings?"

"Yes."

"Well, butter my butt and call me a biscuit," mumbled Precious.

Daphne waved to the men at the truck. "Be with y'all in a moment!"

"Daphne, what do you mean, there's so many 'last-minute' RSVPs?"

"I couldn't figure it out at first," said Daphne from the porch. She straightened a few pillows in the wicker chairs absently. "This meetin' has been scheduled for months. Usually, there's no more than twenty or so folks at these events. However, since you came back, the responses have been pourin' in. Earlene Azalea said folks are comin' because they want to see *you*."

"Me?"

"Yes."

"It's that runaway bridey thing, ain't it?" said Precious.

"I'm afraid so," said Daphne.

"I'm sorry," I said.

"You shouldn't be feelin' bad, Sunshine," said Precious. "There's a tree stump in a Louisiana swamp with an IQ higher than most of these folks in town."

"If that what it takes to get folks here, then I'm willin' to play along," said Daphne. "Now that we have their attention, we need to wow folks with our service, cuisine, and Daddy's olive oils. Actually, I'm seein' it as a marvelous opportunity to promote our new businesses. So, today, if y'all can clean the two suites upstairs, Earlene Azalea and I will take care of the rest of the house. She'll be over to help out while her daughters are recovering."

"Are the twins alright?" I asked.

"They're fine. Just a bit shaken-up. Earlene Azalea thinks they're more tired from the concert than anything else. Now, I need to speak to these folks about the tent." Daphne stepped down the front porch stairs. "Fiddle-dee-dee, someone's left their boots out here. One of the men, I suppose.

Miss Precious, will y'all take these dirty boots out back and set them by the hose? We can spray them off later."

"Sure," said Precious.

Already, Daphne was in the drive, giving instructions to the tent people.

"I'll head upstairs and meet you there," I said to Precious. "I want to disappear before Daphne comes back, changes her mind, and sentences us to the dining room." My ankle and ribs hurt. I wanted to get though the cleaning as fast as possible.

"Sure thing. While we clean upstairs, we can come up with tomorrow's gossip 'bout you." Precious chuckled. Boots in hand, she tromped through the house, toward the kitchen. "I reckon it's gonna be mighty tough followin' today's news!" She laughed out loud.

CHAPTER 21

"Gee willikers!" sighed Precious as we stepped into the Gambinis' suite.

The opulent bath and pink bedroom was a guest favorite. And it had been my room as a girl. Before the upstairs redesign to accommodate guests, the en suite bath had been a small sewing room accessed from the hallway.

"Yup. This is pretty loathsome," I said, looking around at the disheveled bed and piles of soiled clothing on the floor. It was weird to see such a mess in my old room.

"I'm sorry, Precious," I said, turning to her. "I know Daphne is grateful to have your help. We all are. But this is our problem, not yours. I can do this if you want to leave. I'm sure your boss would love to have you back at Greatwoods."

I'd been terribly curious about Greatwoods and Ian Collier. It was frustrating not to remember him. Could Ian Collier be a part of what had happened? This neighbor—a man whom no one in town seemed to know at all—should be every bit as much a suspect as I was . . . maybe more so. After all, he'd been out in the woods during the time the murder happened. And why was he so secretive? Why the barbed wire around Greatwoods?

Maybe Precious could tell me about her boss.

"Aw, Sunshine," said Precious, "don't worry yourself. I ain't gonna leave ya here alone! No offense, but y'all are lookin' bone tired. We got work to do. C'mon. Let's get started. It's only two suites . . . How bad can it be?"

Precious and I each carried a box of cleaning supplies into the bathroom that Daphne had redecorated with pink-striped wallpaper, bronzed fixtures, crystal sconces, and a reclaimed bowfront vanity with a marble top. The room was a shambles. Toilet paper was unwound all over the floor, and bags and boxes of toiletries and shaving paraphernalia were scattered on a counter spattered with creams and beard shavings. And hadn't Bambi said her husband had slept in the bathroom after being sick? I grabbed a can of disinfectant from my cleaning box and sprayed. Everywhere. Precious just nodded her approval as she stood taking it all in, hands on her hips.

"So, Precious, tell me about Ian Collier," I said, putting on a pair of rubber gloves. Opening the shower door with two fingers, I was suddenly grateful for Daphne's tall rubber boots.

"Why do you wanna know 'bout Mister Collier?" Precious pulled up her gloves and threw open the window.

"Well, he did sort of rescue me. I don't even remember seeing him. What does he do?"

"He's a businessman, I guess." Precious flipped up the toilet lid and got to work. I was grateful for her stoutheartedness, remembering Bambi telling the detective that Guido had spent half the night embracing the fixture.

"What kind of business?"

"Something with international security. That's all I know. And more than I should say."

"Securities?"

"That's what I said, ain't it?"

"How did he end up at Greatwoods?"

"Bought it, I guess."

"Where's he from?"

"Not from around here, that's for sure."

After a few minutes and a quick rinse, I stepped out of the shower and grabbed a rag to dry it down. My ribs were aching big-time, so I leaned against the sink for a rest. I stared hard at Precious. "You're not being very helpful, here, Miss Precious."

"Look, Sunshine, I like you and all, but Mister Collier's my boss, and I don't go talking about him. Not for nothin', not for no one, understand? He's been very good to me. *Very good*. He likes his privacy, and I aim to help him keep it that way." She flushed the toilet.

I hobbled back into the shower and polished the fixtures dry. "Well, surely, you can tell me something about him. Is he single? Married? How old is he? He must be good-looking. Daphne nearly melted when she was talking about him. I think she's interested."

"Whether your big sis is interested in Mister Collier or not, Sunshine, Mister Collier's private life is just that, private . . . Ack!"

Precious screamed.

"Precious? What is it?" I turned and saw Precious on her tippy toes, huddled way back in the bathroom corner, shaking and pointing toward the sink.

"Big. Bug. Or a bat!" Her eyes were round, like a night owl's. "Dead bat!" she shrieked.

Cautiously, I stepped out of the shower, went over to the sink, and looked down.

"Hahahahahaha!"

"What? What is it?" Precious demanded. "Tell me!"

I couldn't stop laughing. I laughed so hard, my ribs ached even more. In fact, seeing big Precious cowering in such a state of fear and panic, and realizing what it was that had made her that way, I doubled over in giggles. Still, it literally pained me to laugh, so I tried to stifle my hysterics.

"It's a dead bat in the sink, isn't it!" Precious cried. "Isn't it!"

"Close," I said. A tear—half from laughter, half from pain—streamed down my cheek. "Actually, it's a false eyelash." I burst out laughing again.

After convincing Precious that it really *was* just a giant false eyelash in the sink, we hustled as quickly as we could to finish cleaning the suite. Precious stripped the bed, while I went to the linen closet in the hall and grabbed fresh towels and sheets. Although I was much slower than I should've been due to my wrecked-up body, Precious more than made up for my handicapped effort. While I set up the bathroom with fresh towels, soaps, and glassware, like a great cleaning tornado, she swept over and polished the bedroom floor in record time. And at the end of it all, she mopped the bathroom floor Guido Gambini had slept on while I was short of breath and had to rest in a bedroom chair. Daphne would never find regular help as good as Precious, either in the kitchen or in housekeeping.

Precious lived up to her name.

It wasn't long before we'd moved on to the Malaguttis' suite. Although the bedroom was large—decorated in what I'd call "elegant country" style—every inch of it was in chaos. All of the flat surfaces in the room—the floor, opened suitcases, four-poster king-sized bed, upholstered chairs, my great-grandparents' antique side table, even the opened antique drop-down desk—were draped and covered with clothes, shopping bags, toiletries, accessories, brochures, food . . . you name it.

"Great day!" said Precious with a grim look, as she stepped into the bathroom.

I used two reluctant fingers to remove a chewed-up cigar butt from the marble countertop that was covered in ashes, beard shavings, toothpaste spatter, and dried shaving cream. I tossed the soggy cigar into a little gilded garbage can, already piled high with trash. The grime was a stark contrast to the soft butter yellow walls, floral chintz fabrics, and delicate antiques.

"There's certainly no glory in the hospitality business. This is nasty," I said.

"Just like the last suite. Birds of a feather sure flock together," said Precious, shaking her head. "Only these are dirty ol' birds. Just look at this mess. I gotta tell ya, I ain't got much dog for this fight."

Precious looked around the bathroom, put her hands on her hips, and announced, "Well, I'm not doin' this without some fresh rubber gloves. You wanna pair? I'm goin' down to find me some spankin' new ones. It'll make me feel better."

"I saw a box of gloves in the pantry. We could use some more cleanser, too. There's some in the laundry room. If you don't want to carry it all up, you can use the dumbwaiter."

Precious turned and ducked her head under the doorframe into the bedroom. I heard one of the chandeliers in the bedroom chitter and tinkle as she clomped down the hallway and then down the back stairs. I decided to tackle the bedroom.

When I was a teenager, I had a summer job cleaning half a dozen cabins at a lakeside camp. The crusty old biddy who owned the camp, Miz Poppie, cleaned with high-speed military precision. And she taught me to do the same. I'd stripped all the cabin beds—rotating and flipping the mattresses each time before remaking the beds with fresh linens. Miz Poppie had taught me to first spin the mattress end to end, then lift and flip crosswise. Next, I'd replaced the dirty linens and remade each bed—hospital corners and all—before fluffing the pillows, "chopping" them in the middle with my hand to make sure they looked extra comfy. Also, I'd mopped in a precise figure eight pattern; emptied garbage; washed windows and doors; scrubbed counters, sinks, and showers; hand washed dishes and silverware; cleaned the refrigerator; and restocked cabinets.

Unfortunately, I never managed to maintain my own home with the same verve. Not even close. More recently, I'd been looking forward to the professional cleaning service Zack had promised to hire after we were married. I should've known the promise was too good to be true. Just like Zack. *Stop it, Eva.* Regardless, Daphne's impossible standard of perfection meant that I needed to pull out all the stops when it came to cleaning. Feeling like crap or not, I needed to do better than my best.

I looked at myself in the mirror. My GEORGIA VIRGIN tee had a tear in the sleeve and stains all over it. My hair was a tangled mess. My face was scratched; so were my arms and legs. My eyes were dark and hollow. I looked as bad as I felt. Maybe worse. Like an outlaw. No wonder Daphne wanted to hide me from everyone. *That's not going to happen.*

I needed to suck it up. I channeled Miz Poppie, took a deep breath, and tapped into my cabin-cleaning psyche. I decided to start with the beds. Then, I'd vacuum, dust, wipe the windows, and straighten the furniture before finishing with the disgusting bathroom. Really, I hoped that Precious would cover the bathroom when she got back, so I wouldn't have to step in there again. My injuries were getting the best of me. I was losing steam, fast.

"What a disaster," I mumbled as I shuffled in my sister's green rubber boots over to the bay window. I slid open the floral-patterned chintz drapes. I couldn't help myself. I was worried about Dolly. I scanned the well-kept gardens and lawns below, looking for my pup. It was all I could do to keep from going out and searching for her. Still, Daphne said the pup was in the yard, so I tried not to worry. I'd find Dolly just as soon as Precious and I finished cleaning.

I went to the bed and pulled back the cotton ivory matelassé blanket and embroidered percale top sheet before yanking off the bottom sheet. Given the disgusting mess I'd seen in the bathroom, I decided to swap out the mattress pad for a clean one. I ripped off the soiled pad. The plushy, satin-corded mattress underneath looked to be very pricey. And new.

"Daphne will kill me if I let this mattress get soiled."

I shuffled to the hall and picked up fresh linens and a thickly quilted mattress pad from the closet. Sharp pain shot through my ribs as I carried the load. In my head, I heard Miz Poppie's lecture about the importance of maintaining clean and functioning bedding and the need to guard against dust, bedbugs, dead skin, lumpy linens, sagging mattresses, stains, and more. *Ugh*. I grabbed a fabric-covered cord on the side of the thick mattress. I pulled hard, ignoring the pain in my ribs, and pushed the mattress around, spinning it so the top end relocated to the bottom end of the bed. Then, bracing for pain, I heaved the mattress sideways toward me, so that some of it was off the bed frame. I took a big breath, bent my knees, and, with both hands and all my weight, put my shoulder under the mattress and pushed the long side of the hulking thing straight up into the air.

About the same time I cried out in pain, Precious screamed in hysterics downstairs.

Then I saw the pistol. It was under the mattress, right in the center of the box spring.

CHAPTER 22

"We forgot about the dang-fangled snake in the pantry!" scolded Precious in the bedroom doorway. "Hey! What the hell are y'all doin', girl!"

Precious dropped the gloves and cleanser and clomped over and took hold of the mattress, releasing the crushing weight from my back and shoulder. My ribs felt like they were on fire. I stood, doubled over, next to Precious, as she held the mattress overhead with one hand.

We both stared at the gun on the box spring.

"Pastry guy was shot," I whispered, slowly standing back up. "Do you think . . ."

Of course, she thought the handgun was the weapon used to shoot and kill the man from Boston. We both did. Who wouldn't? Why else would it be hidden under a mattress?

Still holding the mattress above us, Precious looked at me, eyes popping wide. "That, sure as shinola, looks mighty sketchy to me, Sunshine."

I squatted down to get a better look at the pistol. Etched into the black barrel, there was a big "G" with the word "lock" inside the letter. Then, there was a "19."

"It's a Glock 19," I said. "Why would anyone hide a gun like this? Shouldn't it be in a cabinet somewhere?"

"Sounds reasonable."

"A gun safe. We have a gun safe for the guests, don't we? Yes. I know we do. In fact, Daphne *insists* all guns be locked into the safe when people are not using them to hunt. I know she does. She would never let her kids be around guns. And why would anyone *have* a gun like this? Do people hunt with handguns? Besides, it's not even hunting season—is it? Wait! Don't you need a license to carry a handgun in Georgia? Yes. I think you do."

I was rambling. Trying to think. Sort it out.

"Then why am I seein' folks carryin' shotguns and rifles in the back windows of their pickups all the time? You mean *all* those crazy-ass folks got a license to carry guns?"

"No . . . I think you can carry a long gun in Georgia openly. It's just the handguns you need to have a license to carry. Have I got that right? I don't remember. It was different in Massachusetts. Still, you wouldn't hunt with a gun like this, would you?"

"Sunshine, I'm pretty sure that folks'll hunt with any kind of gun they got, this kind included. Heck, folks'll hunt with a peashooter. It's hidin' it under the mattress that's shady."

"Maybe this guy is not licensed to carry a pistol in Georgia. He's from New York; does that matter? Although . . . omigosh, Precious, what if we've got a murderer in the house!" I whispered. "Daphne will die when she finds out about this. We need to get the kids out of here. Think we should take the gun?"

"Take it? Hell no. Don't touch it! Remember what happened to my cousin, Dewanna? Gun went off—*bang!*—just like that, and her man dropped dead. Nuh-uh. No guns for me. Stay away from the dang thing."

"I hear you. Do we call the sheriff's department? Oh, wait. Crap. If this is the murder weapon, I've just destroyed evidence by tearing apart the bed. And they're already gunning for me. Get it? They're already 'gunning for me'? Ha."

"Very funny."

"So, what do we do?"

"Leave it alone. Make the bed. Act like we never saw the cursed thing. I don't want no murderer coming after me 'cause I uncovered his bloody murder weapon. Nuh-uh!"

"Let's think. Maybe we're jumping to conclusions. This could be perfectly innocent. By the way, I heard you scream. I can't believe we *both* forgot about Noose. Is he alright? You didn't kill him, did you?"

"I left the blasted thing right where it was, slitherin' around a big jar of pickled beets. And I ain't goin' back in there until that nasty creature is gone. Now, gettin' back to the conversation we were havin' about the gun here, since when is hiding a gun under a mattress that isn't yours 'perfectly innocent'? Have y'all taken a good look at that Malagutti fellow? He's a gangster if I ever saw one."

"Oh, Precious, that's such a stereotype," I said. "Let's put the mattress down. At least for now."

Precious carefully lowered the heavy mattress back onto the box spring, over the Glock.

"What the hell were y'all doin' liftin' up a mattress ten times your weight, anyway?"

"I was flipping it."

"Flipping it? Sunshine, folks have been making mattresses that don't need to be flipped for a decade or more."

"Now you tell me." I was feeling like someone was sitting on my chest.

"Let's just scrub the place and get the hell outta here," said Precious. "Seein' that gun has given me the creeps. Not to mention, your niece's stinkin' snake."

"Wait. Let's think. Maybe this isn't the gun that killed the pastry guy. After all, do we know that the Malaguttis even *knew* him?"

"Maybe they did. Maybe they didn't. Maybe they killed their guide 'cause they didn't like the fish they caught? Maybe they didn't catch enough fish? Maybe they didn't like the fella's outfit? Or, if he was your pastry guy, like you said, maybe they didn't like the pastries he made. Who *knows*!"

"We need to find out what kind of gun killed Leonard, er, the pastry guy. They should know that at the sheriff's department, right? Can your friend, Tilly what's-her-name, find out?"

"Beekerspat. Tilly Beekerspat, Sunshine. Hell, they got to know somethin' down there, but at this point, I ain't so sure they know anything 'cept how to give speedin' tickets and eat donuts."

"And your muffins." I winked at Precious.

"And my muffins." Precious grinned.

"If I tell the authorities about this gun, and this *isn't* the murder weapon, then I've ruined some potentially important guest relations and killed any sort of business Daddy might have been able to pull off with these guys. And by implicating someone else, I've made myself look guiltier."

"Looking at these folks, I ain't so sure your paw should be doin' business with 'em anyway."

"Even if it *is* the murder weapon, we don't know if it'll have prints on it or not. So, still, I could get blamed, just because I know about it."

"My money says the dweeb detective will try to pin it on y'all no matter what. He's not smart enough to figure it out for himself."

"It makes more sense that Loretta killed Leonard—right? Why else would she disappear? They were running off to get married. They quarreled. The gun went off. He died. And she ran away. Hey, maybe it was actually an accident."

"You mean, she smoked him like Dewanna did to her husband?"

"Like Dewanna. Only Loretta, having just shot and killed her fiancé, runs off in a panic. Maybe he followed her down here? It could be that she knew him in New England, and after she came down here, for whatever reason, he came, too, snowing Daphne into giving him a job as a guide. I don't know where in Rhode Island Loretta is from, but the tiny state of Rhode Island is right next to Massachusetts and only about an hour from Boston."

"I dunno. If you ask me, none of it makes sense. All these folks sound crazy to me."

"Okay. Here's the plan. We find out what sort of gun killed Leonard. If it was a Glock like this, then we say something. If not, no harm, no foul, as they say. We keep our mouths shut and hope Sal Malagutti leaves soon—with his little gun—happy with his stay here and loving our olive oil. Meanwhile, we keep looking for Loretta."

"I didn't know we was lookin' for Miss Loretta."

"We are now."

"We are?"

"Yes. We need to figure out what happened. We need to clear my name. We need to make sure everyone is safe, especially Daphne and the kids. And if she's innocent, we need to be sure Loretta is safe. Although, somehow, I think she's more than capable of taking care of herself. She's a brute if ever there was one. And now, I'm wondering why she came down here in the first place."

"Okay. Whatever you say, Sunshine."

"We need to solve this so we don't kill Daddy's and Daphne's businesses. I owe them both."

"I get it."

"And I've got no faith in Detective Gibbit. Do you?"

"Well, no. Not really. Not at all."

"Maybe Buck Tanner is behind all this nonsense about me being a murderer. After all, he has more reason to want me in jail than he does to find justice. It's not like he owes *me* anything."

"That's for sure."

"So, are you in?"

"Okey dokey." Precious nodded. "So, we leave the piece under the mattress and we case the joint, lookin' for this missing Loretta person—only I don't know what she looks like, and I don't know what we're gonna do when we find her, especially if she's a murderer."

"And we keep our eyes and ears open regarding Sal and Guido. As much as I hate to admit it, I agree; they look like they've stepped straight out of a mob flick. But, of course, we have no real proof of that. Maybe it's all a coincidence."

Precious started looping the ends of the bottom sheet over the mattress corners. "Right. If you say so, Sunshine. But those two give me the jitters. Y'all should see the way they look at your sister, Pep."

"Every man looks at Pep that way. She oozes sex appeal. I call it 'Pep Appeal.' Sometimes, I wish I had a little of it myself."

"Oh, you're fine just as you are, Sunshine. You got your own 'Miss Eva-ness.'" Precious let out a big laugh. "And believe me, those two men have taken notice. Now, help me make the bed. I wanna get out of here quick, like a bunny."

"Sounds good to me."

I grabbed the other side of the bottom sheet and tucked it under the mattress that hid the gun. As I draped the top sheet over the bed, it occurred to me how remarkably easy it'd been to obstruct justice.

CHAPTER 23

"You always drive this slow?" Precious shouted from the backseat.

Driving down the country road with the convertible top down—enjoying the rush of fresh, sweetly scented summery air as it whipped my hair around—I felt a surge of much-needed energy.

"What's wrong with forty-five?" I shouted over my shoulder. "You don't like following the speed limit?"

"Speed limit? Girl, what planet are you on? You been up North too long. Speed limit is sixty around these parts. Step on it!"

Like an oversized carnival doll, Precious had insisted on sitting in the backseat of my BMW 3 Series. And because gargantuan Precious didn't exactly fit in the tiny backseat, we'd put the top down to give her more room during our jaunt to town.

We'd finished cleaning the guest suites, and, at the insistence of Precious, I'd acquiesced and recovered Noose in the pantry before returning him to his aquarium up on the third floor. While Precious met with Daphne in the kitchen,

I'd hobbled around the yard calling for Dolly, planning to bathe and take a nap for the remainder of the afternoon. However, Dolly wasn't to be found. Then, Daphne'd asked if Precious and I could go to town to pick up extra stuff for the Chamber of Commerce meeting the next day while she and Earlene Azalea finished cleaning. She'd promised to have the older kids look for Dolly when they came home from school. After another check around the yard for Dolly, I'd ducked into my cottage just long enough to take two ibuprofen tablets and grab my purse and sunglasses before setting out a bowl of food and some water for Dolly on the cottage steps. In no time, Precious and I were zipping down the country road.

Nodding to Precious in the rearview mirror, I punched the accelerator. She was right. I hadn't adjusted to the faster speed limits. In Massachusetts, a road like this would've been marked forty-five miles per hour. Maybe even thirty-five. However, down in Abundance, unless you found yourself behind a slow-moving tractor, a truck with a full load, or a geriatric driver, you put the pedal to the metal. That was, of course, as long as you weren't on the interstate. None of the locals used it. One of only two ways in or out of the county, it was the sheriff's playground. Or at least it had been when Sheriff Titus ran the show. I'd no idea what Buck Tanner was doing about traffic stops.

"Tell me again," I shouted, "why are you sitting back there, as opposed to up here, in front?"

"On account that unless I'm driving," Precious shouted, "I *never* sit up front. Decided long ago that if folks are drivin' me, I'm goin' in style. Like Miss Daisy!"

"So, I'm your chauffeur?" I asked, glancing back in the mirror again. The fresh air and ibuprofen had me feeling better.

"You got it, Sunshine!" Precious gave me a thumbs-up. "Whoa, watch where you're goin' there, sista!"

I smiled as we swerved around Benderman's Curve, a tight turn on the road in a woodsy area near Benderman's

Campsites between Knox Plantation and town. "Hey, back-seat driver, you said I should speed up!"

"Not around *that* curve. It's bad! Folks come 'round that bend in the middle of the road. Last year a fellow drivin' a turkey truck flipped and landed in the ditch! Turkeys every-where!"

A few moments later, Precious pointed as we passed a deer carcass on the side of the road. Well, part of a carcass, actually. The skin and legs were there, but any part of the animal that could've provided meat had been removed. And if it had been a good-sized buck, there was a decent chance the head and anthers were being made into a wall trophy.

"Poachers!" shouted Precious.

I scrunched my face and nodded. It wasn't uncommon for poachers to hunt deer and process the animal in the back of a pickup in the woods before dumping the unwanted carcass on the side of the road. It always upset me when I came across deer remains like that. Seeing her frown in the rearview mirror, I got the impression that Precious didn't much like it, either.

"I hate guns," I said.

We rode the rest of the way—about fifteen minutes—silently. We whizzed under shady tunnels of live oaks, then flew over bright, sunlit stretches of road past miles of fences and crop fields. Although I was achy and tired, the afternoon sunshine felt good. And except for seeing the deer, I enjoyed the ride.

On the edge of town, I dropped off Precious at the mar-ket. I was to pick her up forty minutes later. That gave me just enough time to drive to the packy on Main Street, where Daphne'd instructed me to purchase some wine and extra glassware. Then, after reconnecting with Precious, I'd drop her off at Greatwoods before heading home with Daphne's stuff.

On Main Street, I pulled up to a sunny parking spot in front of a peacock blue Victorian with red gingerbread trim. There was a blue and red striped awning, and potted red miniature roses in front of the building. A small sign read ABUNDANCE PACKAGE STORE. I stepped out of the BMW onto the boulevard and fished for a quarter out of my purse.

"Nice car," said an elderly man passing on the sidewalk.

"Thanks!"

"I reckon it's a right beautiful day to be out enjoin' the ride."

"Yes, it is."

"Y'all have a nice day, now."

"I will. You, too."

The man moved on, and I put a quarter in the meter before shuffling in Daphne's Wellies across the hot brick sidewalk and into the shade under the awning. I pulled open the glass door, and a little bell jangled. I slid my sunglasses to the top of my head as my eyes struggled to adjust from the bright afternoon sunlight to the darkened shop. The only natural light came in through the glass door behind me. Cool with a dusty smell about it, the liquor store was jam-packed, floor to ceiling, with bottles of wine and alcoholic and nonalcoholic beverages of every kind. There were tall, library-style ladders to reach the highest bottles on shop shelves near the tin-covered ceiling. At the back of the store, coolers filled with ice and beverages hummed and glowed with cool neon lights.

"Good afternoon, young lady," said a husky, fortyish man behind the counter next to the door. He had a blocky head, tiny ears, and big eyes that looked even bigger behind black eyeglasses. His light hair was buzz-cut short. He wore a black bow tie and a name tag on his red short-sleeved shirt that identified him as manager.

"What y'all know today?" he asked. Then, he stopped short. "Oh, hey! I recognize you! You're the runaway bride. The Knox gal. I've seen your picture in the *Supermarket Stargazer* a bunch of times. And on the Internet! Why, you're right famous! And much prettier in person."

He'd caught me off guard. Although, by this time I should've been prepared for it. I ignored his comments and squinted to read the name on the tag. It said WENDEL WILCOX.

"Wendel," I said, smiling, "My sister, Daphne Bouvier, sent me to pick up some glassware. She said that you have some saved for her. Also, she asked me to pick out some wine."

"Of course, Miss Knox. Why don't y'all choose the wine while I get your sister's order together in the back. We've been busy today, so I'm a bit behind. It'll take me a few minutes."

"Thanks."

"No problem. I can't believe I'm seein' you in person! Wait till I tell my family." Wendel slammed the counter with his hand excitedly before he hurried off to the back room.

I was pretty sure that my plastered smile had morphed into a grimace.

While Wendel hunted down Daphne's glassware in the back, I grabbed a mini shopping cart near the door and headed toward an aisle to search for the various wines Daphne had on her list. There were no other customers in my narrow aisle, but I could hear other shoppers talking and sliding bottles off the shelves around the store. Slowly, I pushed my mini cart down the first aisle. I was in the "red" section, passing rows and rows of wine bottles labeled with little signs sticking out from the shelves: BORDEAUX . . . CABERNET FRANC . . . CABERNET SAUVIGNON . . . MALBEC . . . MERLOT . . . I needed to find the sparkling wines. At the end of the row, I pushed my cart around the corner.

Right into Debi Dicer.

"Well, look who the cat dragged in—and, all gussied up like Daisy Duke! Eva Knox, bless your heart. What brings you here, darlin'?" Debi cackled as she took a slender finger and flipped her processed blonde hair away from her face.

Any Southerner knows that "bless your heart" is code for something that rhymes with "duck you." Not nice.

"Debi! You haven't changed a bit in twenty years."

I hoped that would be the end of it and we could both move on. I tried to work my cart around Debi, but the aisle was too narrow, and she made no effort to move. Instead, she just stood, smiling at me as she cradled two bottles of champagne in her perfectly toned arms.

It was a Southern-style standoff.

"Oh, thanks, sweetness. I work real hard to keep my figure just as it was when we were in high school. And my man appreciates it," said Debi with a big wink.

Translation: I look just as young and sexy as I did in high school, and I have a boyfriend. Moreover, the inference is, of course, that the person being addressed—that was me— does *not* look young and sexy and does *not* have a love interest.

Debi wasn't off the mark.

She, was fit, tall, and tanned. Her makeup was flawless, and her long nails were meticulously done and matched her bright pink lipstick. Debi had a sleek "inverted bob" haircut—her hair was shoulder length in the front and just nape length in the back. And somehow, it poofed up at the crown. Kind of modern day, big hair, Southern chic. Quite an improvement from the last time I'd seen her looking like a hedgehog, all foiled up in Tammy Fae's salon. Debi's Lilly Pulitzer shift dress was suitably pert, in a neon floral print with white trim. She wore high-heeled white sandals and carried a straw bag with a designer label. I had to admit, Debi was a very attractive, put-together-looking woman. Her bright blue eyes flashed as she gave me a good once-over.

I was still in dirty cutoffs, my ripped and stained GEORGIA VIRGIN tee, and ugly rubber Wellies, and my tangled hair looked like a rat's nest, not to mention, except for my hands and face, I was still pretty filthy and my skin was scratched and torn from head to toe. Debi's look of disgust wasn't a surprise. She flicked her hair again and licked her pink-painted lips.

"And you! Well, Eva sweetie, y'all are still *exactly* as I remember you in high school. And how *cute*, advertising yourself as a Georgia virgin!" Debi smiled as she fingered her hair again. She made "cute" sound like a dirty word.

There was no use trying to dodge Debi's barbs.

Game on.

"Well, you know, for me, each time is like the first time," I said sweetly.

"Well, I suppose, for you, that it could be so . . . with y'all havin' been with so *many* men and all. How many times is it that you've been engaged now?"

"That's just what it's like, being marriage material. Men just love proposing to me. Has anyone proposed to you, Debi?"

Debi smiled and pretended to not hear my comeback.

"Say, hon, I hear they found y'all layin' next to a *dead* man in your daddy's olive grove. Did y'all love the poor fellow to death, or what?" Debi's high-pitched laugh echoed through the store.

"Actually, I'd never seen the man here before."

"Really? Before what? Before y'all knocked him off after your one-nighter? You go, girl!" Debi winked at me.

I decided Debi's comments were distressingly off-color. I'd had enough of the game we were playing. I didn't answer. I hoped the awkward silence would dissuade her from saying anything else. A moment ticked by. Then two.

"I hear the dead fellow worked for y'all. He was some sort of hunting guide, wasn't he? From up North. Like you."

Now, with the worst of the insults over, Debi was digging for dirt.

"I'm from Abundance, not 'up North.'"

"If you say so. Now, sweetness, forgive me for askin', but who hires a guide from somewhere else? What was your big sis, Miss Daphne, thinking? And y'all know, it's funny, but folks have been sayin' *you* killed that poor fellow."

"Folks are wrong."

"Well then, pray tell, what were y'all doin' out there in the middle of that stormy night?"

"I was running."

"From what? Or from whom, I should say!" Debi cackled again. "Y'all weren't runnin' from *another* fiancé, were you?"

Debi raised her eyebrows and had a cold, fiery look in her eyes. I realized there was nothing I could say that would satisfy her. This kind of insult exchange was sport. If she had her way, we'd be at it for hours.

Then, I remembered the plan.

I scuffled closer to Debi, put my hands on my hips, and smiled. She drew back as I stuck my grimy self in her space.

"Actually, Debi, you're right," I said quietly. "I killed him. I killed him because he was running off with my beloved girlfriend, my sister's chef, Loretta. You see, he and Loretta were planning to get married, and I was jealous. So, I shot him. Right there in Daddy's olive grove. Then, I killed Loretta, too. Now they're both dead."

Debi just stared at me. Her mouth started to drop open.

"So, now I'm free," I said. "For you, Debi." I pursed my lips and kissed the air. "You know, I've been attracted to you since high school. I used to love it when you showed up at the house. Now we can finally go out." I leaned in even closer to Debi.

Eyes wide, Debi was speechless. That's a first, I thought smugly. Finally, after stepping back, she huffed indignantly.

"Well, bless your heart, Eva Knox, y'all really *are* crazy."

"Crazy for you, sweetness."

"No. Folks are right. Y'all are just plain mad as a hatter. Like your crazy mama."

"Thank you!"

Debi backed up another step and sniffed. "Darlin', I don't know what y'all are up to, but I don't have any more time for crazy talk. I've got to get ready for a date. A *real* date. With a man. *My* man. Don't y'all know? We're celebrating our anniversary tonight."

I threw my hands up in mock surprise. "Anniversary? Someone married you, Debi? I had no idea. Congratulations!"

"No, not yet. But very soon. We've been together for six months, and he's about to put a ring on it. He's just waitin' for me to pick out my diamond. Then, I'll marry him. And real quick."

"Yes. At your age, you wouldn't want to wait too long," I said, all sugary.

"Oh, and hon, you'll remember him. I'm sure," she countered.

"I will?"

"Why, yes. Of course you will!" Debi licked her lips and flicked her hair back again.

"Well then, who's the lucky fellow?"

Debi leaned in close to me and lowered her voice. "Before I say, I just want y'all to know, sweetness, that he and I've always loved each other. Always. He just needed some time to sow his oats. And now that he's experienced life, traveled the world, and gotten all that silly, immature boyishness out of his system, he's grown into a real man, ready for a real woman."

I raised my eyebrows.

"Why, it shouldn't surprise y'all, Eva darling, I'm marrying the *first* man y'all dumped so recklessly. I'm marrying Sheriff Buck Tanner." Debi looked like the cat who swallowed the canary. "Now, Buck is finally gettin' the woman he deserves. A sane, honorable woman. A woman who appreciates him. A woman who won't run away."

I felt my face get hot and my neck bristle. I remembered Buck smiling at me, with his cheeky expression and that boyish twinkle in his eyes, as I sat in front of him stark naked in the bed at Greatwoods, hours earlier. Sweet revenge for him—if I hadn't been humiliated enough, it was a double dig to hear he was in love with another woman while he'd stared unabashedly at me. Debi Dicer, of all people. Had he gone back to Debi and told her he'd seen me? All of me? I imagined them having a giggle about my indignity. My chest hurt. I hoped my burning cheeks and neck weren't red. Except I knew they were.

I pasted on a big smile for Debi. "Well, I'm happy for you both. You *deserve* each other. Please, don't let me keep you from your celebration tonight."

My ears were ringing. I was having trouble focusing on Debi's face; so many thoughts whirled in my head. Yes, it had been a long time since my relationship with Buck. And he'd gone off somewhere, for years, and probably hooked up with other women. Still, I had a difficult time wrapping my head around the fact that of all the women Buck could have chosen during all those years, he'd ended up with Debi Dicer.

"Oh, Eva, hon, y'all won't keep us from celebrating. Make no mistake about *that*!" boasted Debi. "Tonight, I've got an extra-special romantic evening planned." Debi worked her way around my cart. "After I pay for this champagne, I'm off to the Lacy Goddess to pick out some lingerie. From France. Of course, *y'all know Buck*! I won't be wearing it for long!"

"Yes. I *do* know Buck. But then, you seem to spend an inordinate lot of time brooding about that fact, so I don't need to remind you," I said dryly.

Debi raised one of the champagne bottles over her head and winked at me before she turned and sashayed down the aisle toward the front of the store. "Tootles!"

Something inside stung. Maybe even hurt. She'd been right about one thing: I hadn't changed much since high school. Debi still managed to make me hot, stinking mad.

I stuck my tongue out at her as she swaggered around the corner.

CHAPTER 24

"Precious, I have a killer headache," I said. "We're stopping at the country store."

Cruising down the rural road, top down in the green convertible—me in front, Precious stuffed into the rear bucket seat sticking high out of the car like a giant warrior maiden in her tiny chariot—we were almost to Knox Plantation. A pile of grocery bags flapped in the wind next to Precious. The tiny BMW trunk had been too full with other groceries and boxes of wine and glasses from the package store to fit in everything we'd purchased for Daphne.

It'd been a long, busy day. I was crashing. Big-time. I figured some sugar and caffeine would ease my achy head and help to keep me awake for the remainder of the afternoon and evening.

Besides, I had a craving for Twizzlers candy and a Coke.

"Fine with me, Sunshine. It's so hot, the hens are layin' hard-boiled eggs. I could go for a Diet Dr Pepper, myself!" shouted Precious from the backseat. Watching the scenery whiz by, she made little waves with her hand in the wind.

About a mile down the road, we pulled into the dirt parking lot outside Carter's Country Corner Store and parked next to a mud-covered blue Chevy pickup sporting a rifle in a rack across the back window. Housed in an old general store built just after the Civil War, open from six in the morning until eleven at night, seven days a week, Carter's was an Abundance institution. The place was a junk food paradise—a virtual smorgasbord of sugary, salty, and artificially colored and preserved confections where one could purchase every imaginable kind of gum, candy, and snack as well as extra sugary or caffeinated beverages. Cheetos, Fritos, nachos, Nekot wafers, Little Debbie cakes, those nasty fake fried onion rings, MoonPies, olive and pimento cheese spread, Honey Buns, Krispy Kreme donuts, and at least three other brands of prepackaged donuts—the kind that stayed "fresh" for months—it was all inside.

Plus, there was a grill and small deli for take-out meals; refrigerators full of carbonated drinks, chocolate milk, and beer; as well as half an aisle stocked with "emergency" cleaning supplies, toilet paper, breakfast goods, pet foods, and cheap kitchen accessories.

In addition to its status as the junk food capital of Abundance, Carter's was the local hub for geezers, hunters, and fishermen. There were cigarettes, cheap cigars, pipe tobacco, and tins of chewing tobacco for sale. Not to mention fish bait, lures, bird calls, knives, and ammo. It was the place where locals read and posted hunting notices; the official location to check in tagged game after a hunting spree; and the spot where good ol' boys bragged about their catch of the day. Old men sat around for the better part of a day, gossiping and hiding out from their wives at home. It was dark, dirty, and smelly. Daphne called it the Man Club. And she, like most of the gentlewomen in Abundance, refused to step inside.

"Let's do this," I said, climbing out of the car. A light breeze blew swirls of gravel dust into the air around us. "I'm sure that I'll be sorry later." Already, I was imagining the first rubbery bite and the fruity taste of my strawberry Twizzler. I'd eat too many of the soft, twisty sticks. Then, I'd have a stomach ache.

I didn't care. *What's one more ache?*

"Gotta have me a Diet Dr Pepper," said Precious, holding her arms out for balance as she carefully picked her way over the gravel in her tight skirt and yellow Louboutins.

A little bell jangled as Precious and I pushed open the door. Dirt, tracked in from the boots of outdoorsmen, rolled under my rubber boots and made little scuffling sounds as I crossed the well-worn wide-pine floor. Just inside the door, a cadre of unshaven old men in dirty overalls sat around an upturned barrel with a checkerboard on top. No one looked up as we entered. I caught a few sideways glances directed toward Precious's spiky heels as she *plickety-plunketied* across the dusty floor. I smiled to myself. Dirty and disheveled, quite the opposite from Precious's city slicker looks, I was a perfect fit for Carter's Country Corner Store.

"How you ladies doin' today?" called out a jolly young woman from the counter. Behind her, a wall-mounted case of cigarettes was surrounded by old license plates nailed to the knotty pine boards. "Can I get y'all something from the deli? BLTs are on special," she said, wiping her hands on her stained apron.

"No, thanks," I said. "I'm just here to load up on sugar."

"Well, that's just fine," said the smiley gal. "Let me know when y'all are ready to check out." She turned to resume a conversation with a man in a cap, muddy boots, and well-worn fatigues standing on our side of the counter.

"You got Dr Pepper?" Precious shouted, halfway down the aisle.

"In the back. Cooler on the far left," said the gal behind the counter.

"Thanks, love," said Precious as she *plickety-plunketied* toward the rear of the store. Her loaded footsteps echoed throughout the store; metal snack racks shook as she clomped by. "You want anything, Sunshine?" Precious called from the back of the store.

"I'd love a Coke, please," I said, scanning the racks for

a package of Twizzlers. The racks were oddly chock-full of candies and bags of snacks in some places, and completely empty in others. "Do you have any Twizzlers?" I asked the woman behind the counter. "I've got a terrible craving."

"I'm sorry, hon. We're all out. We had some vandals over the weekend, and they cleaned out a bunch of our snacks and some beer, as well as some spray paint and hunting knives. Bart and I, we were just talkin' about it, weren't we, Bart?"

"We sure were, Junie Mae." Bart pinched off a huge wad of chewing tobacco and stuffed it in his cheek. He looked like a giant chipmunk gathering nuts for winter. "Damn kids got all my Honey Buns," he sputtered, putting the lid back on the tobacco can and shoving it into his pocket.

"Yep, times sure are a changing. That's fer sure," said the gal as she smiled. "Like that terrible murder they had over at the Knox place—can you imagine that?"

"I heard the fellow was not from 'round here. Heard he was a Yank," said the man.

Quickly, I looked down. *Thank God! They didn't recognize me.*

"Yeah, you know what they say about them Yankees!" said the gal.

"Your move," grumbled a man over at the checkerboard.

"Yep. Them Yanks are like hemorrhoids," said Bart cheerily. He smiled at the gal and then at me. His teeth were yellow. "When they go South and then back North they ain't so bad. But when they go South and *stay* South, they're a real pain in the butt. Hehehe. Maybe that fellow over at the Knox place should've stayed up North."

Bart started laughing hard, then, in no time, he was hacking. He choked on his tobacco and spit tobacco juice into a soda bottle he was holding under his arm.

"All them Yankees are better off stayin' where they are," said the gal. Then she addressed me, "Hey, hon, since we're plum outta Twizzlers, maybe y'all would like some Gummi Bears? We got those. Or how about some Sour Patch Kids? That's what always hits the spot for me."

"Thanks," I said. "Say, can either of you tell me what hunting season it is right now?"

"Huntin'? Not much goin' on now," the man mumbled through his tobacco.

"Oh, now, Bart! You know there's all sorts of stuff goin' on. Some folks don't pay no attention to what season it is," she gushed. "Why, you brought in a whole pile of frog legs just the other night!"

"Well, yeah. I s'pose there's frogs. But that ain't real huntin', Junie Mae. Frog giggin' is just fer fun," he said, smiling as he tried to suck back the tobacco juices in his mouth. "Besides, y'all know I'd never hunt out of season. Why, that'd be breakin' the law!" He winked as a little brown dribble of juice rolled from one corner of his mouth. He wiped it with the back of his hand before he took his soda bottle to his lips and spit the brown juice into the bottle. I couldn't help but notice that his fatigues were stained. Looked like blood. I doubted frogs were all he'd been after lately.

"Here's your pop, Sunshine." Precious clomped up the store aisle and handed me an ice-cold can of Coke. I snapped open the can and took a big fizzy gulp.

"Oh gosh, that's good. Thanks, Precious." I turned and grabbed a bag of Sour Patch Kids from the snack rack. Then, I grabbed a bag of Fritos, a bar of Godiva bittersweet dark chocolate, and two packages of Lance cheddar cheese wafers. They'd balance out the sugar.

"Whoa, there, Sunshine! You aimin' to have a junk food melt down? It's nearly four o'clock now. If you hang on a couple of hours, Miss Precious, here, will make you a real nice dinner."

"Sorry. I'll never make it that long." I grabbed a bag of Poppycock and a small box of Krispy Kreme donuts. "C'mon, let's go. I promised to get you back to Greatwoods."

"King me," growled one of the men playing checkers.

Precious and I paid for our sugary transgressions and headed outside. Precious climbed in the backseat of the convertible as I sat behind the wheel, stuck the can of Coke between my legs, and ripped open the bag of Sour Patch Kids. I popped three or four of the gummy candies into my mouth, and with the other hand, I stuck the key into the ignition.

"We're off like a herd of turtles!" Precious cried from the backseat. I looked in the rearview mirror. She was laughing. In no time, Precious and I were cruising down the road.

"Hey, has Daphne found anyone to replace Loretta?" I shouted back to Precious. I bit the head off another Sour Patch Kid, savoring the chewy, sweet, and salty taste. I grabbed the Coke from between my knees and glugged the candied caffeine. I was going to make myself sick.

"A replacement? Not that I know of," bellowed Precious in the wind.

"How long can you keep helping us?"

"Could be awhile. Mister Collier, he says he don't need me much these days. And I'm kinda enjoying it. Y'all are very entertaining!"

I looked at Precious in the rearview mirror. She ignored me, turning her head to watch the scenery whiz by. She was smiling as her big gold earrings jangled in the wind.

Thank goodness for small favors, I thought. I couldn't imagine how we'd have made it without Precious. But then, what kind of work was she doing for Ian Collier that he didn't need her? Detective Gibbit had called her "estate manager." That sounded like a job that would keep someone busy. I just couldn't figure out Greatwoods at all.

We swooshed around Benderman's Curve, and a few minutes later we passed the modest wooden sign for Knox Plantation. There were pretty pink crepe myrtles in bloom at the entrance to the gravel drive that wound through the woods to the big house, which was set well back from the road. I passed our drive and kept going. The entrance to Greatwoods was only a few more miles down the road.

When we neared the Greatwoods entrance, I pulled toward the center of the two-lane road, stopped, and waited while a slow-moving tractor towing a double trailer of round hay bales passed in the other direction. After the trailer'd gone by, I'd make the left-hand turn across the road toward the huge, black wrought iron gate that marked the front entrance to Greatwoods.

The entry was inset from the road so that one or two cars could park outside the gate and still be off the road, safe from traffic. The double gate hung from two giant brick pillars on either side of a cobblestone drive. I noticed a camera mounted to the top of one of the gateposts. There was more wrought iron fencing on the outside of each pillar. It went along for some fifty or more feet, then jutted back into the woods. Somewhere back there, the decorative wrought iron connected with the barbed wire I'd encountered during my morning trek home.

"Okay, thanks, hon," I heard Precious say into her cell phone from the backseat. She grinned and waved to me as she caught my eye in the rearview mirror. Late-afternoon sun glinted off her big gold hoop earrings. I looked ahead at the road again. Behind the slow-moving trailer of hay bales on the other side of the road, a stream of cars crawled by, one after the other. We waited.

I was anxious to see the mansion from the front. Get the full impression. I'd been so intent on my escape in the morning that I hadn't taken in the place. Maybe now, I could put it all together.

And I was most eager to meet Ian Collier.

The choo-choo train of slow-moving vehicles finally passed, and I pulled across the road and stopped at the closed entrance. On the other side of the gates, a navy blue Hummer with big tires and smoked-glass windows headed toward us down the shaded, tree-lined drive.

Precious tapped me on the shoulder. "This is fine, Sunshine. Thanks for the ride. Mister Lurch will take me on up to the house from here."

"Are you sure . . . ?"

The dark Hummer came to a stop about two car lengths back from the other side of the gate. Like magic, the gate swung inward. Behind me, Precious grunted as she pushed the back of the passenger seat forward. She stood up and leaned forward to grab the door handle of my little BMW.

"It's a little after four o'clock now, Sunshine. Tell your sis I'll be back at five," said Precious, still holding her Diet Dr Pepper. "Miss Daphne said those two ladies from New York were plannin' on havin' Tammy Fae Tanner do 'em up this evening, so they asked for a late supper. We got plenty of time to prepare a killer meal. And you and me got all the ingredients here in the car. You okay to unload it all by yourself?" asked Precious as she lumbered out of the car.

"No problem," I lied.

"Okey dokey." Precious slammed the car door. The car shook. She tiptoed in her Louboutins over the cobblestones and through the open gates toward the Hummer.

Lurch, wearing a little black cap, bright white shirt, black vest, skinny black tie, and pressed black slacks, stepped out from behind the wheel of the vehicle and went around the Hummer to open the door for Precious. Somehow, he looked even taller outside than he had when I'd seen him skulking around inside Greatwoods. As he turned away from me to open the vehicle door for Precious, I caught a glimpse of something at the small of his back under his vest. Was it a gun holster? Did I really see that? The bright sun glared on the windshield. I couldn't tell for sure.

"Thanks for the ride, Sunshine. See y'all later!" Precious called. She waved to me before stepping up into the Hummer. Lurch closed her door and hustled around to the driver's side. Already, the big gates were closing in front of me.

So much for seeing Greatwoods. Or Ian Collier.

I backed my car around, pulled out onto the road, and headed home to unload the groceries.

CHAPTER 25

All was quiet at Knox Plantation. The guests were still out, and I assumed Daphne was up on the third floor with the kids. In the kitchen, after I quickly scanned the yard for Dolly, to no avail, I unloaded the groceries, putting the cold foods in the Sub-Zero and stashing the rest of the food along with the box of glassware in the pantry. I needed to get the wine and champagne out of the trunk and put it in the basement wine cellar.

When Pep had first told me that Daphne had a fancy, climate-controlled wine cellar in the basement, I'd laughed. The basement we grew up in was little more than a catchall for dirt, dust, mold, and a few ancient tools, lawn gear, long-forgotten toys, broken household items, and unwanted furnishings. Growing up, the only way to get to the cellar had been through the outside bulkhead. Once down the stairs, there had been a dirt floor, rock walls, and a single light on a pull string, and it was full of spiders, snakes, and rodents. And although Pep and I had relished the moldy-smelling basement as a place for exploration, adventure, and secret hiding spots, Daphne had *never* deigned to go down there. So, it amused me that, all these years later, this was the place that Daphne had spent so much of her ex-husband's money. And the first time I went outside and stepped through the new basement entry at the back of the house, I was shocked.

Daphne had masterminded an entire basement excavation and renovation, including a poured concrete base floor, new walls, ceiling, lighting, and stabilization of the outer foundation walls. Plus, she'd added a small studio apartment with kitchenette and full bath, an exercise room, storage areas, and a wine cellar. The only caveat was that you still had to go outside to get there. Daphne had sacrificed an in-house stair to keep maximum usable space on the first floor.

I went outside to the car and hoisted up a box of wine. My ribs hurt. My ankle throbbed. I sucked it up, as they say, and hobbled around the house to the basement. Behind my cottage on the other side of the yard, a giant red and white striped tent covered the lawn near the pond.

"Oh my God," I said to myself. "Tomorrow's going to be a circus."

I carried the box down the outside basement stair, went through the unlocked door below, and flicked on the light switch. Daphne's new basement was a generous slate-tiled mudroom with cubbies, shelves, hanging hooks, and a long antique bench that had once been in a local church. On the left was a stained wooden door to the apartment, Chef Loretta's apartment. In front of me, there was a hallway and another wooden door that led to Daphne's climate-controlled wine cellar.

I opened the door to the wine cellar and slid the box inside. Then, I went back out to get the second box from the car. The sugar from the candy and soda I'd consumed was beginning to make me feel sick. Still, I'd long ago run out of energy. I reached into the Krispy Kreme box in the car and grabbed myself a glazed sugar donut. I took a bite. Then another.

Four trips to the car, three donuts later, and the seventh

time I passed the door to Chef Loretta's apartment, my curiosity got the best of me. As anxious as I was to find Dolly and get home to a bath and bed, I wanted to peek into the apartment. Maybe I could learn something about our missing chef.

I closed the door to the wine cellar and went over to the apartment door and knocked. No one answered. I tried the door. It opened. Daphne said the deputies had taken some of Loretta's personal effects for evidence, deciding that Loretta was a murderer, murder victim, missing person, or all three. I wasn't sure that searching her place, and certainly, taking her stuff, was even legal. But this was Abundance. And Loretta was an out-of-towner. If it hadn't been legal, probably no one had cared. I hoped they hadn't done the same in my place. Although, it seemed likely that they'd at least gone through everything. By all accounts, I was an out-of-towner as well. And a damned Yankee, at that. I stepped inside and flipped on a lamp.

With walls painted a soft ivory, the space was neat and tidy. Spotless, actually. And except for a bookcase full of cookbooks and a new wood chopping block in the kitchen area, I recognized nearly all the furnishings. It was all stuff from my childhood. Not the best things—there were no pricey or irreplaceable antiques, for example—but the apartment was outfitted with the sensible, utilitarian furnishings that we'd had growing up. An oak rolltop desk. A painted Windsor chair. Brass reading lamps from the den. The maple dresser from Daddy and Mother's bedroom, only it had been repainted a soft butter yellow color. A side table and a recovered couch from the living room. An old gaming table, repainted for use as a small dining table. There was a braided rug on the floor. And a low four-poster bed, painted white. I remembered the bed before it had been repainted—it'd been left disassembled, scuffed, and scratched, leaning against a dusty shelf in the old dirt cellar. I'd never have imagined that it could've been made to look so lovely again. And it was all Daphne's doing.

Still the most remarkable thing about the apartment, and

what interested me the most, were the photos. The walls were covered with them. Mostly old images of my family. Collectively, they made the apartment look like a Knox family museum. Some of the pictures dated back to more than a century ago. My grandparents, great-grandparents, aunts and uncles, cousins, sisters, friends, neighbors . . . all the people whom I knew, and the ancestors whom I knew about growing up, were captured in images mounted to the walls. Except, of course, my mother. There wasn't a stitch of clothing, a piece of jewelry, personal knickknack, or photograph of my mother anywhere to be found at Knox Plantation. Daphne had made sure of that.

I sat on the couch and took in one wall. There was Great-Granddaddy Knox, sitting in a rocker on the front porch, looking as dapper as ever in his Sunday best and well-trimmed beard. And there was dour-faced Great-Aunt Winnie and her fox terrier standing next to a baby carriage. Grade school–aged Daddy, holding his bicycle, standing next to his Boston terrier. Great-Uncle Somebody-or-other was out in a field with a horse and plow. Or was he a great-*great*-uncle? I'd have to ask Daddy sometime, I thought. There was a photo of Daddy and his three brothers and sisters when they were kids, all sitting on a fence by the road. It'd been a dirt road back then. And there was an antique photo of men working to build an addition onto the house.

I stretched out sideways on the couch and studied the photos next to me on the wall above the back of the couch. These were newer photos—like me, Pep, and Daphne wearing bathing suits, splashing in a wading pool in the backyard. I looked to be only about two years old. In another photo, Pep was leaving for her first prom date, with . . . oh gosh, what was his name? He was in the chess club; that's all I could remember. I giggled. How did *that* unlikely pairing happen? And there was a photo of the house; the pretty dogwood tree outside my bedroom window was in full bloom. That photo was next to a photo of Daddy, Pep, and me carving pumpkins for Halloween. There was a shot of

Daphne standing next to her first car, an old Buick. Another one of me, onstage at my ballet recital. There was a picture of Pep sitting on a John Deere tractor. Me and Daphne standing with a bushel of peaches. All three of us girls, Christmas Day, standing in front of the Christmas tree. Me, holding up my first catfish . . .

Then, I noticed the little photo, at the bottom of a row, just behind the couch.

I'd never seen it before.

It was a small photo, in a cheap black frame. I sat up and looked closer at the two kids, maybe ten or twelve years old. And they didn't look familiar. Dark haired, dark skinned, and bulky, they didn't look at all like anyone in my fair Scottish family. The two little kids were photographed sitting side by side, bundled up in snowsuits, on the steps of a concrete stair to a brick building. Something looked familiar. I took the photo down and turned it over in my hand. Scribbled on the cardboard back was a note that read *Loretta and Lenny, Providence house*.

CHAPTER 26

"Eva! Wake up. It's late!" Pep shook my shoulder. "Eva, baby, c'mon. Y'all need to get up, sweetie. Time to go home now."

"What . . . Where am I? Nooo . . . can't wake up now . . . Not yet!" I mumbled, still only half awake, blinking away deep sleep and dreams of my Scottish prince.

"Eva, what are y'all doin' down here, sleeping on the couch in Loretta's place?" Pep asked. She shook me again. "Daphne told me that she found you down here hours ago, fast asleep. She figured you needed the rest, so she left y'all down here. But when you never came back up, we figured I'd better check on you before I went home."

"What?" I rubbed my eyes. "Is it late? What time is it?"

"It's after eleven o'clock. At night," said Pep. She was wearing a short peplum leather jacket with a high collar and plunging neckline over black leggings and spiky red boots. There didn't appear to be anything under the jacket, and she smelled of leathered perfume and smoke. "I came from the Roadhouse to help Daphne finish setting up the tent for the Chamber of Commerce thingy tomorrow. Daphne said she'd found y'all holed up in here when she came down to the wine cellar to check on the champagne."

"Oh. The Chamber meeting," I sighed. "I bet you both needed my help setting up for that. I'm sorry." I rubbed my bleary eyes again. "And what about dinner?"

"Dinner was the berries! Precious put together an amazing meal—spicy sausage, chicken, and shrimp jambalaya over rice with deep-fried beignets and fresh fruit for dessert. I had some leftovers, and it was the best ever. And—oh my God—Eva, hon, you should've seen the two women from New York! They'd been to Tammy Fae's, and she had 'em all done up with these crazy-ass hairdos! Their hair must've been three feet high!"

"Omigosh."

"Both of 'em had this wacky, king-sized cosmic hair that made 'em look like a pair of hair metal rock queens from the eighties. I think Tammy Fae might've been teasing with them . . ."

"No pun intended?"

"Right."

"Daphne's gonna kill me. I sent her guests to Tammy Fae. I should've known she'd take out her dislike for me on them."

"No. Wait. Here's the best part! The women *loved* their hair. Said they wanted to get their hairdresser in New York to do the same thing."

"Who knew." I rolled my eyes. "Well, I'm happy that we foiled Tammy Fae's wicked plan."

"So, listen, hon, don't worry about gettin' up early tomorrow. We actually managed to get things under control tonight. Just show up midday to greet guests at the Chamber thingy. Daphne wants you showin' your face there. After all, you're the reason most folks are coming. Honestly, I don't know how we did it; Daphne is out of her mind over this. She must've spent a fortune."

"That's our 'DQ.' Everything over-the-top. No use fighting it." I yawned.

"Do y'all feel okay, sweetie, now that you've had some rest?"

"Better. Still, I feel like I've been chewed up and spit out.

And I think I've broken a rib." I started to push myself up. Then, I thought better of it and sank back down into the cushions. "Hey. You know, this couch is wicked comfortable. I don't remember it being like this."

"It wasn't. Daphne had new cushions made before she re-covered it."

"Oh." I yawned. "It feels so good, I must've dozed off while I was looking at all the photos. This place is amazing." I closed my eyes and started to roll over.

Pep shook my shoulder. "Eva, sweetie, I think y'all need to get home to bed. You'll sleep better and feel more rested in the morning. Daphne's countin' on y'all to help in the afternoon."

"I know. I'd planned to be there tomorrow. Although, I'm not looking forward to it. Daphne said nearly everyone in the county is coming. That includes Tammy Fae. And Debi Dicer."

"Debi Dicer? Why are you worried about her?"

"For one thing, she's tight with Tammy Fae. And, well, Debi and I had a bit of a run-in earlier."

"A 'run-in'? Care to share details?"

"No. Not really. Let it suffice to say that Debi takes great pleasure in my discomfort."

"Ah well. Nothing new there. She's always jerking a knot in someone's tail. The woman just makes my ass itch. Y'all will just have to buck up when you see her sorry puss at the meetin' tomorrow."

I shot a dirty look toward Pep when she said the word "buck." She didn't seem to notice.

"Hey, how did the olive oil work out for you and Billy last night?" I asked, changing the subject. "Did it bring the romantic results you thought it would?" I raised my eyebrows teasingly.

"Well, I'm sure that it would've. But by the time I got back home, Billy wasn't there anymore. Pretty much par for the course these days."

"Oh. I'm sorry," I said. "Where could he have gone at that hour?"

Pep shrugged. She seemed to take it in stride. Although, I thought it was pretty weird, Billy running out on his wife in the middle of the night like that. And I couldn't help but wonder if he'd been in the woods with the rest of us. Still, it wasn't my place to upset Pep. I'd mull it over later.

"At least you'll have the oil ready for your next romantic interlude."

"Romantic interlude? You kill me, sweetie." Pep laughed. "Billy hasn't got a romantic bone in his body." Pep sighed. "Although, he did surprise me with some racy lingerie a couple of weeks ago from the Lacy Goddess. Of course, it was two sizes too big. Still, I had to give the guy credit for having nerve enough to shop there. Here," she said, holding out her hand, "let me help y'all up."

I grabbed her fingers and let her pull me forward. Every muscle in my body ached. And my stomach was mad about all the sugar I'd consumed.

"Hey, hold your horses!" Pep said. "What's that?"

I looked down in my lap to see the small photo I'd found before I'd fallen asleep.

"Oh! I forgot. I found this. Tacked to the wall. Like it was part of our family display. Loretta must've hung it on the wall and the deputies missed it when they did their search. Look!"

I handed the photograph to Pep, who examined it in her hands.

"What the . . . ? *Loretta and Lenny*? What does this mean?"

"I'm not sure. But it does seem there's a good chance that our Leonard, my pastry guy, might be Lenny, don't you think?"

"It certainly seems plausible. Hey, why not? But then, if they already knew each other, what were they doing here, acting like strangers?"

"That is the million-dollar question. Of course, I doubt we'll ever figure it out if we can't find Loretta," I said.

"Oh, she'll turn up directly," said Pep. "You can bet your bottom dollar on that, sweetie."

CHAPTER 27

Night creatures screeched and live oaks swooshed in the muggy, moonlit breeze as I labored up the basement stairs to the yard. Exhausted, achy, and groggy, I carried the tiny photo of Loretta and Lenny along with a loaf of Precious's bread and a string bag filled with Daphne's tomatoes that Pep had brought down from the kitchen for me. I slogged across the lawn in Daphne's creaky green rubber boots, hoping that Dolly would be waiting for me outside my cottage.

Dolly was nowhere to be seen.

Maybe after getting out of my wretched clothes, taking another dose of ibuprofen, drawing a warm, lavender-scented bath, and taking a relaxing soak I'd have energy enough to look for Dolly, I thought, opening the cottage door and kicking off Daphne's boots. I plopped the photo, bread, and tomatoes on the Sheridan dresser next to the door. As the screen door slammed shut, I pulled my filthy GEORGIA VIRGIN tee over my head and tossed it to the floor before clicking on the switch to the cranberry lantern overhead.

"Don't let me stop you there, Babydoll."

Across the room, Buck Tanner was settled in my chintz floral armchair under the window. Dolly was curled up in his lap.

Chuckling softly, Buck said, "I must say, I'm tickled pink at your constant desire to undress in my presence."

Dolly jumped down and ran to me, excitedly whining and wagging.

"Dolly!" I cried as I picked her up. Tears of relief fell down my cheeks as she wiggled and whimpered, covering my tears with licks.

I glared at Buck. I felt a confusing mix of relief and elation to finally see Dolly coupled with a sickening humiliation to—once again—be caught off guard and undressed in front of Buck. At least this time, I'd managed to remain somewhat clothed in my black sports bra and cutoffs. I pretended not to care. Or maybe I was too tired to care. I set Dolly down on the floor. In a flash, she grabbed my dirty GEORGIA VIRGIN shirt, shook it wildly, and skittered to her bed with it.

"What are you doing here?" I was chagrined to see my many wads of cried-upon tissues still littered everywhere.

"Why, I'm waitin' to see you, Babydoll. I've been here quite a while." Smiling, with dark, chocolaty eyes fixed on me, Buck leaned back in my armchair, threw one leg up over his knee, and folded his hands in his lap. *Cocky.* He was dressed in black jeans, fitted black tee shirt, and boots.

"Do you always ensconce yourself, uninvited, in people's homes in the middle of the night?" My hands were on my hips. "And, *Sheriff,* are you 'on duty' or 'off duty'?"

"No, I don't usually 'ensconce myself' uninvited, or otherwise, in people's homes," said Buck with a dimpled smile. Then he waved his iPhone with one hand. "This time, I had my cell phone to entertain me. So, there's no need to feel guilty that you missed out on an opportunity to share some of your famous Southern hospitality." Buck chuckled. "And as far as bein' 'on duty' or 'off duty,' I'd say it's a little of both, actually."

My face was getting hot. What nerve. I couldn't believe he'd just waltzed in and sat down. Did he have a warrant? Had he gone through my stuff? Had he proposed to Debi Dicer?

Oh crap. Where did that come from?

I stiffened.

"It seems to me, Sheriff Tanner, that it's either one or the other—on duty or off duty."

"Now, Babydoll, don't get hot and bothered. I'm here to help you," he said, eyes twinkling.

"Help me? How's that? By scaring the crap out of me and stalking me in my own home?"

"Did you know that you look real hot and saucy when you're mad?"

"Stop it."

"I'm here to give you a bit of friendly advice."

"We're hardly 'friends.' We haven't laid eyes on each other in eighteen years."

"Well, yes. I guess you got that right." Buck held my gaze. "At least I don't hold a grudge."

I tried not to flinch. "You don't?"

"No, Eva, I don't," he said softly. Buck gazed steadily at me.

My stomach flipped, and the back of my neck got real hot. I tried to push a million thoughts out of my head. The same million thoughts I'd had, and tried to ignore, for eighteen years. I broke Buck's gaze and looked down at the floor, biting my lip.

I really wanted him to leave.

"What do you want?" I asked, still looking at the floor. I pictured him putting a ring on Debi Dicer's long, slender, perfectly manicured finger—the same way he'd put a little diamond ring on my finger once. I reminded myself that he was *not* my friend. He couldn't be. Not after what I'd done. And certainly, not now. Not with Debi. I could see them laughing together. I started to imagine them, intimately . . . *Stop!* This was all a ruse. He was working a case, I reminded myself. He was here to arrest me. I looked up and glared at him.

"Why don't you sit down and we can talk. You look like you could use a rest," said Buck.

"I don't want to sit down. In fact, I just woke up, so I'm happy to stand here until you leave, which will be any moment now, I'm sure." I looked hard at Buck and crossed my arms, silently daring him to arrest me.

"Have you got something I can eat?" he asked suddenly. "You know, I've been waitin' here for hours, and I'm starving."

"You're kidding, right?"

"Do I look like I'm kidding? I tell you what, since you're not feeling terribly hospitable right now, why don't you sit down while I find us something to eat."

"Good luck with that," I said dryly. I stared over at Dolly, who was happily wrapped in my tee shirt, munching on one of the tissue wads.

In one swift motion, Buck rose up out of the chair and was at the kitchenette. He was like that. Catlike. It looked like he was moving slowly. But really, he was fast. He'd always been that way. Combined with his power, grace, and stealthiness, it was part of what made him such a great athlete. And sportsman. And lover.

Stop it!

"Cute place you've got here," he said. "Was this Daphne's doing?"

Staring at the holstered gun Buck wore tucked into the backside of his jeans, I pushed a strand of hair out of my face and rolled my eyes impatiently.

"Looks like one of her projects," continued Buck. "I remember this place as bein' not much more than a dirt-floor shack."

Buck stepped out from behind the counter and crossed past me to my loaf of bread and string bag of tomatoes on the dresser near the door. "These'll do," he said, picking up the bag and the loaf of bread. Remembering how Buck and I used to make out on the floor of the cottage back when it was "not much more than a dirt-floor shack," knowing my hot cheeks were blushing red thinking about it, only added to my mortification, standing in front of Buck in my sports bra.

Buck stopped short and picked up the little photo.

"What's this?"

"I think it's a photo of Chef Loretta and her brother."

Buck flipped the photo over and nodded his head silently. "Where did you get it?"

"In Loretta's apartment. Your crackerjack detective must've missed it."

Buck studied the photo.

"Stay here."

He pushed open the screen door and stepped outside, closing the door quietly with his hand.

"Like I'm going anywhere dressed like this," I shot back. Still, I doubted he heard me. Already, he was mumbling on his cell phone from the stoop outside. About a minute later, the door squeaked open and Buck stepped back in, placing the photo back on the corner of my dresser.

"I'd appreciate it if you wouldn't just help yourself to all my things," I said. "Although, I'm sure you already have. Are you going to arrest me, now?"

"Tsk-tsk. I don't ever remember you bein' this testy. You need to eat."

Buck brushed my arm absently as he crossed back to the kitchenette. I could feel the familiar heat in his bicep as it skimmed the hair on my skin. He had an energy that could draw me in, like a magnet.

I resisted.

Still, I sensed something different. He smelled different. Cologne? I didn't remember Buck ever wearing cologne. But it was there. Something new. It was a warm, spiced scent that mingled with his honeyed skin. Funny how I remembered his scent so clearly, I thought. But there was something more. Something like patchouli. Sandalwood. Along with something soft and powdery. Following him with my eyes as he crossed behind the counter, I tried to get another whiff of whatever it was he was wearing. I liked it. Even in his black jeans, I could see that Buck's butt was just as I remembered. *Totally pinchable.* I shook my head, trying to erase thoughts of Buck's behind.

It wasn't easy.

"See something you like, Babydoll?" Buck asked from the other side of the counter.

"Shut up."

Buck smiled. How embarrassing.

"I was talkin' about the tomatoes," he said.

Although he'd been devilishly handsome as a young man—with every muscle toned from years of farming, football, and swimming—somehow, all these years later, Buck seemed even more buff than I'd remembered. He'd lost the baby fat. And there was something more mature about him. More honed.

What is wrong with me? The man is investigating me for murder and I'm staring at his ass!

My knees buckled.

"Hey!" Buck shot out from behind the counter and caught my arm before I collapsed. His face was just inches from mine. It was familiar. Like home. Still, there was something different in his eyes. There was more depth. More edge. And for the first time, I noticed little strands of gray in his hair near his temples. And tiny lines on his face—thin furrows at the corners of his chocolaty eyes, the edges of his mouth, his forehead. Smile lines. Or were they worry lines?

"I'm fine," I said. "It's the sugar," I said, pushing myself away from his grasp. "I had way too much sugar and caffeine this afternoon."

I really did feel weak. And my ribs ached every time I breathed in. Still wrapped, my ankle was very stiff.

Buck pulled out one of the chairs at the table under the cranberry glass lantern. "Sit," he ordered. He slid back behind the counter as I dropped onto the chair.

I felt shaky as I put my elbows on the table.

"You got anything to drink? Something stronger than water?" He asked from the kitchenette. I heard him open my little refrigerator.

"I don't want anything," I sighed, putting my head in my hands. All of a sudden I thought I might cry. I was too tired for this. Too unsure. I needed him to leave.

"I didn't ask you if you *wanted* anything," said Buck tersely. "I was asking you if you had any alcohol here."

"Bottom cupboard on the left."

I heard a cupboard door open and close.

"What the hell? 'Georgia Peach Whiskey'? Sounds like the worst of two worlds," chided Buck. "Who would make such a thing? Let alone buy it. Tell me you didn't pay money for this." I heard Buck tear the wrapper off the top of the bottle.

"Daphne did."

Another cupboard door opened. Then a glass clunked on the counter. Followed by another.

"That explains it."

"She's supporting the local economy," I said quietly. I knew that I needed to stay alert. Buck was surely trying to trick me into giving him some sort of information about the dead man. Maybe he thought I'd confess. Lucky for me, I thought, I really didn't know a thing. I saw the ghoulish dead man's face in my mind and started to feel sick.

"Here." Buck set a small glass of the whiskey on the table in front of me. "Drink."

"No."

"Drink it while I fix something for you to eat. Look. It's not poison. I'll even pour myself a shot." Buck went back to the kitchenette.

"I thought you were still 'a little' on duty," I said with a smirk.

"I was." Buck held up a glass half full of peach whiskey and gulped it down before he turned and opened the small refrigerator. "Your turn. It's not all that bad, really."

Good, I thought. I could get Buck in trouble for intimidating me, coming to my house without showing a warrant, and drinking on the job if I needed to. I'd keep the glass with his fingerprints and DNA on it. If he arrested me, the charges wouldn't stick. And it wouldn't be hard to take him down; Daphne had said there were folks in town who didn't want him to be sheriff in the first place. Then, Eli Gibbit would be sheriff. Although, that might be worse.

I picked up the glass in front of me and sniffed the bronzy-colored liquor. No surprise, it smelled like boozy peaches. I took a sip. It burned as it went down. I took another sip. It was surprisingly good stuff. I sipped again while I sorted my thoughts. I was hungry.

"I see that you weren't kidding about there not being any food," said Buck. "Except, what's this army of olive oil on the counter over here? You savin' up for the apocalypse?"

"Very funny. They're samples for work. I'm becoming an olive oil aficionado." I sipped my peach whiskey. It made me feel warm inside. Still, I needed to eat. I heard Buck slicing. Then, he put something into my toaster oven. For the next few minutes, he fussed about quietly in the kitchenette. I heard him chopping and then knocking around with a bowl. Still trying to figure out what to do, I watched the peach whiskey swirl in my glass as I twirled it on the table.

Dolly started snoring from her bed. She was still wrapped up in my shirt, surrounded by her precious collection of tissue wads.

"Where did you find Dolly?" I finally asked.

"She was sitting right on the front step when I got here. Why, was she missing?"

"Yes. I haven't seen her since . . ." I stopped myself short. The last thing I wanted to do was talk about the last time I'd seen Dolly. It had been in the olive grove, right after I'd tripped over the poor dead pastry guy's foot. Should I start calling him "Lenny"? Of course, hearing what I had to say about the dead man was *exactly* the reason Buck had shown up to the cottage late at night. He wanted to get me to talk. Maybe even incriminate myself.

"Never mind," I said. "I have a headache."

Buck came to the table and set down a Blue Willow platter of warm sliced fingers of toast and a bottle of Knox
Liquid Gold Extra Virgin Olive Oil. He went back to the
kitchenette and returned with a bowl of Daphne's fresh tomatoes. He'd crushed the tomatoes into a puree of sorts.
Also, he carried some sea salt and a pepper grinder. The
next time, he returned with two small salad plates and a
spoon that he plunked into the bowl of tomato puree. Then,
he went to the switch over by the door and dimmed the
overhead cranberry glass lantern until it shed a warm rosy
glow across the room. He went back to the kitchenette one
more time before returning to the table with the bottle of
peach whiskey and his empty glass. He plunked down in the
chair across from me and poured himself another whiskey.

"You dimmed the light for a reason?" I asked. "You
wouldn't want me to get the wrong impression."

"You said you had a headache," Buck answered. He
poured peach whiskey into my glass and pushed it back
toward me across the table. He set the whiskey bottle down
and leaned back in his chair.

"Okay, now," he explained, clapping his hands together,
"I've made us some tomato toast." He opened the bottle of
Daddy's olive oil and drizzled it over the toast on the platter.
"Just take a piece with the drizzled oil and cover it with a
glop of the herbed tomato. Add all the salt and pepper you
want on top." Buck swirled his finger into some of the oil
on his plate that'd spilled over from the toast when he'd
drizzled it. He licked the olive oil off his finger. "Good stuff.
I'm impressed."

"When did you start cooking?" I asked. The snack was
simple. Still, the Buck Tanner I knew couldn't make toast
or put together a meal, even a snack, if his life had depended
on it. He'd been more lost in a kitchen than I'd been. Growing up, Buck's food either came out of a box or bag from
Carter's Country Corner Store, or his mother, Tammy Fae,
had made it from scratch. And he'd expected his future wife
to do the same for him.

"When I was overseas, I used to make it for myself every

morning for breakfast," said Buck as he slathered a pile of tomato puree over his slender slice of toast. He salted and peppered his treat and popped the entire thing in his mouth. "Try it," he said, still chewing. "You'll like it. These tomatoes are delicious, by the way. Where'd they come from?"

"Daphne."

"That explains it."

"And the bread?"

"Precious Darling."

Buck raised his eyebrows but didn't say anything as he chewed. He picked up another sliver of toast and dumped a spoonful of tomatoes on it.

I took a sip of whiskey and watched Buck salt and pepper his snack. I was imagining where "overseas" he'd begun to make himself tomato toast for breakfast every morning. I remembered someone saying that he'd been somewhere, left Abundance and gone off for several years. *Who said that?* Had it been Pep? Had she told me where he'd been? How long he'd been gone? I knew he'd become sheriff about a year ago. And hooked up with Debi Dicer six months ago—hence their "anniversary." Hey, I thought, wasn't that tonight? Had he celebrated with Debi then come over here, to me, for sloppy seconds? No, I reminded myself, it was worse than that. He was pretending to be my friend so that he could pry information out of me or get me to incriminate myself in a homicide. I was the town suspect for murder. He was going to arrest me.

I was onto him.

"What do you want, Buck? Why are you here? It must be nearly midnight, and I'm tired."

I took another, bigger, sip of my whiskey. It was going down easier. How could he be with Debi Dicer? Clearly, I didn't know this man at all.

"No, it's not quite midnight." Buck glanced at his wristwatch. It looked expensive. "Actually, it's eleven thirty-two. Here." Buck reached across the table and handed me a toast he'd already slathered with the mashed-up tomatoes. "Eat this."

Before I thought the better of it, I took the toast and bit into it.

"Atta girl. See, it's good, isn't it?" Buck smiled as he watched me. His eyes softened as his dimples deepened.

It was simple and delicious. I nodded as I chewed. The homemade bread that Precious had baked was even better than Loretta's.

CHAPTER 28

"Eva, you ever heard of Anthony 'the Baker' Lemoni?" It was well after midnight, and Buck tossed down his third or fourth shot of peach whiskey.

"No. Why?" I swallowed my last bite of tomato toast.

"You ever hear of Anthony's Awesome Pastries?"

"In Boston? The one in the North End?"

Buck nodded.

"Sure. Why?"

"Tell me about it."

"I don't know. It's a bakery that I used to go to. They won a 'Best of Boston' award a bunch of times . . . Why?"

"What did you use it for?"

"What do you mean, what did I 'use it for'? It's a *bakery.* I bought baked goods there."

"Be specific."

"What . . . ?" I blushed. Surely, if he was asking me about it, he knew that was the place where I'd seen the dead man. And he knew that it was the place where I'd ordered my wedding cake. The cake for *another* wedding that never happened. Did I have to say it out loud? I sipped nearly half a glass of the peach whiskey before I stared hard at Buck.

"Just answer my question. Please," Buck said calmly. He had a serious look in his eyes that I hadn't seen earlier.

"Why?"

Admitting to Buck that I'd run from another wedding was just as bad as owning up to the fact that I'd run from him, and our wedding, all those years earlier. It was the face-to-face moment I'd dreaded for eighteen years. It was worse than admitting that I'd been acquainted with the dead man.

"Because your life could be in danger," he said flatly.

I stared, almost expecting Buck to start laughing, the way he did when he teased and played jokes on people when we were kids. But he just sat still. Waiting for me.

"I . . . I . . . ordered a cake there once."

"A cake?"

I glared at him. "A wedding cake."

Humiliation complete, I expected Buck to make some sort of smirky, satisfied smile. Or say something snarky or sarcastic about my "runaway bride" moniker. But he didn't. His expression didn't change. If anything, he looked even more determined.

"Is that the only time you went in there? To order a wedding cake?"

"No. I don't think so. I've been there several times. Maybe a bunch of times. I don't know!"

"When was the last time you went to Anthony's Awesome Pastries?"

"I don't know."

"Think, Eva. It's important."

I started to squirm in my chair. "Can I have more to drink?"

"Sure." Buck poured me another glass of whiskey. And he poured himself one as well. So much for him being "on duty." The bottle was very low.

"I think the last time I went there was about four weeks ago."

"Why?"

"To check on my cake." I tossed back half the whiskey. "Okay?" I raised my voice. "To check on the stupid, damned wedding cake that—as everyone knows—I didn't need in the first place because *the wedding never happened*. Once again. The wedding never happened. There. Are you happy now?"

Buck ignored my outburst. Poker face.

"Eva, just listen. Did you ever speak with Anthony Lemoni?"

"I already told you. I don't know any 'Anthony Lemoni.' I only spoke with the manager, Tony. And . . . the pastry guy behind the counter." I sighed. "The dead guy."

So, here we were. Finally, getting down to business, I thought. Without thinking, the words had just tumbled out. I'd admitted knowing the pastry guy in Boston was the dead man I'd tripped over in the woods. I never could keep anything from Buck. But why, then, had Buck's expression not changed when I'd said the words? Hadn't he come to arrest me? Clearly, I'd revealed the "connection" Detective Gibbit had been fishing for earlier. However, Buck acted like he hadn't even heard my admission.

"You say the manager was named Tony?" Buck reached into his back pocket and fished out a folded piece of paper. He unfolded the paper and handed it to me. It was a photograph. "Is this your 'Tony' behind the counter?"

"Yes! That's Tony. The manager."

"That's Anthony Lemoni. Also known as Tony 'the Baker' Lemoni. He's the New England crime family boss responsible for all sorts of organized crime. And scores of hits."

"Hits? You mean, like, murder?"

"Yes."

"Aw, come on!" I said, slapping my hand on the table. "Are you telling me that I ordered my wedding cake from a mobster hit man? No wonder the wedding never came off!" I started laughing uncontrollably. "That's ridiculous. Really. Totally, ridiculous. Is this one of your jokes?"

"Eva, I am deadly serious."

"No way."

Buck just looked at me.

"Really?" I wiped a tear from my cheek. "Only me."

"Really."

I shook my head. "So, why are you telling me this? So, I went to a mob bakery. Everyone in Boston goes there. Their cakes are to die for . . ." I burst out laughing. "Get it? To die for?"

"I get it, Eva."

"Besides, I never even got to *taste* my cake."

"Exactly."

"Exactly what? What are you driving at?"

"According to Daphne, you said that you recognized the dead man in the woods as someone who worked behind the counter at Anthony's Awesome Pastries up in Boston. Is that correct?"

He'd caught me off guard. "How . . . ? Did . . . How did you hear this? Daphne said this? When? Where?"

"She told one of my deputies today on the phone."

"She did? Really?"

"Yes . . . she did. The deputy said she was quite dissatisfied with the department's overall handling of the case. Apparently, she used the information you related to her, information Detective Gibbit failed to ferret out, as just one example of our 'slipshod' investigation. She had many examples."

"You mean, she complained?"

"In a word: yes."

"I see."

"So, Eva, did you know this man?"

"Know him? No. I only saw him. Behind the counter. At the pastry shop."

"Okay. So, it turns out, you were right. Our vic in the woods, the man your sister knew as Leonard Leonardo, the man she hired as a field guide, and the man whom you knew in Boston . . ."

"I didn't 'know' him; I just saw him there. At the shop. I said that."

"Right, I got that, Babydoll. Anyway, he was Leonard "Lenny the Doughboy" Lemoni. Anthony Lemoni's nephew, money handler, and 'enforcer' for the New England Lemoni family."

"Enforcer? Wait. What does that mean? Hit man? *Another* hit man?"

Buck nodded.

"What are you saying? I got some hit man to come down here and get himself killed?"

"You tell me."

"Tell you *what*?" I held up my empty glass. "Hit me again. Oh my God, I'm so funny. Get it? I said, 'hit' me!"

"You've had enough."

"No. I haven't. Pour. And why aren't you drinking yours?" I kept rambling. "Wait till I tell Daphne she hired a mobster hit man. Missus DQ Perfect Knox Bouvier will pee in her pants. Does she know?"

Buck poured me half a glass. Then downed what was in his, and refilled it. I daresay, it was probably to keep me from having any more whiskey. My throat was warm and fuzzy. In fact, I was feeling very warm and fuzzy all over.

"Cheers," I said. I took a big sip.

"Cheers," said Buck. And he took an even smaller sip. "Now, why don't you answer my question?"

"What was the question?"

"Why did Leonard Lemoni come down here?"

"I don't have the foggiest idea. I never even saw him here, before I tripped over his foot."

I hadn't meant to bring that moment up. Let alone think about it. I took a big gulp of whiskey and shuddered.

"Hit me again."

Buck poured more whiskey into my glass. As I picked up the glass and downed more of the liquor, he pulled out another photograph and held it up in front of me. It was a photo of a thick-necked, dark-haired, Mediterranean-looking man with a sign around his neck that read RHODE ISLAND STATE POLICE with a bunch of numbers under it. A mug shot.

"Is this the man you knew in Boston?"

I put my glass down and squinted at the photograph. I tried to imagine a body in between the head in the photo and the foot I'd tripped over. I shuddered and turned away from the photo, nodding my head. Buck folded it up and put it back in his pocket.

"Are you sure that you never saw him before last night, except for in the pastry shop?"

"Yes, I'm sure."

"And what did you talk about in the pastry shop?"

"Pastry."

Buck looked at me, exasperated.

"That's it! I swear. All we ever talked about was whatever I was buying or ordering."

"No other 'business'?"

"What? Like, was I ordering a hit or something? Of course not. That's ridiculous."

"And when you came home and saw that your sister had hired him here as a guide, didn't you think that was . . . strange?"

"No. Because, like I said before, I never saw him here. Alive, that is. When I first came home, Daphne told me that she'd hired someone as a guide, except he was out on some fishing or hunting trip for the week. So, I never got to meet him."

"You never saw, or spoke to, Leonard Lemoni here, or anywhere else outside the pastry shop? You didn't see him, living right over there by the pond, in your granddaddy's hunting cabin?"

I shook my head. "No. I'd never seen Leonard, er, Lenny . . . whatever his name is. Or was. I've spoken with Chef Loretta a bunch of times. She's new here, too. I even helped her in the kitchen. Still, I'd never even seen her apartment until earlier tonight. And I haven't seen Leonard, or whatever his name was. And I haven't been to the cabin since . . . well, years ago."

Buck nodded. I wondered if he realized that one of the last times I'd been inside the cabin had been with him. My mind flashed to that late-night tryst when we'd hidden from Daddy and his friends under the secret trapdoor in the floor. First used to hide slaves, and later, moonshine, there were several hiding places like that around the plantation. As scared as I'd been to get caught that night with Buck—I was sure that Daddy never would've let me see the light of day, or Buck, again—I remembered the rush of excitement about it all. It was one of the most romantic nights I'd ever had with Buck. Okay. It was one of the most romantic nights I'd had . . . ever. I remembered Buck's warm shoulder and his arm pressed around me. And how he'd calmly held me steady for hours, stroking my hair. Pressing his lips into my temple. I didn't care about the spiders around us.

Scary had been intoxicating.

Sitting opposite Buck in the cottage, thinking about it, my ears burned and my face got hot. Something in my stomach flipped. Then, all of a sudden, I had an idea. I looked up at Buck. He'd been watching me.

As if he read my mind, Buck said, "It's empty. I already checked under the trapdoor to be sure Loretta wasn't there, one way or another."

"You mean, dead or alive?"

"Something like that."

"So, who is she?"

"We're still waiting for a hit on prints. However, Lenny Lemoni does have a sister named Loretta."

"He does?"

"A twin."

"Like in the photo I found! Then, you know I had nothing to do with this!"

Lenny and Loretta being brother and sister didn't clarify anything, I thought. In fact, it made the note announcing their elopement completely inexplicable.

"Unfortunately, Babydoll, my detective, Eli Gibbit, is sure you're the reason behind all of this. He just can't quite figure out how it all fits together. And I can't convince him to let it go."

"Me? Why?"

"Because you're the only link connecting the Lemoni family to Abundance. And, frankly, although I don't agree with Eli that you're somehow complicit in all this, I do believe that you're the key to the events that happened here. You may have set something in motion unwittingly."

"That's me. Unwitting Eva." I tossed down the rest of my drink.

"Eva, this is serious. These people are cold-blooded killers."

"So, you believe me?"

"Yes, Babydoll. I believe you. Still, I need you to help me. Stop hiding what you know. Your life could be in danger."

For twenty or more minutes, Buck grilled me about Anthony's Awesome Pastries in Boston, Tony Lemoni, Lenny Lemoni, and my quick decision to come home from Boston—the only topic I refused to discuss in any detail with him. And then, of course, I had to recount the events in the woods when I'd tripped over Leonard.

"So, tell me what you know about the note in the kitchen," said Buck.

"I don't know anything about the note. First I heard of it was when Pep told me at about it. And we've all been thinking that it was odd Loretta ran off to marry a guy whom she'd only met a few weeks earlier. Like, for example, I'd prepared dinner with Loretta, and she never said a word about running off to get hitched. But if she's the dead guy's twin sister, then none of it makes any sense at all, does it?"

Buck waited for me to say more.

I gulped more whiskey. "She was kind of weird. Like, when we heard she'd run off to get married, it seemed almost impossible. You'd have to have seen Loretta to understand."

"Meaning?"

"Let's just say, she doesn't strike me as the romantic type. She's kind of a brute, actually. And it isn't so much her physical looks . . . there's something else about her. Scares me to think of her with someone. Anyone."

"Why?"

"Loretta's a big girl. Thick neck. Fat hands. Dour expression. Dark eyes. She has the kind of black eyes that tell you to run. Daphne even said once that Loretta loved to chop meat. Who likes to chop meat? Still, Loretta's a hard worker. And Daphne said she's one of the best employees she'd ever had . . . and my sister's gone through quite a few, let me tell you."

"I'll bet."

"Do you think she's dead?"

"I don't know. But if she's not, she's a force to be reckoned with. They call her 'the Cleaver.'"

"You mean . . ."

"Don't ask. Let's just say she was well-known in the meatpacking business."

I swallowed hard, remembering how I'd stood side by side with Loretta in the kitchen.

"Do you think she killed the pastry guy? But if he's her brother, why would she kill him?"

Buck didn't answer.

"She wouldn't, would she?"

Buck shrugged. "I'll make sure someone talks to Daphne again about Loretta in the morning." "What? No personal nighttime visit for my dear sister Daphne? Aren't you going to intimidate anyone else tonight?" I stifled a yawn. It was well after midnight, the booze had kicked in, and I was getting punchy.

"Am I intimidating you, Eva? You've never been afraid to speak up for yourself."

"Speaking of which, it's late and I'm tired. I can't think anymore. Is there any more to drink?"

"All gone."

"Then, I think you should go now. Or arrest me. Oh, wait!

You know, there is another thing that I forgot to tell you." I heard my words getting fuzzy.

"What's that?"

"I heard gunshots last night."

"What kind of gunshots?"

"I don't know. Just gunshots." I started twirling my hair between my fingers.

"Like a handgun or pistol? Or more of a crack or boom sound from a rifle or shotgun? I know that you know what a shotgun sounds like, Eva."

"Shotgun, I guess. No. Maybe handgun. Oh, I don't know! I thought I heard shots a few times before I left the cottage, but it was so stormy outside that I'd decided some of it was thunder."

Buck looked at me, then closed his eyes. "Okay," he said quietly. "Anything else?"

"Yes. How come everyone is so fixated on me having something to do with all this? It's not like I was the only one in the woods last night."

"I never said you were the only one out there, did I?"

"Not exactly. But Detective Gibbit certainly thinks I was the only one. Except for Loretta."

"Do you think someone else was in the woods?"

"Well, obviously, Ian Collier, from next door. How come no one is asking about him? Or that creepy Lurch guy that works for him. He carries a gun, you know. I saw it."

"Who carries a gun?"

"Lurch. So, why aren't you visiting Ian Collier and his pet, Lurch, tonight? Why me?"

"Ian Collier wasn't involved."

"What do you mean he wasn't involved?" I'd raised my voice. "He found me, didn't he? How could he have found me if he wasn't already out that night? And what was he doing on *our* property, anyway? He's the one I'd be looking at."

"Anyone else?"

"What do you mean, 'Anyone else?' Are you dismissing me? Am I saying something you don't want to hear? *Why isn't Ian Collier a suspect?*" I heard the pitch of my voice getting higher.

"Because, Babydoll, I know Ian Collier. He's not a suspect." Buck never changed his expression.

"You know *me*! And I'm a suspect! Why is that? What makes *me* more suspicious than some gaga mystery gazillionaire from next door? No one in this town knows a thing about him. Where'd he come from? Where'd he get all his money from? Who does he know? What does he *do* over there behind all that barbed wire?" I was throwing my arms around.

"You're yelling, Eva."

"Or is it precisely that he's got money? Money and power. So, no one in this backwater town wants to cross him. That's it, isn't it! He's got everyone eating out of his hand. Including you. Hey, maybe he's the one who got you your job as sheriff! I hear Eli Gibbit was supposed to be sheriff and you stole the job from him. Did Ian Collier pay for your new position? I'll find out what he was doing for myself!" The liquor, combined with my overall exhaustion, was getting the better of me. I knew I was out of control, but I was powerless to stop myself.

"Eva, you'll stay the hell away from Ian Collier. And Greatwoods. Stay outta there, you hear me?" Buck's eyes were flashing.

"Loud and clear. But hearing you doesn't mean I'm listening." I sat back and crossed my arms. Sensing this was territory that I wasn't supposed to venture into, I felt quite sure that I'd uncovered something important. The very fact that Buck was warning me off made me think there was even more reason to investigate.

"I'm warning you, Eva. Stay away from there."

"You're *warning* me? Like, who do you think you are? 'Warning' me? My father? I'm not a child, you know."

"You're beginning to act like one. However, I'm chalking it up to the alcohol."

"How dare you! How dare you spend the evening with your precious girlfriend, come over here, ply me with alcohol, scare me about getting arrested, seduce me for your sloppy seconds, and then—of all things—patronize me! You're way worse than Daphne said you are."

"Daphne? I wouldn't put too much stock in what Daphne has to say about me. I'd expect nothing more than a scathing review. And sloppy seconds? Eva, what the hell are you talking about? You've had too much to drink."

"And you haven't? You're calling me a drunk? You've got nerve. Considering you're the one who poured me the liquor in the first place! Here I am, thinking I'm about to be arrested. Trying to cooperate, even though it's after midnight, and I'm very, *very* tired. And, I don't feel at all well. The booze, if you remember, was all your idea."

"Yes, it was. You looked bad, Eva. I thought a little nip would help you relax. Feel better."

"Relax? I *bet* you wanted me to relax! Relax right into bed with you. I mean, there it is!" I waved toward Grandma's big four-poster bed, taking up a conspicuous chunk of the one-room space. "All of four feet from where we're sitting. Are you trying to get back at me? Humiliate me? It was eighteen years ago!"

"Eva . . ."

"No! Don't look at me like that. Especially when I look 'bad.'"

"Eva, this isn't about that. Believe me."

"Oh really? Come on. I didn't just fall off the . . . what's it called? Oh crappy. Whatever it is . . . the potato truck!"

"Turnip. The expression is 'turnip truck.'"

"Who cares. I mean, really, what kind of sheriff comes into a woman's home late at night, says he's 'a little' on duty, then plies her with drinks? A sneaky womanizer, that's who! You never could play by the rules. People are right. Abundance would be better off with Eli Gibbit as sheriff."

"You're entitled to your opinion. I see there's no arguing with you now."

"Or ever! How dare you. Go on! Go back to Debi."

"Debi? You mean Debi Dicer? What does she have to do with this? Eva, what the hell are you talkin' about?"

Suddenly, my chest heaved. A torrent of tears welled up inside me. What *was* I talking about? I stood up, and the chair fell over behind me. I flailed and turned away from Buck, still seated at the table.

"Go on. Get out," I cried. I put my hands to my face and took a slow breath. "Now. Please. I want you to go," I said quietly. The floodgates were letting loose. Damned if I'd let him see me cry.

"Eva . . ." I heard Buck scoot back his chair and get up. From the corner of my eye, I saw him start toward me. Then he stopped and started to pick up the dishes from the table.

"Leave it! All of it. Just go." I wiped a tear from my cheek with the back of my hand.

Without a word, Buck crossed the room, walked right past me, and grabbed Loretta's photo before pulling open the creaky screen door and stepping outside. The door slapped shut behind him.

Dolly looked at me sheepishly as I went to draw my bath, sobbing every step of the way.

CHAPTER 29

I spent an inordinate amount of time Wednesday morning in front of the bathroom mirror, trying to fix my face. I looked positively ghastly. Although a long bath, a couple hours of sleep, and a good dose of ibuprofen had finally quelled most of the aches and pains from my injuries, I had to deal with a killer headache and a face swollen from crying.

Blubbering for hours after Buck left had uglified me to the point that I was afraid to step out of my cottage without some sort of intervention. I understood how Daphne had felt when her face blew up from the lye. Still, I wasn't going to tie a scarf around my head. Besides, my public portrayal couldn't get much worse than it already was.

Sigh.

Standing at the sink, I pressed the washcloth soaked in cold water and witch hazel to my face. I willed the cold compress to relieve the swelling around my eyes. My hair was still damp from my late-night bath a few hours earlier. I'd coiled and piled it on top of my head and secured it with a single bobby pin. Hoping to divert attention away from my cried-out face, I'd put on a big, dangly pair of Native American silver and turquoise earrings. The rest was simple: a fitted black V-neck tee shirt, a pair of white ankle-length jeans, and thong sandals. I'd replaced the soiled bandage around my left ankle with a black neoprene pull-on ankle wrap that I'd used after twisting my ankle on a Boston side-walk once. Although my twisted ankle was better, I knew that it would be another couple of weeks before I would walk without pain. My cracked rib was another story. That'd be a long time healing.

"It's all over now," I whispered to myself. "Time to start fresh. Forget the past." I took a breath and looked in the mirror. *Ugh.* I felt tears start to well up in my chest again. I pressed the cold compress to my face with more force. *Stop!*

Lazing in the morning sunshine, Dolly snored peacefully on the fluffy bathroom rug in front of the claw-foot tub. Already, it was nine thirty. I'd been up until early morning, bawling and cleaning—oddly, the cleaning had relaxed me more than the bath, or perhaps it had finally worn me out—and I'd slept late and missed breakfast. Thankfully, no one had bothered me. But now, ready or not, I needed to help Daphne prepare for the midday Chamber of Commerce meeting. However scandalous my appearance, it was going to have to do. Besides, getting out and keeping busy would help me stop fretting. And knowing that facing the folks of Abundance was inevitable, I figured I might as well bite the bullet, get it over with, and see as many people as I could at once. It couldn't be any worse than facing Buck after all these years. Hopefully, eating a little crow on my home turf would make it go down easier.

I turned the sink faucet off and patted my face dry in a pale pink towel. I grabbed my sunglasses and slid them on.

"Alright, Dolly, it's time to face the music," I said.

Dolly jumped up from the rug and barked. As she scam-pered out of the bathroom into my "living room" she barked again. And barked. And barked. Shrill and nonstop, she kept barking.

"Dolly! Hush!"

Stepping out of the bathroom, I nearly bumped into the man standing in my cottage.

"Do ya mind shutting up the mutt?" said Sal Malagutti.

Dressed in brand-new camo pants, with tall, lace-up, military-style boots, gray tee shirts, and piles of gold chains across their hairy chests, Sal and Guido sucked up the space in my tiny cottage. Hulking next to my grandmother's four-poster bed with its ivory matelassé cover, Guido slid a big hunting knife out of a holder on his belt. He started picking at his fingernails with the knife, flicking nail debris on my bedcover.

"Dolly, it's alright. Come here," I said quietly.

Dolly scampered around Guido by the bed and then Sal, who stood between me and Guido. When she got to my feet, Dolly jumped up on my leg. I reached down and picked her up—not easy since Sal remained just inches away from me. I was trapped between Sal and the door to the bathroom behind me. Dolly shook and growled quietly as I held her.

Looking up at Sal, I was grateful for the cover of my sunglasses.

"Mister Malagutti. Mister Gambini. Is everything alright?" I asked. Maybe it was all perfectly innocent. Maybe they just had no tact, I thought.

Not for long.

Sal leered at me. I noticed gold caps in his mouth, and his lip looked twisted, due to a scar that angled down from one of his greasy cheekbones. Still, I thought, with less bulk, a neck, and without the scar, he might have been almost good-looking as a young man.

Just inches from my face, Sal mocked, "Sure. Everything is just fine." He turned to Guido, "Right, Guido?"

"Right, boss." Guido didn't look up as he leaned against my bed. His dark, hairy forearms worked the knife fastidiously over his stubby fingers. Guido was a little shorter and younger than Sal. And instead of a scar, he had pockmarks on his face. He was every bit as repellant as his boss. I got the impression that he'd always been that way.

The two of them, whom I'd jokingly thought of as giant, ugly toads in the big house, looked far more menacing up close and personal. In fact, these two toads were more like live gargoyles, with grotesquely cruel, harsh expressions.

Sal turned back to me and bent his head down, closer to mine. His black eyes were mean, and his breath was garlicky. With nowhere to go except back into the bathroom, I leaned away from Sal until my shoulder thudded into the doorframe.

"We just wanted to have a little chat with you, that's all. Didn't we, Guido?" said Sal with a lecherous smile.

"That's right, boss. A little chat." Guido never looked up from his nails.

I slapped a smile on my face.

"Well, I'm happy to speak with you gentlemen. Only, this is my private home. Perhaps we'd all be more comfortable if we chat over in the big house? On the veranda?" I sounded like Daphne.

"This is just fine, right where we are. Don't you agree, Guido?"

"Yeah, boss. I like it here. Nice bed." Guido patted the coverlet on the mattress.

I glanced past Sal and Guido, out the front window, and saw Daphne walking across the lawn. She'd given up the stupid head wrap and was smiling. Her curled, shoulder-length, strawberry-blonde hair bounced in the sunlight as the yellow chiffon skirt of her dress fluttered in the breeze. As she walked, she chatted with one of twins. They were carrying some floral arrangements, probably headed for the tent that was set up for the Chamber of Commerce meeting. I thought about calling to her. But then maybe I was overreacting.

It wouldn't be the first time.

"What is it you want, Mister Malagutti?" I was still trying to smile politely. As if it was perfectly normal to have two wise guys accosting me in my home.

"We just want to send your daddy a little message, that's all," said Sal. "You see, we'd like to do some business together."

"Then why aren't you speaking to him?"

"Well, he ain't here right now."

"He'll be back in a day or two. You can speak with him then. Or give him a call. I'm sure he'd be happy to discuss a business proposal with you."

"Business 'proposal.' I like that," said Sal sarcastically. "Sounds so . . . polite. Don't you like that, Guido?"

"Yeah, boss. That's cute."

"So, lemme make this quick," Sal said to me. His tone was sharp. "I don't usually discuss business with women. In fact, I never discuss business with women. It's not a woman's place."

"Then why are you?" I interrupted.

"If ya shut up for a minute, sista, I'll tell you. Like I was saying, I don't do business with women. But this here, see, this is a unique situation."

"How's that?"

"Well, on account of you being with Lenny the Dough-boy, that's how."

"What are you talking about?"

"Look, Cupcake, don't play coy with me. I knows you're that runaway bride chick from up in Boston. And I knows you and Lenny were up to something, and that means you were up to something with Tony the Baker."

"I don't know what you're talking about."

"Yeah. Right. Look, I don't know whether you was doin' business with Lenny, shaggin' him, or whether you killed the guy, or what. Maybe it was all of it. Maybe you're Tony's moll. I know he's got a few babes stashed here and there. But it don't matter. Here's the deal. I like it here. Don't we like it here, Guido?"

"Yeah, boss. We like it here."

"Originally, I came down here to check out the olive oil business. You know? Thought maybe your old man and I might be able to come to some sorta mutually beneficial agreement. However, now that I'm here, I've decided that I want to stay."

"Lots of people like it here."

"Yeah, well, 'lots of people' ain't me. So, here's the deal: I want this place. All of it. Not just the olive oil. Ya hear me?"

"My father is not selling. *We're* not selling. This is our home. We've been here for six generations. In fact, the state of Georgia has recognized ours as a centennial farm—meaning my family has owned and operated this farm for more than one hundred years. I'm sure there's lots of farms and plantations for sale around here. You need a Realtor to find you another place. Try Debi Dicer in town. She's perfect for you."

"I don't want another place. I want this place."

"Yeah, this place," echoed Guido. He snapped his knife in its leather holder and crossed his arms, glaring at me.

"Why are you telling me this?"

"Because I ain't sure what you got goin' on with Tony the Baker," said Sal. "I knows it must be something, 'cause I read in the paper today that you been seen talking with Tony a bunch of times at his pastry shop up in Boston."

"That was about my wedding cake!"

"I don't give a hoot what you say it was about, Cupcake. And I thinks you're smart enough to say it was about a cake. Maybe you was the middleman between Tony and your father. Maybe your poor farmer daddy needed some money to pay for your fancy wedding up in Boston. I don't know. I don't care. The point is, you're the only connection I see here to Tony Lemoni. That means you're the one who brought Tony's man, Lenny, here. And now that Tony the Baker is involved, I got competition from the New England family, and that translates into a big pain in my ass that I don't need. It don't matter that Lenny's dead. Tony'll just send someone else. Someone else I have to whack. So, you're costing me money, see?"

"Boss don't like it when folks cost him money," said Guido.

"So, the way I sees it, now *you* gotta get rid of Tony. Capisci?" said Sal to me.

"Get rid of Tony?"

"Like you got rid of Lenny."

"I didn't kill Lenny! I didn't even know Lenny. And I'm sure as hell not going to 'whack' somebody."

"Bella donna, I don't care how you do it. You can 'off' Tony just like you did Lenny. I actually respect you for that. Or your daddy can take care of it. It ain't my problem. It's yours. And I don't take 'no' for an answer. You go tell your daddy that. I want this place. I'm gonna have it."

"When the boss wants something, the boss gets it." Guido chuckled with a menacing look.

"Now, Cupcake, you go tell your daddy that I think you're real cute," Sal said with a leer. "And tell him that I might like to have me a piece of that cupcake cuteness. Also, I might want to share my piece of cupcake with Guido when I'm done. Or not. Ya know, sometimes people have accidents. People fall down stairs. People drown in their ponds. Their car brakes fail. Or sometimes, people and their little black dogs just plain disappear. Even pretty little cupcakes like you. Capisci?"

Dolly growled in my arms as the goon put his fat finger up against my temple and slowly drew it down the side of my face, down my neck, to my chest, and right to the vee in my shirt. Then he pressed his finger into me, leaned in to my ear, and whispered, "Bella . . . Bella. You smell *so* good." Still with his finger in the vee of my shirt, Sal drew back and smiled a wicked smile as he looked me up and down. "Yeah, Guido, I think I might like me a *big* piece of this."

"I'll give my father your message," I said dryly. "Now get out."

CHAPTER 30

Sal Malagutti ran his finger up my chest to under my chin.
He put his thumb on top of my chin and pinched it tight as
he lifted my face, put his lips together, and smack-kissed
the air an inch from my face. Then, he let go.

"Till next time, Cupcake."

Gloating, the two mobsters turned and swaggered out of
my cottage, across the sunny lawn, over to their rental car
parked in the drive next to the big house. I was relieved to
see that they got in the vehicle and drove away. I was so
frightened and shocked, after bracing myself against the
bathroom doorframe for a minute or so, all I could do was
cradle Dolly in my arms as I dropped into the armchair
under the window. Shaking, I took off my sunglasses and
sat, dazed, trying to assimilate what had happened.

They'd threatened my life.

I needed to call someone. But who? Of course, the county
sheriff was the logical choice. But that was Buck, the man
whom I jilted and humiliated in front of the entire community. The man who was in love with my archnemesis. The
man who, in a drunken fit, I yelled at and kicked out of my

cottage after making an ass of myself just hours earlier. Or should I call Detective Gibbit? The man who clearly had me pegged as a murderess. The man who wanted nothing better than to sew up the homicide case quickly, so he could garner community support and take over as sheriff.

And if I did call, what would I say? Two guests came over and threatened my life? Threatened me because they think, as everyone else does, that I'm Lenny's murderer? I'd be strengthening the very case that the sheriff's department was already building against me. And I'd have no proof of what the gangsters had said anyway. Without a witness, repeating what had happened would just make me look worse. Of course, Sal knew that. There'd been two of them and only one of me. It was two against one, their word against my word.

"If only you could talk, Dolly." I stroked the top of her head.

No. There was no one to call. No one who'd believe me, anyway. I'd have to figure this out on my own. And quickly.

There was a knock on the door.

"Miss Eva, y'all in there?" One of the twins peeked in the door.

"Yes!" I answered. "C'mon in."

"No need to bother you, Miss Eva," the twin said from the door. She was wearing one of Daphne's official Knox Plantation "uniforms," which consisted of a short black skirt covered in front by a frilly, floral half apron. She wore a white off-the-shoulder blouse with ruffles around the neck and shoulder line. Cute to look at, but hardly practical. "Miss Pep asked me to come get you. She needs your help upstairs in the pink bathroom. The sink is broken."

"Okay. I'll be right over." I didn't know which twin it was. I never did. Charlene and Darlene were identical, both relatively short, with heart-shaped, freckled faces; dark, wavy hair; and wide-set blue eyes. Still, I'd learned quickly that when there was one twin, the other was never far behind. It was a "twin" thing, Daphne'd said once. Always looking out for each other.

Right then, I wished I'd had a twin of my own.

"Also, Miss Daphne wanted me to ask you if you'd seen or borrowed a shovel," said the twin. "We need one out at the tent and can't find one."

"Shovel? No. Sorry. I haven't seen one."

"Okay, thanks!" The twin smiled and stepped off in the direction of the tent.

I went back into the bathroom and turned on the faucet. My hands shook as I drew a glass of water and gulped it down. I checked myself one last time in the mirror.

"What a mess."

I took a deep breath, put my sunglasses on, and headed over to the big house.

CHAPTER 31

There was water everywhere.

"Pep, what happened?"

"That Barbie doll Bambi woman happened, that's what," sighed Pep.

On her hands and knees in the pink bathroom, Pep spread another white towel down on the marble floor and started soaking up the water. Pep yanked up her strapless black corset top. There was a lacy black choker around her neck, and she wore a simple black leather miniskirt over purposely ripped-open black tights and buckled black leather combat boots.

"All this water came from the sink?"

"That bimbo washed so much crap down the drain that the trap busted. Look over there!" She pointed to the little gilded trash can in the corner. I looked inside the can. There was a hamster-sized wad of blonde hair and three or four gigantic false eyelashes, and some other gunk.

"Gross."

"Yeah, right. It was all down in the drain, and I'd just

cleaned the drain yesterday. I just can't fathom how anyone can do this every day," said Pep.

"What do you want me to do?" I asked.

"I've got to get to the Roadhouse in a bit. And Daphne, Precious, the twins, and Earlene Azalea are all so busy prepping for the Chamber of Commerce thingy that they haven't got time to help here. I was hoping that while I clean up this mess, y'all could run into town and pick up the P-trap that I need. Once I have the part, it won't take long to make the fix here. Then, I can be off to work on time."

"Sure. I'll go now."

"Hey, listen, Eva sweetie, before you go, I wanted to tell y'all that our idea is working!"

"What idea is that?"

"The one where we overload folks in town with tidbits of phony gossip about you. Last night at the Roadhouse, I heard folks talking about how the reason you left Zack in Boston was on account of you bein' gay. I cracked up when I heard it."

"Well, that didn't take long."

"Nope. Guess we have Boone Beasley to thank for that."

"Or Debi Dicer."

"Debi?"

"Forget it. Debi's not that stupid anyway. I'm sure it was Mister Beasley."

"Speaking of which, Daphne wants you to take Boone his check today for the meat he delivered yesterday. She left it on the kitchen table, downstairs."

"Sure. I can do that."

"Daphne said Boone called asking for his check. Between you and me, I think he's got some major financial troubles. I see him at the Roadhouse a lot. I think he drinks all his money away."

"Humm."

"Just don't take too long when you're out. I need to get that P-trap installed under the sink before I go to work, and I haven't got much time."

"Okay. Listen, Pep, before I go, there's something important I need to tell you."

"Sure, sweetie, whatcha got on your mind? And why are y'all wearin' those silly sunglasses inside the house? You're kinda reminding me of Daphne." Pep made a silly face.

"Never mind the glasses. The Italian guys came over to my place this morning."

"I thought the ladies were off on a day trip to Tallahassee. Shopping. I saw them leave a couple of hours ago."

"It wasn't the wives. It was the men."

"Why were they over at your place? Daphne told me she'd made arrangements with the guide at Wildman's Lodge to take them fishing on Big Lake today. Did that not work out?"

"They came over to threaten me."

"Threaten you? Why? Oh, hon, are you okay?" Pep stopped mopping and sat up to look at me. "What happened? They didn't hurt you, did they?"

"No. But they scared the crap out of me. Pep, these people are killers."

"Killers?"

"Yes. Buck told me."

"Buck? Whoa, hon, when did you see Buck? *Are* you seein' Buck? Oh! I *knew* it!"

"I'm not seeing Buck. Forget about Buck. It's not important. What's important is that these guys are mobsters and they think that I killed the pastry guy in the woods."

"Why?" Pep looked astonished.

"Because pastry guy Leonard, it turns out, was in the mob," I said. "He was known as 'Lenny the Doughboy.' And the head of the New England mafia family, a guy they call 'Tony the Baker,' is the guy who owned the pastry shop where I ordered my wedding cake in Boston. So, now, everyone in the mob thinks I'm some sort of hit woman. Or, a mob moll who killed another mob hit man."

Pep burst out into laughter. "Oh, Eva, that's a good one! You had me going there for a minute!" She rolled her eyes again. "'The Doughboy.' You're hilarious."

"Pep, I'm not kidding!"

"Oh, come on." Pep looked at me. "'Doughboy'?" She made little pig snort giggles.

"Yes! And it's way better than what they call his sister—we think Loretta was his sister, by the way. They call her 'the Cleaver'!"

"His *sister*? Then what's with the note about their running off to get married?"

"Who knows. None of it makes any sense."

I felt a wave of weakness and looked for a place to sit. I stepped behind Pep over to the toilet where the lid was down—the only seat in town, so to speak. I grabbed a newspaper off the top of the lid before I plunked down.

"Hey, you okay, sweetie? Y'all look like a ghost."

"Not really." I glanced at the paper in my hand. "Oh. My. God. Look at this. See, I told you!" I held up the newspaper for Pep to see. It was the local weekly, the *Abundance Record*. My photo was on the front page.

"Well, don't that just take the cake," said Pep. She took the paper from my hand and studied the page. Then, she started reading aloud, "'Eva Knox, Murder Suspect. Eva Knox, daughter of Abundance County crop farmer, Robert Knox, owner of Knox Plantation, along with a woman known as Loretta Cook, an employee of Knox Plantation, has been named as a person of interest in the death of Leonard Lemoni, also known as Leonard Leonardo.'"

Pep interrupted herself. "Well, now that I see it in print, that's a stupid name. Leonard Leonardo. Daphne should've thought there was something fishy about that."

I nodded in agreement.

Pep shook her head and continued reading. "'Lemoni, a resident and employee of Knox Plantation working as a fishing and hunting guide, was found shot to death early Tuesday morning on the edge of a one-hundred-acre olive grove at Knox Plantation. Eva Knox was discovered by a neighbor lying unconscious next to the deceased. Miss Knox only recently returned to Abundance after nearly two decades residing and working in Massachusetts as a public relations consultant, said a source from the Abundance County Sheriff's Department.'"

"Tell me something I don't know," I said glumly.

"'Loretta Cook has been living and been employed as a cook at Knox Plantation since early spring, said a source. She has not been seen since late Monday night, when her car, reportedly a light blue Honda Accord, also disappeared. Law enforcement officials are asking for the community's help to find the missing woman. One official expressed concern that she may be another victim of foul play, since her personal belongings, including her wallet and cash, were left in her apartment.'"

"Great," I said.

"But there's no mention in the article of her being Leonard's sister."

"Probably because the story was written before I told Buck what I knew about her last night. I gave him the photo I'd found in her apartment."

Pep continued. "'Fingerprint analysis and other evidence recently confirmed that Leonard Lemoni resided in Providence, Rhode Island, and was a well-known member of the New England Lemoni Mafia crime family. Lemoni was also known as 'the Doughboy' and was reputed to be a money-laundering expert as well as mob hit man who had a penchant for gambling. Sources say that although he'd only recently come to town, already there was evidence that Lemoni was running an illegal gambling enterprise in Abundance.'" Pep stopped reading and stared in thought for a moment. "Huh."

Pep and I had probably been struck with the same thought: There was a good chance that Billy had been involved in Leonard's gambling activities. Where had Billy gone when Pep had returned home with the olive oil? Could Billy have been with the pastry guy the night he was murdered? Could Billy have killed Lenny over some sort of gambling debt? No. *Surely not.*

Pep, lost in her own thoughts, finally cleared her throat and resumed reading. "'Lemoni's uncle, Anthony Lemoni, Sr., of Boston, Massachusetts, is reputed to be the notorious New England crime family patriarch known as Tony "the Baker" Lemoni, and is considered to be one of the most powerful and dangerous members of the organized crime syndicate in the United States.'"

"Who knew?" I said dejectedly. "His cakes are heaven-sent."

"'Suspected of racketeering, drug smuggling, loan shark-ing, and money laundering, the senior Lemoni owns several businesses, including a bakery in Boston's North End where Abundance native Eva Knox often visited.'" Pep held up the paper. "Look, Eva, they've got a photo of you going into Anthony's Awesome Pastries. That *is* where you ordered your wedding cake!"

"Yep. That's the place. And I know when that photo was taken. The *Boston Globe* newspaper ran a story about my wedding plans. A reporter and photographer followed me around for a week, recording all the arrangements Zack and I were making for the wedding. The feature was published as part of the *Globe*'s June bridal section.'"

Pep read on, "'Sources say Eva Knox used the mob bak-ery to purchase an expensive wedding cake for a wedding scheduled for this summer. However, in front of hundreds of eyewitnesses, Knox, aka the "Runaway Bride," deserted her fiancé, Boston celebrity and WCVB-TV weatherman Zack Black, just minutes before their ceremony was sched-uled to take place at the historic Beacon Hill Community Church. In a local twist, Eva Knox ran away from Abun-dance County sheriff Buck Tanner eighteen years ago this month on their wedding day. According to a source at the Abundance County Sheriff's Department, authorities are investigating Eva Knox's connection to the Lemoni crime family, as well as her role in the death of Leonard Lemoni.'"

Pep stopped reading. "Oh gosh, Eva, did you see this other photo? Why, that was just taken, here . . . yesterday!"

I grabbed the paper from Daphne and studied the photo. It was a shot of me, standing in the dining room doorway next to Daphne, talking to Judi Malagutti. I looked like some sort of wild beast, all scratched, hair a wretched mess, wearing my torn and soiled GEORGIA VIRGIN tee. And I was making a face at Daphne, with my eyes rolled up in my head.

"Yeah. I look great, don't I? No wonder Daphne had me hide in the pantry. It's a wonder she ever let me out."

"Well, I admit, y'all weren't at your best there."

Kudos for the understatement, I thought.

"That must've been taken by one of those two women that came in here after the highway accident," I mused. "You know, now that I think about it, I saw a camera flash. And there was this one woman who had a camera. She kept walking by as we were talking . . . She had a nose ring, I think."

"Paparazzi?"

"Could be."

"Daphne'll have a cow that she let them stay here. I know that they turned up unexpectedly. I never knew their names. And I think they checked out already."

"Is there a photo credit?"

"Let's see. Here it is, under the photo. 'Tam See.' And the article byline is Pat Butts. Who is Pat Butts? Must be someone new in town."

"Or a freelancer. I attract them like flies to a split-open pie."

"Hey! The caption identifies Judi Malagutti as 'wife of New York mobster Sal Malagutti' and says your Mafia connections appeared to be 'intimate and far-reaching.'"

"Omigosh! They *are* Mafia. We've got the New York mob *and* the New England mob here. Well, crap. Doesn't this just make my day."

I wondered why Buck hadn't told me about the Malaguttis and the Gambinis. Surely, he knew. Of course, I'd forgotten to tell Buck about the gun under the mattress. Neither one of us had come clean.

"Can't see how it can get much worse, hon. Don't y'all

think you ought to call the sheriff's department about the men threatening you? I'm worried about your safety."

"I doubt it'll do any good. At least the good news is, we don't have to come up with ridiculous gossip about me for the day." I tossed the paper in the little golden wastebasket. "It's already in print."

CHAPTER 32

A person can only put up with so much. Then, it's either time to get over it and move on, or give up and have a breakdown. Thinking about it, since I'd been back home, nothing—I mean *nothing*—with the exception of reuniting with my family, had gone right. In fact, nothing had gone right for months. Maybe years. I'd been crying, fretting, hiding—teetering on the edge of total collapse—for weeks. Driving to town that morning, I'd finally reached my breaking point.

I'd had enough.

It was like being hit by a bolt of lightning. In an instant, my life changed. I was over it. All of it. And I wasn't going to have a breakdown. Instead, I was putting on my big-girl pants.

When Guido backed me into the corner—cruelly teasing, scaring, threatening me, and my family—I'd felt like a child. Helpless. Abused. Literally frightened for my life.

I'd wanted to run.

After he'd swaggered out the door, and later when I'd recounted it all to Pep, I'd realized that he only had the power if I let him take it. No one, not even a killer like Sal Malagutti, was going to control me. Or know that he scared me. No one was going to make me feel like that again. Ever. I was done being the tail wagged by the dog. I was done being the hapless victim to circumstance. I was done with running away.

I stepped on the gas as I pulled out of Benderman's Curve. Whizzing down the road in my convertible, with my hair whipping in the warm wind, I felt a huge weight lift off my shoulders. I'd let all the gossip and intimidation suck my life from me. No more.

Eva Knox was back.

CHAPTER 33

Although there were plenty of shoppers in town, it was easy to find a parking spot right in front of Boone Beasley's butcher shop. I hopped out of the car, stuck a quarter in the meter, and went to the door and pulled. It was locked. And the sign hanging inside the glass door read CLOSED. I looked at my watch. Ten forty-five. I double-checked. The hours printed on the door said the shop opened at ten.

"That's funny," I said aloud. "It's Wednesday; he should be open today." Still, the lights were off inside. "Why would he call, asking for someone to bring his check, if he didn't plan to be here?"

As I stood and thought for a moment, I saw Tammy Fae in the Shear Southern Beauty shopwindow next door, peering out from behind a magazine. Seated next to Tammy Fae, back to the window, a woman read a magazine under an old-fashioned hair dryer.

"Hi, Miss Tammy Fae!" I called out loudly. "How are you this fine morning?" I smiled and gave her an energetic wave.

People on the sidewalk turned to see to whom I was

calling. Tammy Fae flapped her hand quickly, then put the magazine up in front of her face and cowered back from the window. I smiled. I was going to be in Tammy Fae's face every chance I could get. You know the saying, keep your friends close and your enemies closer. It'd drive her nuts.

I remembered that Boone Beasley's apartment was above his shop, so I turned and ducked down the narrow alleyway between Boone Beasley's building and Tammy Fae's building. Out back, I emerged in a small gravel parking area for tenants who lived in apartments above the Main Street shops. Something caught my eye, and I stopped short.

Parked on the far side of Boone Beasley's building, right behind Pooty Chitty's business, the Lacy Goddess Lingerie Boutique, I spied Billy's retro red Kawasaki motorcycle. It had to be Billy's bike; upgraded and custom, there wasn't another like it anywhere.

"That's weird," I said aloud to myself. Maybe, I thought, Billy's just too cheap to pay the parking meter out front. Or maybe he thought it was safer to park the bike off Main Street. That's probably it, I decided. Although parking behind the buildings was reserved for residents, certainly, it was easy to find space for a motorcycle without anyone caring, or taking much notice.

"Ugh. What is that!"

Wrinkling my nose, I couldn't help but notice an acrid smell coming from somewhere close. Like the bitter, eye-watering stench of overripe cheese. Behind the butcher shop, at the base of the stair to a second-story deck and apartment, I walked around a black Chevy truck with a license plate that read CHOP. Clearly, the muddy truck with a gun rack mounted in the rear window belonged to the butcher. And the smell seemed to be coming from the truck bed. I went over to the truck and took a look into the bed. Instantly, I drew back, gagging. Randomly tossed about the truck bed were furry animal parts. Legs, ears, tails. Deer. And heaven knows what else.

I spun around, grabbed the stair railing, and raced as quickly as I could to the second-story apartment above the

butcher shop, taking each stair one step at a time, careful
not to bend my sore left ankle. Once on the deck, I rapped
on the apartment door. I wanted to get out of there as quickly
as I could. The rancid smell wouldn't leave my nostrils.

"Mister Beasley?" I fanned my hand in front of my face,
hoping it would dissipate the stench. I was close to gagging
again. Sharp pain shot from my ribs as I coughed.

From inside, I heard something crash.

"Mister Beasley? Are you there?" I knocked again. The
door jerked open.

Boone Beasley, wearing a white sleeveless tee shirt,
striped boxer shorts, and black socks, wiped his red nose in
the doorway. Bleary-eyed and red cheeked, it was clear that
he'd been drinking.

"Well, whaddaya know!" he slurred. "Miz Knox! Howya
doin. Wontchya come in?" Holding the door to steady himself, Boone Beasley threw one of his arms back as a welcome gesture. Looking past him, I knew there'd be no way
I'd step in.

"No, thanks," I said, taking in his squalid bachelor pad.

With the deep green and brown patterned curtains drawn,
the apartment was dark. There was a tray table upturned on
the stained wall-to-wall tan carpeting. Tattered furniture—a
rolled-arm green velvet couch, a gold Naugahyde easy chair,
a blue plaid armchair—surrounded a simple oak coffee table that was covered with old containers of take-out food,
magazines, and empty booze bottles. There was a small card
table with decks of cards, chips, and three folding chairs
under a curtained window. A hunting show was droning on
from a giant wall-mounted television screen.

Except for the television, every speck of wall in Boone
Beasley's apartment was covered with taxidermy and weap-
onry. There were guns in racks, pistols on shelves, and hunting bows hung on the walls. There were stuffed, marble-eyed
deer heads with huge antlers—some were probably twelve
points—and smaller deer antlers of all sizes. Jackets, sweat-
ers, and dirty white aprons draped from a few. Upturned
deer feet with polished hooves held antique shotguns. I saw

bear heads with ferocious-looking expressions, their taxidermic tongues hanging out; sharp-eyed coyote, fox, hare, weasel, and wild boar specimens stared into the room. It was the *Who's Who* of Georgia wildlife.

As much as the sport is important to Abundance economy and lifestyle, I just couldn't wrap my head around what I was seeing. Instead of a being a tribute, of sorts, to the majestic animals who'd given up their lives to the sport of kings, Boone Beasley's collection seemed more like a grotesque carnival of death.

I thrust Daphne's check into his hand, quickly said goodbye, and one-footed it down the stairs as fast as I could, holding my breath as I passed the pickup.

CHAPTER 34

My jaunt down to the hardware store was uneventful. With the help of the store owner, Merle Tritt, I quickly purchased Pep's P-trap and was soon on the road back home with her plumbing part.

As beautiful as the day was, driving under the great live oaks outside town, I couldn't erase the images of Boone Beasley's apartment. How could anyone live like that? With all those poor dead animals in the apartment, staring, day and night. And all the filth.

I shuddered.

Still, I wondered how the butcher had found time to hunt as often as he obviously did. And what about the animal parts in the back of his truck? It wasn't hunting season. Yet, obviously, the remains in the back of his truck were relatively fresh. Could the butcher be killing animals illegally? Then I had a gruesome thought: If he was killing animals illegally, were we eating them?

I shuddered again.

My mind flashed to the night Lenny Lemoni died. I'd been sure I'd heard gunshots before I left the cottage. And again, later, when Dolly and I were running on the trail. Could Boone Beasley have been out in our woods? And there was the other guy, from the Country Corner Store . . . What was his name? Bart. That was it. Bart Somebody-or-other had admitted he'd been out giggin' for frogs. Could he have been out hunting for more than frogs that night?

I shuddered again. I'd have to tell Daphne about Boone Beasley. The man gave me the creeps. Great meat or not, we needed to look into another source. Besides, as drunk as he appeared to be, his reliability was surely in question.

I pulled into the gravel parking area at the big house and hurried upstairs to give Pep her P-trap. Already, the bathroom was dry and, except for the plumbing parts laid out on the floor, the room was immaculate. Pep was sorting her tools on an old towel.

"Is this what you wanted?" I asked Pep.

"Perfect. Thanks, hon," said Pep. "Y'all are a lifesaver. Hey, I filled in Daphne about the stuff you told me earlier— about the mob men threatenin' you. Of course, she was shocked and horrified and went about shrieking and grabbing her chest, you know, the way she does."

I nodded. "DQ."

"Right," continued Pep, "Anyway, we both agree. Y'all need to contact the sheriff's department. Like, right now. These Mafia folks scare the bejeepers out of us, especially with the kids around. Daphne wants to kick them out, but she's afraid they'll all come back and murder us in our sleep. So, we've decided to feign ignorance until they're scheduled to leave at the end of the week. She's gonna tell the kids they're havin' a slumber party and they're all sleeping in her room."

"Good grief. No one will sleep."

"Probably not. Of course, we're all hoping that Detective Gibbit can get his act together and stop focusing on y'all in time to figure out who really killed Leonard, or whatever his name was, before he or she gets away. Or takes out someone else."

"I'll call the sheriff's department first thing after the

Chamber of Commerce meeting," I said. "Promise. Although, I don't have much faith in any of them. I'll be arrested anyway."

"Well, if they arrest y'all, at least you'll stay alive. Besides, why would they arrest you, sweetie? Y'all haven't done anything wrong!"

"Well, yes, actually, I have. Precious, too," I said. Pep waited for me to explain. "And now that I'm thinking about it, can you help me with something?"

"Sure, sweetie. Are y'all gonna tell me what you and Precious did?"

"No. Are you sure that the folks from New York are still out for the day?"

"Far as I know."

"Okay. Come on." Pep followed me out of the Gambinis' pink bathroom and into the Malaguttis' suite. I pointed to the antique bed in the bedroom. "Help me lift the mattress."

"What?"

"Just do it."

Pep and I reached under the side of the bed, and together we pushed the heavy mattress up and nearly over our heads. "Hang on," I gasped as my rib complained. I peeked under the sagging mattress to the center of the box spring.

"Crap!"

The gun was gone.

CHAPTER 35

Not telling Buck about the gun had been an honest mistake. When I came back to the cottage after falling asleep in Loretta's digs, I'd been completely caught off guard to find Buck waiting for me. With the booze and my emotions running high, I'd forgotten all about it.

I wasn't looking forward to coming clean, and I still didn't know whom I should speak to, Buck, Detective Gibbit, or someone else at the sheriff's office. I'd promised Pep that I'd make the call after the Chamber of Commerce meeting. I had just a couple of hours. Still, I was upset that Buck hadn't told me that he knew guests at Knox Plantation were mobsters from New York. He hadn't been up front with me. I didn't know whom to trust.

Walking across the lawn toward the tent, I was still replaying the scene with Sal and Guido in my cottage a couple of hours earlier.

"Eva, baby!" cried Daphne when she saw me. "Here y'all are!" She gave me a big hug and a kiss on the cheek as I stepped into the tent. Then, she whispered, "Pepper-Leigh told me what happened this morning with those terrible mobsters. I am *so* worried for y'all! For all of us, really."

"Me, too."

"You must've been terrified!"

"I was. But I won't let them get to me next time."

"Good gracious, Eva! I certainly hope there never is a 'next time.' In fact, I've already spoken with the sheriff's people earlier today, and they assured me that we're gettin' extra coverage here in the evenings. Have y'all called to tell them what happened?"

"No, not yet. I promised Pep I'd do it after the meeting." It occurred to me that Daphne didn't know about the gun under the bed, either.

"Well, I suppose that's okay. Still, I don't want y'all to wait too long. I'm findin' this all to be terribly frightenin'. I called Daddy. He's drivin' back tonight. He'll be here late tomorrow or early the next day. Says he's got some news about what's been goin' on with the olive trees. And he says he's been tryin' to reach you on your phone. I do wish y'all would check your messages."

"I'm glad he'll be back soon," I said.

"I invited our neighbor Mister Collier over; I hope he shows. I wanted to look extra nice for him, given all he's done for us and all. I'm not sure he's a Chamber member yet, but he should be."

"Speaking of Ian Collier, do you know what he does, exactly?" I asked. "Precious said something about securities."

"Honestly, I don't know," Daphne said with a smile. "But he must do somethin' special to have made all that money. He's just dreamy, isn't he?"

"I don't know. I've never seen the man."

"Never seen him? Why, Eva, of course you've seen him. He *rescued* you from certain death—the forest fire. You stayed in his home!"

"I don't remember any of it," I said.

"Really?" Daphne looked incredulous. "Oh, *dahhwr-ln*', you really were in bad shape, weren't you? That reminds me, have y'all seen the paper today?"

"You mean the one with my ugly mug all over it?"

"Ah, y'all have seen it. Well, I'm glad y'all are here today for the meetin'. We Knox women stick together. We need to be on the offensive."

Cars began pulling up the drive and parking next to the big house. The Chamber of Commerce members were arriving.

"Folks are comin' already!" cried Daphne. She turned and gave me the once-over. "Oh! Eva, hon, is that what you're wearing?" Again, Daphne looked up and down my white jeans and black tee. "I thought perhaps y'all might put on a pretty little sundress."

"No. This is it."

Daphne looked disapprovingly at my outfit again and clucked her tongue. "It'll have to do."

"Good."

"Mornin', ladies!" called Daphne to the guests. "We're ready for y'all under the tent!"

Anyone happening on the scene that day would swear there was a wedding going on. However, it was normal operating procedure for Daphne. She'd offered to host the Chamber of Commerce meeting in hopes that a spectacular event would help put our fledgling family businesses on the map. And she was going all out.

Set up in the small field behind my cottage, right next to the pond, the red and white striped tent was filled with round tables set with china, summery flower arrangements, and elaborately displayed sweet and savory finger foods and beverages. Along with the talented hand of Precious Darling, Daphne had concocted a delicious selection of olive oil treats, including fig and olive crostini, artichoke and olive paste, savory sweet potato skins and bacon, olive oil cookies, and blueberry and peach olive oil mini muffins. Plus, there was a lineup of bottles with speed pourers filled with different olive oils that could be poured into little paper cups for dipping a variety of artisanal breads. Moreover, for each attendee, there was a small gift bag containing a bar of olive oil soap, a container of olive oil hand cream, and a bottle of Knox Liquid Gold Extra Virgin Olive Oil.

Looking at Daphne's lavish gift bags, I had a change of heart. If Daphne wanted me to wear something "pretty," it was the least I could do for her. This event was important to my sister. To our family. So, as more attendees parked their vehicles and headed toward the tent, I hustled off to my cottage where I swapped out my jeans and tee for a floral cotton sundress with spaghetti straps. Daphne'd left it on the bed for me. I even tried to compensate for my rode hard and put away wet appearance by putting on a little mascara and lip color. Unlike many of the women in Abundance, makeup was not something I wore every day; I only bothered with it for special occasions. Or when I needed to hide my face.

Finally, I switched my black ankle wrap for a nude-colored one. Then, I put on a big straw hat and slipped on thong sandals and my sunglasses before padding back over toward the big top.

As I crossed the yard, I saw a couple talking under an ancient live oak tree on the far side of the lawn. Something about the way they were standing—just a little too close—and the way the woman touched the man's arm made me stop in my tracks. Even from far away, their intimacy and attraction to each other was unmistakable. I recognized the man. It was my brother in-law, Billy. Only the woman with him wearing the long, gauzy halter dress was not my sister, Pep. Instead, Pooty Chitty, owner of the Lacy Goddess Lingerie Boutique, shook her wild, dirty-blonde hair as she laughed.

Quickly, Pooty dropped her hand from Billy's arm and the couple leaned back, away from each other, as they undoubtedly saw me heading across the lawn. Still, it was too late. I'd seen them huddled together. I focused on the tent ahead and pretended not to notice them as my mind raced. Pep had told me that after she'd pedaled home from my place on the night of the murder, Billy had not been there. He'd gone out somewhere—she'd assumed he was gambling. Had he been with Pooty instead? And hadn't Pep told me that Billy had given her some lingerie not too long ago? And it was the wrong size? Had he made an honest mistake? Or had Pep stumbled upon something belonging to her husband's . . . mistress? Whichever the case, Billy had clearly gone to the Lacy Goddess more than once. Maybe parking his motorcycle behind Pooty's shop had been more purposeful than I'd first imagined.

I didn't know whether to say something to Pep or not when I saw her next. My own instincts about men were so screwed-up. I was hurting and oversensitive. Maybe I had it all wrong. Certainly, it wouldn't be the first time. Not by a long shot. I didn't want to needlessly hurt Pep, or make her already difficult marriage impossible. Besides, she'd been so excited when she'd taken the olive oil back to her place for a little fun with Billy; she seemed to really want to make things work with him. I'd have to think about it. Regardless, Billy Sweet was on my radar.

I reached the tent and stepped inside. It was shady, but still not much cooler than outside in the sweltering heat. *Time to focus on Daphne's event.* Everything else could wait just an hour or so. Reconciling my anxieties about facing folks in Abundance, especially on the day when I looked like hell and my face was plastered all over the local paper— and not in a good way—I stood right at the entry to the tent and handed each person a program as he or she stepped into the big top. We exchanged pleasantries—I smiled and complimented each guest after welcoming him or her to the meeting. Then I dropped his or her business card into a beribboned basket sitting on the table next to me.

Although most of the attendees had come to catch a glimpse of me, or at least to gossip about me with everyone else, as they came in, most didn't even realize that it was me under the hat, behind the sunglasses, welcoming them. It wasn't until they'd already grabbed their programs and moved on to find their seats for the presentation that it dawned on them. Waiting for the presentation to begin, folks

whispered in their seats and cranked their heads around,
trying to get a better look at the notorious runaway bride. I
smiled and waved, over and over again, as each person
turned to stare at me.

Soon, from the microphone on a little wooden stage,
Daphne was calling out, "Testing . . . testing . . . one . . .
two . . . three . . . testing." She smiled grandly and greeted
the crowd before saying a few words about Knox Plantation,
the new opportunities for overnight guest stays, and all the
health benefits of fresh olive oil. Then, she turned the stage
over to insurance agent and Chamber of Commerce president Heath Hicks, who spoke for about ten minutes before
introducing Abundance native, motivational speaker, and
acclaimed national author Dalia Whipplesnap, who was the
event keynote speaker. She was on hand to hawk her new
book, *How Good Listening Leads to Success*. For nearly an
hour, people in the audience gossiped, laughed, and tittered
to one another as Dalia Whipplesnap droned on about listening skills.

I flipped absently through the business cards in the basket. Wendel Wilcox, Abundance Package Store. Cletis Carter, Owner, Carter's Country Corner Store, est. 1866. Beau
Riddleberger, Esq., Law Offices of Riddleberger and Blan-
kenblatt. I wondered if he practiced criminal law.

I pulled out more cards: Earl Downing, Marketing
Director, Climax Chemical Company. Woody Smart,
Owner, Woody's Gun Shop. Seth Fretwell, Chimney Sweep.
Soletta Overstreet, Owner, Gifts Galore. Merle and Roxxy
Tritt, Abundance Hardware. And my favorite: Angel Pride,
Creator of the Heavenly Bun, "The hair styling aid that
touches souls of women everywhere, bringing bigger hair
closer to God."

I flipped through a few more cards in the basket. I
scanned the tent to see if any of the deputies were there. Or
worse, Detective Gibbit. Or, still worse than that, Buck. I
didn't see any of them. Better yet, I didn't see Debi Dicer
or Tammy Fae Tanner. Maybe, finally, I'd have a day that
went off without a hitch.

After standing for nearly an hour and thirty minutes, I began feeling weak, hot, and fidgety. My ribs were hurting and my ankle throbbed. And no breakfast and too much alcohol the night before was taking a toll. No more Georgia Peach Whiskey for me, I thought.

I figured a breeze would bring some relief, so I slipped outside. Slowly, careful to not bend my ankle much, I picked my way across the grassy lawn toward the pond where I watched the sun's rays dancing on the water rippling in the breeze. I was happy for the shade of my big, floppy hat. Standing on the water's edge, looking toward the far side of the pond near the cabin, I could see a little red dinghy, tied to a rickety old dock, bobbing in the water. I remembered how Pep and I had spent entire summers swimming and fishing off that dock. I'd caught my first catfish there. And, of course, I'd spent plenty of time in the cabin, especially in high school, with Buck . . .

As I reminisced, and my mind drifted to happy times growing up on the plantation, I heard polite applause behind me as the crowd in the tent broke up for refreshments. After another hour or so of socializing and "networking," the meeting would be over. After that, I was going to have to come clean about the gun under the mattress, and contact either Buck or Detective Gibbit. Kind of like trying to decide between the better of two evils.

"Eva, Knox, *here* you are!" a familiar voice cried out.

I spun around to see grim-faced Debi Dicer in a bright green and pink Lilly Pulitzer shift marching toward me from the tent on the knoll. Her fists were clenched. And she looked really, really angry. Sour-faced Tammy Fae Tanner was in stride, right behind Debi.

"You bitch!" hissed Debi to me. "Eva Knox, just who do you think you are!"

I saw people in the tent turn toward us. I doubted they could hear Debi, but the way she was marching across the lawn had to attract attention. Her lack of decorum was almost unprecedented in Abundance.

"Debi. How nice to see you," I said. "You, too, Tammy

Fae." I waved to Tammy Fae, who stayed a bit behind Debi. "Sorry we didn't get a chance to talk earlier today in town."

I put on my "bestest," brightest smile. I'd never seen or heard Debi be so . . . blunt before. Her usual game was to spar with subtle double entendres. Hissing ugly words was not her shtick. Nevertheless, I wasn't going there. Especially not on Daphne's big day.

Tammy Fae stopped short in the yard and glared while red-faced Debi continued working her way toward me, stomping and aerating the lawn with her pointy heels. Finally, she stopped in front of me by the water's edge, haughty chin held high, manicured hands gripping her narrow hips.

"Don't be cute, Eva. You know exactly what you've done." She spat the words out.

"Perhaps you can enlighten me," I said brightly. I wasn't going to give her an inch. "I can't imagine what I've done today to put such a burr under your saddle, Debi. And I thought we had such a *lovely* chat yesterday."

"Oh, sugar pie, like hell you can't imagine what you've done. Y'all are nothing but a man-whorin' harpy! I told you yesterday in the package store that Buck and I were going to celebrate our anniversary last night. And y'all just couldn't stand it, could you?"

"Debi, you are ridiculous, if not completely paranoid."

"You little hussy! Y'all went right under my nose and tried to seduce him!"

"What on earth are you talking about?"

"Y'all know exactly what I'm talking about, sugar pie," seethed Debi. "Buck never showed up last night for our celebration. That's 'cause he was at your place!"

"And how would you know that?"

"Because I came over here lookin' for him and saw his car out in the drive. He was here for *six hours*!"

Wow, I thought. He *was* here a long time. I remember he'd said that he'd been waiting for a few hours. Guess he hadn't lied about that. Score one for Buck. But, of course, there was no need to concede anything to Debi.

"Well, Debi," I said, "if you have to go out to hunt the

poor man down every time he's not where you want him to be, that certainly doesn't seem like a sound basis for a marriage, now, does it?" I admit, I was being smug. I figured she had it coming to her. "Maybe it's all for the best."

"Well, *you* of all people would know about *not* gettin' married!" she shrieked. "Buck and I've been datin' steady for six months. I've *always* known where Buck was, and I've never, *ever*, had to go lookin' for him. That is, until *you* came slitherin' back into town." Debi raised her voice again. People were definitely looking from the tent.

"Kind of like old times, I guess, huh?"

"When he finally got home last night, he was chock-full of alcohol!"

"And you know that because . . ."

"Because I was sittin' there, waitin' for him! And then he said he was 'too tired' for me. For us! And on our special night. He actually sent me home. I'd been plannin' our special night for *months*!"

"Just goes to show you: It takes two for romance."

"You skank," Debi hissed. "You'll do anything to get him back!"

"I don't want him back."

"Right. And you've been tryin' to cover your tracks, tellin' folks you're a lesbian. Well, you aren't foolin' me, sister!"

People were wandering down from the big top to where we were at the pond. Tammy Fae started to back away. We were becoming a scene. A bad scene. Tammy Fae had enough sense to know that she didn't want to be a part of it. She'd let Debi do her dirty work.

"You're so desperate, you spent half the night pryin' him with liquor, tryin' to seduce him. Hours and hours you tried to spin your nasty web around my poor Bucky. And, Lord knows, he may have taken a little taste of what you were offerin'—you can hardly blame a man when a woman shamelessly throws herself at him. Still, my Bucky wouldn't stay the night with you," seethed Debi. "No man wants to wake up next to a skank. When the deed was done, obviously, he didn't care for it. At least he got *that* right."

Way up at the tent, I saw Detective Gibbit. He was talking to Daphne, and she was shaking her head.

"Well, then, you should be happy about that, shouldn't you?" I said. Debi was getting into my space. I took a step backward.

"You're nothin' but a man-stealin' whore!"

"It's not my fault, Debi, that you can't keep your 'Bucky' happy. That's on you, sweetheart. Maybe, you should stop calling the grown man 'Bucky.' That might help."

Debi stepped up to me and slapped me across the face so hard that my hat and sunglasses flew off into the pond. I was sure I heard a camera click from somewhere. I wasn't going to let her see me flinch.

"Hey, at least I saved you from wasting two very pricey bottles of champagne—or did you finish them yourself?" I smiled and took a step toward her. Really, I wasn't sure what I would've done. I never had a chance. All of a sudden Debi started screaming for me to let go of her. I hadn't touched her. The next thing I knew, I felt a hard shove to my shoulders and I fell backward into the pond.

Things happened quickly after that. Debi was shrieking that I'd hit her and she wanted me arrested for assault. There was a photographer taking pictures—I recognized the woman with the nose ring who'd stayed at the big house. A crowd rushed forward. At some point, I glimpsed poor Daphne's horrified expression in the mob. My hat was floating upside down on the water. My three-hundred-dollar Maui Jim sunglasses had disappeared. I dove back down to see if I could find them. Opening my eyes underwater, it was too dark to see. I felt around on the murky bottom. There was something wooden. A pole? No sunglasses. I swam back up for air. Debi was still screeching. The crowd was jabbering. My ribs were screaming in pain. A few people started to come into the water, thinking I was in trouble. One of my thong sandals floated by. I dove back down again to try to find my sunglasses. I wasn't giving up on them. I'd never be able to afford another pair. I felt around. There were sticks, leaves, rocks, the wooden thing again . . . a branch?

No, a pole of some sort. I snagged it and realized it was a shovel.

I went back up for air, shovel in hand. Someone grabbed my other arm and yanked me hard toward the muddy shore. I released the shovel as I looked up to see stony-faced Detective Gibbit, up to his knees in pond water, shaking his head with disgust as he hauled me toward the muddy shore. For a geeky skinny guy, his strength surprised me.

"Arrest her!" shrieked Debi. "She threatened me and assaulted me!"

"Please, let go, you're hurting my arm." Detective Gibbit gripped my arm so hard that I could feel his bony fingers making impressions in my skin. He didn't let go.

"Miss Eva Knox," whined the detective through clenched buckteeth, "you're under arrest for disorderly conduct and assault." He gave me a disdainful look and, in a flash, snapped handcuffs on my wrists. The weedy, jug-eared man wrenched my arm and started dragging me across the lawn.

"What the . . . ? What are you doing?" I cried. "I haven't done anything! What about *her*!" I gasped for a breath as a sharp pain shot from my ribs. "Ow! Go slow! I can't walk this fast!"

I still remember Debi's gloating sneer as the detective dragged me across the lawn, hobbling barefoot, muddy, and dripping wet with my soaked sundress stuck tight to my legs. He was reciting my rights. I was going to jail.

CHAPTER 36

"So, how was it?" shouted Precious from the backseat. "Did ya set that weaselly little detective straight?"

"I think we agreed to disagree," I said. "At least he didn't really arrest me." And I was genuinely grateful for that. I stepped on the gas to the convertible. I was hungry, dirty, exhausted, and eager to get home. And I could smell the whiff of pond mud coming from my filthy sundress.

"Well, that's good, Sunshine! I figured that fella's got more bite than bark. In fact, Tilly Beekerspat—she works in dispatch, remember?—she tells me he's about as useful as a screen door in a submarine. Most folks outside the department just ain't caught on to him."

"Thanks for picking me up."

"No problem. Miss Daphne sent me in your car 'cause she needed to stay with her kids. She wants you to check in with her as soon as you get home. You still look damp. I wish you'd let me drive. You warm enough?"

"I'm fine. Better now that I'm out of the air-conditioning. One of the deputies brought me a blanket. I wrapped myself

up in it for most of my six-hour 'interview.' They didn't even
let me go to the bathroom. That would have been nice."

"Sunshine, 'nice' isn't on the list of stuff to do in the
po-leece interrogation room. In fact, I hear they bring criminals a lot of soda to drink just so they'll have to pee.
Once the bad guys confess, then they get to pee." Precious
chuckled.

"I won't ask where you heard such a thing." I remembered
how the detective kept insisting I drink the Mountain Dew
he'd slammed on the table in front of me.

"I know all about it, Sunshine. I'm a crime expert 'cause
I read murder mysteries."

"Got it." We soared past a white board fence and a big
field with corn.

After I'd been dragged off muddy and soaking wet,
someone had called the sheriff's department to complain
about Detective Gibbit manhandling me. Probably Daphne.
Amazingly, someone else said that I hadn't laid a hand on
Debi and that Debi'd been the aggressor. The coup de grâce
was that someone had videoed the whole thing. I hadn't
touched Debi. In any event, by the time Detective Gibbit
and I got to the station, the detective had been ordered not
to proceed with the assault case. Had Buck called him off?
Still, since he had me handily in his clutches, the detective
wasn't going to let his opportunity pass by. After all, he had
bigger fish to fry.

For six hours, he'd interrogated me, over and over again,
with combative, grueling, and often absurd questions about
the murder, and my alleged connection to organized crime.
Even after I'd told him about the mobsters threatening me,
the rank detective never let up. He'd just sneered and said it
was my word against theirs. Then, finally, after getting nowhere, the detective agreed to let me go home. Albeit, with
a strong warning not to leave town.

He'd only quit because it was probably his dinnertime, I
thought. And as Precious and I rode past a big white farmhouse and I smelled barbeque in the air, I wondered if there

was a Missus. Gibbit waiting at home to serve her hubby homemade fried chicken, green beans, mashed potatoes, gravy, and fruit cobbler. I hadn't eaten all day. I was hungry. I thought about stopping at Carter's Country Corner Store. But when I got there, I decided to keep going. It brought back memories of my sick stomach the night before, after all the sugar. And I couldn't bear to be in my mud-sodden dress another moment. I'd take a warm, scented bath at home and then grab a snack from the big house. Maybe I'd order a pizza.

Although I hated to admit it, the questions Buck had posed to me during his unexpected visit the night before had inadvertently helped prepare me for Detective Gibbit's interrogation. And, much to my surprise, the detective didn't seem to know my answers ahead of time; it was as if Buck hadn't shared what I'd told him. So, due to my newfound, intense distrust and dislike of the detective, I'd decided not to tell him anything that he hadn't asked about directly or specifically. I didn't tell him about Loretta's photo, which he probably knew about anyway. Or about the missing gun under the mattress, of which I was sure he didn't know.

Maybe I'd cut off my nose to spite my face.

I glanced in the rearview mirror. Precious was using the camera in her sparkly gold phone as a mirror, painting a fresh coat of bright coral-colored lipstick on her lips. She pursed her lips together before smiling, apparently pleased with the look. She saw me watching and flashed a big white grin. "Gonna be a pretty sunset tonight," she said.

"Yep!"

Precious snapped a selfie in the backseat.

We whizzed around a corner and swooshed under a tunnel of great live oak trees. We were almost home. Just before Benderman's Curve, I slowed down to look at the side of the road as we passed another deer carcass. What a shame, I thought. And my mind flashed again to Boone Beasley's apartment.

"Here we go again," laughed Precious. "Miss Eva's drivin' as slow as turtles!"

I looked up at the curve ahead.

Out of nowhere, a black car appeared on our side of the road. It was speeding right for us. There was no time for me to get out of the way.

CHAPTER 37

The small black car must've been going at least seventy or eighty miles per hour. It was impossible to imagine how it could have made it around the curve without the driver losing control. And at that speed, no one could have seen it coming any sooner than Precious and I had.

Right before the impact, I remember hearing Precious say, "Holy shhhh . . ."

Then there'd been that terrible sound of crunching metal and plastic.

Afterward, I was afraid to look down. The air bag hadn't worked. Surely, I'd been injured.

"Sunshine!" Precious said from the backseat. "You alright?"

"I think so," I whispered.

I was frozen. My arms, which had taken the brunt of the front-end impact, were still outstretched, fingers clamped tight around the steering wheel. My left collarbone, breast, and lower abdomen ached where the seat belt had locked and stopped me from flying forward. I'd hit and cut my left knee on either the bottom of the dashboard or the steering column. Already, it was beginning to swell. I looked at Precious in the rearview mirror. She was still holding her phone in the air, just like she had when she'd been taking her selfie.

"Precious, are you alright?" I asked.

"I'm fine," said Precious. "Didn't feel a thing, actually. Good thing I'd already finished puttin' my lipstick on. I'd have been pissed if I'd messed up my makeup."

I tried to laugh, but nothing came out.

"Goddamn, that little bitty black car was going like a bat outta hell!" said Precious.

After careening around the wrong side of the sharp curve, the black car had plowed across the front of the BMW and pretty much taken the entire front end off. Especially the driver's side. The front end of my engagement gift-car was lying twenty feet away on the other side of the road, near the edge of the woods. After hitting us, the black car had kept going another hundred feet or so, until it finally ran off the road and flipped over in a ditch.

Precious was on her phone. "Mister Collier! Mister Collier! Miss Eva and I've been in an accident at Benderman's Curve! Come quick! Miss Eva's car is totaled!"

I was still gripping the steering wheel. Frozen. And, remarkably, my car was still running. And the air bag hadn't deployed. I turned the key, shutting off the engine, and fumbled around for the emergency flashers.

"C'mon, Precious, we've got to see if the other driver is okay."

I'd said it but still hadn't managed to move. I heard Precious rustling around in the back, and the passenger seat flipped forward as she began climbing out of the car. The passenger-side door didn't open, so she hoisted herself over the side of the car and onto the pavement. Finally, still shaky, I managed to ungrip the steering wheel and push open my door. I stumbled out of the car and began hobbling slowly down the road toward the flipped car. Adrenaline. Huffing and puffing, Precious passed me. As she marched ahead of me, wearing tight jeans, an orange silky top with slits that exposed her big shoulders, and matching orange Louboutin pumps, she was still on her phone, talking with Ian Collier.

"No," she said, "I don't know. Some crazy driver plowed right down the middle of the road goin' the other way, like a streak of greased lightnin' . . . Wait . . . We're almost there . . . No, we haven't called 911 . . . okay. Thanks."

We were about halfway to the wrecked car when we saw someone behind it running toward the woods. All of a sudden, the person turned to look at us.

"Oh my God." I called out, "Loretta! Wait!"

Precious and I stopped short, breathless, in the middle of the road. We watched as fleeing Loretta, wearing jeans and a black jacket with a gold and white Boston Bruins "B" emblem on the back, ran deeper and deeper into the woods until she'd disappeared.

"What the hell! Is that your cook?" asked Precious. "The missing Loretta woman?"

"Yes."

"The woman everyone says you killed?"

"Yes."

"Well then," huffed Precious, "there's one damn thing for certain."

"What's that?" I bent over and put my hands on my knees to try to catch my breath and keep from fainting.

"That ol' bitch sure as hell ain't dead!"

CHAPTER 38

Less than five minutes later, Precious and I were waiting on the side of the road by my crushed BMW when the navy blue Hummer motored around the curve and pulled off the road. The driver stepped out.

I nearly fell over.

Wearing a rumpled white button-down shirt with rolled-up sleeves tucked into a pair of faded denim jeans over cowboy boots, it was the mysterious man from my dream. My Scottish woodsman prince.

In the flesh.

"Oh! Mister Collier, we're so glad you're here!" Precious called over to her tall, dark, handsome boss.

"Are ye alright, Precious?" asked the familiar Gaelic voice as he clasped her hands.

"Yessir. I'm just fine. Didn't even smudge my makeup."

"I'm happy to hear it," he said to Precious as he held her shoulder. Then, he turned, and with big, sure steps, headed toward me.

My mouth gaped open as I stood in the road, unable to

move. Broad shouldered with a slender waist, at least six feet three inches, with intense green eyes, dark, wavy hair, and a ruggedly handsome face, my dream guy had come to life. My best dream—the one when my woodsman prince held me in his arms, carried me through the woods, and, eventually, stripped me of my clothes—wasn't a dream after all. The thought hammered me numb. The man was standing right there. My mind raced to try to sort reality from what I'd imagined. I must be dreaming now, I thought.

He stepped in close to me.

I froze.

"Eva, are ye alright, lass?"

I couldn't seem to answer. Suddenly, I felt hot and the ground was whirling. Ian took me by my shoulders and looked me up and down. His green eyes flashed as he leaned forward and cradled my face in his hands.

"Eva?" Ian said. He was speaking to me.

Yes. It was him. Same face. Same eyes. Same arms. Same voice. Same scent. Except it wasn't a dream. My knees felt weak. I needed to sit down. Fast.

"I . . . I . . ."

"Ooooh, Mister Collier," shrieked Precious. "Lookit! Miss Eva don't look too good. She looks white as a ghost. I swear, she's gonna keel over!"

"Ahh, drookit! I should've known." Ian's familiar arms were around my waist in a flash. "I gotcha, Eva. Just stay with us." I couldn't seem to focus on anything that was going on.

"I think she's in shock, Mister Collier!"

"Precious, would ye open the door to the Hummer."

I heard them talking, but it was like I was somewhere else.

In one quick motion, Ian Collier swept me up into his arms. I smelled the familiar woodsman scent from my "dream." I felt Ian walk effortlessly as he carried me to the vehicle. Precious opened the passenger-side door. Ian slid me into the seat before he gently pushed my head between my legs and told me to breathe as he rested his hand on the back of my neck. I heard them talking but couldn't make out what they were saying. Then, there were sirens.

I pulled up my head. A fire truck, an ambulance, and a bunch of other vehicles all rumbled up at once. As red and blue lights flashed, busy people in uniforms started poking me and asking me questions: Do you hurt? Where? How did it happen? Where did the other car come from? Where were you? How fast were you going? Did you see the other driver? Where is the other driver? Then, someone else in a different uniform said, "Do you want to go to the hospital? You should go get checked out." Someone looked at my eyes and took my pulse. Another someone wrapped my arm and checked my blood pressure. They explained that I would bruise badly where the seat belts had been. And I'd be very sore for a couple of weeks. Then someone asked for my license, registration, and insurance card. I pretended to read something they handed me and scribbled my signature on a paper form. I heard them wondering why the air bag hadn't deployed, but all the same, if I was not seriously hurt, I was better off that it hadn't worked. Someone said I was lucky because when they'd pulled up, they'd been sure I was seriously hurt, or worse. I heard Precious loudly repeat what had happened over and over again. I heard Ian Collier's Gaelic tones. After a while, I put my head back on the headrest and closed my eyes. An EMT handed me a couple of ice packs.

"Here, hon," she said. "Put one on your knee. The other one is for later. Please, reconsider going to the emergency room to get checked out."

"Thank you," I whispered, eyes still closed.

"That was quite a jolt you got," she said. "Your body absorbed a lot of the impact because you were holding on to the steering wheel. And the fact that you hit your knee means you encountered a lot more force than you may realize. You're going to be sore."

All in all, I have to say they were wonderful. All of them. Professional. Courteous. Attentive. But I really wasn't paying attention. I was grappling with the confusing realization the dreamiest guy in the world had taken my clothes off. And, more important, just minutes earlier on a backwoods country road, I'd been *this* close to death.

CHAPTER 39

I handed a one-hundred-dollar bill to the young, pimply-faced pizza delivery guy. It was the last of my emergency cash. Thirteen dollars and ninety-nine cents of it was to pay for the medium veggie pizza I'd ordered. The rest was the pizza delivery guy's tip. His eyes had gotten real big when he'd recognized me as the runaway bride lady from the paper, and probably, like everyone else, he also thought I was a mob moll. Maybe even a murderer. I'd decided that if I were going to be known as a man-stealing, murdering mobster, folks in Abundance would know that I was a damn good tipper, too. That'd be my self-made gossip for the day, I decided. "Eva Knox, spendthrift." Although, it would hardly overcome the stories I'd already generated that day.

At least, I thought, I wasn't wet and covered in stinking mud anymore. I smelled good after my lavender-scented bath. And I wore clean jeans and a pristine white V-neck tee shirt. Best of all, I'd cheated death. I was still alive.

Although I'd clearly been dazed after the accident, I'd

refused to go to the hospital for a checkup. I'd ridden silently in the Hummer as Ian and Precious had driven me home to the cottage, Precious babbling all the way. Then, before I could draw the water for my bath, Daphne and Pep had shown up and fluttered around for an hour or so, trying to assure themselves that I was alright. And Daphne's kids came over to deliver a big bowl of fresh fruit and some gourmet chocolates—they'd raided Daphne's stash of welcome treats for her guests. As I sat in my mud-covered dress, quite sure I reeked of wet, decayed leaves and the excrement of frogs and fish, the kids sang me a well-rehearsed feel-better song before they ran back across the yard, up to Daphne's bedroom in their big-house slumber party. As instructed, Meg called Daphne on the phone to report they'd all made it safely to the third floor.

Then, Daphne and Pep had me recount what had happened at the sheriff's department with Detective Gibbit, followed by what had happened at Benderman's Curve on the way home. Afterward, we speculated about where Loretta had been the past couple of days and why she'd run off after the accident.

"Well, I think it's obvious," said Daphne. "She killed that poor man and she's been hiding from the law."

"Daphne, that 'poor man,' as y'all say, was a hit man for the mob," said Pep. She rolled her eyes. "I'd hardly think that you need to be feeling sorry for him." She yanked up her strapless top, popped a chocolate bonbon into her mouth, and tossed the wrapper on my glass coffee table.

"Well, yes. However, now that the poor fellow is dead, I can be more sympathetic toward him," retorted Daphne, glaring at the offending wrapper on the table. "Poor Leonard," Daphne sniffed. She ran her slender palm down her chiffon skirt.

"Poor 'Doughboy,' you mean," I said. "And he was Loretta's brother. Why would she kill her own brother?"

"I don't know. If I killed someone, I sure wouldn't hang around to get caught," said Pep, her mouth full of chocolate. "Where's Loretta been hiding all this time, anyway?"

"Exactly," said Daphne. "Pepper-Leigh, why would she hide at all if she didn't kill him?"

"Because we know there are other killers here," I said softly. "Remember, Sal Malagutti admitted to me that he wanted our farm and that he was willing to kill for it. And Leonard—Lenny, 'Doughboy,' whatever his name was—he was problematic for Sal. And now, Sal wants me to kill mob boss Tony the Baker back in Boston. Omigosh, am I really saying this? This is all completely nuts. I swear, life was easier back in New England."

"Easier, maybe," said Daphne as she patted me on the knee. "But y'all definitely weren't any happier."

"Right," said Pep. "So, my money is on the wise guys from New York, Sal and Guido, whacking our Leonard. Maybe Loretta was there when it happened. After all, if you'd been there when someone offed your brother, wouldn't you hide? I sure as heck would." Pep grabbed another chocolate.

"No. I think this is a case of a quarrel gone bad," said Daphne. "Loretta did it. Just because someone's a sibling doesn't mean you can't lose your temper with him. Pepper-Leigh, please leave some of the chocolates for Eva."

I remembered the creepy way Sal had looked at me, the way he had run his thick, fat finger down my face and neck to my cleavage.

"Sal Malagutti or his goon, Guido, would kill someone in a heartbeat," I said. "They are evil to the core. My money's on them. I just need to prove it. I owe them that much."

"I agree," said Pep. "And why, Daphne, are y'all tolerating them stayin' here? Just kick their fat mob asses out," said Pep.

"Given the fact that they appear to be cold-blooded killers, I don't want to aggravate them," said Daphne. "Besides, they'll be on their way back to New York in a few days. It would be foolish of them to harm any of us while they're stayin' on here, wouldn't it? If they are as bad to the bone as y'all say they are, then they'll surely not kill us while they're payin' guests here."

"Unless they decide to kill us all by making it look like some kind of terrible accident," I said. "Where are they now, by the way?"

"They went out to dinner in town. They should be back late this evening," said Daphne.

"Has anyone seen the gun that Precious and I found under the bed in the Malaguttis' room? Why hide it in the first place unless it's the murder weapon?"

"After Pepper-Leigh and I talked about it, I had the twins case the joint," said Daphne. "No gun."

"Daphne, you had the twins 'case the joint'? Why, I'm impressed!" laughed Pep. "Daphne the debutante detective."

"Pepper-Leigh, I don't appreciate y'all makin' fun of me, just because my erudite and comprehensive terminology outshines your elementary parlance," sniffed Daphne. "You, of all people, criticizing me—why, y'all talk about 'whacking' people! Very crass, indeed. And, now that I think about it, since you've been working at that nasty Roadhouse place, your language—not to mention your demeanor in general—has deteriorated tremendously. I daresay, by the end of the year, your dearth of social graces may prove to be irreversible."

"I'll be sure to turn in my library card," said Pep as she popped another chocolate in her mouth, tossing the wrapper on the table again.

"Has anyone heard what caliber gun killed Leonard?" I asked.

"Actually," said Pep as she chewed, "funny you ask that. One of the deputies was in the Roadhouse today, and I overheard him say something to his buddy about it bein' nine caliber. I think that's what he said, anyway. He got quiet when he saw me headin' their way." She licked chocolate off her fingers.

"Pepper-Leigh, please," mumbled Daphne. "Show a modicum of manners."

"But the gun under the bed was a Glock 19, I think," I said. "Or was it a seventeen? I'm sorry. My mind is all mush."

"Isn't a Glock 19 a nine-millimeter-caliber weapon?" Daphne asked.

"Last time I heard," said Pep, tossing another chocolate into her mouth.

"Omigosh, none of this makes sense," I said, holding my achy head.

"It's alright, Eva dear," said Daphne. "I still think it was Loretta who did it." She patted me on the knee.

"Ow!"

"Oh, Eva, dear, I'm sorry. I didn't mean to hurt you."

"C'mon, Daph, we need to leave now. Eva is fading."

"Of course." Daphne turned to me and smiled sweetly as she stood to leave. "Eva, dear, do be sure that you bathe tonight. I hesitate to tell you this, but you smell like a dirty fishbowl." Daphne blew me a kiss before following Pep out the door.

After Daphne and Pep left, I'd drawn a bath and gone to soak in my warm, lavender-infused tub water. I'd closed my eyes, taken some deep breaths, and let my mind wander, listening to Dolly rhythmically chewing on her bone over on the rug.

As the night darkened outside, in my mind, I saw the black car racing toward us at Benderman's Curve over and over again. I remembered taking my foot off the gas. It'd been all I had time to do. Like a rocket, the car had sped toward us out from nowhere. Scary fast. I tried to remember how far into the curve the car had been when I'd first seen it. I must've replayed the scene a hundred times. It never changed. There'd been no warning. One moment the road had been clear. The next moment the car was screaming toward us. Half an instant later, I'd felt the jolt in my arms and back as I heard the terrible crunching. In the end, I was grateful that I'd slowed down to look at the deer carcass before I'd gotten to the turn. If I'd been going just a teeny bit faster, or hadn't looked up exactly when I did—the outcome would've been very, very different.

After my soak, I decided to splurge and order a veggie

pizza. And I'd ended up eating all of it, except for the crusts I'd shared with Dolly. I'd just tossed the empty pizza box into the trash and was washing my hands with a bar of Daphne's sage-scented olive oil soap when I heard a firm knock on the screen door out front. Dolly woofed once.

CHAPTER 40

"Eva?" A man's voice called quietly. "I've got a little something for ye if you feel up to havin' some company."

My heart skipped a beat. I crossed to open the door.

"Please, come in!"

Ian stepped into the tiny one-room space. I was extremely conscious of how tall he was. And how awkwardly prominent my big four-poster bed was, up front in the tiny cottage, and just steps from the door. I felt like a kid, back in my college dorm room. For all sorts of reasons.

Ian didn't seem to notice. In the same jeans and cowboy boots he'd worn earlier, he'd added a dark vest that was hanging open over a pink button-down shirt of the most exquisite cotton fabric. I blushed from embarrassment, realizing that he'd probably changed his shirt from earlier after it'd taken on the fishbowl stench from my sundress when he'd carried me to the Hummer.

"How ye feelin'?" he asked. Ian held out a huge bouquet of dahlias as he put his other hand on my arm and looked me over. "I stole these from the greenhouse. Don't ye go tellin' Precious."

"How lovely!" I gushed. "Thank you. I have the perfect vase." I took the big bouquet in my arms. "Have a seat." I motioned past the bed, toward my "living room" on the far side of the room.

"I'll not come in and keep ye, lass. It's late, and ye must be tuckered." Ian smiled softly and lowered his voice. "I've been worried about ye since ye left Greatwoods yesterday— that was no wee tumble ye took off the balcony. And now the accident. How ye been holdin' up?"

"Oh!" I felt my face get hot. Had he seen me jump from Greatwoods? Of course he had. There was security every-where. I should've known. I was mortified. "I'm sorry about your wisteria. I'll pay for the damage."

"Aye, forget it. I enjoyed the show. Ye're quite the gym-nast." He chuckled. "I just want to be sure ye're okay. I can't imagine having a couple of days like this and still bein' chipper."

I smiled. "Well, 'chipper' isn't a word that exactly comes to mind right now. I'm just a bit worn out, that's all." Of course, that was the understatement of the century. Every muscle in my body was screaming out in pain. I could feel my cheeks burning as Ian watched me.

I had a cupboard in the kitchenette open, and the blue and white Spode vase I wanted for the flowers was high up on the top shelf. Normally, I would've climbed on a chair or jumped up on the counter to reach it. This time, I wasn't up for it. Not even close.

"Let me." Ian came up behind me in the kitchenette. I felt his palm on the small of my back as he reached up and around me to grab the big vase with one hand. With his touch, I felt tingles run up my spine to the back of my neck. I could smell his "wealthy woodsman" scent. My mind raced to the dream. The part in the car wash. When he'd taken off my clothes. I remembered the feel of his hands, the way his long, gentle fingers had caressed my skin. Thinking about it made me feel weak in the knees. But how? When? Where? Surely not in a car wash. Maybe I did dream some of it. It was frustrating not to remember. Still, I could hardly ask about what happened. I mean, how would that sound: *Excuse me, neighbor, can you tell me if you took off my clothes in a car wash? I'm having trouble remembering.* I still needed to sort it out.

"I'll fill it for ye."

Ian put the vase in the sink and turned on the faucet. When it was full, he took the big bunch of flowers from me and slipped them in the vase. I couldn't get over how he smelled just the way he had in the dream, of rich leather and woods.

"I'll not even attempt to arrange these," he said. "I know better. I'm sure ye'll get it looking just right. He carried the flowers over to the table. Do ye need anything else?"

"No, thanks. I'm . . . I'm just kind of recalibrating. Trying to make sense of everything. Sort through my priorities." I thought for a moment. "You know, like, trying to figure out the meaning of life." I rolled my eyes.

"Aye, coming close to death can do that to a soul," he said. His green eyes were deep and quiet. I couldn't tell what the man was thinking. Still, there was something . . .

"Okay, lass. I'll be leaving ye now," he said abruptly as he stepped toward the door.

"Wait!"

Ian turned and waited.

"I . . . I have a question."

"Aye?"

"What is it that you do over at Greatwoods? I certainly don't mean to pry. Precious told me that you're into securities?"

"Did she now?"

"That's all she would say."

"Aye."

I waited for him to say more. He didn't. I barged on. "I've been wondering about the barbed wire. There's bound to be miles and miles of it. None of it was there when I was growing up."

Ian said nothing for a moment. Instead, he closed his eyes. Then, he said, "I purchased Greatwoods to create and maintain a sanctuary of sorts . . ."

"You mean, like a nature preserve?"

"Aye. Ye could say so. I'm working to protect certain species."

"Endangered species?"

He stepped close and tipped my chin up. His hand felt gentle and warm. His bright green eyes mellowed as he looked down at me. Something in his face softened, and his voice grew husky. "I need to go now, Eva. Don't let this— don't let them—get ye down." He bent down and lightly kissed my forehead. "Life's too short." In two strides, he was at the door. "Get some rest, lass."

"Thanks for the flowers."

I doubted he even heard me. Already outside, he was halfway across the lawn.

CHAPTER 41

Ian Collier made my insides ache. In a good way. I heard sexy music when I thought of him—the slow seduction of low, thumping Celtic drums. And on an evening when I should have crashed and gone to bed, our encounter only made it more difficult for me to sleep. I felt like a schoolgirl. I replayed how his hand had felt on the small of my back as he reached for the vase. How his lips had felt as he'd kissed my forehead. The soft throatiness of his deep Gaelic voice when he'd last spoken to me. How he'd smelled. Earthy. Woodsy. Intoxicating. He had my attention, that's for sure.

I couldn't sleep.

"C'mon, Dolly, we're going for a walk."

I pulled my hair into a ponytail, slipped on an ankle wrap, and slid into my flip-flops. Dolly and I were out the door. She stayed with me as I hobbled toward the trail in the woods.

A sliver of moon peeked in and out of the clouds. Unlike the afternoon, which had been unusually crisp and dry, the night air was thick and muggy—heavy with the sweet aroma of rosebushes and scented crepe myrtle trees. Crickets chirped as I followed Dolly into the forest, and the scent changed to musky dirt and tangy pine. The air felt cooler, especially at my feet. In a daze, I thought about Ian's small waist and broad, toned shoulders.

A dark figure slid out from behind a tree, blocking the path in front of me.

"Where y'all going, Babydoll?"

"Hey!" I cried out, startled.

"It's not safe for you to be out here," purred Buck in his smooth Southern drawl. In lace-up field boots, black cargo pants, and a fitted black tee that hugged his brawny shoulders, Buck looked neat, sleek, and flawlessly honed. Nothing extra. Nothing out of place. He glided toward me, like the consummate black panther. His catlike movements were almost military-like in their precision. He'd always been that way. Scrupulous. Attentive to detail. A stickler for perfection. His remarkable assiduousness had come easily to him.

I was sure he had a gun holstered somewhere.

"I'm going for a walk. That's all. And why are you out here scaring people? Last time I looked, our place was private property."

"Well, Babydoll, after she called half a dozen times, I promised Dame Daphne that we'd keep an eye on things."

"And you just forgot to tell her that it'd be *you* watching the farm? Night watch detail hardly seems fitting for a sheriff. What happened? You draw the short stick back at the office?"

"Something like that. Why don't you tell me what you're up to, hobbling alone in the woods."

"I'm not alone. I have Dolly with me. And, apparently, like it or not, I have you, too. So, like I said, I'm just going for a walk."

"Yeah, right," Buck said sarcastically. "I know you too well, Babydoll."

"I just want some time to unwind. I've had a long, crappy day. As if you didn't know that."

"Yeah. I know all about it. You feelin' okay?"

"Do you mean am I okay after you plied me with drinks that gave me a killer hangover this morning? Or am I okay after I was accosted and my life was threatened by a pair of mob hit men? Or am I okay after the fight I had with your girlfriend, who shoved me into the muddy pond and tried to have me arrested? Or am I okay after the witch-hunt interrogation your detective spearheaded for six hours while I sat, soaking wet, covered in mud? Or am I okay after the car accident that nearly killed me and Precious? Which one is it?"

"I'm sorry, Babydoll. About all of it."

"Fine. Then get out of my way, please. I'd like to go for a walk with my dog. I've earned it."

"Wait a minute. What hit men?"

"What do you mean?"

"You said you were accosted and your life was threatened by a couple of hit men. What are you talking about, Eva? Why don't I know about this? Did Malagutti or Gambini threaten you?"

"Yes. I told your crackerjack detective all about it. He laughed."

"What? Babydoll, I've been trying to get a line on 'em and get 'em all locked up since I found out they were here. Did they hurt you?"

"No. And thank you for not telling me—anyone in my family, actually—that you knew there were convicted criminals staying at our place."

"I thought you'd be safer not knowing anything. All of you."

"Right. So, you knew there was a pair of dangerous criminals staying at the house, and that there'd been a murder. Still, your hotshot detective spends all his time chasing me, accusing me of killing someone, accusing me of being in the mob. Then, you go and give the information to the *Abundance Record*, so that everyone in town knows before we do. What the heck! That was a crappy thing to do. Get out of my way. I'm going for a walk now, Sheriff Tanner."

"I didn't leak the story."

"Well, someone in your ace establishment sure did. And our second-rate newspaper editor was only too happy to publish the poop. Overnight, no less."

"I'll get to the bottom of it. I promise."

"Sure you will. And just for my amusement, do these thugs, Sal Malagutti and Guido Gambini, have nicknames like everyone else in the mob who's been staying here?"

Buck looked down.

"Well?"

"Gravedigger."

"What!"

"Well, there was a story about how Malagutti became a made man when he had some poor sap dig his own grave before . . ."

"Are you frigging kidding me? What's Guido Gambini's name?"

"Dumbo."

I sighed. "Well, that fits."

"I'm sorry, Babydoll. I should've told you."

"But you didn't. That's because you considered me a suspect for murder, right?"

"Right. Well, officially, that is. Not personally, Babydoll. Besides, I've been watching."

I rolled my eyes. "Well, that's reassuring."

"What happened with Malagutti and Gambini?"

"They scared me nearly to death, that's all. And I know they meant it."

"Did they touch you?"

"It doesn't matter."

Buck swore, and a storm crossed his face.

"I'm just mad that I didn't kick Sal in the nuts, that's all. But I will next time."

"Christ." Buck put his head in his hands. "Don't even think like that. They'll kill you. Just stay out of their way. I'll take care of Malagutti."

"You mean Gravedigger. And how am I supposed to stay out of their way? This is my home. And they walked into *my* house!"

"They were in your place? The cottage?" Buck swore again. "Just give me a few more hours, alright? I want you to tell me everything you know about them. Where they've been, what they've done since they've been here. Everything. Can you do that? Can you just trust me . . . for once?"

"Do I have a choice?"

Buck waited.

"Fine," I said.

Now was as good a time as any to tell him about the gun under the mattress. So, I spent the next twenty minutes standing on the trail relaying all I knew about that and the New Yorkers. I told him the details about Sal and Guido's visit to my cottage; how they wanted to take over our farm; and how they wanted me to get rid of their Boston family competition.

"Jesus, Eva. Why didn't you come to me? Why? They could've hurt you. Badly. Or worse."

"Maybe if I'd known they were thugs to begin with, I'd have said something. But you kept that little ditty to yourself."

"I could've had them arrested. Or at least brought them in."

"You didn't trust me enough to share. Besides, at the time, I didn't think you'd believe me."

"Not believe you? Eva, what were you thinking? Why wouldn't I believe you?

I shrugged. "No one else in this town believes me. Except Pep and Daphne, although I think Daphne had her doubts for a while. And Precious Darling. And Ian Collier." I even surprised myself when I mentioned Ian.

"What's Ian Collier got to do with this?"

"Nothing, I guess. He seems to care about me, that's all. I like him."

"I warned you, Eva. Don't be getting too close to Ian. It won't end well for you."

"What's that supposed to mean?"

"Just heed my warning, that's all. Understand?"

I didn't answer.

Buck put his hand on my shoulder. Like a giant bear paw, it felt warm and reassuring.

"Why didn't you tell me about finding the gun under the mattress? How are you gonna feel if that turns out to be the murder weapon? Or if someone else gets killed with it?"

I was too embarrassed to answer. He was right. I guess we were even.

"I'm sorry. I was afraid you or one of your gung ho goons would arrest me. Are you going to arrest me now?" I couldn't look Buck in the eye. I'd been selfish and stupid. Too much overthinking. Too many crime dramas. My overactive brain had been my worst enemy.

"Never mind," he said. "Don't ever mention the gun under the bed again, unless I ask you. Only me. Got it?"

I nodded.

"We'll find it. And I forgive you for calling my deputies 'gung ho goons.' There are some first-rate people on the force. I'd trust them with my life. And yours. Just not all of 'em—Eli's got a couple of his own loyalists."

"Why does that not surprise me?" I asked.

"I've learned to watch my back. And if you're going to stick around these parts, knowing you like I do, you should learn not to antagonize them. If you're poking around, it's not a good idea, especially if it makes Eli look bad. Let me handle that."

"Let you handle what? Making Eli look bad?"

Buck didn't answer right away. Then he said, "Just give 'em enough rope. They'll all hang themselves. Wait . . ."

Buck stepped away, took out his cell phone, and spoke quietly to someone. I heard the words "warrant" and "plantation." He put his phone in his pocket and turned back to me.

"Why did you fight with Debi? She told me you hit her at the Chamber meeting today."

"What!" I cried. "I never, ever laid a hand on her. It was all a setup. She wanted to humiliate me in front of everyone. Probably wanted to wreck Daphne's big day as well. It was payback."

"Payback for what?"

"Never mind. You wouldn't understand."

"Try me."

"I'd rather not get into it. Let's just say that Debi and I are a bit like oil and water." I shuffled some dirt with my foot. "And we always have been."

Buck raised his eyebrows and waited for me to say more. I hadn't planned to embellish my thoughts; however, since I was still angry with Debi, I added, "By the way, are you sure she isn't waiting for you out front, in her car? In case you haven't noticed, she seems to have a bug up her butt about your not being where she expects you to be at all times. You might want to check your vehicle for a tracking device."

Buck just stared at me.

"I'm just sayin' . . ." I shrugged.

He burst out laughing. Buck laughed harder than I'd seen anyone laugh in years.

"Ahhh, Babydoll! I knew it. You haven't changed a bit! No wonder Debi's so fit to be tied these days." He smiled, and I had to laugh myself. Damn, Buck had a killer smile. And dimples to die for. It felt good to make him laugh; a little like a peace offering. And maybe, I thought, I could forgive him just a bit for being with Debi.

There was a soft *beep-beep* sound, and Buck reached into his pocket and pulled out his phone again. He pressed it to his ear and turned away. After a few mumbles, Buck put the phone back in his pocket and turned to face me.

"I gotta go. C'mon. I'll walk you back home."

"Debi calling to check up on you?"

"No. It's business." Still, I saw him smile as he turned away.

"You can leave me," I said. "I'll be fine."

"No, Eva. We're going back to the cottage. Together. But I've got to hurry back. Can you keep up alright?"

"I'm fine. I'll just hobble along."

"Atta girl."

Although I was sore all over and I still wobbled when I

walked, I tried to step up my pace to keep up with Buck. Dolly followed right behind as Buck escorted me back to the cottage, where he instructed me to go inside and lock the door.

"There's one more thing, Babydoll," said Buck. He took my arm and looked at me hard. "I'm not sure what it all means yet, but you should know that the car Loretta was driving tonight had a sloppy spray-paint job. It was originally light blue."

"Loretta's car was blue. So, that's the same car, right? Her missing Honda Accord? Why would she paint it?"

"I don't have the details. If it is her car, she probably painted it when she figured we were looking for her in a blue car. And she didn't want to be found."

"Right."

"Here's the thing, Babydoll—the brake lines had been tampered with. She flew around Benderman's Curve and ran into you like that because she had no brakes."

"What?"

"It looks like someone wanted her dead. Like I said, these folks play for keeps." Buck pulled out his phone and looked at the time. "I gotta go now."

"But . . ."

"Eva, listen to me. *For once.* Go inside and lock the door. And keep Dolly with you. Now. I'll either be back later or send someone else to watch the place. Meanwhile, Malagutti and Gambini haven't returned tonight, and I don't want you out and about when they get back. Hopefully, they don't know we're onto them. We're planning to pick them up when they come up the drive."

Before I could say anything, Buck turned and sprinted off toward his vehicle parked at the big house. With Dolly at my feet, I opened the screen door and stepped into my cottage. I waited three or four minutes and listened as Buck's car flew down the gravel drive. I grabbed two ibuprofen tablets and chugged them down with some water. Then, I snuck back outside. Only this time, I left Dolly behind.

CHAPTER 42

Note to self: Order a pair of decent running shoes; walking the woods in flip-flops is for the birds. I pushed a low-hanging branch out of the way and continued slowly making my way down the moonlit trail toward the cabin. An owl hoot-hooted, and I jumped.

Buck had confirmed that Sal Malagutti and Guido Gambini were career killers. And they wanted something from me. Were they the ones who killed Lenny? Or had it been someone else? I knew that I'd never sleep until I figured out what happened to Lenny, and how Loretta was involved. Had he and Loretta quarreled, like Daphne suggested? After all, not all siblings get along. But if Loretta had killed her brother, why go to all the trouble to paint her car and then stick around?

If Loretta wasn't the killer, could it have been Ian Collier? Surely not. He seemed like a gentle soul. And he was protecting endangered species. Isn't that what he'd said? He hardly seemed like the type of person to kill someone. Still, why was he on our property that night in the first place? Certainly, he had enough of his own land to wander about in the middle of the night. And why did Buck keep telling me to avoid Ian?

And what about Ian's gun-toting henchman, Lurch?

Or could Leonard's death have been a total accident? Had he been shot by someone poaching in the woods? I was sure I'd heard gunshots that night. More than once. Boone Beasley? Bart, the frog gigger? Could there have been someone else out there?

I sighed. It was beginning to look like half the county had been out in the woods that night.

Still, I had to start with what I knew. And I knew that Loretta had been at Knox Plantation long enough to be pretty familiar with it. She had known the pastry guy, most likely her own brother, Lenny, way better than any of us had known him. And now, after hiding for two days, she'd run off into the woods and disappeared again. Where could she have gone? I may not have understood the "why," but I could certainly check out the "where."

I reached the clearing on the other side of the pond and stood in front of the log cabin where Lenny had been living. Some sort of small animal scratched in the leaves on the ground by my feet before darting into nearby undergrowth. I curled my toes in my flip-flops.

Typical of cabins built by Southern Georgia's early settlers, not much more than ten or twelve feet high at the roof peak and about twenty-four feet long by twelve feet wide, the old log cabin was set on a thin foundation of stone. Extending out on the long side of the structure was a wooden platform that formed the base for a covered front porch. There was one door and several windows, and on one short side of the building there was a crudely built stone chimney.

A couple of bats squeaked overhead. When I ducked, I misstepped and stubbed my right toe into a pine tree stump.

"Ouch!" I cried out loud. "Yikes! That hurt." I hobbled up to the porch, flopped into a rocking chair, and held my sore toe. I uttered a few bad words as I rubbed the sticky sap off my toe. If I hadn't been so angry at myself, I would have laughed. Stubbing my toe made me madder than when I'd been in the car accident earlier in the day.

"I need to cover myself in Bubble Wrap," I groaned. Every part of me ached.

The oak rocker squeaked as I rocked back and forth, nursing my toe and taking in the moonlit clearing. I'd loved spending time at the cabin when I was a little girl. And, of course, there were the times later, with Buck.

I scanned the moonlit yard, looking for clues regarding Lenny's murder. There was a big oak stump with an axe wedged into the top, and some wood logs scattered on the ground. Also, a Weber kettle grill squatted between a pair of old wooden sawhorses topped with some wooden planks. I remembered how Daddy used to clean fish and other game on that sawhorse table. A rope hammock hung between two pine trees. And over by the corner of the porch, a hand pump hovered over a small cistern for water. I knew that there was an outhouse, just in the woods, around back. Nothing unusual, I thought, forcing myself out of the rocking chair.

"Eli Gibbit missed the gun under the mattress in the big house. Maybe he missed something here," I said under my breath. "Okay, now I'm talking to myself. Get a grip, Eva."

There was a wad of yellow police tape on the porch next to the cabin door. I lifted the iron latch to the door. The door wouldn't budge.

"What?" I said aloud. "How can the door be stuck?"

I tried the door again. And again. It wouldn't budge. I threw my weight against it. "Ow!" Still, the door was shut tight.

"That's weird." I knew there was no lock on the door. Never had been.

I went to the window closest to the door and peeked inside. There was enough moonlight shining into the windows to see that the place looked just about the same way it'd looked when I was growing up. Inside, under the window, there was a small, rough-hewn oak table with an oil lamp on it. Four chairs flanked a table littered with cards, poker chips, and open beer cans. Seeing the cards and chips, I thought of the newspaper reporting Leonard's illegal gambling outfit. Then I remembered Billy and his chronic gambling. Could he have been in the cabin with Leonard that night? Or had he been busy making a "Pooty call" with his mistress in town?

Stop, Eva. Innocent until proven guilty, right?

The opposite wall was lined with a wooden upper cupboard and two lower cabinets with some stuff scattered on the countertop. An interior sidewall nearest to my window had a door to the bedroom. On the opposite side of the cabin, there was a ratty brown leather couch and two mismatched leather armchairs facing a stone fireplace.

"I've come this far. I'm not going back now," I said as I tried to open the window. It was stuck. I moved over to the next window and pushed. It wouldn't budge, either. Then, I went around the corner to one of the two windows on the end of the cabin. Again, I pushed up on the window frame. *Success!* I pushed the window open wide and hoisted myself up and into the cabin.

I landed on the grimy wooden floor in the bedroom. Barely large enough to hold a twin-sized cot and a small upright dresser with an alarm clock, the tiny room was littered with dirty laundry and smelled of musky body odor.

I plugged my nose as I looked around. And I wondered why I hadn't thought to bring a flashlight. Or my phone. Still, I poked around as best I could. It was hard to tell whether the place had gotten messed up from when the deputies combed through everything, or whether that'd been the way Leonard had kept the place.

"Gosh, I hope Daphne hasn't seen this," I said aloud, still holding my nose. "She'll die."

Regardless, I had to agree with Detective Gibbit: It certainly didn't look like a place belonging to someone who wasn't planning on coming back.

Dirty clothes were littered on the bed, on the floor, and

sticking out of open dresser drawers. A Boston Bruins sweatshirt, a green Celtics tee shirt, a couple of wrinkled flannel plaid shirts, a pair of rumpled blue jeans, boxer shorts . . . I made my way through all the clothes, picking through each pocket. Nothing turned up except an unopened can of snuff, a couple sticks of gum, some twigs, pebbles, and lint. As I grabbed a gray sweatshirt off a doorknob, something dropped to the floor and rolled under the bed. Gingerly, I got down on my hands and knees and felt around under the bed. I put my fingers around the small metal object and pulled it out. I held it up to see in the moonlight. My heart stopped. It was Pep's ruby and gold skull ring. She'd said she suspected Billy had taken it to pay off gambling debts.

"Jerk."

So, Billy had known Leonard. Could he have killed him? What a terrible thing to think about a family member. Billy'd always been an irreverent sort. That's what drew Pep to him in the first place. Still, it was a far cry from being a killer. Up until that point, I'd been on the fence about sharing what I knew about Billy and Pooty with Pep. However, finding her ring made me mad. Family or not, Billy had betrayed his wife. In more ways than one. Pep could do better. She needed to know. I shoved the ring in my pocket.

There was a worn Red Sox baseball cap on the floor. I lifted up the cheap mattress on the metal cot and found a *Penthouse* magazine. I looked under the bed again. There was an open, empty suitcase, dirt, and dust balls. I emptied each drawer in the dresser and looked underneath. Nothing. There were a couple of dollar bills and some change on a small table next to the bed. A *Playboy* centerfold was tacked to the door.

I went out to the main room. The counter was littered with dirty paper plates and used plastic silverware. There were stinky, opened cans of tuna fish, empty Budweiser beer cans, an open bag of bread, a jar of peanut butter, crumpled potato chip bags, and several large containers of salt littered everywhere. And there was a hunting knife. I walked past the gambling table under the window, headed across the room where moonlight illuminated a couch and two chairs clustered together on an old rag rug in front of the fireplace. There was a stool in front of the fireplace, a fire poker, and a stack of logs.

Then, I remembered the door. As I walked toward it, something about the rug caught my eye, but I was still focused on the door, so I didn't give it much thought. Against the wall next to the door were five or six fishing poles, a rake, and several tackle boxes on the floor. I stood on the welcome mat in front of the door, pushed up the latch, and tried to pull the door inward. Nothing.

"What the heck?"

I stood back and studied the door. There was no way to lock it, so it had to be stuck somehow. Then I saw it. Near the top on one side, something was wedged between the door and the frame. I tried to get ahold of it with my fingers, but it was too high for me to get a good grip, and it was jammed tight. I went to get the stool by the fireplace so I could climb up and get a better look. As I neared the stool, the moon outside must've gone behind the clouds, because suddenly, the room became inky dark. I stopped in the middle of the room to let my eyes adjust. And that's when I noticed the rug, again. It was rumpled and out of place. And the trapdoor was exposed.

Most people would never have noticed it—especially in the dark. The little door was so well integrated into the wood floor that you almost had to know it was there to recognize it as anything but the floor. I remembered Buck indicating that after the deputies had been through the cabin, he'd checked under the trapdoor himself, looking for Loretta. Still, something about the way the rug was—half on and half off the door—just didn't seem right to me. Buck never would have left it that way. It was just one of those quirky things that I knew about him. We'd snuck in and out of that cabin so many times ourselves, and I remember the way he made sure that the rug was "just right" before we'd left the cabin after hiding from my dad.

I forgot the front door for a moment, dropped the stool on the floor, got down on my hands and knees, and started feeling around the edges of the trapdoor in order to raise it.

Suddenly, the door flew open—knocking me backward.

CHAPTER 43

I scrambled to pick myself up off the floor. Loretta was in full attack mode, making guttural Godzilla-like sounds as she climbed forcefully from the cavern below. She quickly raised herself up from the hole and squatted down between me and the rest of the room with her hands in the air—ready to lunge. There was nowhere to for me to go. With a menacing look, she stepped toward me as I backed toward the fireplace.

"Loretta! What are you doing!"

"I'm takin' care of business, that's what," she growled. Still in her black Boston Bruins jacket and jeans, her face looked banged up, her lip was cut, one ear was bloody, and she had bruises on her neck. Probably from the car accident.

I blindly snatched at the space behind me, and my fingers found the wrought iron fire poker. Quickly, I whipped it around and pointed it at Loretta.

"Don't come any closer! I've had a *really* bad day!" I tried not to freak out as I remembered Loretta's mob nickname: "the Cleaver."

"Not half the day I've had," snarled Loretta. "And I can

tell you right now, little miss, that my day is gonna end better than yours!"

With a giant growl, Loretta lunged at me. I swung with the poker and hopped to the side.

"You killed Lenny, and now you're gonna pay for it!" she screamed.

Loretta lunged at me again. I swung the poker hard and scuttled to the next corner.

"I didn't kill him! But I know who did. Wait! I'll tell you!"

Truth be told, I still had no idea who killed Leonard. I was just trying to buy time until I could find a way out of the cabin. I needed to either disable Loretta—which was highly unlikely—or make my way back to the open bedroom window where I had a chance to escape the cabin and run like hell. Okay, hobble like hell. Hopefully, my adrenaline would kick in; even crippled, I was an experienced and fast enough runner to get away from Loretta, who looked formidable but not necessarily quick on her feet. And she looked like she'd been injured in the accident. Maybe that'd slow her down. I pointed the poker at Loretta and jabbed it a few times.

"Let's just talk."

"Okay," she said. "I kinda like you anyways. You're not all stuck-up like your big sis. And since you're not goin' anywhere, and I got time, we'll talk."

Loretta stood up and put her hands on her hips, still blocking me from the rest of the room. She'd surprised me.

"Okay. Good," I said, taking a deep breath.

I kept the poker raised in front me, waving it slowly back and forth. I thought for a moment about where to start. Then, I remembered the photo back in Loretta's apartment.

"You didn't just meet Lenny here, did you?"

"No," sighed Loretta. She repositioned herself in a "ready" position, arms out in front, knees bent, looking like she'd pounce on me at any moment.

"You've known him a long time, haven't you?"

"Yeah, you could say so."

"Brother?"

Loretta nodded.

"Are you . . . twins?"

Loretta nodded again.

"Lenny and me, we came down here after Uncle Tony told us to check it out."

"Check it out? Check what out?" As Loretta thought about Leonard, she seemed to soften. Still, I kept my poker at the ready.

"You ordered your wedding cake at Uncle Tony's shop in the North End," she said. "And you mentioned that your father owned some big plantation in Georgia where he grew olives and made olive oil. My Uncle Tony, he's been wanting to get into the olive oil business for*ever*. He's diabetic. Pastries aren't good for him. Anyway, this olive farm is a gift from heaven, he says when he calls me later. He says there were olives right here on the East Coast and he wanted 'em. Wanted to get outta the bakery business—with all that sugar and all—and get into olives. He said he had a plan, and he sent me down here to check it out.

"Your uncle is Tony Lemoni? Tony the Baker?"

Loretta nodded.

"Go on." I kept waving my poker. So, everything Buck had told me had been right, I thought. We had two mob families visiting Abundance, The Lemonis from New England and the Malaguttis and Gambinis from New York. And they'd all followed me to Knox Plantation because of my dad's olives.

"Great," I said under my breath as I shook my head.

"I got down here a few months ago, and it all looked pretty legit," said Loretta. "People in town were bragging about the farmer guy who was growing the best olives in the country. They told me his oil was winning awards. Then, I saw an ad for a chef to work at the Knox place—the very place I was supposed to be checking out. I stayed up for two nights studying Southern recipes on the Internet before I showed up asking for the job. If there's one thing I can do it's cook!"

"I'll give you that," I said. Loretta almost smiled.

"Once I had the Southern recipes under my belt, it was a snap. After I cooked her a 'real' Southern meal, your sister nearly fell all over herself to give me the job. Even gave me an apartment down in the basement after I told her I had no place to live. Sweet."

"And . . ."

"I reported back to Uncle Tony that I was 'in' and prospects looked good. After a couple of weeks, he called me and told me he wanted to send Lenny down here, too. Uncle Tony had some kinda plan, and he wanted to start the ball rolling with our 'acquisition.' As it turns out, at the same time, your stupid sister tells me she's looking to hire a field guide. I told Uncle Tony that maybe Lenny could come down posing as a guide. Heck, the woman hired me; why not give it a try?"

I rolled my eyes.

"So, I said to Lenny, 'Lenny, to look the part, all ya need to wear is some camo, like a vest or something, and one of those Day-Glo orange caps with some fishing lures stuck into it—these country folks really go for that stuff here.' And I told him to stick some snuff into his mouth."

Loretta broke down for a moment and sobbed. "He did it all, and he didn't even like snuff!"

Then Loretta lost it. She was crying like a baby. I started to inch along the wall and planned to make a break for it. Except, Loretta looked up before I could get moving. She wiped her runny nose with the back side of her hand and stepped closer, looking like she was going to grab my neck.

"Don't even try it!" she snarled at me with a menacing look.

I froze. "I'm sorry for your loss. Tell me more about Lenny," I said. I needed to keep her talking.

Loretta didn't come any closer. She started talking again. "Anyways, next thing you know, my brother is down here."

"What happened the other night?"

"I was finishing cleaning up the kitchen. Lenny comes in and says we got a problem. He says some wise guys from New York are staying here and they knows what we're up to."

"The Malaguttis and the Gambinis."

Loretta nodded.

"I says, 'I know!' I'd just served the damn West Side guys and their wives dessert! So, Lenny and I agreed we needed to fast-forward our plan—'specially 'cause it looked like we'd be taking it to the mattresses with the West Side bunch. We're thinking, with no crew down here, we needed to bug outta the place for a while before the West Siders took a swing at us."

I raised my eyebrows. Was Loretta actually predicting some sort of mob war? Here? At Knox Plantation? All this over olives?

"So, we write this note that says we're running off and getting married. You know, so's not to arouse any suspicion with the locals about why we left so sudden. We leave it on the kitchen counter. We think we can meet with Uncle Tony up in Boston and regroup. Then, later, we can finish business down here when we've got some 'associates' with us. Eventually, we'd all move down here, live on a real Southern plantation, and Uncle Tony would have the olive oil industry by the balls. He'd own the whole place, lock, stock, and barrel."

Loretta grinned, then wiped another tear from her face with the back side of her massive arm. She sniffed hard.

I flicked my poker. "Go on. What happened next?"

"So, after I'm done in the kitchen, I follow Lenny to his cabin here—he's gonna pack and then we're gonna go back and get my stuff from the house, load my car, and go. See, Lenny don't have a car. He never learned to drive. But then, Lenny says he promised Uncle Tony that he'd salt the olive trees real heavy that day, and he forgot to do it. So, before he packs, we grab some salt he had stashed in the secret place we found under the floorboards, plus we grab a couple of shovels. Then, Lenny shoves his Glock in his jacket pocket, and we head out toward the olive trees, planning to salt the ground around the trees one last time before we pack and leave."

"Salt? I don't get it. Why were you putting salt around the trees?"

"To make the trees sick. It was all part of Uncle Tony's plan. Don't you see? By makin' the trees look sick, we'd slow down production, depress the value of the olives and the farm, drive your father's business under, and then Uncle Tony would be able to buy out the farm for next-to-nothing. Of course, if that didn't work, we'd do business in the 'usual' way, you know, give everyone the deep six. But that gets messy."

"I see. Thanks for small favors." I rolled my eyes. So, the "sick" trees that Judi and Bambi had mentioned were actually trees that Lenny had been salting. I didn't say anything to Loretta about how salting the soil was stupid if they'd wanted to continue growing olive trees in the same soil later.

"Only, that night the weather is real bad . . ." continued Loretta. It was almost as if I wasn't in the room with her. Loretta just rambled on. She seemed to need to talk. At least it gave me more time, I thought. I stayed silent, studying the room, waiting for my chance to make a break for it.

"Like a hurricane, it was," Loretta said. "Raining hard that night. The wind was blowing and the lightning was crazy."

"Tell me about it," I said quietly. Again, I rolled my eyes. Loretta didn't seem to notice me.

"I didn't have a raincoat or nothing," said Loretta. "So, Lenny says I can wear his old Bruins jacket that he's got hanging back in the cabin, the one I gave him for Christmas once. So, I run back here to get Lenny's jacket. This jacket. See? I'm still wearing it." Loretta wiped another tear. "The plan was, I'd catch up and meet Lenny where we'd been salting the trees."

"Anyways, inside the cabin, I grab Lenny's jacket. Then, when I step outside, I was reaching for my shovel, only I didn't see it. All of a sudden something hard hits me in the back of the head. Like that, I'm out like a light. That's all I remember. And I got the bump on my head to prove it."

I nodded. Afraid to move. Still waiting for my opportunity to make a break for it. As if she read my mind, Loretta's eyes darted back and forth before she continued.

"Anyways, next thing I know," said Loretta, "I'm waking up out in the yard. The rain has stopped and I smell smoke everywhere. There's a dog barking like crazy somewhere and a fire that looks like it's near where Lenny was supposed to be. So, I get up and go tearing through the woods to find Lenny. Only, I can't find him anywhere. I didn't dare call him 'cause we didn't want people to know we were out there. But there's this big tree on fire along with the brush around it. So, I go closer, worried about Lenny. Then, all of a sudden, I sees him, lying on the ground, next to this woman with pink hair—it was you. I call, 'Lenny! Lenny! Lenny!' But even through the fire, I could see that he was . . . dead."

Loretta teared up again and sobbed heavily. Then she shook her head.

"Damn! Anyways, seeing Lenny like that, I felt sick. Even barfed up my dinner. But before I get a chance to figure out whether you were dead or not, or to look for Lenny's Glock, I hear someone calling out. And he's pretty close. I couldn't tell if it was one of the West Side guys or not, but without a piece, I wasn't going to hang around and end up like Lenny. And the fire was gettin' real big. So, I ran back to the big house, jumped in my car, and took off. I'd planned to figure out what to do about Lenny later. Turns out, Lenny's cell phone and wallet were in the Bruins jacket pocket, so I had his phone and some cash. I dumped his phone right away. I figured the cops would be looking for it."

"Then what happened?"

"When I got to the highway, it was shut down—both directions—on account of some big accident. Since it's the only way I know outta this backwoods place, I was trapped. Once folks found Lenny, and figured out who we were, they'd be looking for me and my car. So, I drove real fast to the Corner Store place, broke in, and grabbed some spray paint, drinks, and junk food. Then, I drove to that old camp-site road by the big curve and pulled off into the woods. I spray-painted the car. I've been living in it. I figured I could finally get away today. Then, you came along on the road and hit me. So, if it wasn't you—then who killed Lenny?" asked Loretta.

"I wish I knew."

"What do you mean?" shouted Loretta, her eyes flashing angrily. "You said you knew who killed my brother! I told you that stuff 'cause you said you knew! Now you're sup-posed to tell me!"

"Well, I have an idea, but I'm still not sure. Why didn't you run? Why stick around?"

"First, like I said, I couldn't get out of town. Then, I hung around because I wanted to pay back whoever it was who killed my brother. After I heard you were alive, I figured it was you."

"Well, I assure you, it wasn't me."

"Then why were you out in the olive grove with him? I figured you'd caught him salting the trees and then you whacked him."

"No. I didn't 'whack' him. I'm sorry, but I literally tripped over your brother. That's all. He . . . he was already . . . there."

"Well if it wasn't you, then who killed Lenny?"

"It looks like it was Sal Malagutti or Guido Gambini. I don't know which one."

"I'll kill the both of 'em!"

"If they don't get you first. It looks like they almost did."

"What do you mean?"

"Didn't you know? Someone cut the brake line in your car." I sounded almost smug. For once, it felt good to know something that my opponent did not. I waved the poker again.

"What? That's why I couldn't slow down or nothing? Those bastards! I'll ice 'em!" roared Loretta.

I started to inch sideways along the wall.

"Hey, where do you think you're goin', little missy?" Loretta cried.

"I'm leaving. I didn't kill your brother. I told you that."

"That doesn't mean you're goin' anywhere. You know way too much about Uncle Tony's operation. You're toast!"

Loretta lunged toward me. I stabbed my poker toward her, but she grabbed it with her massive hand and tossed it away. It was child's play for her. I realized she'd been toying with me, and my silly little poker, all along. I tried to duck under her arm, but she had me pinned. Then, I smashed my knee up into her groin—not the perfect defense when dealing with a woman attacker, I know. I'd just had it on my mind since my meeting with Sal Malagutti, and it was the first thing that came to me. The move gave me a split second to duck under Loretta's arm when she flinched, but not much more.

"Owwww!" she cried. "Come back here, you little wench."

I flew across the room, headed to the bedroom, when all of a sudden I felt Loretta grab my shirt from behind.

"I'll make it quick," she yelled. "You won't feel a thing!"

As my shirt stretched out behind me, somehow I managed to reach the bedroom doorway, towing Loretta behind me. Suddenly, I felt her massive hand clamp onto my shoulder. It felt like she would break my bones if she squeezed just a bit harder. I tried to wriggle out of her grasp. Then, with all my weight, I twisted my shoulder free and threw myself forward through the bedroom doorway. That's when I smashed into something.

Or, rather, someone. Big. Hard bodied. Solid as a tank.

"Evenin', ladies. You two wrasslin' for fun?"

Buck.

In a split second, Buck had somehow tossed me behind him before grabbing Loretta in some kind of choke hold.

"I would've come in through the front door, 'cept I see you've got it jammed shut," he said, smiling. "Mind if I play, too?"

Before I knew it, Loretta was crying out and Buck had her handcuffed.

"Wait! How long have you been standing here?" I asked as Buck spun Loretta around.

"Long enough. And she's most definitely Lenny's twin sister, Loretta 'the Cleaver' Lemoni. We finally got a match on prints."

"Which means she probably didn't kill Lenny."

"Of course I didn't kill Lenny, you idiot!" huffed Loretta.

"Aw now, calling names isn't nice," said Buck with a smile. "But since you're a guest in our fair county, we won't take it personally. We'll just chalk it up to your Yank manners."

"So, you've just been standing there?" I asked, hands on my hips, "watching me fighting for my life?"

"Now, Babydoll, I wouldn't put it that way, exactly. Let's just say that I was weighing my options."

"Great," I said sarcastically. "And when Loretta 'the Cleaver' said I was 'toast,' you did nothing? Were you still 'weighing your options'? I could've been killed!"

Loretta spat at Buck's face.

"There y'all go with those nasty Yank manners again," he said.

Loretta kicked Buck in the shin. He ignored her and turned back to me.

"Babydoll, you're still here, aren't you? Full of piss and vinegar, too." He looked at Loretta, then back at me. "I'm not sure which one of you is worse."

"That's a terrible thing to say!"

"Although, I'm afraid I'm going to have to change your name to 'Hop-along,' Babydoll." Buck chuckled.

"Nice. Really nice," I said.

"Maybe we'll call you 'Eveready.' Or 'Timex.' I never saw anyone take such a lickin' and keep right on tickin'. You should be real proud." Buck smiled.

"Do I get a prize?"

"No, babe. And if you did, I'd have to take it away from you. You didn't play by the rules. I do recall someone tellin' you to stay home and lock your door. What happened? I thought we had a deal."

"First of all, I didn't know that we were playing a game. And second, I couldn't sleep. And since I've been the only suspect Eli Gibbit is looking at, I took a wild guess that your ace detective and his cronies might have missed something when they looked around up here. So, I came to look for myself," I sniffed.

"Did you find what you were lookin' for, Babydoll?"

"Very funny."

"Have you stopped to think what would've happened if I hadn't come lookin' for you?"

I ignored his question. "I hate you! How could you be so cruel! Standing there all that time watching me scared to death."

"It wasn't all that long. Really. And you looked real sexy, wavin' your little poker around."

Loretta snorted.

Tears started to fill my eyes as the realization set in that I could have been killed. Again.

"Now, don't go all soft on me. You know I had your back." Buck winked at me. With one hand on Loretta's shoulder, he whipped his phone out of his pocket with his other hand.

"You two need to get a room," Loretta said. "I don't have time for all this backwoods drama. I want my lawyer."

Loretta tried to wrench herself free from Buck's grip. I backed away. Buck must've done something, because Loretta whimpered and stood still again.

"Come on, darlin' we're off to the station, as they say." Buck punched a button on his phone. "But first, we'll pull out that little wedge of wood that you've got jammed in the door. Otherwise, Babydoll and I are gonna have to stuff you back outside through the bedroom window."

"I choose option number one," I said.

CHAPTER 44

Dolly was waiting outside the cabin.

"Dolly!" I cried out as she ran and jumped up on my leg. Then, I looked at Buck, who was leading handcuffed Loretta off the cabin porch. Buck had called for help, and soon a deputy would be there to meet us. "How did Dolly get here?"

"How do you think I found you so quickly," Buck said, looking at Dolly. "That dog has the nose of a bloodhound when it comes to you."

Fortunately, we hadn't needed to stuff Loretta out the bedroom window to get out of the cabin. Buck had reached up and pulled out the piece of wood Loretta had jammed in the cabin door. She'd put it there to keep people from entering her hideout. It'd given her the time she needed to slip into the secret cavern under the floor. She might have stayed hidden for as long as she liked if she hadn't run into the only two people who knew the cabin and the cavern better than she did.

I heard a beep, and Buck pulled his phone out of his pocket and punched a button.

"Yeah? What is it?"

Loretta tried to head toward the hatchet in the stump, ripping one arm from Buck's grasp. Still talking on his phone, Buck kicked one leg in the air and swept Loretta's legs right out from underneath her. She fell hard, like a sack of potatoes, to the ground.

"Hang on a minute," he said into the phone. He yanked Loretta her to her feet. "There's plenty more where that came from, sweetheart." Then he put the phone back to his ear. "Okay. Go on . . . Uh-huh . . . Got it . . . Yeah, she's here . . . Okay, put her on." Then he held out the phone to me. "It's for you."

"Me?"

"Your big sister. Be quick. There's something goin' down. Eli's got a blockade set up in the drive. My deputy can't get here. So, Miss Loretta and I gotta run, don't we, darlin'?" He looked at Loretta and grinned. Loretta spat again.

I took the phone. "Hello?"

"Eva, baby, it's me. Daphne. Where are y'all? Are y'all alright?"

"I'm fine. We're over at the cabin by the pond. Buck has Loretta. What's going on?"

"I've been so worried! Remember when I said I was going to wash the pair of boots someone left on the front porch?"

"Yes."

"Well, I did. I took them out in the yard, then I hosed them off."

"Okay . . ."

"Well, to be honest, I forgot about them. And then, tonight, I found them where I'd left them in the back next to the hose to dry. I felt terrible! What if someone had been missing their boots, I thought?"

"C'mon, Timex, we gotta start back," said Buck over my shoulder as he led Loretta toward the trail back home. "Talk and walk. Or hobble."

I shot Buck a dirty look and kept talking to Daphne as I shuffled in my flip-flops as quickly as I could behind Buck and Loretta. I felt like crap. My body was stiffening and my aches had intensified. My sore ribs were bad. Really bad. Not to mention everyplace the seat belt had been. Once I stopped moving, I'd feel even worse.

"Daphne, Buck needs his phone back soon," I said.

"So, I picked up the boots, you know," continued Daphne, "to put them back on the front porch. And one felt heavy. So, I looked inside. Y'all know what I found inside one of the boots?"

"What?"

"A gun!"

"What?"

"Yes! A pistol! Right there, stuffed down inside one of the boots. It was a Glock 19. What if one of the children had found it!"

"Where'd it come from?"

"No one knows. Precious thinks it's the gun y'all found in the bedroom upstairs! Anyway, Detective Gibbit and the deputies are here right now. They're going through the entire house. What if it's the gun that killed poor Leonard?"

Buck's phone beeped again.

"Daphne, I've got to go now. Buck's phone wants him."

"Alright, Eva. I'm worried about y'all. Please, be careful! And stay away from Buck!"

I handed Buck his phone. "Yeah," he said into the phone. Then, he grunted and hung up.

All of a sudden, Dolly made a U-turn and bolted into the woods, barking.

"Dolly!" I cried out. "Dolly! Come back!"

"Leave her, Babydoll. We gotta get back," Buck called out as he marched down the trail with Loretta. "You know I can't stop now."

"I'm not leaving Dolly!" I said.

"Like hell you aren't. She'll come home. C'mon, Eva. Keep up." Buck continued to hustle Loretta down the path toward home.

"Dolly!"

"Eva!"

"You lovebirds just work it out. I'll sit here and wait. I promise!" Loretta laughed wickedly.

"Shut up," said Buck.

"You go on ahead. I'll catch up," I said. "Dolly won't be long."

"Dammit, Eva. I can't come back and wait for you now," called Buck. "It isn't safe for you out here. This is not a game!"

"Sure it is. You said so, remember? I'll be fine," I called. "Dolly!"

"Eva!" I heard Buck curse as he marched Loretta around a corner and disappeared. "Eva!"

Then, I heard it. From deep in the forest, toward Greatwoods. The same noise I'd heard the other night before I'd tripped over Leonard. It was a low, rhythmic rumbling. Only this time, I recognized the sound for what it was.

"How stupid am I!" I said aloud. I set off in earnest. Hobbling as fast as I could in the direction of the sound, I cursed at my flip-flops, trying to grip them with my toes to keep them on in the thicket of wire grass. From farther away this time, I head Buck call my name. I ignored him.

"Dolly! No! Come here! Ouch!"

I stumbled along a narrow trail, probably a deer path, trying to follow the sound. Moving deeper into the woods, I called for Dolly and stopped to listen every few minutes. Then, somehow, I lost the trail. A few minutes later, I looked around and it was dark. Really dark. And everything looked the same. Flat land. Acres and acres of wire grass under tall, spindly pine trees. The night creatures were screeching like mad. Cicadas, frogs, bats . . . you name it. They were having a party.

"Dolly?"

Nothing.

I heard the noise again. I spun around. The moon popped out. Finally, I saw it. Loping between the trees, heading right toward me, was a huge chestnut horse with a big, white blaze.

Then, just a few feet in front of me, I heard the unmistakable ratcheting of an old-style rifle as the shell casing hit the ground and a new shell popped up. Then, the recocking as a shadowy figure jumped up out of the wire grass.

I was in the air, diving toward the man, when his rifle went off.

CHAPTER 45

I heard the horse gallop away. Underneath me, the man hiccupped.

"Aww, shoot!" he said. I recognized the voice.

I jumped up and snatched the rifle from his hand. "Mister Beasley, what are you doing out here?" I cried. "You know, you could've killed someone!"

"Whoz dat?" slurred Boone Beasley. "Whoz out there? I gotta gun, ya know!"

"Mister Beasley, it's me. Eva Knox. Robert Knox's daughter. I was at your apartment today. Remember? With your check from my sister, Daphne Bouvier?"

"Ohhh, ye-ahhhh. I remember you. Whacha'll doin' out here, pretty lady? Say, aren't you the gal that killed that poor fellow workin' for Miss Daphne? What was his name? He was a Yank, I think. Poor bastard. Y'all ain't gonna shoot me too are ya?"

"I'm out for a walk, Mister Beasley. What are you doing out here? Surely you're not hunting?"

"Damn right, I'm huntin'! And y'all just let the biggest

whitetail I ever seen git away! Damn y'all, girl! You're as much a pain in the ass as your old man!"

"That wasn't a buck, Mister Beasley. It was a horse. And Daddy? What'd he do?"

"I been huntin' these woods *fer* years. Dammit. These are some of the best huntin' grounds in the county. Got some of my best meat out here. And your pa, he's gone an' spoiled it all!"

"Meat? You mean to sell? You've been poaching our land for meat? And then selling it?" My heart sank. My family had purchased meat from Boone Beasley for decades. "How could you do such a thing?" My ribs were hurting real bad. Throwing myself onto Boone Beasley had worsened the pain.

"It ain't easy bein' a butcher these days, ya know! Everyone wants 'grass fed,' 'organic,' 'free-range'! That stuff is pricey as hell, and I ain't got the cash or the business for it. That's why I source stuff myself. Been makin' ends meet by sellin' wild game and my fresh breakfast sausages. The pork's been comin' from the wild boar that's been runnin' though these parts."

"Wild boar?" I shuddered. As far as I knew, the meat from wild boar tasted like . . . sweat. Not at all desirable for consumption.

"Yep. If the hog ain't been eatin' carrion or too many pine tree roots, I can carve off the fat, remove the loins, and eat 'em just like deer loins. And I make a roast outta each back leg. Ribs go on the grill for a couple hours. Just baste 'em and cook 'em low and slow. I grind the rest and use my special seasonin' fer breakfast sausage. My sausage is an eighty-five to fifteen lean-to-fat ratio; that'd be leaner than anything folks can git 'round these parts. Customers eat 'em up."

Boone Beasley reached into his pocket, pulled out a flask, untwisted the top, and took a swig. Then another.

"Everything was goin' fine until that fellow from outta town next door put up a big fence. Except fer one or two spots, he's got the entire Greatwoods place surrounded. I used to hunt all over that place. This one, too. And where the feller ain't got fencing, he got little *cam-er-ahhs* in the trees. I seen 'em, watchin' me. I don't go there no more."

Buck took another swig.

"And what does my dad have to do with all this?"

"Your pa went and cleared one hundred acres of the best huntin' grounds I'd ever known. Now, he's usin' it for his blasted olive trees. Whoever heard of olive trees in Georgia! It's gittin' so a feller cain't do a decent days huntin' no more. Damn! And now, you just let the finest buck I ever saw git away. Double damn." Boone Beasley took another swig from his flask.

"Mister Beasley, like I said before, that was not a buck you were aiming at. It was a horse."

"Horse? Whatchyou talkin' bout, young lady? There ain't no wild horses 'round these parts. I'dda seen 'em."

"Believe me, Mister Beasley, it was a horse. And I've got a good idea who . . ."

I heard the hoofbeats again. They were trotting. Closer. The horse snorted from somewhere nearby. I looked into the darkness and tried to see. Then, from behind me, I heard the voice.

"Ye folks lose a round tonight?"

I spun around, still holding Boone Beasley's old rifle.

And there he was.

Ian Collier. Sitting high above us, on a great blaze-faced chestnut mare. Ian had no saddle. No bridle. There was just a halter over the mare's head and a lead line that led to Ian's hand. And the mare was just as calm and obedient as she could be. With a scorching look, Ian tossed a bullet to the ground by my feet.

"Better luck next time. I'm afraid ye missed me by just a meter or so."

CHAPTER 46

Ian jumped off the mare. "Eva Knox, I never expected to find it's been *ye* out here." He sounded like something between disappointed and angry. I couldn't tell.

"I . . . uh . . . I was looking for Dolly when I stumbled on Mister Beasley here. I'm afraid he'd mistaken your mare for a big whitetail buck. The gun went off when I tackled him. I'm sorry. I had no idea anyone else was in the woods."

"Tackled him?" Ian looked surprised.

"Damn girl flew outta nowhere!" cried Boone Beasley. "Knocked the wind clear outta me just when I had that buck in my sights! Biggest whitetail I ever seen, too!" He took another swig from his flask. "Ahhhh. Dammit. Buck got away, he did."

Slowly, a smile made its way across Ian Collier's face and his eyes twinkled mischievously.

"Good going, lass. Looks like I owe ye one." Ian chuckled and put an arm around my shoulders, giving me a squeeze and a peck on my forehead. "You see, Kyrie here is my pride and joy." He patted the great mare on the neck.

"Kyrie? That's the mare's name?" The back of my neck was hot. Something somersaulted deep inside me.

"Aye. It's short for Valkyrie."

Kyrie put her huge head down, and Ian stroked the big mare's face. Boone Beasley hiccupped.

"Except she's a bit of an escape artist and likes to take 'erself for evening jaunts. She seems to enjoy it and always comes back to her stall in a couple of hours, so I'd not worried about it much until lately, when I heard someone hunting over here. Kyrie knows the secret trail out of Greatwoods."

If only I'd known the "secret trail" out of Greatwoods, I thought. Would've saved me from fighting the barbed wire.

"Is that what happened the other night?" I asked. "When you found me?"

"Not exactly. I'd tacked up Kyrie and come out lookin' for a poacher after I heard shots. Had him on the run, too, didn't we, Kyrie? Then, when I heard the lightning strike and smelled the smoke, I came over here lookin' to see what happened—checkin' to make sure there wasn't a fire."

"And there would've been a big one, if it hadn't been for you," I said.

"Aye. Scots luck, that's all."

"And you took me back to Greatwoods on Kyrie?"

"Aye. I did. Ye don't remember?"

"No. I don't remember anything about that night. Not after I tripped over . . . well . . . not after the lightning."

I still hadn't figured out the car wash part, so I chalked it up to being a dream. And it would stay a dream, at least until I was able to get it straight in my mind.

"Aye, I'm sorry, lass," said Ian. His eyes went all soft.

Boone Beasley belched.

"So, Mister Beasley," said Ian, "is it you who've been out here all these nights hauntin' the wood folk?"

Boone Beasley didn't answer. Sitting on the ground, he just hiccupped and belched again. So, I explained to Ian all that Boone Beasley told me, about how he'd hunted illegally for years.

"That makes sense," said Ian. "Yer father told me he was sure someone was huntin' out here. I told him I'd keep an eye out. Thanks for saving Kyrie. I owe ye."

"Let's just say we're even," I laughed.

Celtic music thumped and quickened in my head.

CHAPTER 47

My suspect list was shrinking by the hour. It hadn't been
Loretta who killed Leonard. And I couldn't believe it'd been
Ian, either. After Ian and I sorted it all out, it appeared that
although he'd been out and about in the woods that night, it
hadn't been Boone Beasley he'd heard. The gun was all
wrong, and Ian was pretty sure Boone had been hunting
nearer Greatwoods Monday night, because Ian had found
shell casings on Tuesday. And if I believed him, Ian assured
me that his employee Lurch was not my man, either. In fact,
he'd actually laughed when I mentioned it. Seems Lurch had
had the night off and was at a ballroom dance class somewhere. It was all easily corroborated.

So, it was looking like my wise guy visitors, Sal and
Guido, were at the top of the suspect list again. Seems like
while their wives were sipping peach whiskey in the living
room at the big house, they'd been out and about stalking
mobsters. Hopefully, Detective Gibbit had already tied the
gun Daphne found in the boot to the gangsters.

"Sure ye don't want a lift, lassie?" asked Ian with a smile.
He was still wearing the vest and pink shirt he'd had on

earlier. He bent down to pick up Boone's flask from the ground, and I decided that in his faded Wrangler jeans, Ian looked pretty awesome from every angle. The sultry tribal music of Celtic pipes, fiddle, flute, and drums rocked on in my head.

"I'll put you up on Kyrie while Mister Beasley and I hoof it alongside the mare. It's hardly proper for ye to be out alone late at night like this," said Ian. He was talking, but I was staring hopelessly at his green eyes, slender waist, and broad shoulders. I was hearing nothing but my Celtic music, and the tempo was quickening. I watched Ian's strong, slender fingers stroking Kyrie's neck.

"Eva?"

Boone Beasley hiccupped from somewhere behind me.

"Eva?" said Ian, again.

"Oh, right. Sorry," I said. "I was thinking."

"Were ye now?" Ian raised his eyebrows and flashed a wicked smile. "Aye, something's put a twinkle in your eye."

I blushed.

The plan was for Ian and Boone to head to Greatwoods, where Ian would put up Boone for the night while he slept off the alcohol. In the morning, Ian would send Lurch out to find Boone's truck, which was stashed somewhere in the woods, just off the main road. After that, Ian said he'd contact my dad and they'd decide together how to handle what Boone had done. Ian said he thought that maybe some time in a decent rehab center, rather than a fine or jail, would do Boone Beasley the most good. And he even talked about paying for it. Which only made the mystery of Ian Collier more mysterious.

What the heck does this guy do?

Anyway, I knew that if Ian and Boone walked me home, it would take them as much as forty-five extra minutes to get where they were headed. And none of us were sure that Boone could last that long. Already, Boone had admitted that it wasn't unusual for him to pass out during his nighttime hunting forays. So, I argued for several minutes with Ian about how I'd get home.

"I'll make it fine on my own," I said. "Besides, after the day I've had, what else could possibly go wrong?"

"Ye got a point there, lass. Although, it's still not right, leaving ye out here . . . all alone."

"How about a compromise?" I asked. "I admit, I'm a little turned around right now. If you wouldn't mind leading me back to the main trail, I'll be able to get back on my own from there."

Against Ian's "better judgment," compromise is what we ended up doing. Ian slid his hand under my raised foot and gave me a leg up on the mare's back, and I grabbed the end of Kyrie's mane. Like a spoiled princess, I rode on Kyrie bareback as Ian led us from the ground. Although I'd ridden as a girl, it had been years since I'd been on a horse. Normally, I'd have been in seventh heaven, riding a beautiful mare like Kyrie. However, my mind was so preoccupied with everything that had transpired, I barely noticed the great creature, all powerful and soft, moving beneath me.

Ian kept hold of the rifle as Boone Beasley dragged himself along behind us. We went that way for about ten or fifteen minutes, until we got to a spot in the woods where I recognized the trail. Then, I dismounted to walk—or hobble, as Buck would've said—back home for the remaining ten or fifteen minutes that it would take to get there. Ian objected to leaving me, but I insisted that I would be fine. After all, I was just a few minutes from home, and Boone Beasley was losing steam fast. Ian grabbed a big stick, snapped it into just the right length to make a cane and handed it to me.

"There ye go, lass. Watch yer step and have someone call me when ye get back home safe. Yer sister Daphne has my number."

"Thanks." Daphne works fast, I thought. Already, she had the man's number. I'd been right about her thinking Ian Collier was husband material. I chuckled to myself.

I turned and headed down the trail while Ian hoisted Boone, them himself up onto Kyrie. They stood and watched me until I rounded the first corner before I heard them canter off in the other direction. All was looking good.

That is, until five or ten minutes later when I ran into trouble.

Sal appeared first, huffing and puffing, as he jogged around a corner on the trail.

"Well, lookee who we found here, Guido!" Out of breath, he huffed with a big sneer before accelerating and lunging toward me.

"Oh yeah, boss! Lookit who we found!" wheezed Guido as he chugged up the path.

"Help!" I turned, tossed the stick and moved as fast as I could, off the trail into the woods. I yelled again.

"Call . . . all . . . ya want . . . Cupcake!" taunted Sal as he huffed behind me. "No one's . . . gonna hear ya. Way . . . out . . . here. They're all inside . . . back at the house . . . tearing it up . . . By the time . . . they quit . . . you'll be long . . . gone. So will we."

"So . . . will . . . we!" repeated Guido from farther back.

Despite the fact that he sounded quite tired, Sal wasn't tired enough. He was only about ten feet behind me. I needed to move faster.

I was sure my quota for adrenaline had been used up for the day. Still, I tried to speed up. I imagined myself flying over the ground, as I zigzagged recklessly between the trees. Speed was all I cared about. I never even noticed when my stupid flip-flops fell off my feet. And I didn't feel any of the briars scratching and tearing at my feet and ankles. After a minute of brainless, frantic crashing through the wire grass, I couldn't hear Sal's wheezing breaths and thumping footfalls. I was making progress. Even injured as I was, I'd pulled away.

Then, I stepped into nothingness.

And fell.

Deep into the ground.

CHAPTER 48

Hidden from above by darkness and wire grass, the pit in the woods was no less than six feet deep and at least as long, by about three feet wide.

It was an open grave.

At the bottom of the grave, I'd landed face-first into the dirt next to one of our missing shovels from home—one of the ones that I remembered Daphne and the twins had been looking for earlier in the day. I'd found the other one at the bottom of the pond. Sal's crashing and wheezing, from somewhere in the woods above me, was coming closer. I grabbed the shovel and scrambled to my feet, pressing myself back against the short wall of the coffin-sized pit. Maybe he wouldn't see me, I thought. Better still, maybe he wouldn't see the pit and he'd run right by.

"C'mon, Cupcake, don't be hiding!" Sal huffed. His steps pounded the ground as he tore through the wire grass. It sounded like he'd almost reached the grave. Would he just pull out a gun and shoot me? I heard him pick up his pace. "Cup-caaake!" he teased. "We're gonna have a real good time to-nighhhhh-yaaa . . . !"

Sal Malagutti tumbled down into the hole, right in front of me. He landed standing on his feet. And he didn't seem too fazed by the fall. In fact, the very moment he realized I was there, he charged at me.

"Oh yeah! I'm havin' me my piece of cupcake tonight!" Sal said with a lecherous grin.

As burly hands forcefully grabbed my neck and shoulders, he pressed himself into me—all of him. His garlicky breath huffed in my face. I felt his unshaven face against mine. His nasty, massive body crushed me against the dirt wall of the grave.

I looked past Sal and threw myself back against the dirt behind me. "Copperhead!"

Sal hesitated. And when he tilted his head just a bit to look back and check for the snake that I'd pretended was behind him, it was my moment.

Pinned flat, with all the force I could muster, I raised up my knee between his beefy thighs. With all my might, I jabbed my knee fast and hard into his groin. I must've practiced it a hundred times in my head since he'd first threatened me in the cottage. As he cried out and staggered back, clutching himself, I tried to get away from the wall as I grabbed the shovel. Before Sal had time to lunge at me again, I closed my eyes and whacked him on the head as hard as I could.

Sal Malagutti crumpled in front of me and didn't move.

I stood still, shaking, pinned between Sal at my feet and the short wall of the grave behind me. Then, up above, I heard Guido, headed in the same direction.

"Oh my God!"

I was having trouble breathing; my rib felt broken and, exhausted as I was, I was having trouble thinking on my feet. There wasn't enough left of me to hold up against another attack.

"Boss? You gotcha some o' that cupcake cutie?" called Guido between his huffs and puffs above us. Thrashing and wheezing through the wire grass, I could hear him getting closer.

"I want some of that cupcake, too . . . Hey? . . . You alright? Boss? Where are ya?" He coughed and wheezed some more as he neared the grave.

He was closer still.

Almost on top of us. I held my breath. Shaking.

"Boss?"

And wouldn't you know it? Guido let out a yelp and tumbled down into the grave, landing right on top of Sal in front of me. Only, I didn't have to whack him with the shovel. He just started hollering about how he'd broken his leg.

Then, off in the distance, I heard Dolly barking.

CHAPTER 49

I'd never been so glad to hear a barking dog in all my life. Just a minute later, Buck reached down into the grave and, with one muscled arm, hauled me out and away from wailing Guido, who was going on and on about his broken leg. Sal was stirring awake in the bottom of the pit underneath his blubbering buddy.

"Aw," said Buck softly. "We gotta stop meetin' like this, Babydoll."

I was sobbing. I couldn't help it. Scared out of my wits, I was humbled and angry at having been so helpless.

"Talk about havin' one foot in the grave!" joked Buck. "Looks like you jumped in with both feet, Timex!"

He put a big arm around me and hugged me as I heaved and sobbed uncontrollably. I could barely breathe with my achy rib; still, I didn't care. Buck felt just as warm and safe as he had eighteen years ago. Only he was bigger, stronger now. He held me close and snuggled his head down next to mine.

"Eva? Y'all alright?" he whispered. "Did they hurt you?"

With two hands, he tried to pull my head away to look at my face, but I buried it deeper into his chest, shaking my head and clutching onto his shirt. I didn't want him to see me. Still, I didn't seem able to let go. He wrapped his arms around me and held me as I wept.

Finally, Dolly jumped up on my leg and whimpered.

"Someone's tryin' to get your attention," whispered Buck. He slowly released me. Before he could look at my tearstained, blotchy face, I bent down to Dolly.

"Hey, Dolly girl, what ya got there?" I wiped my eyes and hugged Dolly before she wriggled free and licked my face.

"Oh shoot!" I jumped up, grabbing my front pocket. "The ring! I can't feel the ring!" I shoved my hand in my pocket and felt around for Pep's ring. "Oh. Phew! It's here." I pulled out Pep's skull ring and studied it.

"What's that?"

"It's Pep's. I found it in the cabin."

Buck raised his eyebrows. "The cabin we were in earlier?"

"Yes. The same one your detective and his cracker-jack crew checked so thoroughly." I rolled my eyes. "I think Billy might have given this to Leonard to pay off a gambling debt. I've been worried that Billy might have killed Leonard over it."

"You lost me, Babydoll."

"Well, I suppose I should've mentioned it earlier—but it was family and all."

"You mean, there's *more* you haven't told me?"

I sighed. "Pep told me that Billy had gone out on the night of the murder. She thought he might have gone gambling. And initially, I was concerned that he might have had something to do with all this murder business. Still, he's family. So, I didn't say anything. Later, I figured out that he might be having an affair."

"An affair?"

"He made a Pooty call that night. At least I thought so,

until I found Pep's ring. Now, I don't know what to think. Maybe he was gambling in the cabin."

"A 'Pooty call'? You mean he's been doin' Pooty Chitty?"

I shrugged. Buck started chuckling.

"It isn't funny! Pep's my sister, and she deserves better," I sobbed.

"I'm not laughing at Pep. You're right. She does deserve better. Billy's a cad. I'm laughing at your 'Pooty call.'" Buck stopped for a moment. Then he chuckled again and said, "I've always called it a 'Pooty Chitty Bang Bang.'"

I looked up at Buck. His eyes twinkled mischievously, and his dimpled smile was broad.

"Omigosh! That's terrible! Besides, why would you ever say such a thing? Unless . . ." I looked at Buck and frowned. "You? And Pooty?" My mouth dropped open.

Buck shook his head. "Forget it. Let's just say Pooty has a rep for having been around the block. More than a few times."

"Well, you would know, now, wouldn't you?"

"Thatta girl, Babydoll. See, you're feelin' better already."

"Is someone gonna help me!" Guido yelled from the grave. "I'm gonna *die*!"

Buck pointed to a boulder about thirty feet away. "Eva, can you walk?"

I nodded.

"Help!" Guido wailed from the pit.

"Go sit over there, please. And don't move." He watched me scuffle to the boulder as he punched a button on his phone and stepped back to the grave. "Thanks for dropping in, boys," he said to Sal and Guido. He mumbled something into his cell phone.

I sat numb on the boulder, trying to compose myself, while Buck stood at the edge of the pit, sometimes on his phone, sometimes with his arms folded, as Guido wailed and blubbered about his leg and the fact that he'd heard Sal mumble something about a copperhead being in the pit.

After several minutes, Buck turned to me and said,

"Don't worry, Eva. Billy's a cad and a cardsharp. He's no killer."

I just nodded. Then, a minute or so later, Buck said, "Give me your phone number."

"What?"

"I said, give me your phone number. I'm callin' you."

"But I'm not there. I mean, the phone's not here. You know what I mean. I can't answer. I don't know where my phone is."

"I know that, Babydoll. I'm just callin' so you'll have my number."

"I don't need your number."

"Yes. You do."

"I won't call."

"Yes. You will. Unless you want to have another night like this."

"I'll never have another night like this." I waited a beat. "Besides, if I call, what if Debi answers?"

"She won't."

"Don't bet on it."

Buck chuckled. "No one knows this number 'cept a couple of my deputies."

"I bet Debi has it."

Buck didn't answer.

"And anyway, like I said, I don't need your number."

Buck shook his head and walked over to me on the rock.

"Girl, I never had to work so hard to get a number in my life. I'm tryin' to keep you safe. That's all. Give it up, Eva." He put his hand on my shoulder.

I mumbled the number.

"Now, I want you to carry your phone. And I want you to call me when you get into trouble. Lord knows, you will. This was too close for comfort."

"I won't get into trouble."

"Yes. You will, Babydoll. You're a magnet for disaster. And I'm not sure how many lickin's like this you can take before you stop tickin'. No one can keep this up."

"Keep what up?"

"This attraction to danger that you have. You're like a bug at night chasin' the light. Honestly, I'm not sure how you managed to keep landing on your feet these past few days without gettin' yourself killed."

"Maybe I'm special."

"Well, if that's what it is, 'special' nearly put you in your grave, Babydoll. Permanently. Next time, at the first whiff of trouble, I want you to call. It's not hard; you just push the little button. Like this, see?" Buck smiled teasingly as he held up his phone and demonstrated. "I'll answer."

"Fine."

"Fine? What does that mean, Babydoll?"

"I will."

"I will, what?"

"I will carry my phone."

"And?"

"And I will call you when I get into trouble. Except, I won't."

"You will, Babydoll. A leopard can't change her spots."

Suddenly, Guido's blubbering over in the grave was drowned out by the deafening sounds of fast Honda utility ATVs carrying deputies. They were followed by a slower, bigger John Deere Gator painted in camo colors. A uniformed deputy drove while Detective Gibbit, wearing a Backstreet Boys tee shirt, sat on the passenger side. Later, an even bigger orange four-seat Kubota with a dump bed in back mashed its way through the wire grass and pulled up next to the grave. Deputies and EMTs were running through the woods, people were shouting orders, taking out equipment, flashing spotlights, and, eventually, everyone gathered around Buck and the grave with the gangsters.

No one seemed to notice Dolly and me, and I was grateful to stay out of the fray, off to the side on my rock. Once Guido, and then Sal, had been pulled out from the grave and handcuffed—Guido with a group of EMTs working around his leg, Sal with EMTs taking his pulse and flashing little lights in his eyes—I hobbled over a little closer to the group, to listen.

"This is a mistake!" cried Sal, full of his usual vigor again. "We flew down from New York to celebrate Judi and my's thirtieth wedding anniversary! We're just vacationing."

"And how come you came here? To the Knox place?" asked Detective Gibbit. Along with his Backstreet Boys shirt, he wore baggy, plaid Bermuda shorts that hung below his knees and lime green plastic Crocs with black socks.

"Eli, this isn't the time," said Buck. "We'll do this down at the station."

"No! Wait! This is all a setup!" said Sal. "That crazy runaway bitch set up this whole thing!"

"Explain," said Detective Gibbit. "And we know *all about* you being wise guys."

I saw Buck grimace before he put a hand to his face. In that one moment, I realized Buck shared my opinion regarding Detective Gibbit. Well, that was something, I thought.

"Monday morning, Guido and I met up with the guide here to go fishing. Only the guide turns out to be Lenny from the family back up in Boston. I says, 'Lenny, what are you doing here?' And Lenny says, 'What a coincidence,' that Guido and I should turn up in Georgia, right where he's got his new job. Right then and there, I figure he's scoping out the place for a business acquisition."

"That true, Mister Gambini?" asked Detective Gibbit.

"Sure," said Guido. "Whatever the boss says. Owweee! Watch it there! My leg!"

"Either of you folks know who hit Miss Loretta Lemoni—formerly known as Loretta Cook—in the head? And any of you know what might have happened to the brake line in her car?"

"That was her car? Shoot. I thought it was Lenny's car."

"Stick a glove in it, Guido," said Sal.

"You folks decide to make something look like an accident?" asked the detective.

"This here, this was gonna be *our* olive farm. We thought of it first," said Guido. "Owww!"

"Jesus, Guido, would ya shut up? If it weren't already broken, I'd go and break your leg for ya!"

CHAPTER 50

"Morning, everyone!" I slipped out of Daphne's Wellies and padded barefoot across the kitchen floor over to the coffee-maker. "Is there coffee?"

"Hey, girl!" said Pep. She was sitting on the red kitchen counter, snacking on some packaged pork rinds, wearing a lacy black choker, strappy black dress with a fitted top and tulle skirt, and black high-top basketball sneakers.

"Pep, I have something for you." I reached into my pocket, pulled out the skull ring, and put it in her hand.

"Hey, thanks, hon! But how did . . . Where did you get this?" Pep looked at me intently.

"I found it on the ground."

I hadn't decided how I was going to handle what I thought knew about Billy. I wasn't sure if I could trust my instincts. Especially when it came to men. Although I wanted to tell Pep about Pooty and where I'd found Pep's gold ring, I needed time to sort though the facts. Besides, I knew Pep wanted her marriage to work and I didn't want to be the reason it didn't. I decided to hold off saying anything, for the time being anyway.

"Eva, dear, it's twenty minutes past noon," said Daphne over by the sink. "The coffee's been gone for hours. Let me make a fresh pot." Her hair was loose around her shoulders. She wore a white sleeveless linen blouse over creamy silk capri pants and a pair of Tory Burch sandals. Gold earrings, each shaped like a little Buddha, complemented her gold bangle bracelet.

"Thanks," I said. I pulled out a chair at the kitchen table and dropped into it. I was back in my cutoffs and a plain white tee.

"And, my, my! Don't you look better today," continued Daphne. "Even all scratched and bruised as you are. Eva, you've got a sparkle in your eyes that I haven't seen in years. A little family, some down-home excitement, and a few hours of sleep has done you a *world* of good!" Daphne dumped a pile of coffee beans in the grinder and flipped the switch.

"I'd say it's on account of a little Buck . . ." teased Pep.

Daphne scowled at Pep.

I ignored Pep's comment. "I feel like I've been hit by a car . . . Oh, wait, I was!"

"Do you have much bruising, Eva?" asked Daphne as she dumped the coffee grinds into the coffeemaker.

"That's a dumb question, Daph," said Pep. "Look at her legs. And I can see some up near her collarbone. Does it hurt much?" asked Pep.

"Everywhere the seat belt was. And my arms, shoulders, and back are sore. But the EMTs said to expect it. And none of it is as bad as my ribs. I'm just glad to be alive, that's all."

"Amen to that!" called Precious as she came in from the back door. "Whew-wee! It's hotter out there today than butter on a biscuit! Miss Daphne, I got the roast you asked for, and some country-style ribs. The grocery store was havin' a special."

Wearing a hot pink blouse over fitted white and pink polka dot capris, Precious marched in lime green Louboutins to the counter, where she began unloading packages of food.

"What? Not using Boone Beasley anymore?" I chuckled.

"What y'all shared with us last night about that man is positively stomach turning. I can't think about it anymore," said Daphne. "And I tossed the sausages he brought over. To think . . . we'd been eatin' wild boar!"

"That just plum curdles my guts," said Precious. "My grandpappy made us eat wild boar once. It smelled and tasted like piss." Precious shuddered.

I laughed. I'd have laughed harder, but my insides were killing me. If it weren't for ibuprofen, I'd never have made it out of bed.

"Hey, if Boone's wild boar tasted good enough to eat, then I don't see the problem," said Pep. "When he gets out of rehab, he should market his secret spice. He'll be rich in no time."

"You see, Pepper-Leigh? It's just like I told you. Working at that bar has not only tainted your sensibilities, it's adulterated your senses as well." Daphne poured water into the coffeemaker and snapped on the switch.

Pep rolled her eyes. "Hey, Precious, are there any more blueberry scones? I'm starving."

"If you wait thirty minutes, hon, I'm whippin' up a special picnic lunch for the New York ladies after they get back from the *po-leece* station. I can make you a sandwich and some nibblies."

"Sounds good!"

"Oh, that reminds me," said Daphne. "I need to pull some sparkling wine from the basement to send with the ladies. It's the least we can do, given their husbands are in the slammer, and all."

"Daph, did you say, 'slammer'? Really? And you're giving me a hard time about *my* lingo?"

"Miss Daphne's been readin' some of my mystery books, ain't ya, hon?" Precious smiled.

Daphne opened her mouth but decided instead not to say anything.

"Speaking of mysteries, anyone heard any more news about last night?" I asked.

"I was goin' to ask you that," said Pep.

"I slept all morning and haven't heard a thing. Although, I haven't seen my phone in days, so I wouldn't even know if anyone is trying to reach me with any news."

"Tilly Beekerspat said the two mob guys, Sal and Guido, are gettin' booked this morning."

"Did they figure out what happened?" Pep asked.

"The detective says they had Lenny dig his own grave, 'cept he got away and almost to the olive grove before they caught up with him and took him out. Then, Miss Eva and the lightning showed up before they could finish the job and dump the body in the grave."

"That sort of makes sense," I said. "Buck told me they call Sal Malagutti "the Gravedigger.""

"Oh! We need a plaque to hang over the bed upstairs that reads GRAVEDIGGER SLEPT HERE," teased Pep.

Daphne wrinkled her nose. "Pepper-Leigh, must you be so uncouth?"

"Yes."

Daphne shook her head before she looked at me and said, "Eva, dear, don't you think you should carry a phone with you? After all, it does seem that if you'd had your phone with you last night, you could have called for help. More than once. You could've been killed by those thugs!"

"Yeah, you owe Dolly big-time. And Buck, too," said Pep.

"I don't think you owe Buck Tanner anything. However, I'd say that if you owe anyone, you owe our wonderful neighbor, Ian Collier," said Daphne. "He's *such* a gentleman. If he hadn't called Buck Tanner because he was worried about leavin' you out in the woods last night, who knows what may have happened when those two killers came running up to you."

"What'd the men do? Hop outta their car comin' down the drive and run into the woods when they saw the *po-leece* waitin' for 'em here?" asked Precious.

"That's what I heard," said Pep. "Then, when they ran into Eva in the woods, the Malagutti thug thought he could grab her and use her as a hostage to negotiate his way out of Abundance."

"Eva, you really need to carry your phone." Daphne sounded stern.

"The only people calling me are reporters looking for runaway bride dirt. I hate my phone."

Daphne sighed. "You're gettin' to be kind of a hammer-head, Eva. Like Daddy. He should be back later today, by the way. He's been tryin' to call y'all on your phone. And he was glad to hear you're alright. Also, he was interested to know about how the salt got into the olive grove. They'd figured out at the lab that there was salt in the soil; still, they couldn't figure out how it got there."

"So," I asked, "now that their husbands are in the can, how long are the ladies from New York staying on?"

"Seems like they'll be here for at least another few days," said Daphne. "Until formal charges are brought against their husbands for Leonard's murder and attempted kidnapping and for assaulting you. My friend Sadie Truewater—she's in my book club and volunteers with adult protective services down at the station, maybe you met her last night? Anyway, she told me this morning that folks at the station were all talkin' about how Mister Malagutti's fingerprints were on the gun that killed Leonard. And it was the Glock 19, the one I found in the boots. It seems likely that it's the same gun that you ladies found under the bed. Anyhoo, Detective Gibbit has a whole laundry list of stuff he wants to charge them with. And he's goin' after that nasty Loretta, too. I'm disappointed in myself for lettin' the whole lot of 'em stay here."

"Yeah, hopefully ol' Eli can make everything stick," said Pep.

"If anyone can make charges stick, that ol' weasel can," said Precious. "That fellow's slicker than deer guts on a skinnin' knife."

"Well, if y'all ask me, Eva, you should press charges against Debi Dicer as well. What she did to you here at the Chamber of Commerce meetin' was a travesty. What kind of a grown woman behaves that way?"

"A jealous one," smirked Pep. She winked at me.

"I'm sorry that I ruined your party, Daphne."

"Well, at least, the whole scene generated some publicity for us."

"You've all generated enough badass news about yourselves to last weeks!" chortled Precious.

"Debi's so stuck-up, she'd drown in a rainstorm," said Pep. "Hooking up with Buck has only made her worse. The woman thinks she's plumb invincible."

"Ain't nothing more annoyin' than a biggity woman with her feathers ruffled," said Precious.

"She's got nothing to be ruffled about," I said. "This silly jealousy thing is all on her."

"I certainly hope so, Eva." huffed Daphne. "Y'all washed your hands of Buck Tanner years ago! And quite wisely, I might add."

"Still, I don't know what Buck sees in her," I said.

"I hear Debi's as limber as a wet dishrag," Pep said brightly.

"Pepper-Leigh!"

"Well, it's true. Y'all wouldn't believe the things folks say at the bar. I hear all kinds of stuff."

"If you ask me, the two of 'em are well deservin' of each other," said Daphne. "The perfect couple. Good riddance to the both of 'em from the single, upstandin' folks of Abundance."

"Speaking of which, I heard Debi can do it standin' up as well," smirked Pep.

"Pepper-Leigh!" scolded Daphne. Precious tittered as she laid out her sandwich ingredients.

"So, Pep," I asked, "what do they say about Ian Collier down at the Roadhouse?"

"Ian? Oh, let's see . . . Actually, folks don't know what to make of him, mostly. Not many folks have ever seen him in person, and most just wonder where he got all his money."

"That gorgeous man can do just about anything he wants," sighed Daphne. "I bet he'd make a wonderful husband and father."

"And by coincidence, you just happen to have an instant family for him. Right? Ha!" laughed Pep.

"Well, I hate to burst your bubble, but I ain't seein' that happening," said Precious.

"Precious, what's the big secret about Ian Collier? Are you gonna fill us in?" asked Pep.

"Pep, I tried that . . . It's no use," I said.

"Well, y'all are right about one thing. Mister Collier's got enough money to burn a wet mule," said Precious. "But it's like Sunshine says. Mister Collier pays me a lot of money to do my job, run his household, and keep my mouth shut. And that's what I intend to keep doin'. Still, to save you the trouble, Miss Daphne, and I mean no offense, he ain't gonna be addin' on any family."

"I see. A confirmed bachelor?"

"Daph, did he show up to the Chamber of Commerce meeting yesterday?"

Precious laughed. "*My* Mister Collier?"

"No, I'm afraid not, Eva. We'll just have to keep tryin' to get the man out and about. With all that money, it'd be nice to see him become active in our little community."

"Now, Precious," said Pep, "don't y'all go thinkin' that my sister has dropped her designs on your boss just because y'all told her to do so."

Precious shook her head and smiled. Daphne threw a disparaging look toward Pep.

"With no help from Precious, it looks like we'll just have to embrace the mystery of Ian Collier," I said. "At least for now." I was eager to find out more about him for myself. But, of course, there was no need to let anyone in on my plans.

"Well, anyhoo, I'm delighted Mister Collier has allowed for you to be here, Precious. Do you know how much longer you'll be able to help us out?"

"Long as I like, I reckon."

"Really!" said Daphne, surprised.

"Greatwoods is a big place and all, but to tell you the

truth, it gets lonely over there. And day to day, I ain't got much to do since I'm in charge. We got other folks to do nitty-gritty stuff."

"Oh. I see," said Daphne.

"This place is gooder'n grits over here. So, I'm plannin' on stickin' around as long as you'll have me." Precious chuckled. "If things get any better over here, I may have to hire someone to help me enjoy it all!"

"Well, in that case, hurry up with my sandwich, Miss Precious," said Pep, laughing. "I'm so hungry I could eat a bear!"

CHAPTER 51

The good thing about farm living was that there were always all sorts of useful vehicles around. Tractors, trucks, ATVs . . . whatever was needed to do the job at hand. And on that particular sunny day, I was happy about Daddy's many farm vehicles for two reasons. First, I had no car of my own. The BMW was totaled. Moreover, because I'd forgotten to pay my insurance and I was flat broke, prospects for a new replacement car were not looking good. So, for the foreseeable future, if I needed to drive to town—or anywhere off the plantation—I'd need to get a ride or borrow a vehicle.

The second reason I was grateful for Daddy's motor vehicles was that he owned a Kubota RTV utility vehicle—kind of like a mini two-seater jeep, with a roll bar and a dump bed in back. It was the perfect conveyance for tootling around the farm. I was too beat up for any long walking—any walking at all, really. Still, I wanted to revisit the place where Leonard had died, to pay my respects and to spend some quiet time setting the events of the past few days straight in my head.

Although I'd finally gotten some sleep in the morning after the craziness in the woods, I'd spent several hours tossing and turning as my mind raced, trying to figure everything out. I still hadn't put all the pieces together. The Kubota was just the ticket for a little me-time and some fresh air.

So, after Precious Darling's delicious lunch in the big house and a quick stop in the cottage, I headed out on the bright orange Kubota with Dolly standing next to me on the bench seat, her nose to the air, ears flapping in the wind. As we cruised over the lawn, headed for the woods, I caught a glimpse of two giant heads bobbing in the gazebo near the pond. Judi and Bambi were having their quiet picnic together. And Pep had been right. Tammy Fae had gone all out. The women from New York had the biggest, poofiest hair I'd ever seen. If Bambi's hair had been pink, she'd have looked like a cotton candy cone. From across the lawn, I saw Judi raise a champagne flute to her lips.

"Looks like the ladies are content to have their husbands locked up, Dolly. Now, there's no one around to yell at them anymore."

I jammed the brake hard. Dolly nearly fell off the seat next to me. I remembered how the women had been clear with Detective Gibbit about how they'd *not* been with their husbands for several hours on the night of the murder. They said they'd been together in the living room. Then, both men had slept alone in their respective bathrooms. In fact, it was the wives statements that had been the most damning with regard to their spouses whereabouts during the night in question. And now their husbands were surely going to jail.

Dolly and I sat there, idling in the Kubota, watching across the lawn as the women talked in the gazebo, with their giant beehive heads close together. I thought about what I wanted to say for another minute or two. Finally, I decided that a "Northern" approach would be best. I turned the steering wheel hard and headed toward the gazebo.

Decked out in their gold jewelry, wearing their velour running suits, Judi and Bambi were seated inside the raised octagonal pavilion at a little wrought iron table. The table was set with a pretty floral tablecloth and some of Daphne's best china place settings. Already, their crystal champagne flutes were nearly empty. There was an open picnic basket with more desserts and another bottle of sparkling wine on a smaller table. Daphne'd figured with their husbands in the slammer, the two women could use a special treat and some bubbly. She'd gone all out to try to make them feel better. The duo looked up as I motored over to the gazebo.

"Hi, ladies."

I parked alongside the six-sided folly and shut off the Kubota engine. Yankee-style, I didn't waste any time getting to the point.

"I want in," I said.

"You want what?" Judi Malagutti stared at me, sandwich in hand, surprised.

"I said, I want in. Your business, that is." I slid out of the Kubota and climbed the gazebo stairs, which were flanked with potted pink geraniums. Dolly followed me and started sniffing the painted wooden floor under the table for crumbs.

"I don't know what you're talking about," snapped Judi. She put her sandwich down and took a gulp of the sparkling wine. It was pink and had a big strawberry floating in it.

"Sure you do. I'm talking about your new olive oil business. I've heard you two talking about it a bunch of times. Everyone has," I said.

The two women looked at each other.

"And now, with your husbands safely locked away—I doubt they'll be getting out anytime soon—you can go ahead with your scheme. Only, I know that it'll mean you still plan on taking over my family's plantation." Already, the bottle of bubbly was about half empty. I poured more of the sparkling wine into each of their glasses. "And I want a piece of the action."

Judi and Bambi stared at me in stunned silence.

"Ahh, a Pol Roger rosé. One of my favorites! I see that Daphne's sent you some of her best."

I reached into the basket and pulled out a champagne flute. There'd been four in the basket. Apparently no one had removed the extras. I poured myself a little champagne and raised my glass.

"Salut!"

"Why would we give you a piece of *our* business?" asked Bambi, raising her glass and sipping her champagne. She dipped a crostini into some feta and olive salsa and pushed the treat between her pouty lips.

"Shut up, stupid," whispered Judi.

"Because I know what you did," I said.

"And what's that?" asked Judi.

"You killed Lenny the Doughboy, then framed your husbands for the murder."

Bambi's mouth dropped open. Judi shot her a glance.

"That's crazy," said Judi.

I reached into my pocket then pulled my hand out and opened my palm. "Look here," I said.

"What's that?" asked Judi.

"Oh! I know!" said Bambi.

"I bet you do, Missus Gambini," I said. "It's a bat-sized false eyelash. And it's one of yours."

"Where did you find it?"

"Yes, well, that's where this gets interesting," I said. "I found it late last night. In the woods, of all places!"

"Really?" said Judi, raising an eyebrow.

"Yes. It was on the ground. Next to the grave that I was in. The same grave your husbands fell into when they were chasing me. But I digress," I said. "My dog, Dolly, was sniffing the eyelash when the sheriff pulled me out of the grave."

The two women just stared at me. Then, each took a drink.

"Lucky for you two, I neglected to share this little ditty with the sheriff." I held up the eyelash and smiled wickedly. "And if I had, that'd mean that he'd have found out, like I did, that you'd been out in the woods, at the grave."

"Really? And why would you do us the favor of keeping your mouth shut?"

"You've done a great job framing your husbands. They

deserve it. And, I'd hate to see them wriggle free. After all, they threatened me and my family and I owe them one." To be honest, I'd been so distressed and out of my mind after Buck had hauled me out from the grave that I'd neglected to give him the eyelash when I'd discovered it. I'd just shoved into my pocket and forgot about it until morning.

"I see."

"Besides, even if I were to let the authorities know, given the choice of who to prosecute, I'm willing to bet that they'd choose to go after hardened known criminals over a couple of disgruntled housewives. You might spend a little time in jail for something; however, your husbands will still probably go down for the murder."

Judi sipped her sparkling wine.

"Anyway," I continued, "I can read the writing on the wall. You two are too smart and powerful for the likes of Southern backwater folks like my family. My folks don't stand a chance of fighting your family 'associates' for the plantation."

"You got that right!" squealed Bambi.

Judi put her hand on Bambi's arm as she narrowed her eyes.

"So, you know how the saying goes . . . If you can't beat 'em, join 'em. Right? The way I see it, once your 'associates' from New York help you to expand your territory to Abundance, and you manage to 'acquire' my family's farm, you're going to need some help with public opinion. That's where I come in."

"Really? How's that?" asked Judi. She sipped her drink thoughtfully.

I had her attention.

"As you know, I've spent years living up North. And I'm a lot savvier than most folks down here. Including the bumpkin sheriff and his ridiculous sidekick Detective Gibbit. After I help you swing local public opinion to your side, I can come up with a national marketing campaign that will blow your minds."

"Maybe we got our own marketing people. Maybe that's

what I'm gonna do myself," said Judi. "Of course, I'm not saying that any of what you're saying is true."

"I hope not. You're too smart for that—doing your own marketing, I mean. Working on the marketing would only be a distraction to what you do best. You're the business brains; you need to focus on running your business. Let me handle the fluff."

"Well, I *do* have a great mind for business."

"Of course you do. And, obviously, I know how to get the word out. After all, I've gotten myself coverage in all sorts of media."

"You got a point there."

"What about me?" asked Bambi. "What am I gonna do?"

"You're the face of the business," I said. "Kind of the public spokesperson. You'd do the personal appearances, commercials, stuff like that."

"Aww, I like that!"

Judi looked at Bambi and rolled her eyes.

"And, assuming that what you're saying about us is true, why should we let you in?"

"Because if you don't, I'll tell the sheriff what I know. If your fingerprints aren't on the shovel that I used to hit your husband, I know where the other shovel is."

"The other shovel?"

"Yes. The one at the bottom of the pond."

Judi and Bambi exchanged glances.

"And it was probably the one you used to hit Loretta on the back of the head when she stepped out of Lenny's cabin the other night."

"You said the sheriff was a bumpkin."

"He is. But then, there's only so much evidence that even a bumpkin can overlook."

"I still don't think anyone around here would believe you," said Judi.

"Yeah, we heard all sorts of stuff about you when we had our hair done," said Bambi.

"Right. Exactly, no one around here much likes me. And

the feeling is mutual. Then again, people are talking about me all over the country. And I can have them talking about you and your business, too. That's what counts, right?"

"Oohh, we could be famous!" cried Bambi.

"What about your family?"

"I've never fit in. Look at my sister Daphne. Do I act like her?"

"Well, no . . ."

"Miss prim and proper. No one is good enough for her. Even me. And my other sister, Pep. Who can take anyone who looks like that seriously? She's an embarrassment. I'm happy to take this place from them. Besides, are you willing to take the chance that no one would believe me?"

"Well, certainly, if you're dead, no one will be the wiser." Judi smiled.

That was the magical moment I'd been waiting for. The moment when I knew that I'd been right. I didn't know how or why; however, the two of them had killed Leonard. I was sure of it. So, for another ten minutes, the three of us batted threats and innuendo back and forth. Judi and Bambi finished their bottle of champagne, and we opened a second bottle. They didn't seem to notice that I drank less than a quarter of what they drank. I poured them each another full glass—we were nearly through the second bottle.

I figured it was now or never.

"Of course this sounds corny, but you both must realize that I've got this all written down," I said. "And it's in a safe place. You know, just in case something 'unfortunate' were to happen to me. I didn't just fall off the turnip truck, ladies."

"I'm not saying that you're right about any of this. Regardless, your offer does intrigue me," said Judi with a polite smile.

"So, do we have a deal?"

"We might consider it."

"Good. Because I'm not wanting to stay down here in bumpkinville for the rest of my life. A product like yours has international appeal. Women all over the world will love it. Especially if it's a company started by women, run by women. I aim to help you get rich off it."

"Ooooh, I like the sound of that!" cooed Bambi.

"Look, we've all gotten the shaft from the men around us. It's time that we take the business that should've been ours in the first place. I tell you what. I'll share a secret with you. Something guaranteed to rid you of your competition and put you ahead in your business right off the bat. In fact, why don't we trade? As a show of good faith."

"Trade what?" asked Judi.

"As an act of good faith, I'll tell you a secret about Tony the Baker up in Boston, a real easy way he can be eliminated, ousting competition and clearing the way for your business down here. Then, you share something with me."

"Like what?"

"If I share a secret, you share a secret."

"We don't have any secrets, do we, Bambi?" Bambi shook her head. And her hair wobbled back and forth.

"No secrets? Really? You surprise me. After all, I've got lots of secrets. Every woman does." I paused. "Okay, how about you tell me how you got rid of your husbands. We all know you did it. And, frankly, I am in awe of you both. What really happened Monday night?"

"I dunno. You first," said Judi. "What's the secret about Tony the Baker?"

"First, do we have a business deal?"

Judi and Bambi looked at each other.

"I'm not sharing what I've got on Tony the Baker unless you give me something in return. And if you don't, I'm going to the sheriff. And if something 'unfortunate,' as you say, were to happen to me, and I don't make it to the sheriff, someone will open my letter, detailing what I know about you. Still, of course, it's your choice."

I smiled and took a sip from my champagne glass.

"You say what you got on Tony is good? Sure to get rid of him?"

I nodded.

"Why not," said Judi. "I kinda like you, anyway. It'll be fun. Besides, there's only one of you and there's two of us here. Probably if you squeal, no one will believe you anyways." Then, she thought for a moment. "Hey, you're not wearing a wire or anything, are you?"

"A wire? Like in the movies? Are you kidding?" I laughed. Then, I stood up and lifted my shirt to show my jog bra underneath. Hell, I'd been doing it all week; what was one more time, I thought.

"Wowie, Those are some bruises ya got there. Did my Sal do that to you?" Judi seemed like it was an everyday occurrence.

"It's nothing," I said. I pulled my shirt down. "You ladies still have cold feet?" I'd let her believe what she wanted to believe about the bruises.

"Nah, We're cool," said Judi with a sly grin.

"Yee! We're all in this together now!" said Bambi, clapping her manicured hands together.

The three of us clinked our champagne flutes.

"So, what's the big secret about Tony the Baker?" asked Judi eagerly.

"He's diabetic. Big-time. It'd be easy to bump him off. No one would be the wiser. It'd look like a medical issue. No mess, and your competition would disappear." I smiled and raised my glass.

"Huh. That *is* real good. You know? Real good." Judi raised her glass and clinked mine.

"Your turn. What happened Monday night?"

"Monday night, when we got downstairs, we heard voices in the kitchen," said Judi.

"So, we decided to take a peek through the crack in the kitchen door, didn't we, Judi?" said Bambi. "That's when we saw Loretta and Lenny talking."

"Yeah. We already knew Lenny was here because Sal had told me about the fishing trip, and how Guido was going to 'do' something about the New England family poaching our future olive oil business. But I was shocked to see Loretta when she served dessert the other night. Of course, I'd known them both since we were kids; we'd met at a couple of funerals and other 'family' stuff. I should've guessed if he was here, she'd be here. They were usually never far apart."

"The twin thing," I said.

"I guess so."

"Anyways," said Bambi, "Judi and me, we heard the two of them talking about doing something to the olive trees that night. Then, they went outside."

"'Cause we were in our bare feet, Bambi and I slipped into Sal's and Guido's boots on the porch," said Judi.

"We followed them to a cabin, where they grabbed a pair of shovels," said Bambi.

"Then they went back on a trail. We'd gone about two or three minutes when the rain and wind started to really pick up. Bambi started whining that she wanted to turn back, when all of a sudden Loretta turned and started heading for us. We dove into the brush real quick, and Bambi started blubbering because she got her hair weave all tangled in some of the prickers."

"Yeah!" Bambi giggled. She pushed a big strawberry through her puffy pink lips.

"Loretta didn't see us. I promised Bambi a day at the beauty parlor and some Botox treatments if she'd follow Lenny while I stuck to Loretta."

"Guido's been cutting back on my Botox funds," said Bambi. She tried to furrow her brow.

"While she went off with Lenny, I followed Loretta back to the cabin where she left her shovel next to the door before she went inside. I was looking in the window when I accidently fell into the cabin. I heard Loretta heading for the door, and I figured she'd heard me. The woman's an animal; I heard that she clipped one of her own cousins! Anyways, I grabbed the shovel, and when she stepped out of the door, I whacked her real hard in the head. Honestly, it felt kinda good, so after she fell to the ground, I whacked her again. And again. It was like, all this anger I had at Sal came out, and I suddenly felt a giant rush of calm."

"I see," I said. "Remind me not to cross you during a board meeting."

Judi laughed raucously.

"Loretta didn't move," said Judi.

"So, I bent down and listened to hear her breathing. When I didn't hear nothing, I figured she was dead," added Bambi.

"That's when it first occurred to me—we could get rid of two . . . heck, maybe three birds . . . with one stone, so to speak," said Judi. "We'd get rid of Loretta and Lenny *and* our stupid husbands, then we could start the olive oil beauty business we wanted. So, I grabbed the shovel and ran off to catch up with Bambi. My idea was for us to come back and take care of Loretta's body later. First we had to deal with Lenny."

"Only, along the way, you heard something," said Bambi.

"Yeah, right. I heard gunshots, and I was worried that Lenny had shot Bambi. When I got to Bambi, she was fine, standing behind a tree in the woods crabbing about some nail she'd broken somewhere, watching Lenny light up a cigarette in the olive grove. So, I whispered my plan to Bambi, and she liked it. Except, she didn't want to hold the shovel. I figured Bambi probably couldn't lift the shovel to do much damage anyways, and it was starting to rain real hard again. And I was getting impatient. So, I decided arguing was useless, and I stepped out with my shovel."

"I don't think you're talking very nice about me, Judi," said Bambi. "It costs a lot of money to have my nails done. At least Guido keeps telling me that."

Judi and I both ignored Bambi.

"So, we're out there in that stormy weather, standing at the far end of the olive grove. I says to Lenny, 'What ya doing out here?' He turns around and pulls out a Glock. Only I was ready for him, and I smash his hand with my shovel and his Glock goes flying. Before he can move to grab it, Bambi steps forward and grabs the gun, and points it right at Lenny.

"I says, 'So, Lenny, you gonna answer?'

"And he says, 'Leave me alone. I got a job here. And you better get running before Loretta catches you here. She'll burn you if I don't do it myself.'"

"And he called us the B-word," said Bambi.

"Yeah. It's not like I'm not used to it. Sal calls me that, and worse, all the time. Men are pigs. So, I says to Lenny, 'Loretta ain't coming. Ever. Now, march!'"

"I waved my shovel, and Bambi and I walk Lenny at gunpoint for a few minutes over into the woods where we had him start digging a hole. 'Big enough for two,' I told him.

"Of course, Lenny was digging his own grave, and one for Loretta, too," I said.

"Judi said that we still needed Lenny to finish the hole before we whacked him for good," answered Bambi.

"I whispered to Bambi that if he pulled any funny business to shoot him in the leg, 'cause we needed him to help us move Loretta out here," continued Judi.

"I was only gonna shoot him if necessary. Then, when the hole was dug, Judi could take care of him with the shovel, like she did his sister. Judi is real strong."

I nodded.

"Except, all of a sudden, Lenny chucks his shovel in the ditch and starts running," said Judi. "So, we're chasing him through the woods in this terrible storm, and we're losing ground because we're both wearing our husbands' big boots, which are falling off our feet. Then, we lose him. So, we're out in the pouring rain and wind in this friggin' forest, Bambi is whining about her hair again, when all of a sudden, there he is . . . Lenny, mad as hell and standing right in front of us. That's when Bambi shot him. Bull's-eye. He dropped like a rock. Right there, near the olive grove. Then, Bambi starts blubbering, sayin' her nail got caught in the trigger and she never killed anyone before and she needs to get out of there. And she's not helping me move Leonard to the hole."

"That's right," said Bambi. "It was all an accident, really. He just surprised me so, well . . . I shot him."

Judi rolled her eyes. "So, we left Lenny and ran back to

the house. I threw my shovel into the pond. I thought Bambi tossed Leonard's Glock, only I found out later she forgot and she still had it. Anyway, we put Sal's and Guido's boots back where we found 'em on the front porch. Then we high-tailed it upstairs and into bed. I shoved the Glock under the mattress. Sal was snoring away. He never even woke up. It was like nothin' ever happened."

"We should've put Leonard's Glock back in his hand—made it look like suicide, isn't that what we said later?" said Bambi. "Oh well."

"No. It worked out better this way." Judi rolled her eyes again. "Although, we never made it back to move Loretta's body. We figured folks would think Lenny killed her."

"Yeah. We couldn't believe it when we heard she was still alive," Bambi's eyes bugged out.

"If the detective had deputies looking though the house, why didn't they find the gun under the mattress?"

"'Cause when we heard the cops asking questions and looking through the place, Bambi hid the gun in her boobs."

"My boobs are awesome! Guido tells me that all the time."

"Of course, after the cops left, we wiped our prints off Lenny's Glock, and while he was sleeping last night, we wrapped drunken Sal's hand around it. Later, when no one was looking, we dropped it in Sal's boots, hoping some-one would find it. Bambi wanted to drop the gun in Guido's boots, but it didn't fit. Besides, I said, 'cause Guido worked for Sal, chances were that if Sal went down, they'd both go down for Leonard's murder."

"It was the perfect crime," said Bambi.

"More bubbly, ladies?" I asked, as I filled their cham-pagne flutes with the last of the bubbly.

"I just love this Southern hospitality!" Judi sighed with a contented smile. "Yes, siree, we did it," she said, clinking her glass with Bambi before they each took another sip of sparkling wine.

"Yes, you did. But don't you know?" I smiled. "Ladies, there *is* no perfect crime."

I reached down in my lap and tossed my cell phone on the table.

"Oh gosh!" I cried out. "It looks like I accidentally hit the 'call' button when I sat down. And wouldn't you know, it's *still* connected!"

The lit screen on my phone read, BUCK.

I raised my champagne flute and winked.

Judi and Bambi sat speechless.

"At any moment now, my bumpkin sheriff will be comin' down the path to show you ladies even more of our Southern hospitality."

Bambi froze, bug-eyed, holding a big strawberry in the air, while Judi gave me "the stare."

"Cheers!"

Dolly jumped up. As the familiar figure in uniform strode across the lawn, Dolly barked once and wagged her tail.

RECIPES

Loretta's Tapenade

A simple, savored treat since Roman times. Serve as an appetizer with crusty bread and crudités or prepare as a condiment to complement many dishes. May be prepared a week ahead and stored in refrigerator with a thin layer of olive oil poured on top. Before serving stored tapenade, stir in extra olive oil and add a few drops of lemon juice to brighten, then serve at room temperature.

- 1 pound brine-cured black olives, Niçoise, Gaeta, or Coquillo. Do not use canned Spanish or California black olives, which lack the flavor and texture you need.
- 1 2-ounce tin anchovies, packed in oil, drained
- 2 tablespoons drained capers, rinsed
- 2 garlic cloves, peeled and crushed
- 6 small dried figs, coarsely chopped
- 2 tablespoons fresh mint leaves
- 1 tablespoon fresh basil leaves

- 2 tablespoons fresh Italian or flat-leaf parsley
- 1 tablespoon dried Herbes de Provence, or any combination of dried thyme, marjoram, tarragon, basil, oregano, rosemary, lavender
- Fresh coarsely ground black pepper to taste
- Coarse sea salt to taste
- ¼ cup extra virgin olive oil
- 1 tablespoon lemon juice, plus more to add to stored tapenade just before serving

1. If olives are not pitted, using sharp knife, slit each olive and squeeze out pit. Discard pits.
2. Combine olives, anchovies, capers, garlic, and figs in food processor. Pulse briefly until ingredients make chunky paste.
3. Add herbs and several grinds of pepper and sea salt to taste.
4. Add olive oil and lemon juice. Pulse briefly to combine to coarse-textured paste.
5. Use immediately or store in refrigerator for up to one week. If stored, add lemon juice and stir before serving.

Buck's Basic Tomato Toast

Simple and yummy anytime. Tinkering with herb ingredients makes it a unique delight every time.

- Tomatoes
- Fresh or dried rosemary, oregano, basil, lavender, parsley

- Sea salt and freshly ground black pepper to taste
- Crusty baguette or artisanal bread, thick sliced
- Fresh extra virgin olive oil, or garlic-infused olive oil, or herb-infused olive oil, such as basil or rosemary

1. Cut tomatoes into large chunks.
2. Add tomatoes, herbs, salt, and pepper into bowl and mash with pastry cutter or potato masher until chunks are soft and mushy but not pulverized.
3. Toast bread slices.
4. Drizzle olive oil on warm toast and top with spoonfuls of tomato mash.

Loretta's Pan-Seared Georgia Trout with Pecan Brown Butter

Best fresh caught, be sure to select only the freshest market filets with pristine, vibrant flesh and shiny skin that is resilient to the touch. Trout is mild tasting and delicately textured.

- 2 tablespoons olive oil, plus 1 tablespoon more
- 1 cup pecans, finely chopped and lightly toasted
- 1 cup panko bread crumbs
- ¼ cup chopped fresh Italian or flat-leaf parsley
- Coarse sea salt and freshly ground black pepper
- 4 trout fillets, 6–8 ounces each with skin on one side
- ½ cup buttermilk
- Loretta's Pecan Brown Butter (optional, recipe pg. 330)
- Lemon wedges for garnish

1. Preheat oven to 200°F. Brush rimmed baking sheet with 1 tablespoon olive oil and place in oven to warm.
2. Combine pecans, bread crumbs, and parsley in a shallow bowl or pie plate.
3. Season trout fillets with salt and pepper.
4. Brush flesh side of trout with buttermilk, or dip each fillet into shallow pan of buttermilk.
5. Press the flesh side of each fillet into the dry pecan mixture, coating in a thick crust.
6. Heat 2 tablespoons of oil in a large skillet. Adjust heat to medium.
7. Place 2 trout filets in skillet, crust side down. Cook until golden brown, 2 to 3 minutes. Turn and cook until fish is opaque in the center and just cooked through, 2 to 3 minutes more.
8. Transfer cooked trout, crust side up, to prepared baking sheet. Place baking sheet in oven to keep filets warm.
9. Repeat the skillet process with the remaining 2 tablespoons of oil and the remaining 2 trout fillets.
10. Place 4 cooked filets, crust side up, on warmed serving plates. Drizzle with Loretta's Pecan Brown Butter (optional, recipe below).
11. Garnish with lemon. Serve immediately.

Loretta's Pecan Brown Butter

Perfect complement to fish. Makes 4 servings.

- ¼ cup unsalted butter
- Finely grated zest and juice of 1 lemon

- ¼ cup chopped pecans
- ¼ cup fresh flat-leaf parsley
- Coarse sea salt and freshly ground black pepper

1. Wipe skillet that trout was cooked in with paper towels.
2. Add butter; melt over medium heat until butter foams and turns medium brown, swirling pan occasionally.
3. Remove from heat; add the lemon zest and juice, pecans, and parsley; season with coarse salt and black pepper.

Loretta's Buttermilk Coleslaw

This Southern classic is wonderful with fried fish, chicken, and barbeque. Makes about 8 servings.

- 1 medium to large green cabbage, washed, with outer leaves removed
- 2 large carrots, peeled
- 1 tablespoon sugar
- 1 teaspoon celery seed
- Sea salt and freshly ground black pepper to taste
- ½ cup mayonnaise
- ½ cup buttermilk
- 2 tablespoons fresh-squeezed lemon juice
- 1 tablespoon apple cider vinegar

1. Cut off stalk from bottom of cabbage.
2. Cut cabbage in half lengthwise, then cut each half lengthwise in half again.

3. Cut out cabbage stem from each quarter.
4. With flat side facedown on cutting board, thinly slice each quarter from top to bottom.
5. Collect all slices and place into large bowl.
6. Grate or shred carrots by hand or in food processor.
7. Add carrots to cabbage and mix well.
8. In small bowl, combine remaining ingredients and stir until smooth.
9. Pour buttermilk mixture over cabbage and carrots and toss until well blended.
10. Cover with plastic wrap and refrigerate at least two hours.
11. Serve cold.

Loretta's Easy Cracklin' Biscuits

Self-rising flour makes these rich biscuits easy and quick to prepare. Makes about 1 dozen.

- 2 cups self-rising flour
- 1 cup heavy whipping cream
- ¼ cup finely diced salt pork cracklin's (recipe pg. 333)
- 1 egg white, lightly beaten with a whisk

1. Preheat oven to 400°F.
2. Butter or grease baking sheet and set aside. Or, for crustier biscuit bottoms, place a skillet in the oven to warm for 10 to 15 minutes.
3. Add flour to large bowl. Make a well in the center.
4. Pour cream into the well, stirring with a spatula until flour is moistened.

5. Stir in cracklin's. Mix until dough pulls away from sides of the bowl. If flour remains on the bottom of the bowl, add additional cream, one spoonful at a time.
6. Transfer dough to a lightly floured surface. Sprinkle a little flour on top of the dough.
7. With floured hands, pat dough down to ½ inch thick. Fold in half. Pat to ½ inch thick again.
8. Brush off visible flour from pressed dough top.
9. With 2½-inch biscuit cutter, or rim of a drinking glass, cut out each biscuit round. Roll dough scraps together and flatten to ½ inch thick to make more biscuits.
10. Place rounds about 1 inch apart on buttered or greased baking sheet or in warmed skillet.
11. With a light hand, brush egg white on tops of rounds.
12. Bake biscuits in upper third of oven for 10 to 15 minutes, or until golden brown. Serve warm.

Southern-Style Salt Pork Cracklin's

A delicious, crunchy Southern staple to enhance vegetables, legumes, barbeque, and breads.

- ¼ cup or more finely diced salt pork

1. In small, heavy skillet, stir-fry diced salt pork over moderate heat until well browned and crisp, about 10 minutes.
2. Remove from skillet and drain cracklin's on paper towels.

Loretta's Pork-Seasoned Simmered Crowder Peas and Butter Beans

Hearty and delicious, seasoned peas and beans make for a perfect Southern-style side dish. Careful not to overcook!

- 2 cups shelled fresh crowder peas
- 2 cups shelled fresh butter beans
- 1 ham hock or 2–3 ounces salt pork
- 1 small hot red pepper, seeded and minced
- Sea salt and freshly ground black pepper to taste
- 1 small onion, quartered
- Butter to taste
- 1 tablespoon fresh parsley, chopped

1. Place peas and beans in a large bowl of water and stir with fingers, picking out any debris as well as blemished peas and beans. Drain.
2. Place peas and beans in a large saucepan with ham hock, red pepper, salt, and pepper. Cover with three times as much water as the volume of beans and peas.
3. Bring water to boil and reduce heat to low. Cover and simmer until peas and beans are tender but not too soft, about 20 minutes.
4. Add onion and cook past the rubbery stage, but not until mushy, another 10 to 20 minutes.
5. Drain. Discard ham hock or salt pork.
6. Transfer peas and beans to serving bowl. Top with butter. Garnish with parsley.

Loretta's Pan-Fried Okra

A thick coating of batter helps keep each bite-sized okra slice crisp on the outside and prevents it from wilting on the inside. Stirring or turning okra while frying will knock off the coating and burn the okra. One medium okra makes about 8 to 10 slices. Serves about 6.

- 2 pounds okra, rinsed
- 1 egg, beaten
- 2 tablespoons water
- 2 cups buttermilk
- Hot sauce, such as Tabasco pepper sauce or cayenne pepper sauce, to taste
- 4 teaspoons salt, divided into two equal parts
- 2 cups cornmeal
- 2 cups panko bread crumbs
- Freshly ground black pepper to taste
- Olive oil, vegetable oil, or shortening for frying
- Sea salt to taste

1. Slice stem ends off okra and cut okra into ¼-inch slices.
2. Mix egg, water, buttermilk, hot sauce, and 2 teaspoons salt in large bowl.
3. Add okra slices to the buttermilk mixture.
4. Into another bowl, mix cornmeal, panko, pepper, and remaining salt.
5. With slotted spoon, remove okra from buttermilk mixture and add to cornmeal.
6. Toss okra in cornmeal mixture lightly to coat.
7. With slotted spoon, remove okra pieces to cake rack to allow excess cornmeal mixture to fall through rack.

8. In large, heavy iron skillet, add oil to reach about ½ inch up the sides. Heat until deep-frying thermometer reads 350°F.

9. With large spoon, add small batches of okra to pan without overcrowding the pan.

10. Fry just a few minutes until golden brown; resist urge to turn frying okra so batter will remain undisturbed. Turn with slotted spoon only as necessary.

11. With slotted spoon, remove browned okra from pan and set on paper towel covered cookie sheet to drain.

12. Sprinkle with sea salt to taste, if desired.

13. While frying remaining okra, keep cooked pieces warm in 200°F to 250°F oven.

14. Serve warm.

Precious Darling's Garlic Smashed Potatoes

Sure to be a favorite you'll want to prepare again and again.

- 2 pounds Yukon Gold potatoes, about 6 ounces each
- 3 cloves garlic, lightly smashed
- 2 teaspoons sea salt
- ⅓ cup extra virgin olive oil
- ¼ teaspoon freshly ground black pepper
- 1 teaspoon fresh basil, chopped, or dried basil
- 1 teaspoon fresh thyme, chopped, or dried thyme
- 1 teaspoon fresh rosemary, chopped, or dried rosemary
- 1 tablespoon fresh parsley, chopped

1. Preheat oven to 450°F.
2. Bring large pot of water to boil. Add potatoes, garlic, and salt. Simmer until just tender, about 10 to 15 minutes.
3. Drain water. Save garlic. Let potatoes cool for 5 to 10 minutes.
4. Mince boiled garlic and set aside.
5. Rub baking sheet with olive oil.
6. Place just-cooled potatoes on oiled baking sheet and lightly smash each potato with the palm of your hand or bottom of a glass so that the skin breaks open with the potato remaining relatively intact.
7. Drizzle potatoes with half the olive oil; sprinkle with salt and pepper. Carefully turn over potatoes to coat both sides.
8. Roast 15 minutes, then drizzle again with remaining oil.
9. Roast another 20 to 30 minutes until edges of skins begin to brown and crisp.
10. Remove from oven.
11. Combine minced garlic with chopped herbs.
12. Place potatoes in serving bowl or on individual plates and sprinkle with herbs and garlic; serve immediately.

Boone Beasley's Boneless Wild Boar Tenderloin

Leaner than domesticated pork, with care not to overcook, wild boar boneless loin may be prepared like domesticated pork loins.

- Tenderloin of wild boar, trussed to maintain even thickness throughout

- Sea salt and freshly ground black pepper to taste
- 1–2 tablespoons extra virgin olive oil

1. Preheat oven to 400°F.
2. Lightly season tenderloin with salt and pepper.
3. Heat oven-proof skillet over medium-high heat with olive oil.
4. Sear tenderloin for about 2 to 3 minutes per side.
5. Transfer tenderloin in skillet to oven. Roast until center of loin reaches temperature of 150°F. Depending on size of roast, this can take as little as 10 and up to 35 minutes.
6. Remove roast from oven, transfer to serving platter, and loosely tent with foil. Rest roast for about 10 minutes before serving with Boone Beasley's Creamy Mustard Sauce (recipe below).

Boone Beasley's Creamy Mustard Sauce

Perfect and classic for many cuts of domestic pork or wild boar.

- Warm skillet drippings from roast tenderloin
- ½ cup dry white wine
- ¾ cup heavy cream
- ½ cup low-sodium chicken broth
- ¼ cup Dijon mustard or country-style mustard
- 1 tablespoon brown sugar
- Sea salt and freshly ground black pepper to taste

1. Pour off any fat in the skillet.
2. Add wine to skillet.

3. Scrape up browned bits from the bottom of the pan with a wooden spoon.
4. Increase heat to medium-high and boil 2 to 3 minutes or until wine is reduced to about 2 tablespoons.
5. Stir in cream, chicken broth, mustard, and sugar.
6. Boil until reduced to a saucy consistency, about 5 minutes.
7. Season to taste with salt and pepper.
8. Return meat and any juices to skillet. Turn meat to coat with sauce. Transfer back to serving platter.
9. Drizzle any remaining sauce over meat and serve.

Georgia Peach and Pecan Olive Oil Cake

This Knox Plantation signature treat is Southern and sweet, made with healthy olive oil. May be prepared with or without pecans. Serve plain or with fresh whipped cream, vanilla ice cream, or yogurt. Makes yummy breakfast treat. Or, for dessert, prepare scrumptious frosted layers with brandy and Dreamy Peach Frosting.

- 1 cup extra virgin olive oil plus more for coating parchment paper
- 3 ripe peaches, thinly sliced
- 1 teaspoon vanilla extract
- 1 cup plus 2 tablespoons sugar—½ and ½ mixture of packed light brown with white granulated
- ½ teaspoon kosher salt
- 1 teaspoon ground cinnamon
- 2 cups all-purpose flour, plus more for tossing with fruit

- 3 duck eggs or 3 extra-large chicken eggs
- ½ teaspoon baking powder
- ½ teaspoon baking soda
- ½ cup Pan-Roasted Pecans (optional, but oh-so-good; see recipe pg. 341)
- ½ cup peach-flavored brandy (optional, to accompany Dreamy Peach Frosting)
- Dreamy Peach Frosting (optional, see recipe pg. 342)
- Garnish (optional): peach slices tossed in lemon juice and fresh mint sprigs

1. Preheat oven to 350°F.
2. Line 9-by-13-inch baking pan with parchment paper.
3. Coat paper with olive oil.
4. In a bowl, toss peaches with ¼ cup olive oil, 1 teaspoon vanilla extract, ¼ cup plus 2 tablespoons of sugar, salt, cinnamon, and pinch of flour. Let stand about 15 minutes or until juicy.
5. In a large bowl, whisk eggs, remaining ¾ cup sugar, and ¾ cup olive oil.
6. In another bowl, whisk the flour, baking powder, and baking soda.
7. Whisk dry ingredients into bowl with egg mixture.
8. Fold in pecans, peaches, and juices.
9. Scrape batter into pan; bake 35 minutes until golden and toothpick inserted into the center comes out clean. Let cool.

For brandied and frosted cake, cut cake lengthwise in half. Place bottom layer on cake platter. Brush with half the brandy. Spread half the Dreamy Peach Frosting (recipe follows) on cake layer. Place second cake layer on top. With toothpick, poke holes in top cake layer. Brush cake top with remaining brandy, letting it seep down toothpick holes. Spread remaining frosting on top layer of cake. Garnish with mint sprigs and fresh peach slices soaked in lemon juice to preserve freshness. Fabulous dessert paired with vanilla ice cream and served with coffee.

Pan-Roasted Pecans

Delicious alone or as an addition to sweet or savory dishes. Make extra; you'll be eating these goodies right out of your hand!

- Olive oil
- ½ to 2 cups pecans, chopped
- 2 tablespoons butter, melted, for each ½ cup pecans
- Ground cinnamon to taste
- Natural brown sugar, such as turbinado, to taste
- Pinch of ground red pepper

1. Preheat oven to 350°F.
2. Lightly coat baking sheet with olive oil.
3. Toss pecans in butter and sprinkle lightly with cinnamon, brown sugar, and ground red pepper.
4. With fingers or a slotted spoon, spread pecans on baking sheet in even layer.
5. Bake 10 to 15 minutes or until fragrant. Check frequently; toss once with spatula to avoid burning.
6. Remove from oven. Let cool on rack a few minutes (pecans will continue to cook for a bit).
7. Spoon buttery pecans into coffee filter over paper towel to soak up any extra liquid.
8. Cool until spiced butter hardens onto pecans.

Dreamy Peach Frosting

Rich and creamy delight! A perfect complement to Georgia Peach and Pecan Olive Oil Cake or angel food cake.

- 1 cup heavy cream
- 16 ounces cream cheese, softened
- ½ cup butter
- 3½ cups confectioners' sugar
- 2 teaspoon grated lemon peel
- 2½ cups fresh or frozen peaches, sliced, or 2 16-ounce cans of peach halves, drained and sliced

1. In large bowl, beat heavy cream at high speed until stiff peaks form; chill.
2. Use same bowl to beat cream cheese and butter at medium speed until smooth.
3. At low speed, gradually add confectioners' sugar. Beat just until frosting is of spreading consistency.
4. Fold in whipped cream and lemon peel.
5. Chop peaches; place in small bowl.
6. Fold 1 cup frosting into peaches.